CW00862996

MOON*FLAW*

A NOVEL

STEVE GODSOE

 FriesenPress

Suite 300 - 990 Fort St
Victoria, BC, V8V 3K2
Canada

www.friesenpress.com

ISBN
978-1-5255-6775-9 (Hardcover)
978-1-5255-6776-6 (Paperback)
978-1-5255-6777-3 (eBook)

1. FICTION, SCIENCE FICTION, HIGH TECH

Distributed to the trade by The Ingram Book Company

Also by Steve Godsoe:

The Turnstile

AUTHOR'S NOTE

Eight long years ago, essentially on a whim, I embarked on a lofty mission. "I'm thinking about writing a novel," I'd said to my wife hesitantly as she sat opposite me at a local restaurant. Considering my prior writing experience included no more than some wishy-washy song lyrics, she took a few seconds to absorb my out-of-left-field utterance, and then replied with a deadpan expression, "Well, make sure it's a bestseller and we make lots of money." I chuckled along with her wilfully humorous (and clearly idealistic) reaction. But all the while I couldn't help but take something more from it. Somewhere below the surface of her tone, I sensed a sort of unmapped faith that perhaps I could actually tackle this thing. We both didn't know it at the time, but upon looking back, all I really needed in that moment was something—*anything*—affirmative. So, I'd like to thank my wife, Lindsay, for inadvertently lending this project a springboard, for it ultimately shot me to the moon.

—SG

For Lindsay, affirmatively

I saw it written and I saw it say
Pink moon is on its way
And none of you stand so tall
Pink moon gonna get ye all

—Nick Drake

Hell is empty and all the devils are here.

—William Shakespeare

PROLOGUE

The Fall of the Aerialist

Dear reader,

Who I am is not important at the moment, but I'll be your guiding voice through this tale.

It all began when I was jolted from my slumber to find a wash of brilliant autumn moonlight gleaming through the heart of the halcyon night. The radiant light poured in through my dormer window, silhouetting the ancient white oak that stood in my yard like a contorted behemoth.

Disoriented and clammy, I rose from my sweat-moistened bedding for a choice view of the lunar glow. The orb hung low and polished before me, and feelings of wonder bubbled to the surface of my soul. As I became enthralled in its luminescence, the moon suddenly triggered a recollection of the daunting dream that had ultimately awoken me.

I vividly recalled the horror of feeling myself fall in ethereal slow motion from my familiar tightrope. To this point, it was as if I'd lived the very definition of a balanced life, and I'd always crossed this vast chasm of the mind with the greatest of ease. The next thing I knew, I was helplessly flailing in a sea of lava beneath a baleful, reddening moon, from which balloon-sized drops of blood fell into the roiling magma around me like crimson napalm. Though I could see and smell my skin burning, there was no pain whatsoever, and I miraculously maintained full movement of my limbs and extremities.

As if I wasn't in enough trouble already, a tidal wave of molten lava had emerged in the distance and was picking up steam like a runaway locomotive as it barrelled toward me. Distressed by the oncoming swell, I suddenly noticed a rope gently swaying within reach like a listless pendulum. It appeared to dangle from the blood-shot moon above. As I took hold of it and hoisted myself free of the caustic sea, lava licked at the timely twine with a venomous tongue.

The burgeoning tsunami continued to close in as I frantically scaled the fraying cord. As I climbed, the rope began to feel rather familiar in my grasp, and I realized that it was *my* rope—the one I'd been traversing, one steady foot in front of the other, before I had fallen. The moon's bloody tears continued to fall; one grazed my shoulder and exploded with a sickening sound, like flesh tearing from bone. The pain was sudden, shooting through my entire body. It was with that pain that I was lurched from my sleep.

Now fully alert, I walked through the frosted light of the moon and entered the bathroom, ready to rid myself of the last traces of the dream. Just the thought of a cool, late-night shower induced a sense of calmness in me—an ease that I presumed would see me through the balance of the night.

Afterwards, with the nightmare washed from my memory, so to speak, I was ready to drift back under to the Land of Nod. It was then that I realized something was amiss. Returning to the bedroom, I encountered an acute roseate glow. *The moonlight certainly wasn't this tinge ten minutes ago,* I thought to myself. I haltingly continued past my bed and pressed my once-again-clammy palms to the window frame.

I stood spellbound as the pink moon stared me down with asperity, piercing my vulnerable spirit to the core. I blinked, and a rigid tightrope appeared out of thin air, bridging the base of my second-storey window to the distant orb, bloated and buoyant on the horizon. An angry crimson hue was already pushing through the pink, and with an anguished mind, I began to wish it all away.

It was then and there I knelt—a non-believer on the brink of prayer, trapped between my dreams and the impossible yet undeniable reality before me—and prepared to walk the line.

PART I

I'm bein' followed by a moonshadow

—Cat Stevens

CHAPTER 1

From the Morning

Doing her best just to keep her umbrella from flying away like an untethered kite, Shelly Madison-Lowe hurled herself underground and into the cover of the subway station nestled below West Seventy-Second Street. Conveniently for her, the entrance was located only half a block from her spacious condo, where her view from the fifteenth floor gracefully overlooked the 840-acre doormat that was Central Park.

Running late for work was nothing new to Shelly, but on this morning, it wasn't her typical snooze-button trifecta forcing her to move at such a nimble gait. Not only New York City, but also Long Island—and most of New England, for that matter—were still being doused by the remnants of Hurricane Allan, a bruising Category 3 storm that had already wreaked havoc on the Caribbean and the Southeastern United States.

Countless pools of run-off rain had accumulated throughout the subway, mixing with rust and God knows what else. The depths

7

of the city had taken in a lot of water during the storm, and the resulting stench had become near dizzying.

Now clumped in the hustle and bustle of the morning commute, Shelly had no choice but to shift her thoughts to her *Careers* column, and her current article's stagnant state within an already extended deadline. She was presently a month shy of completing twelve years with the *Wall Street Journal*, and she generally met her deadlines with ease. But on this particular assignment, she consistently felt herself pulling from a dry well, and she was now feeling the pressure pushing down from her administrators.

Though in recent years there had been spells where her passion for writing seemed to go adrift on some unknown sea, her column in the *Journal* was what defined her. After graduating from New York University (NYU) with an MA in English and American literature, Shelly had reams of job offers on the table before she hit twenty-three. She jumped at a reputable editorial position with *Newsday*, but quickly found that Melville, New York, lacked the big-city buzz that had fuelled her writing through her university years. Coincidentally, a *Journal* executive had Shelly tabbed as a coveted prize from the moment her work at *Newsday* first appeared in published form. Playing on his hunch that the young writer would apply should an opening in her line of work become available, the executive posted the position of "*Wall Street Journal*: Entry-level Correspondent."

Shelly caught wind of the opportunity by means of a chance encounter with a former English literature professor at NYU. After bumping into each other and catching up on the streets of Brooklyn, he'd asked her if she was aware of the current opening. She wasn't, and her initial reaction was that it was too good to be true. She'd figured that the odds of landing a position with the mighty *Journal* would be astronomically against her. Every aspiring writer in the Greater New York City area would surely apply.

Little did she know that the *Journal* was pursuing *her*—and if she failed to apply, they would proceed to cross that unwritten boundary between contending agencies.

In the end, Shelly gathered her courage and applied. After all, it was her dream job, and she knew that if she balked at the opportunity for simply fearing the odds, she'd grow to regret her passive stance. The job at the *Wall Street Journal* was handed to her the day following her one and only interview. A day after that, Shelly was giving *Newsday* her notice of resignation.

The southbound subway train came to a screeching halt at Rockefeller Center Station, and the metallic smell of brake dust and ozone added to the sodden atmosphere. For Shelly, the cheerless morning weather had slipped her mind, as the subterranean passage often worked well in giving the impression of an isolated underworld.

Now ascending the steps towards the exposed gloom, umbrella cocked and ready, she locked into the mindset that this would be the day she'd buckle down and finally put the long-standing assignment behind her. The creative juices were stirring, and she was certain that with one last push, the piece would be ready to submit by noon—just in time to head out for a well-deserved lunch date with her husband, Jeremy.

Though the morning of October 29 dawned ominously, it still marked a long-awaited day for a freshly tenured professor at Columbia University. Jeremy Lowe, finally free of both the "Assistant" and "Associate" tags he'd been toting through the school's prestigious halls for over a decade, was set to be one of seven recipients at a morning commencement ceremony honouring newly appointed faculty. Though he'd technically held the rank of full professor since early September—when the fall semester began—Jeremy had this particular day marked as an equally momentous affair.

The uphill journey to this esteemed platform began with a PhD and postdoc from Brown University. Then, following two more years at Brown as a graduate student, Jeremy applied for a transfer within the Ivy League circle. Having grown up in Yonkers, New York, Columbia University offered a return to his roots, and was first on a short list of options. The request was granted, and six short months later, despite fierce competition for advancement, Jeremy was offered a teaching assistant position at the school, where he immediately began netting a minimal income. With the tenure track now in motion, the goal of becoming a full professor was waiting in the attainable distance.

Two years later, upon his promotion to assistant professor, a young correspondent from the *Wall Street Journal* approached the Columbia administration in the hopes of interviewing a range of aspiring professors for a "Steps to Success" column. The piece would focus on the long, arduous road to full professor status.

The school executives were conscious of the columnist's reputable work, and she was granted full permission to proceed with four complying members of the faculty. Little did Shelly Madison know that when she sat down to consult with Jeremy Lowe, she was not only interviewing a professor on the rise, but she was also interviewing the man who would one day become her life partner.

From the moment their careers intersected, the two felt an unmistakable connection. A few dates developed into a relationship, and shortly thereafter, amid a florid autumn twilight, Jeremy proposed an engagement atop Central Park's Bow Bridge. A year later, they were happily married—the ceremony taking place in the park's sumptuous Conservatory Gardens.

Backstage at Columbia's Roone Arledge Auditorium, ten minutes before the ceremony was set to begin, Jeremy decided to squeeze in a quick phone call to Shelly.

As if she were expecting it, Shelly picked up after a single ring.

"Hey, Shel," Jeremy began, "just wanted to hear your voice before this thing gets underway."

"Aww, that's sweet," Shelly replied with an apprehensive note somewhere not far below the surface. "I was thinking maybe they'd decide to postpone it due to this weather. You should see the rain comin' down as we speak. And the *wind*—my *God*."

"No, it's still a go," Jeremy continued. "You wouldn't believe how many people are here. I swear they disregard the fire code when they really wanna pack 'em in this place."

Shelly had a knot in the pit of her stomach that felt like it was being pulled from both ends, tightening by the second.

"Honey, this is gonna sound so stupid," she said as she began to unravel the mass in the form of words, "and I realize that the timing couldn't be any worse, but I feel like this storm is some kind of . . . some kind of bad omen, what with the timing of your official commencement."

Caught a little off guard, Jeremy pondered his wife's choice of words, and the shadow they suddenly seemed to cast over his impending moment in the sun. He realized that it wasn't so much the storm that had him down, but rather Shelly's unseemly absence. "If I *did* regard such things as bad omens, I'd have to say that the only one hanging over my head today is the fact that you're not here to support me."

A sharp pang of guilt stabbed into Shelly's spirit, offering a few seconds of silence before she forged a response. "I've already said I'm sorry I couldn't make it. They're crawling down my back for this piece, and I practically promised I'd have it in by noon today. Again, I'm sorry. I want to hear all about it over lunch. That *is* why we planned to meet at Petrocelli's, right?"

Jeremy could feel the tension blossoming like a field of unwanted weeds, and he did his best to promptly defuse it. "Of course it is, honey. Listen—no worries. You just bear down and nail that article like I know you can. I'll catch you up on everything in a few short hours, but I'm gonna call you again first, around eleven thirty. If the weather doesn't improve before then, I think it would be wise to just hunker down until the end of the working day. I can always tell you about the ceremony this evening, over a cognac."

"I should be there for you, Jeremy." In her own mind, Shelly's voice now seemed to skate the periphery of her hollow words. "Good luck, and I love you. Talk to you soon."

When Shelly hung up, she exhaled a long breath and continued with her morning. She knew that when it came to her article, she'd have to struggle through a layer of contrition in order to finally finish the piece. She prayed the weather would turn. The sooner she could see her husband, the better. Having to pass up on lunch would stretch the day into an eternity of pedestrian writing and self-reproach.

On this day, aside from the forthcoming ceremony, Jeremy had woken with an ulterior matter on his mind. He'd spent the entire morning trying to piece together fragments of the most peculiar dream he'd ever experienced. Sure, there are some that rise above others as far as eccentric ambience, but this dream was somehow . . . *conscious*. It left him puzzled in a way that he failed to define. And whenever he tried to repress it, it simply wouldn't go away.

In the short time between the quick phone call and taking the stage, Jeremy resolved that he would share the dream with his wife the next time he saw her. An unrelenting gut feeling told him that the vision held some kind of underlying significance, and maybe all it needed was a fresh perspective from Shelly's end to help conjure up an interpretation.

CHAPTER 2

The Relinquishing Reality Tour

It had been one year to the day since Linden Maddox's wife, Vera, had wailed, "You can stick that goddamn telescope up your *ass!*" and marched out the front door for good.

Their inevitable downward spiral had taken root nearly two years earlier, when Linden's obsession with astronomy took flight. Ironically enough, it all began when Vera insisted that they move from Las Vegas to Albuquerque, New Mexico, after Linden had wandered into the Bellagio one night and casually hit a $294,000 jackpot with the single pull of a $25 slot machine arm. Knowing the history of her husband's addictive personality all too well, she felt she couldn't chance him handing it all back to the casino in slow, incremental donations; besides, Linden himself knew deep down in some forsaken crevice of his mind that, just as his wife perceived, he'd ultimately succumb to Vegas' artful draw.

To Vera's relief, when it came to dictating a six-hundred-mile upheaval from the only city they'd ever known, Linden didn't plead the slightest of protests. In fact, he was graciously on board from the moment she proposed the populous New Mexico city. They were already quite fond of—and familiar with—Albuquerque, as they made consistent excursions there to visit Vera's twin sister, Ruth. Their house was put up for sale the following week, and not a month later, when it was officially sold, they sealed the deal by quitting their jobs: Linden, a Sports Authority store co-manager, and Vera, a medical administrative assistant.

Albuquerque proved to be the perfect abode, and in the short time before Linden fell under the spell of its starry firmament, all was well. Ruth and her husband, Gerald, played gracious hosts, as they took them in until they found a charming ranch-style house in the North Valley. Vera didn't miss a beat, promptly finding work in her field at the Desert Hills Medical Center. Linden dawdled in his employment search, but an eventual thirst for the open air led to a position with Duke City Roofing.

One Saturday night, Ruth and Gerald invited Linden and Vera over for a barbeque and a few drinks. As the evening was waning, and the sky was fusing into that sort of inscrutable semi-darkness, Gerald introduced Linden to what he personally dubbed his "Skyfinder." The intricate apparatus was a mounted, high-end Celestron telescope, and Linden was simply enthralled just by the look of it. "You can't live in Albuquerque without a quality lens, my friend," Gerald asserted as he fixed the mount into position and aimed the optical tube skyward.

"Boys and their toys," Ruth quipped while shaking her head and motioning Vera to come inside for tea. The two men remained outside, swilling beers and scanning the celestial void into the wee hours of the night.

For Linden, though he didn't exactly know it at the time, the seed of obsession had been planted deep in the loam. And that seed would go on to flourish beyond anything Vera could have ever foreseen.

The following morning, clouded in the haze of a hangover, Linden took his brother-in-law's advice and purchased a telescope of his own. Sticking with the Celestron brand, he chose to keep things simple, and went with a NexStar beginner's model. All parts included, the scope ran him a reasonable $250.

From that day forward, like clockwork, Linden would follow dinner by grabbing a few beers and losing himself in the wonders of stargazing for hours on end. Like a child, he was wholly captivated, lost in the limitless phenomena of the cosmos. Despite rising at six o'clock in the morning, Monday to Friday, to be on the job for seven, it would be a rare occasion for him to pack it in and be in the house before the clock struck midnight.

Now several months into what she comically called his "Relinquishing Reality Tour," Vera, feeling the burden of her husband's constant neglect, began delivering her first of many ultimatums. "You'd better start toning it down with that shit," she'd emphatically warn, "or I swear I'll leave your ass!"

Unfazed by his wife's seemingly feeble threats, Linden continued on his quest to attain more knowledge in the field. His hobby was filling more than just leisure time, steering dangerously into a full-blown obsession. Investing more time and money than ever into his research, he now found himself delving into such themes as celestial navigation, planetary systems, selected moons, and a plethora of other cosmic trends and tendencies.

Vera's warnings escalated still, and though they were no longer ignored, they were met with scorn. "Don't tease me," or "Take what's yours, and keep the change," Linden would reply to her fiery divorce threats.

The final straw came crashing down on a night when Linden had vowed to accompany Vera to an annual Desert Hills charity banquet. She'd bought a new dress specifically for the event, and fancied nothing more than her husband's arm to escort her to their designated table. Dressed to the nines and ready to head out for the evening, Vera became enraged when she found Linden out in the backyard, garbed in shoddy jeans and a stained T-shirt, arranging his telescope for what appeared to be yet another night of superfluous sky watching.

"Are you *kidding me?*"Vera roared from the patio like a woman possessed. "You know we have the *fucking* banquet tonight—*right?*"

Jolted from his preparations, Linden swivelled to face the heat, and for a few seconds, absorbed the effort of his wife's elegance. "Wow! You look great, honey," he finally declared. "But we must've gotten our wires crossed on this one. Tonight's the *supermoon!* I've been waiting—"

"You self-centred son of a bitch,"Vera said, arresting his words, her own voice reducing to a throaty, feral snarl. Through with her ineffective string of ultimatums, it was here that she severed the twine. Regaining her fiery cry, she told Linden exactly where to stick his telescope, and from that day forward, not once regretted the unfortunate yet necessary decision she had to make.

———

After the inevitable separation, Linden became a man of free rein. No longer was he the bridled observer, but rather a boundless enthusiast of the skies. Gone were the late-night guilt trips that he'd eventually come to tune out like monotonous static. And gone were any restricting boundaries that once threatened to contain his lust for the craft.

Besides his near-nightly ritual of a minimal four hours of stargazing, he began to spend weekends frequenting New Mexico's circuit of astronomy shops and vendors. Early one Sunday morning, while making a small purchase at The Cosmic Lens—Albuquerque's marquee destination for all things astral—Linden was politely canvassed by the checkout clerk.

"Say, my friend, I've noticed you in the store quite a bit of late." The man was a gentle giant with suspenders that stretched up and around his torso to a dangerous degree. A trusty grin paired with his pleasant approach. "Therefore, I'd be obliged to ask if you're familiar with TAAS?"

"TAAS?" Linden replied slowly, uncertain if he'd even heard the word correctly. "Can't say the term rings a bell."

Always buoyant with the prospect of recruiting a new member, the clerk, who introduced himself as Terrance Barlow, continued, "TAAS—The Albuquerque Astronomical Society. I've been involved since '98, and the society itself originated way back in '59."

"Go on." Nodding, Linden urged the man behind the counter to elaborate. "I'm all ears."

"What we are is a three-hundred-plus-member group that gathers once a month to study New Mexico's constellation activity. Then we share our findings through public education. We start our evenings with an abbreviated meeting based out of Regener Hall, up at the University of New Mexico, and then we disperse throughout the state to selected observation stations."

It didn't take long for Linden to be sold on what Terrance was briefing. He'd heard more than enough to convince him that this fraternity would be right up his alley, and likely a door to a whole new world of cosmic exploration. "The name's Linden Maddox," he stated, reaching over the counter to offer a firm handshake. "Where do I sign up?"

Terrance chuckled. "All you have to do is show up at Regener Hall at four o'clock on the twenty-seventh of the month. You'll be welcomed as a new member, and made to feel right at home." While handing Linden his receipt, along with a handful a change, he continued, "Listen, I'm gonna venture out on a limb here and guess that you're relatively new to the hobby."

"Well, I wouldn't go as far as to say *new*," Linden conceded, somewhat embarrassed before the likes of an accredited pro. "But I'll admit to still being green when it comes to playing with the big-boy toys. I can only hope your generous invitation will rid me of the colour."

"Oh, I'm pretty sure you won't be disappointed, Linden. Remember, the twenty-seventh. Four o'clock. Regener Hall. I hope to see you there."

Perhaps subconsciously channelling the spirit of what now seemed like a distant, former life—where all that ruled the night was *neon* light—Linden replied, "You can bet on it!"

CHAPTER 3

A Flight of Fancy

On a crystal-clear fall morning such as this, the aerial view of Boston was nothing short of breathtaking. Nevertheless, to Luke Sheehan, the lofty perspective would play second fiddle to his mere presence in the remodelled Martin B-26 Marauder.

Over the past six months, the "Travelling Museum" of vintage warplanes had hiked its way across the country, finally arriving in Boston for the final stop along an eight-city tour. For the event, a $300 weekend pass would grant first-hand access to over fifty classic World War II fighter planes and replica models. Also included in the fee were state-of-the-art simulations of a wartime take-off and landing scenario, viewed from the cockpit of an actual Boeing B-17 Flying Fortress. But when it came to the museum's complete ensemble, what Luke regarded above all else was the twenty-minute flight aboard one of a dozen operational models.

An abundant number of proficient tour pilots were set for two days of airborne navigation. The circuit would carry enthusiasts high over the skyline and along the North Shore, concluding with a manoeuvred swoop over the historic jewel at the heart of the city: Fenway Park.

Various fighter planes were at Luke's disposal, all primed and polished for what would be the tour's swan song. Thinking solely of his grandfather, he had little doubt that the B-26 would be his scenic shuttle.

While gliding majestically over the city, Luke had the luxury of communicating with his tour pilot. He told him how back in 1942 his grandfather had flown the exact same model in the Pacific War, and how the veteran was still alive and speaking of prodigious war stories like they were as fresh in his mind as the day they had taken place.

After politely hearing him out, the pilot suddenly pivoted, shifting his eyes from the sky and fixing his gaze firmly on Luke. The look was bloodless and cold, like that of a spectral spirit, causing a slow chill to run down Luke's spine and then seize him with a crippling fear. "Pardon the pun," the aviator began to disclose in a cavernous voice that suited his sunken eyes, his hands now edging the yoke forward to initiate a descent, "but I've been trying to pilot my way through this entangled nightmare since the day of my grim demise. Unfortunately, you're already in the network, but if you're lucky enough to wake before your *own* passing, consider yourself—at least temporarily—free of the moonflaw's more *sinister* approach."

While trying to discern the pilot's baffling delivery, Luke caught his first glimpse of the renowned ballpark, resting just in front of the famous Citgo sign in Kenmore Square. Rising before him in all its stateliness was the Green Monster, the imposing wall in left field where home runs go to die. Observed from this rarefied perch, the red hue of the vacant seats and the green shades of the perfectly manicured grass complemented each other with their sleek pres-ence. Closer now, there appeared to be a man and a young child sitting together in the left-field bleachers.

Having put them in position to launch the manoeuvre, the tour pilot performed the sophisticated swoop that dipped the Marauder between a pair of towering light stanchions. After plunging within a hundred feet of the playing surface, they regained the sky as swiftly as it had been relinquished.

A crackling snap of thunder stole Luke Sheehan from his plagued slumber and initiated what would be his fourth consecutive day of combatting Boston's harsh elements. With Hurricane Allan's intensity now downgraded to a dwindling storm, the morning of October 29 still greeted the Fenway Park groundskeeper with a weighty, leaden sky, and a saturated field awaited his upkeep after yet another night of steady rain. Intermittent thunderclaps continued, seemingly serving as a reminder that the tempest still held rage in its belly and wouldn't fully cease without a prolonged fight.

A demanding job on the best of days, head groundskeeper duties at Fenway were a trying test whenever the skies opened and dumped a substantial deposit. Now in his ninth year of overseeing the beloved landmark's playing conditions, Luke oversaw more than just keeping the field in tip-top shape for game days. Apart from the constant nurturing of all grassy areas, as well as watering and re-levelling the various clay surfaces, he was also in charge of hiring, training, and evaluating his staff. The training procedure was extremely thorough, as the calculated use of mowers, aerators, irrigation systems, and pesticide application was not to be taken lightly—especially during the last two seasons, as state laws had tightened considerably on pesticide, herbicide, and fertilizer use.

Every March, while the ball club was gearing up for the regular season down in Fort Myers, Florida, Luke would convene with the team's brass to formulate the annual budget; having to remain within this restricting allocation of funds would be the biggest challenge his position would present, year in and year out. After all, for the groundskeeping crew, the "season" stretched far beyond the customary six-month term that encapsulates a full baseball calendar. Advanced preparation on the grounds can begin as early as February, and the mandatory procedures that consist of the field's winterization process can run well into late November.

Fortunately for Luke and his crew, this current spell of uncompromising weather fell upon the city when they wouldn't be pressed for time. The Red Sox, having failed to advance to the postseason, had played their final home game over a month before Allan roared up the coast.

Around eight o'clock in the morning, while pulling onto the rain-slickened course of Yawkey Way and into a garage only accessible to Red Sox personnel, Luke was suddenly rattled by a cursory recollection of a dream from the preceding night. As he tried to recall the hazy image, he caught no more than sporadic fragments that quickly evaporated before he could decipher their context. The desire to crack the dream passed, and before he knew it, he was out on the field, immersed in his work, surveying the extent of the latest barrage upon his drainage system.

The dismal morning bled into the noon hour without a hint of improvement, as the apocalyptic clouds progressively pressed down in a suffocating fashion. While squeegeeing pools of stagnant rainwater into a dugout drain, Luke once again began to recall fractional winks from his dream—only this time, when they swam to the surface, they endured. With some intricate configuration, the curious vision was now coming together like a twisted puzzle: the vintage warplanes, the flight above the city and the pilot's chilling impressions, the Fenway swoop and the two people alone in the stands.

He'd held a fascination for historic planes for as long as he could recall, and his connection to Fenway Park needed no explanation. But there was still the odd bit about his grandfather—how he'd piloted a Marauder during the war and was still alive and kicking. The reality was that Luke had never had the honour of meeting his grandfather, as he'd passed in Ireland some years before Luke was even born.

CHAPTER 4

The Qualm After the Storm

Remarkably, over the course of three hours, the New York City weather had reformed from tropical storm-like conditions to a tranquil autumn afternoon that appeased the urban core. The sun was even gracing the sky for the first time in days, its rays streaming through skyscrapers like blazing beacons. Light glistened upon a city still soaked to the bone.

The break in the clouds was like an adrenaline shot of hope. The city that never sleeps hadn't exactly slipped into slumber, but the streets and pedestrian walkways were quickly regaining the familiar clip of a weekday lunch hour.

"Listen, I know you want to hear about the ceremony," Jeremy Lowe began to explain to Shelly as they leafed through their lunch menus at Petrocelli's, "but something's been eating at me since this morning." By now, they both had one less burden to bear: Shelly had finally wrapped up and submitted the piece for her column, while Jeremy had breezed through his emotional commencement speech without a hitch. The professor planned to elaborate on the ceremony, but first things first. "If you don't mind hearing me out for a minute or two, honey, I need to get your take on a dream I had last night."

"Okaaay," Shelly acknowledged hesitantly, somewhat perplexed by the timing of her husband's request. "This seems a little odd, but I guess if it's important to you . . ."

Jeremy nudged his menu off to the side of the table, as if it threatened to divert his full attention. A slow, deep breath followed before his eyes locked in on Shelly's, and then he stepped into the dream recollection like walking into the vaults of his own memory. "I seemed to be the only soul sitting in Boston's Fenway Park," he began, "which is weird in itself, because I fucking *hate* the Red Sox. I was high up along the left-field line, close to where Fisk hit that famous home run in the '70s. I was at the foot of a column supporting the upper deck. How I'd gotten there, or why I was alone, I can't say. As you know, dreams don't exactly set the scene."

As if her facial muscles were unfreezing, Shelly had slowly been forming an expression that could only have said, *This is the lead story? Really?*

"Anyway, it was a beautiful morning, and I could feel the autumn air cleansing my lungs. There was an almost eerie silence, until the unmistakable whine of an approaching plane leaked into the setting and spoiled the serenity. Then suddenly, my eyes locked in on the source of the sound: a magnificent warplane swooping down into the bowl of the ballpark like a hawk after its prey—and I felt the impression of a hand resting delicately on my left shoulder."

"Uh-huh." The utterance that leaked out of Shelly's mouth was barely audible.

"Oh, I'm sorry—am I keeping you awake, dearest?" Jeremy quipped. "This *is* leading somewhere, I promise." He drew a breath and went on. "So, in that instant, I was of two minds: to follow the plane's course, or to turn and identify my unexpected company. I chose the latter. The curiosity of another presence was just enough to draw my attention from the riveting bomber."

Just then, a young waitress with impeccably poor timing approached the table to take their orders. "Two specials and a couple glasses of ice water, please," Jeremy said promptly, eager to expand on his subliminal events.

For Shelly, this slight interruption brought about the realization that part of her was actually buying into the dream. "Well, go on," she stated with raised eyebrows before the waitress had even gathered the menus. "Do tell who was stalking you at your private airshow."

"Okay, this is where things really started getting strange. When I turned, there was a young girl, all by herself—couldn't've been more than seven or eight years old. She was an adorable little thing, but her eyes were grievously sad. She was sporting a pink Red Sox cap that was doing well to shade her eyes from the morning sun. She had fairly long blonde hair and was wearing a light-blue T-shirt with a NASA decal—of all things. The child quickly pulled her hand from my shoulder, and I noticed a circular fishbowl—half-full of nothing but cloudy, brown-tinged water—resting in her lap. The first thing she said was, 'Don't worry. The plane will be precisely where you left it—it has to be.' I had no idea what she meant by that, but when I turned back around, it quickly became evident. Expecting the warplane to have travelled some distance, I found it in the exact same position in the sky as when my eyes had abandoned it. It was as if time itself had offered a brief pause for me to acknowledge this child. The plane continued its kamikaze descent, levelled out, and then vaulted back up and out of the stadium like a stunt only seen in the movies. From there, the droning buzz of the engine slowly dissolved as it reclaimed dizzying heights and flew off into the ether.

"The young girl was now nestled into the seat next to me, as if she'd been there all along. She was waving in the direction of the all-but-diminished plane, while her other arm still balanced the fishbowl. I immediately noticed that its contents had changed from the murky brown colour to a reduced red, like heavily diluted blood. It was at this point that she asked me two questions. She first asked if I'd seen her goldfish, Cleo. I told her I hadn't, and with that reply the entire dream began to take on an unnerving quality. A great darkness had seemingly crept in undetected and morphed the atmosphere to that of a cataclysmic nature. The air turned cold, and a brisk breeze seemed to whip right through me, carving up my bones in the process. I noticed tears welling up in the young girl's eyes, and then she asked me in the saddest voice imaginable, 'How many people will die when the moonflaw is upon us?' I remember being utterly baffled by the question—still am, for that matter—and I wanted desperately to ask her what she meant by it. The thing was—I could no longer speak. I'd been robbed of my voice and was left to just stare at this forlorn child, watching *her* eyes practically beg for an answer that, even if I *could* speak, I couldn't offer." Jeremy paused and became uneasy in his seat, shifting and fidgeting like a child. He felt haunted by the memory of his own dream, as he continued to fight his way back upstream in search of a deeper understanding.

After the waitress arrived with their drinks and some warm bread and butter, Jeremy continued: "So, that's pretty much the last thing I can recall. I've been racking my brain for more, but only to a hollow end. Still, there's something more. I wouldn't be bugging you with all this if it weren't for a more pressing incentive. I would've normally shaken it off as just another dream, but the thing is, I've seen this young girl before, and it's killing me that I can't put my finger on *where* or *when*. I know this probably sounds a little excessive, but I was hoping you could help me place her, because it's damn near driving me mad. Shit, even when I was reading my speech, I kind of flicked the switch to autopilot and let part of my mind wander about like a search party."

"Okay," Shelly began after drawing a breath of her own, realizing that somewhere along the line she had become fully engrossed in the narrative. "Let me start by saying that that got dark in a *hurry!* Talk about a sudden wrong turn into the land of nightmares. Secondly, I have absolutely no idea who your little blonde friend might be—your description doesn't match anybody *we* know—so I can't help you there. But I think after everything you just described, what I *really* want to know is . . . what the hell is a *moonflaw?*"

Jeremy hesitated, and then started slowly, as if anticipating that the words themselves might taste a little sour. "Before today, I'd never heard the expression before in my life. I did look it up on my phone, though. It's an obsolete term, defined as an attack of lunacy, induced by the moon."

Shelly didn't like the sound of that at all; the chill that had permeated Jeremy's dream had somehow found its way down her spine, as if it had wafted in through the restaurant's slightly ajar windows. The breeze seemed to carry cracked images on its wings: baying wolves, underground asylums, and ice-pick lobotomies. She shook the horror from her mind and then said, "With all due respect, honey, I think maybe *you're* the one having an attack of lunacy— trying to dissect some trivial dream and all. I mean . . . who cares, really? Start tellin' me about your ceremony, already."

The Lowes conversed for another forty minutes. They spoke, among other things, about the commencement ceremony and the hot topic of the passing storm—but not once did Jeremy return to the dream in question. Shelly had courteously heard him out, and that much was appreciated, but it was quite evident that he'd already heard all the input she cared to offer on the subject. They vacated the restaurant and returned to their respective professions.

Still, Jeremy knew he wouldn't be putting this thing behind him anytime soon. There was an underlying significance here, and it was burning to be found. And though he realized he'd now have to decrypt the vaporous clues on his own, it somehow made the challenge that much more intriguing.

CHAPTER 5

Saferock
(Gavinia's Grave)

YESTERYEAR

They say the loneliest soul is the soul of a lighthouse keeper. Sadder still is the soul of a keeper manning an *offshore* lighthouse some seven miles from the mainland—as was the case for the man simply known as Teaghue.

Saferock Lighthouse was built on a small, rocky islet in 1888 to prevent shipwrecks. It stood directly south from Mizen Head—Ireland's most southwesterly point. Known as "Ireland's Teardrop," the islet was the last piece of home soil that nineteenth-century Irish emigrants saw as they sailed to North America. The lighthouse, with its Cornish granite walls, was situated on a clay-slate islet with quartz veins, towering over 150 feet above the sea's low waterline.

Though Teaghue was in his seventh year as Saferock's sole attendant, he was still considered relatively green by the Commissioners of Irish Lights' standards. But when you considered his complete résumé involving the briny deep, manning the navigational guidepost was far from his first kick at the nautical can. At the tender age of eleven, his father, Greagor, thrust him into the world of deep-sea fishing. By the time he'd reached his mid-teens, he'd already logged half a dozen seal-hunting expeditions. At twenty, Teaghue was offered a once-in-a-lifetime opportunity when his father arranged for him a six-month stint up at Roche's Point Lighthouse. There, Teaghue worked as a general helper for the designated term and was ultimately offered an additional six months, as his workmanship proved to be a great asset to the trade.

A few years later, Teaghue was blessed with a son of his own: Colin. Unfortunately, two months after Colin's birth, the child's mother ran out on the two of them, and Teaghue was left to raise the toddler on his own. Naturally, Colin was brought up with the salt of the sea instilled in his veins, as a handful of coastal dwellings formed the loose roots of his youth. Fishing expeditions were a way of life, and as a young lad in the late 1950s, Colin had found employment with the Irish Boat Preservation.

In January of 1953, Teaghue was offered the permanent position of lighthouse keeper at the renowned Saferock. His experience at Roche's Point had placed him far above the other candidates.

For three weeks, Teaghue shadowed the skilled hand of Lonan Roarke—Saferock's preceding keeper, who'd manned the beacon for sixteen years. Learning the ropes came easy with Teaghue's prior understanding of the general operation and his orderly obligations: the light signals and their precise timing mechanisms, the fog signals, the constant cleaning of windows and polishing of brass fittings. Also, a daily logbook, required by government standards, was to be kept in great detail. The exact time of lamp lightings, any fog lamp usage, and the presence of passing ships had to be accurately documented. More so during Teaghue's early days on the islet, it wouldn't be beyond the Irish Lights to turn up unannounced for scrutinizing inspections: their way of ensuring a systematic operation.

Teaghue devoted much of his spare time to both reading and writing. He had a novel in the works that was bound to resonate with fellow seafaring enthusiasts. It had become a near-formality to throw back an ale or two at twilight, while surrendering to the afterglow. It was also during these early days of Teaghue's tenure at Saferock that he began sporting his old brown sea cap; for years to come, he'd be virtually unrecognizable to his peers if he wasn't donning his weathered crown that epitomized the essence of a life at sea.

Just when Teaghue felt he had settled into the role, an event occurred in which no training could have ever prepared him for. It was October of 1953. He'd gone about his day like any other, except he'd consumed a significant number of ales before the sun had dissolved below the horizon. In a small addition attached to the foot of the lighthouse, he dozed for an hour in a blue-and-white hammock eerily reminiscent of Norman Rockwell's *On Leave* painting. When he awoke to a curtain of heavy fog he was lost in a sea of disorientation. As if still enveloped in a hazy dream, he frantically lurched his way up the spiralled stairs to load the necessary fog signals.

During Teaghue's slumber, the serene waters of the day had mutated into a procession of violent surges, crashing up against the reef with an unyielding aggression. Like a great eye in the sky, a colossal moon peered down through the murk, unblinking, as if it were the author of the upheaval. The night had turned sour, and its sudden rage—coupled with Teaghue's ill-timed negligence—had left Saferock in an extremely vulnerable state.

Teaghue began his attempt to make up for lost time by firing the electrically detonated fog signals at will, as if an abundance of sudden charges would rectify his lack of attentiveness. The sea below was in a fury, and by midnight the full embrace of the thickest brume he'd ever seen would seemingly suffocate every breath the fog signals had to offer. Then, approaching the one o'clock hour, the inevitable calamity occurred.

The bloodcurdling sound of snapping wood accompanying the frenzied cries of countless sailors was what drew Teaghue to the tower's south window, nearly a hundred feet above. A prolonged study through the haze ultimately revealed the horror that was a shipwreck of epic proportions. The reef's jagged armour was slashing through the underbelly and starboard side of an imposing three-masted schooner, and like rotten candy launched from a punctured piñata, the vessel's contents spilled over Saferock in a grave fashion.

In utter distress, Teaghue rushed down the coil and into the bedlam suddenly thrust upon him. Precious seconds passed as helpless strangers were hurled into the seething waters with every thunderous wave, while others were tossed upon the unforgiving crag, breaking like fine porcelain figures in the process. Immersed in the chaos, Teaghue clawed his way through the mangled debris for any signs of life, all the while treading the slippery rock with painstaking caution.

With fragments of the crippled ship scattered over the reef, Teaghue would go on to spend the next several hours rummaging through the remains. All told, the distraught keeper recovered five bodies; two were broken beyond repair, likely killed upon impact, while three souls had miraculously survived the carnage. Two seamen of Scottish descent and a young American were all found in their own dire condition, but with the immediate actions of both Teaghue and the Irish Lights (who Teaghue had promptly contacted), they all recovered and lived to tell the harrowing tale.

When the dust settled the following morning and the dense fog had rolled out, the Irish Lights began their investigation into the particulars of the tragic mishap. After some time, they concluded that the wreck had occurred by no fault of Teaghue, as the ship had run aground due to "unfortunate, weather-induced circumstances."

The combination of the initial lacerating blow and the repetitive pounding from the raging sea was what ultimately brought the Scottish schooner *Gavinia*, and most of its crew, to its demise. As the details emerged from the survivors, the captain and his mates had been whirling blindly for hours in the turbulent swells, perfectly oblivious to their surroundings before the sudden encounter with a steadfast Saferock. Sadly, twenty-three men had perished on that fateful October night.

The days following the tragedy brought about feelings of great despair and guilt to Teaghue. Though the storm had come about unexpectedly, he had no doubt that he should have been more prepared for such an event, and therefore more productive in his rescue efforts. Vowing to never again be caught off guard with senses dulled, he swore off the drink until the day he'd no longer call Saferock his home.

Teaghue gradually began collecting tokens from the wreckage that still littered the reef. Scavenging the rock and researching his findings proved to be an essential distraction from the ingrained images of the disaster that would forever plague his spirit. He converted a mini steel crate—which had previously been used to store non-perishable food items—into a chest to house newfound relics, trinkets, and assorted nautical gadgets. Among the salvageable artefacts: a nineteenth-century mariner's astrolabe, an operable marine sextant, and a remarkably unscathed marine sandglass in a four-column stand. And perhaps the most intriguing find of the litter was a timeworn, three-draw pocket telescope with the word "moonflaw" haphazardly scratched into its brass surface. The tool was from an indeterminable era, and the mysterious, etched-in scribble only added to the allurement. Due to its severely cracked lens that essentially rendered the eyepiece useless, Teaghue chose to mount the instrument up above his Wedgewood stove like a revered keepsake.

A little over six years would pass before the night of the Heartmoon dream, where Teaghue would seize the pocket scope and behold a ghostly manifestation of his terror and guilt.

CHAPTER 6

Bartering Blues

The morning of Linden Maddox's first TAAS meeting had finally arrived, and as he'd expected, it dawned with a medley of emotions; his excitement was running rampant, while a spell of bad nerves was seemingly balancing the pots. He looked forward to meeting up with Terrance Barlow once again—the man who'd soft-tossed him the invite from across the counter at The Cosmic Lens. Soon he'd be rubbing shoulders with a whole new circle of astronomy enthusiasts—all the while hoping he wouldn't stick out like a sore thumb as the society's obvious newcomer.

Since he didn't have to arrive at Regener Hall until four o'clock, Linden chose to fill the day by leisurely cruising the streets of Albuquerque, popping in on occasional pawnshops and used sporting goods stores. He had a set of used Callaway golf clubs kicking around his garage (even though they'd only ever fought their way through one forgettable round), and the goal was to dump them somewhere along the line for some quick cash. He'd be content to collect $50 for the set, and then grab a bite to eat before topping up his tank and heading up to the hall at the University of New Mexico.

While heading along Gibson Boulevard, Linden pulled into Mrs. B's Pawn & Trade. This stop brought about some cursory bargaining, but rather than strike a deal in the first inning, he chose to move on and test other waters. An unexpected Closed sign greeted him at the door of Valley Sport and Recreation. A handwritten message was taped to the interior glass that read: *We'll re-open at 12:30. Sorry for any inconvenience.* Linden glanced at his watch and found this odd, considering that at this point it was already pushing one o'clock. He knew of one other pawnshop in the area—The Treasure Trove—and decided to take one last crack at selling his clubs on this day before surrendering to his growing hunger.

"The Trove," as the locals knew it, was a thriving, family-owned shop that had been operating for over fifty years. Sammy, the Trove's well known and respected owner, knew his merchandise like the back of his own hand. He was getting on in years—seventy-seven, to be exact—but he was still the one turning the key to open and close the shop six days a week.

Linden parked his Jeep Grand Cherokee in the rear lot, rolled his golf clubs around to the front, and proceeded through the main entrance under a sign that read: *Buy, Sell, Trade, and Loan— Albuquerque born, Albuquerque grown.* Upon entering, he immediately noticed two things: the first being an old Welsh terrier who was distinctly beyond the horizon of the breed's typical lifespan. The canine greeter was curled up in a cozy dog bed with the words *Lounging Libby* embroidered into the fabric. His right foreleg and paw were wrapped in a bandage. With a pair of cloudy cataracts, the dog still seemed to give Linden a quick once-over as he entered *his* store. The second thing Linden noticed was the direct contrast to his previous pawnshop visits—both earlier in the day and in days past. Unlike his prior stop at Mrs. B's, which had come and gone without another customer in sight, this place was buzzing with potential buyers and sellers.

Given the shop's current activity, and the fact that there appeared to be only a single clerk manning the lengthy counter, Linden figured a stroll around would suffice for the time being. While doing so, distracted by other odds and ends within the shop, he clumsily stumbled over the corner of a dusty cardboard box that was jutting out into a customer aisle. The words *Assorted Junk* were faintly scribbled on each of its two visible sides. It was quite evident that the contents were not on display, but the box was half-heartedly tucked away, nevertheless.

With curiosity aroused, Linden hunkered down to venture into the seemingly forsaken load. The top flaps were already folded open, and a double layer of bubble wrap veiled the interior. He peeled back the wrap to unearth a plenitude of dust-coated "junk" that surely hadn't seen the light of day in some time.

Still crouched, Linden paused to survey his surroundings and then was suddenly gripped with paranoia, as if the unfrequented box was somehow forbidden. With the clerk still engaged at the counter, Linden shook the apprehensive bout and continued to rummage through the cardboard tomb. That was until he spotted an old brass pocket telescope buried in the depths, its cracked lens a cloudy cataract of its own. He promptly rescued his find, and instantly began to ponder its origin. The curio was caked in dust and chipped, but there was something . . . *more*. Something that ran far below the surface of the moment, like an underground water supply that serves an entire city. Linden suddenly felt averse to returning his discovery to its boxed grave, and he rose from his crouch to the simultaneous *pop* of two cracking knees.

Caught up in his fascination like a child in a toy store, Linden, thinking he'd lost track of time, remembered the TAAS meeting. He quickly checked his watch and realized that only a few short minutes had ticked away; there was still plenty of time to press the clerk for some information on what he guessed was a rare and obviously obsolete nautical telescope that possibly dated as far back as the late nineteenth century.

When the crowd had finally dispersed, Linden wheeled his set of Callaways up to the main counter, along with his newfound treasure in hand. A noticeably exhausted Sammy, spent from a long day of ceaseless activity, awaited.

"The help left me high and dry today—haven't even had time to take a leak," the pawnbroker groaned, now hunched over with both forearms resting on a glass-planed display case. "What can I do for you?"

"Well, sir, I've got two things, but I'll make it quick," Linden replied, as hunger pains began to bark in his belly. "I'm looking to sell this set of practically brand-new golf clubs—leather bag and all. And I'd like to inquire about *this* item." He gently placed the pocket scope down on the glass, and then the clubs rattled in their cage as he hoisted them up to be assessed.

"Well, I'll be damned!" Sammy stated with a smile and a shot of restored life. The golf clubs drew no more than a cursory glance as he picked up the eyepiece. "This one goes *waaay* back. If I'm not mistaken, it's been kickin' around the shop since shortly after we first opened the doors in the early '60s. And if we're speakin' truths, I didn't even know it was still in my possession. Was it in that box-a-junk over there? Been meanin' to rummage through it for any salvageables, so I can clear it the hell outta here." He now brought the scope to within a few inches of his straining eyes. "If you wipe off the dust here, and look hard enough, you'll notice the word *moonflaw* has been etched into the brass—though like it was the very day I received the piece, the expression is lost on me."

The term "moonflaw" didn't register with Linden either, but the peculiar engraving still worked in adding another wrinkle to the artefact's mystery. "Okay, how does this grab ya?" Sammy continued, his expression shifting on a dime from a look of wonder to one strictly ready for business. "For whatever reason, I've never had much luck turning over golf clubs in here, so unfortunately I can't offer you cash. But here's what I *can* do: I'll take the clubs off your back in a straight exchange for Mr. Moonflaw here."

Linden smiled thinly and took an extra second to absorb the offer. "No disrespect, sir," he began, "but I'm certain these clubs still hold at least a $400 value. Shit, the bag *alone* has gotta be worth $200. All I'm askin' for is an easy fifty—for the whole shebang!" He discerned a growing impatience in Sammy's eyes. "Now don't get me wrong, this old scope would make for an interesting conversation piece; but if we're speakin' truths, it can't be worth a salty dime."

"In case you didn't hear me, I'll say it again—I don't *need* any damn clubs!" Sammy was quickly coming to a boil. "I've given you my only offer—take it or leave it."

Though irked by the exchange, Linden drew a deep breath and calmly countered with a final inquiry: "All right then, forget about the clubs. How much to buy the scope outright?"

Sammy chuckled briefly and then snarled in contempt, "An easy fifty." He then turned and walked into a back room with the instrument grasped firmly in hand. Then, as if it were a distant, delayed echo, "And we're closed for lunch!"

Linden's clubs felt twice as heavy and half their worth as he rolled them back to the rear lot. Despite the discourteous dealings of the pawnshop clerk, he quickly found renewed hope in his journey up to the university, and the promise of his inaugural TAAS meeting. His loose plan would be to make a few acquaintances, hopefully check out some impressive new equipment, and when the moment was right, casually mention to Terrance about the curious relic he'd literally stumbled upon at a local pawnshop, along with asking him if he was familiar with the equally curious word that was engraved in its surface.

After a hearty soup and sandwich at Chloe's Cuisine *(Dine and Dash, but Not before Cash!)*, Linden Maddox approached the pink doors that fronted Regener Hall at ten minutes to four. And little did he know at the time, but he was on the cusp of entering a whole new world of cosmic exploration.

CHAPTER 7

Janelle

A PAST LIFE AGO

Ten long years had passed since Janelle Crawford had wilfully chosen to abandon the only city she'd ever known, leaving behind the tragic events of a cruel autumn night that had stolen her beloved husband, Andy. In vowing to never return to Hartford, Connecticut, again, the door to that chapter in her life would be forever sealed—a chapter that was supposed to introduce a lifelong tale of love and happiness.

Before the accident, life for the Crawfords couldn't have been better. Janelle was a stunning thirty-one-year-old who was reputably known for her uncanny resemblance to Gwyneth Paltrow. (More than a few times she had to rather regrettably disappoint suspecting fans of the actress with the mistaken identity. And once—only once—she did some acting of her own, signing a hysterical young fan's school binder before kneeling to join her in a photo.) She consistently hit the gym five days a week, and her career as a clinical perfusionist was thriving. Janelle's parents had moved to Hartford from nearby Waterbury when she was an infant, and it was here in the Connecticut capital that she'd grown into a woman, graduated from Trinity College, found the love of her life, and eventually began a family of her own.

Andy, two years Janelle's junior, was in his third year with the East Hartford Fire Department (EHFD). Following what seemed like a lifetime of trying to prove his worth through the certifying steps—the EMT courses, the volunteer hours, the endless written and physical testing—he'd finally inaugurated his career as a certified firefighter. Andy's towering, brawny frame fit the position's stereotypical requirements to a tee, and his sense of humour was fast becoming legendary within the department ranks. Though barely beyond the probie stage himself, he was nominated as the station's chief coordinator whenever a new line of hazing was in order.

The couple lived comfortably in a gorgeous ranch-style house situated in a cozy suburb of the big city, and were proud parents of their adorable two-year-old daughter, Ashlyne. Also keeping them on their toes was a mischievous pair named Kody and Alias—their ten-month-old black Labrador retrievers.

Everything was right in the world, until the day when everything changed. The day a dark axe fell and severed Janelle's life into clear-cut segments of before and after.

Just as he'd done before every twelve-hour night shift, Andy gave Janelle a long kiss and then offered a joke to lighten the inevitable concerns he could always read in her eyes. His jokes were corny and cliché, and he knew it; but the last thing he always saw on his wife's face as he was leaving was a smile, and on most nights that was enough to see him through the grind.

Janelle was happy for her husband, as he was doing what he always wanted to do—what he *loved* to do. But in the back of her mind lurked a demon, a malevolent spirit that always had her fearing the worst. She'd heard the horror stories; she wasn't ignorant to the cold fact that firefighting was a dangerous profession. All she could ever do was just hold faith in her husband's judgement when it came to working safely.

"If H_2O is on the *inside* of a fire hydrant, then what's on the *outside?*" Andy calmly asked before heading out for this particular shift.

Sometimes Janelle would chuckle before even hearing the answer. It was a nervous giggle that, in reality, was a struggle to fight off that ever-present demon that ruled in her husband's absence. "I don't know, Andy. I never do," she replied through her anxious laugh.

"Well, it would certainly have to be K_9P!"

Not once did Janelle ever mention how she thought her husband's jokes were trite; she just sent him off with a warm smile and prayed that he'd return home safely and get the chance to tell another.

CHAPTER 8

Discovering Dream Threads

Having returned from her lunch break that she'd spent with her husband at Petrocelli's, Shelly suddenly found herself depleted by the stresses of the morning. She contemplated using the afternoon to declutter her workspace, but that big idea quickly sank like a weighty stone. Rather than put some rare free time to good use, she rested her head down between her folded arms and allowed a brief, feathery curtain of sleep to encompass her.

As her subliminal sense leaked into a cheerless, foggy atmosphere, Shelly found herself sitting alone, her legs draped over the edge of a pier that seemed to extend straight into the ashen mouth of gloom. The old wooden structure creaked and swayed with the breeze as it stretched high above the stirring sea on frangible legs sleeved with moss. The last shades of daylight were being devoured by darkness as the night was met with the raucous cry of circling gulls.

Shelly's eyes were suddenly drawn to the heavens, as through an ethereal mist and sinister clouds an angry full moon with a reddish-pink tinge now ruled the ambience. It was odd; rather than hovering gracefully in its place, the glowing orb appeared to be drawing nearer, growing, as if gliding earthward along some invisible zip line. From somewhere in the cold distance, she faintly began to hear the panicked voice of what seemed to be an old man. Through his shortness of breath he seemed to be shouting the same phrase over and over, but the rumbling skies and the choppy waters below muffled his words. Though the man's figure had yet to emerge through the haze, his footfalls grew louder as they clanked along the pier towards her. With his approach, his words finally became discernible. "The moonflaw is upon us! The moonflaw is upon us!" the stranger bawled repeatedly.

As the unhinged moon continued to close in, it began to reveal what could only be described as a giant surface fissure. Like an inky scar on its florid face, the black slit appeared to be spewing forth a grainy substance into the atmosphere. The discharge not only littered the skies, but it also eventually showered into the sea like pernicious hail. Amidst the commotion, the pier began to teeter and tremble as loose planks spilled into the brine below.

"The moonflaw is upon us!" Though still void of a source, the words now seemed to be right on top of her.

With the fissure now gushing particles like some cosmic geyser, all was now a fiery red as an imminent collision was—

As most dreams go, the moment of impact, or climax, is often harshly interrupted, severed by a quick cleavage and a painless splice back to consciousness. In this case, it was the piercing ringtone of Shelly's cell phone that cut her slumber short. Startled awake from her brief but unsettling repose, she answered the call that displayed nothing more than the frustrating "Unknown Caller" caption. She was still groggy, and her breath had turned stale.

"Hello?"

"Hello, um . . . hi." An anxious and unfamiliar male voice on the other end filled Shelly's ear. "Listen, first off, I have to say that I know how absurd this is all gonna sound."

"Excuse me?" she replied swiftly. "How absurd all is *what* gonna sound? And who the hell is this?"

"There's no time for questions," the stranger continued in his troubled tone. "I need to get hold of your husband—and right away! It's beyond urgent! All I can say for now is that everything will soon make sense—just give me his cell number and we can all stay ahead of this."

"Whaddaya mean, 'stay ahead of this?'" a confused Shelly questioned. "Stay ahead of *what?* And I thought I asked you to tell me who I'm speaking with. Make it the next thing outta your mouth, or this conversation's over."

"Okay, I understand. Let me start again, but all I ask is that whatever you do—just don't hang up. My name is Luke Sheehan, and I'm calling from Boston. You don't know me, and I don't know you, but I believe your husband and I are—or should I say *were*—linked in some bizarre dream experience."

Shelly, now pondering the notion that she was still adrift in her *own* midday siesta, struggled to make the slightest grain of sense out of what this wacko was going on about. She pulled the phone away from her cheek and held it out at a distance, as if upon returning it to her ear the stranger might kindly begin to cut through the gibberish.

"All right, Luke from Boston," Shelly began in a tone that affirmed she'd be the one calling the shots from here on out. "You say you're in a hurry, so I'll make this quick. There's no way in hell I'm giving you my husband's number. But what I *will* do is this—I'll give him *your* number so he can call *you* on the off-chance that he deems you worthy of his time."

"Deal!" Luke practically shouted without a moment's hesitation. "The number's 617—"

"Not so fast, buddy," Shelly cut in before he could spill his digits. "I'll only go through with this if you tell me exactly how you got *my* number."

"Listen, I told you this will all make sense," a persistent Luke now pleaded. "But like I also said, there's no time for me to sit and answer a buncha questions right now. We're wasting precious time here—so I'm begging you, take down my number and then call your husband right away! And be sure to emphasize the urgency in my request."

Against her better judgement, Shelly permitted the stranger from Boston to issue the number where he could be reached. With a skeptical hand, she scribbled the digits down on a Post-it note as he rattled them off. During the process, she was still contemplating if she was actually going to take this thing any further. She considered how Jeremy would respond to all this nonsense—how he'd react to some outsider calling his wife and suggesting they all had to act fast to "stay ahead" of a seemingly impending threat.

Shelly was still on the fence when Luke suddenly dropped a bomb on the entire situation, ultimately forcing her hand. "There's one more thing," he abruptly asserted before she had the chance to hang up, "and it's absolutely critical that you mention this piece of information."

"This better be good."

"In his dream—the one he would've had just last night—it was *me* that was flying in the old warplane that swooped down over Fenway Park. He'll know what you mean—trust me. Tell him I not only saw *him* in the empty bleachers below, but I could also see a ghostly impression of a long-deceased young girl sitting next to him."

Shelly broke into a sudden cold sweat and nearly dropped her phone in the process. She wanted to ask her caller if he was playing some kind of sick joke, but her mouth had gone dry, and the words perished in the stale cavity. Instead, she instinctively ended the call and considered tossing her phone across the spacious office. The device had admitted the intruder and his meddling words into her head, and she now found herself wishing she'd never taken the call in the first place.

What was the true identity of the man behind the desperate voice? Shelly ruminated in her unnerved state. And how in God's name could a stranger over two hundred miles away, in Boston, know such exclusive details about her husband's dream?

CHAPTER 9

The Empyrean Vault

Just as he'd initiated nearly every meeting since joining The Albuquerque Astronomical Society back in 1965, Ernest "Ernie" Cowarth began this month's session with a brief rundown of all imperative news, and then followed with the welcoming of new recruits. Luckily for Linden Maddox, there were two other first-time guests, and they were received as a trio.

Following Ernie's words, the hall's large gathering of roughly two hundred members suddenly dispersed into groups of twenty, and then promptly fled through the exits as if someone had cried fire.

Linden was caught at a momentary loss; one minute the place was buzzing like a hive of bees, the next it was like a deflated balloon. This was when Terrance Barlow, alongside Ernie and two other certified TAAS members, came over and personally greeted Linden and his fellow newcomers. Terrance kindly filled them in on what exactly had just taken place—why an abundance of grown men and women had just made tracks like children informed of a nearing ice cream truck. "We have a dozen observatory stations at our disposal—all located within a ninety-minute drive from here," the owner of The Cosmic Lens explained. "Our members have been strategically grouped based on experience and skill set. These groups rotate through the stations every other time we gather, and as you just witnessed by the stampede-like exit, everyone's eager to man their new posts by early nightfall."

With a neck swivel and a nod, Terrance handed the floor to the old man who had held the podium for the evening's announcements. Ernie Cowarth was a frail yet spirited senior who always seemed to find another gear whenever the topic was TAAS related. The Society had run in his blood for more years than he dared to remember, and the fact that he was now pushing eighty-one only meant that his time spent in this familiar circle was more precious than ever. "What we plan to do with *you* fellas is to try and gain an understanding of where you stand as far as knowledge and experience in the field. We'll be touring our campus observatory shortly, and then hopefully by the end of the evening we'll have a better idea as far as an appropriate grouping for your next session."

As if on cue, another of the TAAS members—a towering man of six foot eight—stepped forward. "Gentlemen," he began with a confident professionalism, "my name is Aubrey Mills, and this here is my assistant, Angel Ferroia. What we'd like to do is let you experiment a little with our instruments here on-site—familiarize yourselves with some new equipment. It's calling for a cloudless night, so let's get after it while the gettin's good!"

While the masses had decamped the hub in search of stargazing euphoria, Terrance led the group of newbies through a maze of hallways that eventually wound to an imposing set of steel doors marked The Empyrean Vault. Aubrey stepped forward and tapped a six-digit code into a mounted keypad to the right of the entrance, and the doors swung slowly inward. The group navigated the threshold, and what lay beyond was enough to render Linden speechless and frozen in awe.

The observatory was an enormous open-concept space, capped with a retractable dome ceiling. A giant window along the west wall awarded a stunning view of the seemingly boundless valley below. The picturesque vista was a sight in its own right, but it was essentially playing second fiddle to the grand collection of state-of-the-art astronomical equipment within. A profusion of multifaceted telescopes, mounts, cameras, and focusers all formed a broad band around the room's centerpiece: a Meade 16-inch LX200-ACF telescope with a permanent pier.

"Welcome to the playground, gentlemen," a proud Aubrey boasted to the new recruits, his rangy arms forming a giant *V* as he spoke. "That bad boy taking centre stage is our latest acquisition— a sixteen-inch Meade that I've personally dubbed the 'Supernova Seeker.'" He then pointed up to the domed ceiling. "Pretty soon we'll be peeling the lid back on this tin can, and at that point you should feel free to sample any of the toys you feel comfortable with—and to ask questions about the ones you don't, of course."

For Linden, the next few hours flew by like a dream. He acquainted himself with the new equipment as he sampled the night sky with nearly everything he could get his hands on. It quickly became apparent that though he'd been in the game for some time now, he was now getting his feet wet in a much higher league.

Before wrapping things up around eleven o'clock, the group gathered for a brief question and answer period. Here, as they'd done from the moment the others departed for the lookout stations, the two newcomers Linden had been grouped with monopolized the conversation. Brothers Karl and Ian Burleson continuously spewed asinine questions and remarks like verbal vomit. After a solid ten minutes, Linden had finally heard enough. "Excuse me, fellas." He managed to wedge into the Burleson wall of prattle, speaking to the group. "I have a quick question."

"Certainly, Linden," Terrance replied without hesitation, the look on his face suggesting that the know-it-all brothers were long overdue for a gag cloth.

Ignoring the Burlesons' indignant stares, which implied he'd interrupted their rightful floor, Linden continued. "Well, it doesn't really concern the Society—or *anything* we've dealt with tonight, for that matter—but I'm curious to know if the term 'moonflaw' holds any relevance with anyone here."

Terrance scrunched his eyes, fighting to summon a memory that he conceded was never there. Disappointed he couldn't help, he shook his head meekly. Ernie just pivoted around without a response and gingerly hunched over to sample a drinking fountain. Aubrey and Angel momentarily met eyes before shrugging in unison, while the Burleson brothers offered nothing more than sullen faces.

"For my own curiosity, where did you hear the term being used?" A now noticeably shaken Ernie returned from his swill and immediately questioned Linden. Sweat was forming on the old man's brow and his eyes were swimming in pools of panic.

"You all right there, Ernie?" Terrance jumped in and spoke. "Looks like ya just seen a ghost."

"I'm fine, Terrance," Ernie replied, assuring his fellow TAAS leader without as much as a fleeting glance away from Linden. "Linden, answer my question—where did you hear that *word*?"

"It's no big deal, really." Linden, discerning the urgency in Ernie's tone, tried to downplay his own inquiry. "I just happened upon this old pocket telescope this morning, and it was hand-etched into its surface."

"Do you have it with you now?" Aubrey queried from on high.

"No, unfortunately I don't. It was kicking around a pawnshop downtown, and I . . . well let's just say I didn't have much luck on any front while I was in there. The fact that it was so old is what grabbed me in the first place. Christ, it was *ancient*. The peculiar inscription only added to my curiosity."

An awkward silence suddenly fell over the group. Even the long-winded Burlesons were at a loss for words, as a general lack of interest appeared to have rendered Linden's report moot. Terrance broke the lull by reminding the newcomers of a slight time change for the following session, and the night concluded with a round of handshakes before the pack parted ways.

Linden left the hall beaming. With the TAAS program, a great resurgence had taken form in him, and the next session couldn't come soon enough.

Approaching his vehicle after an invigorating walk through the crisp autumn night, Linden paused to turn, as he thought he could detect a faint panting sound in his wake. With the agonizingly weak breath now gaining and growing louder, he sharpened his gaze on the slow, advancing figure. "*Wait!* Linden, please *wait!*" the yet-to-be-identified man pleaded with all he had left in his lungs. Linden cautiously stepped toward his pursuer and, to his great astonishment, found it was Ernie Cowarth, who nearly collapsed upon his feet.

"Shit, man, *what is it?*" Linden questioned the evidently perturbed TAAS leader. With the old man still winded and unable to reply, Linden rested his hand on Ernie's shoulder and carried on. "No offense, Ernie, but you're a little too old to be chasin' people down in parking lots."

Again, Linden awaited an explanation for the drastic approach. When his heavy breathing finally began to subside, Ernie slowly revealed his motive through minimal gasps and wheezes. "I'm terribly sorry it had to come to this, Linden. I just couldn't risk the others gaining any further information."

"Further information?" a bemused Linden echoed. "Information on *what?*"

"It's about the object you claim to have found earlier today."

"You mean the old telescope? Unfortunately, there's no further information to offer—I've basically told all there is to know."

Ernie broke into a light chuckle, and then struggled to keep it contained. It was the sort of inward snicker of someone who holds a deep, dark secret—a secret that, if it were ever to become known, would rip the accessible threads of sanity from the recipient, and then unravel the whole ball of yarn straight to the bughouse. After a moment he smothered his laughter, bringing a sternness back to his approach. "If there's any truth to what you're saying—that you actually saw the scope with your own two eyes—then we desperately need to get our asses back down to that pawnshop first thing in the morning and get our hands on it!"

Linden was finding it harder and harder to wrap his head around Ernie's pressing state. "I have to admit, you're losin' me here," he asserted. "Care to elaborate on your urgency?"

"Assuming the shop opens at nine o'clock, I need you to pick me up in this very parking lot at eight. I'll explain as much as I feel I can on the ride down. And for Christ's sake, whatever you do—don't be late! I wanna be waiting by the front doors when they flip the sign." Ernie had one last piece of information for Linden to digest overnight, and though vague in its measure, he needed it to really hit home. "Son, I'm sure it's all fuzzy to you now, but your little discovery may just clarify *everything*."

———————

Following his chance encounter with Linden Maddox, Ernie Cowarth raced home to Santa Fe, hobbled into his study, and went straight for the file long secured under lock and key. Before this rather fortuitous wind came blowing, he'd accepted the fact that the file containing years of in-depth research and pinpoint-accurate findings would remain unstirred until the end of his days—unless, by some extraordinarily bizarre twist of fate, someone either came querying about the elusive blonde children, or, as in this particular case, one of the *two* hallowed artefacts.

CHAPTER 10

A Lack of Light

It was Ardmore—a quaint fishing village on Ireland's south coast—where Teaghue had planned to end up in after riding off into the sunset. His retirement destination lay less than a hundred miles from his current post at Saferock, and when the day came that he finally tired of the islet, he'd return to the mainland, where he'd peacefully settle into his twilight years. But unbeknownst to him, waiting like an immovable blockade before the great wide open was a massive heart attack that struck one night in late October, 1959—the night another storm snuck up like a thief, and a ghostly recollection of *Gavinia* suddenly made the promise of Ardmore—and the usual serenity of Saferock—fade away into a premature eternity.

Eerily, just like the squall in '53 that had rocked *Gavinia* into extinction, this storm seemed to generate with an abrupt flick of a switch. Come twilight, ominous black clouds riding gale-force winds suddenly rolled in over Saferock like a floating quilt, blotting out the last traces of the day. Treacherous waves relentlessly

55

pounded the rocks, and a driving rain opened over the bound-less sea.

Despite the vile ocean and its thirst for ruin, there would be no shipwrecks on this night. Though the mistakes Teaghue had made back in '53 would forever plague his spirit, not once did he ever duplicate his costly lapses. On this night, the weather-related warnings were fired in abundance, and they were done so in the utmost of clear-headed mindsets. Not until all was safe and sound did Teaghue finally rest his head.

Now deep into the small hours, long after the storm had advanced to the east, a vivid impression of *Gavinia* sailed into the restful harbour of Teaghue's dream.

A low-lying crescent moon was seemingly resting on the horizon like an oversized reaping hook, lighting the setting with a haunting maroon tinge. The sea below was a vast, silent sheet of glass, yet it still seemed to whisper of how it could—and *would*—deform into a virulent pool should it be provoked.

Then suddenly, in the great distance, as if breezing in on some languid mystical zephyr, Teaghue caught his first glimpse of *Gavinia*. As it emerged in all its glory, the prow cut through the tranquil waters toward Saferock like a hot-tipped blade, breeding soft ripples that sparkled in the moonlight. To Teaghue, the sight of the unblemished schooner was the most beautiful he'd ever beheld. In his haste, he snatched the pocket scope from the wall behind his stove for a closer look. Training its cracked, defective lens on the nearing vessel, he distinguished a skewed view of his surroundings. What to the naked eye was nothing more than a calm, moonlit marine climate was now a churning sea of sanguineous fury. Tidal surges rocked *Gavinia* as she stretched for Saferock, posing a dire threat to the crew.

The crescent moon had mutated into the form of a human heart, still kindling the night with its crimson hue. The organ pulsed with life, but it was also shuddering with an increasing pressure from within. *The Heartmoon,* Teaghue thought, not knowing how he knew its name.

From high above the turbulence, Teaghue tweaked the scope to its maximum magnification, but all it did was magnify the horror. He saw that the *Gavinia* crew had transmuted into an enraged army, their intentions clear on attacking the vulnerable lighthouse. Like Vikings invading by longship, the warriors wielded spears, swords, and battleaxes. Their cries pierced the night as they sought revenge upon the rock's sole occupant for their expirations. As the ruddy glow of the Heartmoon reflected upon the advancing mob, Teaghue found that their faces were strange deformities of the most lurid design: wooden skulls, mouldy and eyeless. Shaken by the contorted images, he'd seen enough of the revulsion that was the view from the pocket scope. He lowered the spyglass and, expecting to once again see a crescent moon hovering above placid waters, witnessed instead the culmination of the nightmare.

As the vessel dropped anchor, and the barbaric crew began to take the rock, the Heartmoon suddenly detonated with a resounding blast. A myriad of black-and-white particles gushed into the atmosphere as the explosion vaporized the ship and its savages in an instant. With the grave concussion, a violent, sharp pain in Teaghue's chest suddenly stripped away the image and pulled down the eternal curtain with the same stroke.

Though in the end it was no more than the devilish mindwork of a nightmare, the trauma of the vision was enough to drag Teaghue's life away with it—the heart attack causing him to perish in his sleep.

The following evening, an outgoing cargo ship notified the Commissioners of Irish Lights of Saferock's uncharacteristic lack of light. The report was met with an immediate investigation, as a pair of members made the short voyage out to the islet. As they approached the jagged rock, it was evident that something was amiss. The beacon, which should have been glowing high above the brine, was nothing more than a cold ember.

The Lights members proceeded to mount the lighthouse in search of its keeper. What they found when they reached the sleeping quarters was best described by one of the men as "peacefully disturbing." A deceased Teaghue was lying flat on his back on a collapsible bed—his eyelids limp, yet still half-open. What should have been the whites of his eyes were a ghastly deep crimson, and his cold expression still appeared to register fear.

The two members of the Irish Lights put their trouble and grief aside and proceeded in the best manner they knew. They lit the lamp that would see Saferock through the night, and then solemnly returned to the mainland with Teaghue's body in tow. A coroner's inquest was promptly arranged, and the lighthouse's keeper position was filled on a temporary basis before a permanent successor was appointed.

It was a mournful period for all, as many had come to know the kind and dependable lighthouse keeper who had manned the country's most storied post for nearly seven years.

CHAPTER 11

Cellular Activity

Shelly chose to immediately contact her husband following her disconcerting phone conversation with the stranger from Boston. A simple *CALL ME ASAP!* was forwarded via text message.

After a dreadfully long twenty minutes for both parties, Jeremy paced to the campus' nearest common area and addressed his wife's urgent request. "I got your text, honey," he began with evident concern when she answered. "I would've gotten back to you sooner, but I was in the middle of a class. Is everything all right?"

"Well, to be honest, I'm not really sure," Shelly replied, and then took her best stab at explaining the situation. "Before I sent you the text, some guy from Boston named Luke Sheehan called my cell and practically demanded to talk to *you* right away. He was damn near frantic about it. Luke Sheehan—does that name ring a bell with you by any chance?"

For Jeremy, a hot stew of interest began to stir. He went silent on the other end of the line and then began repeating the name aloud, as if to rouse a connection. When there was no relation to be found, he started firing a barrage of questions at a faster rate than Shelly could absorb, let alone answer. "Why would somebody from Boston want to talk to *me?* And what the hell does he want, anyway? If he wanted to speak to *me,* then why is he calling *you?* How did he get *your* number? Did you get *his* number?"

Having survived the bombardment of curiosity, Shelly attempted to summarize the ordeal. "I guess the bottom line is this bizarre bit about how he thinks the two of you are—or rather, *were*—linked in a dream, or something. And that we need to 'stay ahead of this.'"

"Stay ahead of this? Linked in a *dream?* What the hell are you goin' on about?"

"Hey, listen—I'm just the bloody messenger stuck in the middle here. Now loosen up, I'm tryin' to break it down for you. When I returned to my desk after lunch, I put my head down for a quick snooze. I went out like a light—got to dreaming. A few minutes later, my phone woke me. I was a little dozy when I took the call, and it was this guy—this stranger, Luke—all in a tizzy, pleading to get in touch with you. Trust me, I almost hung up on him a couple of times, but he kept roping me back in with these . . . particulars."

"For Christ's sake, Shelly, I need a little more here." Jeremy didn't realize it, but he was now squeezing his phone so tight that it was on the verge of suffering damage. "It sounds to me like this crackpot is taking you for a ride. Let's cut through the shit—tell me right now, what else is there?"

Knowing that what she had yet to mention just might send her husband to the tipping point, Shelly felt reluctant to proceed. But she was already in too deep—*they* were already in too deep, and to suppress any information at this point would only be detrimental to both. And perhaps even to Mr. Crackpot, calling all the way from Boston. "Well, he *did* mention another thing—something that turned my flesh cold," she finally conceded, as the chill still lingered. "And this is the main reason why I followed through with contacting you. He insisted, above all else, that I mention that in your dream last night, it was *him* in the old warplane that flew over Fenway Park. He also said he could see you sitting in the empty bleachers next to the ghost of a dead little girl."

Jeremy took a moment to mull over the seemingly impossible information he was receiving from his wife, and then responded heatedly, "Whoever this son of a bitch is, he must've overheard me at the restaurant, and then decided to play a little game with us."

"Quite possibly—I mean, it sounds like the only logical explanation here," Shelly concurred, but a small seed of doubt still lingered. "But how the hell did he get my number? I asked him repeatedly, but he kept brushing it off by saying there's no time for questions, and that everything will eventually make sense."

"Did you get this creep's number?" Jeremy asked again.

"Yes, I have it, but I'm not so sure I want you calling him back. The more I think about it, the more I figure it might be best if we just steer clear of this guy. I think maybe we should be calling the police, if anybody."

"I get what you're sayin', but as far as I'm concerned, this guy ain't gettin' off the hook that easily. I promise I won't do anything rash. I just want to feel him out a bit. I'm willing to bet that this guy was in the restaurant and is still in the city. He *had* to've been— you're the only person I've told about that dream."

Shelly collected her thoughts before throwing something else into the growing fire. She knew Jeremy would shoot it down, but he hadn't heard the sheer desperation in Luke's appeal, and as of yet he hadn't heard the significant details of *her* most recent dream. "All right, I'll give you his number, but just hear me out for a minute, first. What are the chances that there's something . . . more? I mean . . . just consider that maybe there's another hand at play here."

"Another hand at play?" Jeremy repeated sarcastically. "I think we've already established *that*, honey."

"You know what I mean, wise-ass—besides our caller. All I'm saying is that maybe we should approach this with an open mind. The more I think about it, I don't recall anybody sitting anywhere near us at that restaurant—place was practically empty. Unless we at least start *considering* other possibilities, there's just no explanation for this."

"Okay, consider it considered. Now, the number, please."

Shelly obliged with a gut full of trepidation, and then offered her husband one last piece of information before leaving the situation in his hands. "There's one more thing, and then I'll let you go. Like I said—when I received his call, I was in the midst of a dream, myself. It was similar, in a way, to the one you described from last night."

"Similar in what sense?"

"Well, maybe not *similar*, but that curious word surfaced in it. What was it again? Moonflow? Some old guy kept yelling it over and over, like a lunatic advertising the end of the world."

"Flaw," Jeremy revised. "Moon*flaw*. Listen, honey, I hate to cut you short, but I've only got a few minutes before I have to head to a meeting. I'm gonna call this guy back right now, and hopefully get to the bottom of this. As soon as I get a chance, I'll let you know how it went. I love you, and I'll talk to you soon."

Jeremy Lowe loved his wife indeed. He essentially fell in love with her the day she sat across a table from him and, for twenty minutes, peppered him with questions about progressing in his career. He hoped this nonsensical matter would be settled soon so their lives could go on as usual. But a sense of dread was now simmering in his stomach like a peptic ulcer.

INTERLUDE

Debating the Perigee-Syzygy

Hello again, reader.

Let's dip into some theory, shall we? You'll get varied opinions on whether or not a supermoon can influence the earth's delicate balance, and therefore be responsible for natural disasters of varying forms.

Technically termed "perigee-syzygy," a supermoon is the coincidence of a full moon with the closest approach the moon makes to the earth on its elliptical orbit. This offers stargazers a bigger (roughly 14 percent) and brighter (roughly 16 percent) perspective of our natural satellite. The term "perigee" is defined as the point where the moon is nearest to the earth, and "syzygy" means an astronomical alignment of three celestial bodies—in this case, the sun, earth, and moon.

Richard Nolle is an American astrologer who coined the term "supermoon" in 1979. Highly regarded in the field, his published works date back to 1973. Below is an excerpt from a recent *Mountain Astrologer* article pertaining to the lunar spectacle.

> Within three days—either way—of the exact syzygy, as a general rule, supermoons are

noteworthy for their close association with extreme tidal and seismic forces during the phenomenon. From extreme coastal tides, to severe storms, to earthquakes and volcanic eruptions, the entire natural world surges and spasms under the sway of the supermoon alignment.

Examples of a supermoon connecting with major storms and seismic events abound. The Mount Pinatubo eruption that spewed ten billion tonnes of magma in 1991, the devastating earthquake that struck Turkmenistan and killed over 100,000 people in 1948, and the deadliest natural disaster to ever hit the United States—a hurricane and tidal surge that struck Galveston, Texas, in 1900, all took place within three days of a supermoon. These events only begin to scratch the surface of the great number of catastrophic occurrences within the past two centuries.

Though Richard Nolle's name is practically enshrined within the halls of astrological lore, scientific naysayers continue to loom, ready to pounce on his latest works and deem them erroneous or unverified. These scientists dismiss his supermoon theories and predictions as utter nonsense, stating that although it presents a great photo opportunity for astronomers, the seemingly swollen orb has no more of an impact on our planet than when it's in its apogee orbit (the greatest distance from the earth). They go on to assert that natural disasters that occur within the supermoon's window are purely coincidental.

Perry Vlahos is the media liaison officer for the Astronomical Society of Victoria in Melbourne, Australia. He is a renowned astronomy educator, author, and broadcaster. Below is an excerpt from his recent "Overstated in Orbit" article from the *Sydney Morning Herald*.

> Neil Armstrong never used the term "supermoon,"
> let alone the freshly minted "extreme supermoon."
> The reason is because these, and other decorative
> terms, have been mostly coined by non-astrono-
> mers to capture headlines. It's nothing more than a
> cheap publicity trick—come up with a new phrase
> for an age-old phenomenon to attract attention.
> As far as the myth that the moon's perigee orbit
> attributes to various forms of natural disasters, well
> I've researched the 10 earthquakes with the largest
> magnitudes in the past 400 years, and not one of
> them occurred when the moon was anywhere
> near being the closest to earth for that given year.

The supermoon debate is undoubtedly a touchy one within astronomy circles. And while all parties produce sufficient proof to defend their arguments, the thesis of the perigee-syzygy and its ramifications remains equivocal. The topic becomes a case of causation versus coincidence, where the mediator stands between science and chance.

Carl Jung, the Swiss psychiatrist and psychoanalyst who founded analytical psychology, considered the opposing theories in his book *Synchronicity: An Acausal Connecting Principle*: "Meaningful coinci-dences are thinkable as pure chance. But the more they multiply and the greater and more exact the correspondence is . . . they can no longer be regarded as pure chance but, for lack of a causal explanation, have to be thought of as meaningful arrangements."

I'll leave you with this, reader: On a late October evening in 1953, a young Ernest Cowarth, alongside a mélange crew of Scottish and fellow American mariners, embarked from Scotland's Port Bannatyne on a seafaring expedition aboard the splendid schooner *Gavinia*. With a roseate reflection of a cherry moon gracing the tranquil waters, the ship's company set out for the Irish Sea. Little did they know that when they were to meet the open waters of the North Atlantic the following night, the sea would turn without warning and thrash their vessel into irrevocable ruin.

PART
II

All along the all along
The mountains of the moon

— Jerry Garcia & Robert Hunter

CHAPTER 12

Marketing Misfortune

Sipping a cold Samuel Adams from a frosty mug, Travis Kellogg of Keene, New Hampshire, leaned back in his squeaky old computer chair and started into a brief silent prayer. He didn't beseech the heavens so much for a hefty return on his item for sale, but rather for a buyer whose shipping address was a great distance from his own—preferably in another time zone. Convinced that his artefact listed on eBay was the source of his current run of misfortune, he anxiously ogled the computer screen as four unsuspecting candidates duelled to outbid one another for the cursed prize.

Travis felt no chagrin in his self-proclaimed status as a secluded loner. He led a simple life that was fuelled by his passion for all things collectible. Anything from vintage casino dice to rare European stamps could be found on display in the cozy confines of his den.

Though he had bought and sold curios over the internet on a near-daily basis, Travis struggled to recall ever purchasing the article that had mysteriously arrived on his front porch three weeks earlier without as much as a knock on the door. The item was a globe—but not your run-of-the-mill, three-dimensional scale model of Earth. This was a *moon* globe, and it was delivered not in a box, but rather curiously exposed, and resting upon a weathered wooden pedestal that was about twelve inches in height. There were no customary forms attached to confirm receipt, as all that accompanied the object was a hand-scribbled note in red ink stating his address. Travis had acquired globes—and even *moon* globes—in the past, but he was baffled when he went to grab the mail and *this* globe innocently awaited outside his front door like a morning paper.

A further inspection revealed the orb's impeccably detailed surface. It was undoubtedly the work of a steady hand, as mountains and craters were carved to perfect scale and then coated in suitable shades of grey.

After receiving the peculiar delivery, Travis made it his mission to trace the item back to where it had come from. He reviewed a record of all his recent online purchases on the off-chance that he'd bought the globe with an erroneous click of the mouse—perhaps at three o'clock one morning, when the computer screen often becomes a cloudy aberration of itself.

When the purchase history revealed no such acquisition, he contacted the postal service, as well as the major delivery service companies in the Keene area—all to no avail. He even went as far as asking a few neighbours if they'd witnessed the globe's arrival.

Though Travis didn't have the slightest inkling as to how or why, the moon globe was now his. Accepting this fact, he continued to dig into the mystery, searching the internet for any information he could find on this specific model. He was amazed to discover that moon globes had been in existence for over sixty years, but nothing even remotely matched the lunar replica that he began to believe had arrived by some fortuitous stroke. If he only knew at the time that the only "good fortune" it would bring was that it would ultimately spare his very existence.

During the three-week spell in which Travis held the globe in his possession, he'd experienced a lifetime's worth of mischance and affliction. First, it was the immobilizing flu that seemingly arrived on his doorstep alongside the alien artefact. The intrusive illness had sunk its teeth in deep and failed to relinquish its hold until a solid ten misery-laden days had passed. The sickness appeared to be heading into a remission by the fourth day, but he relapsed with a high fever and chest pains that led to bacterial pneumonia.

On the heels of the flu and lung infection was the hair-raising highway incident. Travis was travelling east along Route 101 when he suddenly heard the front end of his Honda Prelude begin to cough and choke in a combustive fit. Before he could swerve toward the shoulder, he was abruptly blinded as the hood thrust upward and into his direct line of vision. As thick smoke began to billow from the engine like an industrial stack, Travis angled the wheel clockwise to avoid the imminent perils of oncoming traffic. Following a run-in with a Deer Crossing sign, he secured the vehicle along the roadside and immediately offered the heavens a gesture of gratitude.

Also crammed into Travis's twenty-one days of hell were a pair of broken fingers (the pinky and ring finger both squashed in the car door of his rental), the premature death of Buster—a golden retriever who was his one and only companion, and a minor kitchen fire that was deemed the result of an overloaded circuit.

For some, a quick trip to the local dump or an easy swing of a sledgehammer would be enough to quell a cursed entity. Not so for Travis Kellogg—not by a long shot. Even if the globe were smashed and then steamrolled into grainy bits, it wouldn't be enough to put his mind at ease. It was solely about *distance* now. If he could expel it to the moon itself, he'd gladly pony up the shipping fee.

After taking multi-angled pictures of the orb, Travis took to his computer, bluffed his way through the product description, and had it up for sale in no time at all. He opted for a twenty-four-hour bidding window as, quite frankly, anything longer would be pushing the limits of his sanity.

Some twenty-three and a half hours later, with beer in hand, Travis returned to the eBay site for a front-row seat at the results table. He'd listed the globe the day before with a minimum bid of $50. Not expecting any action quite yet, he nearly choked on his suds when he noticed that four applicants were currently duelling it out in a bidding war. The current leader had just raised the stakes another $25, bringing the figure up to a whopping $775. He could already sense the lubricated movement of gears in his reversal of fortune. The bedevilling sphere and its substructure would soon be on its way out of town, and a lucrative return would be the icing on the cake.

Ten minutes later, the bidding had reached a tidy $900. At this point, Travis decided to venture a closer look at the candidates by viewing their accessible information. He shuddered when he noticed that not one, but *two* of the potential buyers were from the neighbouring state of Vermont. *Waaay too close for comfort*, he thought. Furthermore, a third was from within the *same* bloody state—a mere sixty miles to the east, in Manchester. *Not for a $10,000 return, thank you very much.* Then there was lucky number four. In stark contrast to the others, this sphere seeker was clicking his bids from all the way across the country, in beautiful Bellevue, Washington— currently the greatest location in the *entire fucking world*! Like a kid on Christmas morning, Travis could hardly contain his excitement. Shipping the globe to a consumer some three thousand miles away would be just the ticket—the *one-way* ticket.

Upon reviewing this critical information, Travis Kellogg knew he had to promptly pull the plug on the live auction and arrange a fixed outcome. Exporting the ill-fated object to the Pacific

Northwest was now the *only* option, and by removing the item from the board altogether, the three bidders in his proximity would be instantly expunged. He would follow this step with a personal congratulatory message to the Bellevue bidder, stating that he'd won the auction and the moon globe was now his. And not only that, but his bid that had reached $900 would be nearly slashed in half to an even $500—no questions asked. *Sold*, to the distant dupe who would surely think it was his lucky day.

CHAPTER 13

The Dream Trilogy

For Ernie Cowarth, something was suddenly happening—something *big*. A perfect stranger had just sent him into a tizzy by mentioning the whereabouts of a simple telescope—a telescope that, in truth, was anything *but*, simple. With the discovery, Ernie began to dig into the past. The past, in this case, was retained in the pages and reports that comprised his Reverie Redeemer file. After flipping through the file's contents with a nervous excitement, he revisited his inaugural report, which he hadn't regarded in some thirty years. It read as follows:

FEBRUARY 1981

For definitive reasons that remain unknown, I, Ernest Cowarth, received a series of mysterious dream visions in the fall of 1980. These visions—or rather, admonitions—were recognized in the form of a trilogy, all viewed in a sequence over three consecutive nights. I perceived these dreams with great clarity, and they struck me with enough emotional fervour to remain in my psyche until the day I die.

With their often-disconcerting interpretations, I was never one to put any *real* merit into dreams. But following these particular visions, I threw that notion to the wind, as I've since embarked on a cognitive journey to construe this curious, three-part puzzle.

Mere moments after waking from the second dream, I established a link between it and the previous night's vision—what with the particular apparition that so candidly graced the two. But it wasn't until after the trilogy's final instalment—where the pocket scope, moon globe, and child were all united—that I truly began my quest to grasp its subliminal meaning.

The enigmatic scope and globe were coined "Reverie Redeemers" in the initial dream by an innocent-looking little girl who politely introduced herself as Isabel. Having seemingly materialized from the ashes of conscious thought, the unfamiliar child with glistening, golden-blonde hair had spoken with a most refreshing candour. "Though I wish I could've reached you in a sentient state, I've recently been deprived of such an ability," Isabel began, then paused to survey her surroundings—which, from my point of view, appeared as nothing more than a fog-drenched cavity. She continued in her cultivated tongue, which was years beyond her apparent age. "I'm here to inform you of an imperative reacquaintance, if you will. Twenty-seven years ago, you unintentionally parted with an item; an extremely consequential item that you—and *only* you—must redeem. In due time, this artefact will be crucial to the developments within the real world, and I have faith that if it falls into the right hands—*your* hands—the Deceivers won't prevail."

As if to jog my memory, Isabel then proceeded to describe the pocket scope in detail, focusing on its more intricate traits, such as the cracked lens and unmistakable engraving. Then, before the dream dissolved into conscious thought, she concluded with some must-follow instruction. "This quest will likely take you many years, but you *must* follow through with finding the scope, no matter what. And do not—I repeat, *do not*—tell a single living soul about your search until the eyepiece is firmly in your possession."

After I woke from the first of these dreams, the words of the child resonated with me in a powerful way. Without a single thought of dismissing the strange counsel, I promptly put ink to paper to document her instruction.

The following night, during the second of my three enlightening dreams, the young Isabel emerged in the same fashion as the first. The child, failing to miss a beat, continued as if the two dreams had never bridged a conscious divide. "I now must briefly acquaint you with the ways and wonders of the *second* Reverie Redeemer—and you'll soon understand why."

Rather than use a descriptive manner, Isabel revealed a holographic visual of an orb. With outstretched arms the child cupped her hands, and with a brilliant blue flash, a globe seemingly materialized out of thin air. Then following a brief bout of gibberish, as if she were casting a foreign spell, the glowing light diminished, and the moon globe settled nicely into her awaiting hands. "Carrying an equal relevance to that of the aforementioned scope, this—the second Reverie Redeemer—is a miniature model of our moon." She paused briefly while slowly lowering her arms to her sides, sanctioning the sphere to hover once again. "Though this object is a distinctly different chapter within the depths of the same tale, it doesn't pertain to you until you find the scope. Then, and only then, will the two forces unite to reveal the genesis of the moonflaw. This isn't to say that at this juncture you should be ignorant of the globe's detail. From both the skilled hand and troubled mind of a long-deceased NASA employee, this miraculously precise lunar model, when observed through the engraved scope of which you now seek, will expose what truly happened in late October of 1953."

Invigorated by the mystery, the promise of my assigned quest has jumpstarted my days in a way that has been years overdue. At the time of the dreams, I scribbled notes to trap every last drop of data that was subliminally sent my way. I knew that if it all weren't somehow logged, it would only be a matter of time before it would sporadically pick up and fly away to the wastelands of lost recollection. Though I was eager to jump headlong into the search, I knew that in order to move forward, I had to start by taking a step back. It had been twenty-seven years since I'd last seen my scope, and given the circumstances of that fateful night in Irish waters, another twenty-seven could pass before it could be proven to be anywhere other than resting in a deep, salty grave.

Before I knew it, another night was upon me, and I wondered if I'd once again be graced with the child's presence in the depths of slumber. As I slowly slipped under, she was there, as if waiting impatiently for my arrival. In an evidently anxious state, Isabel opened round three with a word of caution. "Before I leave you with a demonstration, I must forewarn you of the 'Redeemer Deceivers'—this being their *official* title." As she whispered her words she glanced about, giving me the impression that, for whatever reason, time was now of the essence. "They look and act like ordinary everyday people, but you can decipher them by their eyes—their cold, *unresponsive* eyes. In your search for the scope, these Deceivers will stop at nothing in keeping you from attaining even the slightest grain of information regarding its whereabouts." While continuing to speak, Isabel was now working her magic once again. This time it wasn't one, but rather a *pair* of holograms that were floating before her. "You see, I was cursed with a twin sister named Estella. Just recently, in a selfish fit of rage and jealousy, she murdered me with our own father's pickaxe. Overwhelmed with guilt, she went on to kill herself shortly thereafter, and suddenly here we are—impelled into the dreams of the living, as we try to out-scheme one another. Inequitable as it is, unlike me, Estella was gifted the ability to return to the real world as a spectral being, if only in short spells. She has the capacity to mislead the living—hence the 'Deceiver' designation."

The next thing I knew I was standing before the holographic scope, pressing it to my eye and training its lens on the floating moon globe. In a strange way I could sense a change in the atmosphere, like the dream was suddenly dying all around me—crumbling to dust and ash. "You *must* recover the scope," the child pleaded in a waning voice that seemed to be losing contact like a failing radio signal. "Act now, and mind the ever-growing army of Deceivers. Good luck, and may you—" Her voice had flatlined mid-sentence, and in the same manner she'd suddenly appeared amidst the fogginess of the late-night dreams, the child had vanished. As of the day of this writing, she has yet to resurface in my subconscious weavings.

In the dying breath of that final dream, I was left with a vague, foreboding image. It was the perspective offered by the holographic scope, and it was surprisingly not that of the moon globe it was aimed at, but rather that of a *man*. Enrobed in a haggard, black trench coat that grazed the gossamer surface, the eerie figure was skulking in the hazy distance, like a stalker in the depths of a dank alleyway. His sinister glare—which derived from lifeless eyes—could be spotted below the weathered flap of an old brown sea cap as it burrowed into my soul by way of my *own* eyes. His countenance was frustratingly vague, yet still somehow the epitome of what lies at the root of all nightmares, and I was shocked back to consciousness with the horror.

I found myself constantly pondering the identity of this fiendish spirit. With all the information I'd compiled over the three nights, the vision of the ghoulish figure seemed to linger over the collected works like a dark cloud. Seeing as the child had fashioned the holograms, had she also *intended* for me to witness such a dispiriting apparition? Was the image a stark impression of these so-called Deceivers she said I'd encounter at some point down the road?

I found myself struggling to shake the sick notion that perhaps my most recent dream had been breached by this dead-eyed demon. After all, the child had been frequently looking over her shoulder, as if she sensed someone might be closing in. And I can't help but wonder if she had other intentions as to what I was to *actually* witness through the holographic scope—presumably something more along the lines of a moon-related phenomenon. Regardless, keeping in mind Isabel's cautionary advice, the man in the sea cap had given me the overwhelming impression of an intruder—an intruder that perhaps reigns superior over a myriad of other revenants.

CHAPTER 14

Sphere Amasser

Like winding his way through a road course, the FedEx driver squealed his rubber around a sharp corner before hitting the brakes in front of Mason Greene's gated estate. The spacious manor within the iron palisade was a visual highlight along Bellevue, Washington's 134th Avenue, where even the behindhand driver paused for an eyeful before buzzing the intercom to announce his arrival.

Mason, a seasoned pilot in his twenty-sixth year with Delta Air Lines, was in the midst of a three-week vacation, of which he was dedicating a share to his collection of rare and estimable globes. Since the purchase of his first model nearly ten years ago, he'd amassed over 120 globes in total—all varying in a wide range of style, age, and value. The hobbyist's beautiful rec room exhibited a majority of terrestrial models, along with a number of planetary and celestial globes. There they all sat, perfectly spaced behind dust-free glass, basking in the pot-light glow like a marshalled cluster of planets in some untold distant galaxy. When it came to his globes, Mason was more than your typical collector. He knew the history and surface condition of every model he owned like he knew the cockpit of a Delta plane.

Mason had recently been aiming his search engines toward early-twentieth-century models, but today's arrival was a most intriguing exception. Listed and shipped all the way from the country's Northeast region, he had purchased this particular *moon* globe on a whim, as its specifics were cloudy, and its appearance differed from any lunar model he'd ever possessed.

"I have a package here for a Mister M. Greene," the driver's voice crackled through the intercom's interior speaker.

Mason briskly made his way out to the gate and signed for his prize, and then rushed back inside for the unveiling. It had been exactly six and a half days since his purchase was finalized on eBay, and now time seemed to stand still as he began to extract the moon replica from its cross-country confinement. After slicing through a dense layer of tape, he folded back the box's top flaps and revealed the bubble-wrapped globe and accompanying stand. A wide smile followed a quick survey of his newest acquisition. He knew its backstory would require a lengthy study, and it was finally time to dive in: a moment he'd eagerly awaited since blindly throwing $500 at the mysterious, handcrafted orb.

In the days leading up to its arrival, Mason had pre-arranged a home for the lunar model, as the plan was to situate it on an eye-level shelf alongside his "marked landings globe." (Originating in 1978, this NASA-approved moon replica accurately depicted the precise location of all Russian and American landing sites, as well as geographical features such as impact craters, mountain ranges, and "seas.")

Following dinner, Mason put on a fresh pot of coffee and accompanied himself downstairs to his orbital lair with a steaming-hot mug of Columbia's finest. With his wife and only child away on their annual mother-daughter retreat (this year's trip was a change of pace from the Caribbean sun, as they were aboard a rail tour of the British Isles), he still had eight days to himself, and a cozy autumn evening with a computer and his newest toy was shaping up quite nicely.

During a meticulous inspection of the globe's surface, Mason suddenly noticed a tiny scuff mark that, being the perfectionist he was, irked him to some extent. Though the dark blemish was smaller than the size of a BB pellet, it still gnawed at him, as repeated attempts to banish it from the varnished shell were futile. The stickler in him even went as far as to contact the seller to see if *he* was aware of the facial flaw; and though the gentleman from New Hampshire came across as contrite, he proved ignorant of the imperfection.

Perplexed, Mason's next move was to refer to the marked landings globe. He found himself leaning on the long shot that he'd discover a connection of sorts—a visual relation between the same spot on each of the two models.

Now situated side by side on a small table, the two distinctly different moon globes shared the main stage. A floor lamp with its shade removed towered above the table, its exposed bulb radiating heat and light like a high sun. Mason arranged the orbs in alignment with one another and was justly intrigued when he found the blemish was in perfect correlation with the site of one of the American moon landings. It was the Apollo 15 mission—landing in the Hadley–Apennine region, near the Apennine Mountains.

To Mason, this was more than just an uncanny coincidence; there was something deeper at play. With his ever-reliable Electro-Optix magnifier in hand, he opted to augment the defect. Through the convex lens, he noticed that the blemish appeared to be more than what the naked eye could have possibly distinguished. It was a form of print, and though the characters remained fuzzy, a few subtle adjustments to the eyepiece revealed a single, legible word: *moonflaw*.

What he'd initially deemed a minimal yet aggravating defect on the globe's surface was, in actuality, an improbably diminutive engraving. In the hope that the foreign term would cling to some residual root of memory, Mason bounced it around the forest of his mind. With no such luck, he began to speak it aloud. "Moonflaw . . . moonflaw," he recited while surveying his great wall of globes, as if the answer lay deep within the cosmic collection. "Moonflaw . . . moonflaw. What the hell does it *mean?*" His words withered back into thought: *And how is it possibly linked to Apollo 15?*

CHAPTER 15

An Unsuspecting America

YESTERYEAR

"I've been in this dispiriting business for longer than I care to remember," the hardened coroner mournfully declared through his thick Irish accent. "And these are the rare cases that escape the very sense of reason—the ones that defy the logic of the craft."

After his body had been returned to the mainland, Teaghue's post-mortem examination ruled out any possibility of foul play. With a more or less inconclusive diagnosis, he appeared to have simply passed in his sleep. The autopsy confirmed that there were no signs of blood clotting, nor any suggestion of internal organ damage. In the end, sudden cardiac arrest was deemed the official cause of death, but still a shadowy cloud of skepticism and uncertainty seemed to hover over the case.

As requested in his Last Will and Testament, Teaghue was laid to rest by his only son at a private sea burial. Only eighteen at the time, Colin Sheehan ferried his father some ten miles from the

Irish coast and disposed of his remains into the eternal depths of the North Atlantic.

In the time that followed, Colin was overcome by a desire to start anew. It wouldn't be a rebirth that would commence on the Irish mainland, but rather in America—specifically, the renowned Irish communities of Boston. But before his lengthy journey across the great pond, there were imperative orders of business to address—both with his commitment to the Irish Boat Preservation, and to honourably closing his father's chapter at Saferock.

The Commissioners of Irish Lights were extremely gracious in their efforts to assist Colin, allowing him adequate time to withdraw Teaghue's belongings. He surely wouldn't be toting any major appliances to America, so he offered to leave them in their place, thus making things easier on both himself and Saferock's new attendant. As he planned to transport the minimal amount of baggage across the Atlantic, only the absolute essentials made the cut.

For Colin, rummaging through his father's furnishings and prized possessions was no easy task. A single return trip out to the islet was enough, as it was about all his emotions could endure. He transferred a pair of generously sized wooden crates out to the lighthouse, one to charge with linens, which he intended to donate, and a second to collect a plethora of keepsakes. Knowing Teaghue's cherished mementos hung proudly on his kitchen walls, Colin made sure that every last one of them would accompany him overseas.

Less than a week after gathering his father's goods from Saferock, Colin boarded a trans-Atlantic steamer with the crated stock in tow. The crate that he'd crammed with Teaghue's linens was now replenished with his own belongings. When he set out from the Irish coast, all he had to his name was a suitable share of provisions—as well as enough of his father's nautical knick-knacks and gadgets to support a mini maritime museum. Little was Colin aware that when the westbound steamer passed within a quarter mile of Saferock, he was exporting a world of misfortune away from his beloved homeland and onward to the shores of an unsuspecting America.

———————

Colin Sheehan touched the eastern coast of the United States in November of 1959, where the city of Boston welcomed him with open arms. Within four days he'd not only found employment, but a downmarket basement apartment in the North End, as well.

After a revitalizing two-year stay in the big city—one that saw a total of eight different jobs and a half-dozen dwellings—he was once again consumed by wanderlust. Boston had been exactly what his soul required, but the winters of '60 and '61 were unrelenting, and the charm of sunny California was calling him from afar. Now travelling alongside his girlfriend, Dolores, Colin sat behind the wheel of his temperamental '42 Ford sedan as the couple set about for the Golden State. With a load of goods packed to the hilt and exactly $834 in cash to their name, they were freewheeling it in the truest sense of the word.

Colin and Dolores wed in the spring of 1964—two years after they'd arrived in sun-drenched San Diego. The scenic, southern city served as home for an additional eight months, which in turn preceded a full year of rootless living within the state's southern regions.

By '66, with anti-establishment and psychedelia in full swing, the couple had found themselves facing financial hardships. The timing couldn't have been worse, as Dolores was now pregnant with their first child. With no reliable funds coming in, and no place to firmly call home, the two agreed that a return trip to the familiarities of Boston was the only logical course of action.

The Sheehans were on the road once again—heading back to the city in which they'd met, the city where employment would still be a certainty and they could start a family with the freedom of security. The old Ford had finally kicked the bucket back in San Diego, and in their attempt to span the country in a swamp-green '52 Volkswagen Transporter, Colin and Dolores departed from Moreno Valley, leaving the stunning lakes and mountains behind them. With the weight of their recent economic struggles seemingly pressing down harder with every tick of the odometer, Colin concluded that he had no choice but to hawk some of his father's antiques along the way. Though consciously conducted against his better judgement, the moves were necessary to gain money for food, or to top up the ever-dwindling fuel supply.

While making their way through Boulder City, Nevada, on fumes, the Sheehans pulled into a little dive of a shop called Orvel's Odds 'N' Ends to try their luck. There, after some minimal bargaining over a marine sextant, Colin was rewarded with enough fuel money to not only *reach* Flagstaff, Arizona, but to also fill their bellies handsomely once they arrived. While regrouping there in the City of Seven Wonders, he parted with two more relics that also returned a pretty penny. A hulk of a man who surely wasn't Anna from Anna's Antiques offered Colin $28 for a pair of ancient planispheric astrolabes.

The Sheehans were on a roll as they continued to sell their way eastward. With plenty of his father's gadgets still in his possession, Colin figured that, though he'd have to draw the line sooner or later, he could part with at least a few more items.

Now gearing through the streets of Albuquerque, New Mexico, Dolores spotted a wooden lawn sign that advertised The Treasure Trove - Pawn 'N' Trade - 1 Mile on the Left in faded, hand-painted lettering. After the misleading mile that was more like *three*, Colin pulled into the lot and prepared a couple of random items for possible sale.

A young man named Sam—whose name was sewn on a patch above his breast pocket—worked the counter, and he immediately passed on Colin's initial pitch: an outdated, yet still functional Brunton compass. But when the young Irishman placed his father's antiquated pocket telescope on the counter, it promptly drew a contrary reaction. "Now, what have we *here?*" Sam asked inquisitively, sharpening his own focus to gauge the small magnifier.

"Honestly, sir, all I know about this particular piece is that it was salvaged from a shipwreck some thirteen or fourteen years ago. My late father manned a lighthouse on an islet just off the coast of Ireland. There was a terrible storm one night, and a Scottish schooner got lost in its way—smashed hard into the jagged rock. I believe over twenty perished."

"Fascinating tale indeed," said Sam after a moment, nodding slowly. "But if you don't mind me sayin' so, don't you think you might wanna hold on to it? I mean . . . seems like a keepsake, if I've ever seen one."

Colin explained to the pawnbroker that though he respected the angle, he still had an abundance of similar items he planned to retain, and that he just needed a few bucks to keep their wheels spinning toward Boston.

For Sam, it was a no-brainer. He was drawn to the curiosities of the scope—particularly its exotic, freehand inscription—and he now felt obliged to sponsor the couple's skip across the country. In the end, his $7 offer wasn't quite what Colin had anticipated. But on the other hand, he wasn't about to start dickering over the value of an old instrument about which he knew no specifics, other than a grim piece of its history.

Like back in Flagstaff, and Boulder City before that, the funds from the Albuquerque shop bought them fuel, and the fuel bought them directional distance. Over the course of the next twelve days, the Sheehans scraped and clawed their way toward the East Coast in a similar fashion. And what a feeling it was when they finally arrived. The couple had conquered the country, and they agreed that they were not only home, but they were home for *good.*

Just like they'd planned, the Sheehans resettled comfortably in Boston, and Colin found solid employment within two weeks of their return. Three months later, Dolores gave birth to their first child, Chelsea, and the following year they were blessed with a son named Luke.

———————

To Colin Sheehan, the pocket telescope he'd once parted ways with in an Albuquerque pawnshop was nothing but a long-forgotten object when he succumbed to colon cancer in 2003; he was sixty-two. Fortunately for him, he was spared the true magnitude of its power.

CHAPTER 16

Rolled Pennies and the Holy Grail

PRESENT DAY

Winding his way through the cool, refreshingly placid Albuquerque night, Linden Maddox's journey home from his inaugural TAAS meeting was blemished with reservations. The evening had been an absolute blast—like none he'd ever experienced. But it had concluded with the unforeseen, somewhat frenzied actions of Ernie Cowarth, an elder statesman within the esteemed organization who urgently wanted his hands on the pocket telescope Linden had excavated from the pawnshop.

Reiterating Ernie's words in his head like a broken record, Linden tried to decipher the message the old man had desperately uttered through short-winded gasps. According to the animated senior, Linden's discovery had the potential to "clarify everything."

The following morning, Linden was brusquely stolen from his slumber by the reverberating racket of his home phone. Sluggish in his actions, he glanced at his watch before finally ceasing the unwelcome clamour. "Hello?"

"*For the love of Christ!*" The sheer volume of the voice on the other end of the line was enough to shake Linden's morning haze away in an instant. "What are ya still doin' at *home*?"

Like a paralyzing jolt, it suddenly dawned on him that he'd forgotten all about Ernie and his desired re-engagement. Discomposed, Linden replied with a half-hearted apology, then stammered in asking, "H . . . How'd you . . . How'd you come by my number, Ernie?"

"What didn't you understand when I *stressed* not to be late?" Ernie ploughed forward, as if he should be the only one asking questions at the moment. "Get yer ass up here and pick me up— the shop's already open!" The line went silent. In this intermissive moment, Ernie realized that though he was angered by Linden's untimely disregard, he had to cool it with the contentious approach. The truth was that he needed Linden a thousand times more than Linden needed him. "Linden? Linden, you still there?"

After a few seconds: "Yeah . . . yeah, I'm still here. Hang tight, I'll be out the door in five."

"Great! Listen, whaddya say we start over? The answer to your question is that you filled out your name and number."

"Come again?"

"You asked me how I ended up with your phone number. You filled out your name and number on the TAAS registration form prior to yesterday's meeting."

"Aaahhh, right, right. Gotcha."

"I apologize for my outburst when you picked up the line."

"As do I, for leaving you hangin' up there. I'm on my way."

Both curious and concerned as to what the day would have in store, Linden shook off the lingering cobwebs of sleep and harnessed his senses for the hike back up to Regener Hall, where a resolute old man would surely be awaiting his arrival with all the composure of a caged lion.

Following Linden's return to the parking lot where Ernie had nearly collapsed in his effort to chase him down the night before, the two used the fifteen-minute ride down to The Treasure Trove to bounce a slew of questions off each other. Ernie now wanted to know—in much greater detail—what kind of shape the pocket scope was in, and how exactly it had been packaged within its cardboard confinement. He also wanted to know what Linden knew of its current possessor—that is, what kind of temperament they would be dealing with when inquiring about the relic. Linden, on the other hand, was still trying to wrap his head around the big picture. The old man's vague remarks on the situation were quickly becoming subtle jabs at his patience. And as if one uncooperative senior wasn't enough, he'd soon be face to face with Sammy once again—the disgruntled shop owner who'd basically regarded him with the same respect as a teenage shoplifter.

As Linden approached the pawnshop for a second consecutive day, Ernie deemed this an appropriate time to ease Linden out of the dark and finally start shedding some real light on the matter. "Now listen up," he began with conviction in his delivery. "I've no doubt you're probably seeing me as some *crazy* old man with more than his share of loose screws and faulty wires. But you need to trust me when it comes to why we're here today. You see, over parts of the past sixty years, I've dedicated countless hours to investigating the prospects of an event that, because of your very actions here at this pawnshop, may suddenly be on the verge of actually taking place—and consequently changing our world as we know it."

Linden was fortunate to find a prime parking space in the already congested lot, and while bringing his Cherokee to a halt, he acknowledged the recent tier of confusion Ernie had added to an already teetering stack. "Well, I must say that that sounds rather riveting and all, but you're gonna have to expand on the significance of this damn scope already!"

93

Sensing Linden's cynicism and lack of respect for the situation at hand, Ernie seared a sinister glare in his direction and raised his voice like an angry parent. "That scope is *so much more* than you could ever begin to perceive! It's merely *disguised* as an old nautical instrument. Its tired brass shell serves a supernatural element within—one that would surely put the fear of God in any nonbeliever. It's one of two key pieces to a puzzle that's been laughing in my face since . . . well, since the early fifties, when I nearly lost my life in tragic fashion. And now *this!* I could never have imagined that at my age I'd still be granted an opportunity to get my hands on it again."

A suddenly intrigued Linden now had more questions of his own, and they rolled off his tongue with a growing enthusiasm. "Get your hands on it *again?* You're sayin' this thing used to be *yours?* Why didn't you just say so in the first place?"

"I'll tell you what," Ernie replied, rather collectedly. "If we walk out of here today with that scope, and it's not a phony of some kind—trust me, I'll know—we'll head straight up to my place in Santa Fe and I'll tell you all about its history on the way. Once we're there, I'll show you my file with all the critical information I've gathered over the years on this whole phenomenon. I'll put on a pot of coffee and we'll go over it word by word. Oh yeah, and by the way—hope ya didn't have any other plans today."

Once again, the Trove was a lively pot being stirred by the almighty dollar. Items were assessed on glass countertops and then exchanged for loan, credit, or hard cash. "Point me to the scope, Linden," Ernie requested impatiently, the shopkeeper's bell still jingling softly behind them.

Linden was busy gauging the surroundings. It had been less than twenty-four hours since he'd last set foot in the place, yet he found it somehow lacked the same . . . *air.* For one thing, there was no sign of Lounging Libby—the aging canine greeter whom Linden assumed wouldn't have left his cozy dog bed even if the place were on fire. Additionally, the room seemed to be under a spell of shadows, like it was riding the low end of a dimmer switch. "Can't say I know where it is at the moment," he ultimately responded, under the assumption that the targeted item was still in Sammy's possession, whether it be hidden somewhere in the back room, or up front, under glass. "I don't see the miserable prick I dealt with yesterday. Let's wander—I'm sure he'll pop out of his hole soon enough."

The two spent the next few minutes shuffling through a maze of seekers and sellers. Linden found the place a lot easier to navigate now that he wasn't carting his weighty clubs around. He distinguished a man and a woman working behind the giant U-shaped counter, but there was still no sign of the shop's owner. Ernie, now becoming visibly irritated with their lack of progress, requested the name of the man Linden had dealt with. "Sammy," Linden replied, then added, "a crusty old bugger like yourself."

In an attempt to ask the whereabouts of the proprietor, Ernie shouldered his way past a browsing customer to score a prime position up front. Then suddenly, as if an alarm had wailed through the shop's spacious back room, a sour-looking senior emerged by way of a narrow, doorless frame. "Who do ya think you are, buddy?" Sammy barked as he met Ernie at the counter.

Ernie immediately raised his arms as if to express remorse. "I apologize," he then stated rather tactfully. "You must be Sammy."

"Don't apologize to me," Sammy replied, shaking his head in disgust. "Apologize to the fella you just downright disrespected by shoving your way through."

At this point, Linden met up with Ernie at the counter and immediately drew a share of Sammy's ire. "Now here's a pair cut from the same cloth," the owner remarked, his steely gaze bouncing back and forth between the two.

"Listen, we're not here to cause trouble," Linden began in a composed manner. "And I assure you I'm not here to continue haggling over my clubs. The reason I've returned this morning is because my friend here would like to purchase that old pocket telescope from yesterday."

Sammy absorbed the request, and then broke into a slow, derisive chuckle. "Ya know, gentlemen, this crazy world can still amaze a man," he then declared through his waning laughter. "Even an old fossil like myself."

"How do you mean, sir?" a bemused Ernie asked.

Now leaning forward with both palms resting flat on his glass countertop, Sammy replied in a sobering tone, accompanied by a single raised eyebrow, "Like I mentioned to your friend yesterday, that scope has loitered in the land of frivolous accumulation for years. Now all of a sudden—in less than twenty-four hours—I've had *two* people inquiring the old piece of junk like it's the Holy Grail."

"Sir, you've understandably mistaken our situation here," Ernie politely began to advise the man behind the counter. "The two of us aren't here to *compete* for the item. We're here *together*, and would like to make the purchase *between* us."

Sammy consciously hung a few seconds of silence over the conversation before responding with a crippling blow. "Well then, I'm quite sorry to've misled you," he feigned penitence in his tone, "but I didn't mean *you* two." He now aimed an arthritic finger at Linden. "I meant *you*, and the person I sold it to first thing this morning."

Upon receiving the debilitating news, Ernie's face blanched to a bloodless veneer. He was momentarily rendered speechless, and felt as if his knees were about to fail him.

"You sold it *this morning*?" Linden questioned with heavy suspicion. "Sold it to whom? And for how much?"

"Well, generally that kind of information is confidential," Sammy replied, still holding the slightest of smirks—a smirk that Linden now wanted to wipe away with his knuckles. "But given the circumstances, I guess I could make an exception. Before I left the shop last night, I put the scope back where it belonged—in that cardboard box that you shouldn't've even been snoopin' through in the first place. Then shortly after opening up this morning, a young child—I assumed to be accompanied by an adult—found her way to the same box. I suppose with most things in here either hanging too high or locked up behind glass, it was a rather feasible target. Considering I left the cardboard flaps hanging open, and the scope resting in plain sight on top of the heap, she must've scooped it up and taken a quick liking to it. She brought it up to the counter armed with a cute little smile that could've lit the dark side of the moon. We jokingly negotiated its value, and in the end, I sold it to her for a grand total of one whole American dollar. Well, one hundred *rolled pennies,* if you really want to know the *intricate* details of the sale."

"Let me get this straight." Requesting validation from the top, Ernie found his voice. "You held in your very possession an old brass pocket telescope that had the word 'moonflaw' scratched into its surface?"

"Since Johnson was president," Sammy sharply acknowledged.

"And you just sold it this morning for a *lousy buck?*"

"Well . . . yes and no—there's really no such thing as a *lousy* buck in my line of work." While Ernie was still teetering from the news of the transaction, Sammy delivered the knockout punch that would conclude their conversation, and ultimately Ernie and Linden's visit to The Treasure Trove. "Besides, what would you have had me do? Shit, she couldn't've been more than seven or eight years old—I'm sure as hell not gonna gouge an innocent little blonde-haired girl."

CHAPTER 17

The Fallbrook Recollection

Given the fuzzy array of recent information, Jeremy Lowe was livid, and he wanted all the answers in an instant when he reached Luke Sheehan by phone. But on the receiving end of the line, having foreseen his caller's justifiable anger, a composed Luke already had another plan in mind.

Along with his attempt to convince Jeremy that they desperately needed to meet in person, Luke expressed his gratitude for meeting his request to contact him. He stated that though the road ahead was surely about to get rocky, the phone call was a crucial step in the right direction. He also mentioned—or rather *insisted*—that Jeremy mustn't tell a single soul about their current conversation, or more importantly, about the prospects of their forthcoming rendezvous.

Though reluctant to take this matter on the road, it was quite evident to Jeremy that the mysterious stranger from Boston wasn't about to cough up any relevant answers over the phone. Conscious of the fact that his own curiosity could be leading him deeper into some formidable scheme, he caved nonetheless. "All right, buddy," he finally declared in a resentful tone, "I'll continue to play along with your little game here. But let me just say this upfront—I already hold you in an extremely dark regard, and if for one *second* I suspect that I'm in any kind of danger, I'll make initiating this whole affair the biggest fucking mistake of your life!"

Following Jeremy's thorny word to the wise, the two agreed to split the 225-mile trek between New York and Boston in half and convene at the Hilton Hotel in downtown Hartford. To the best of their knowledge, the Connecticut capital was roughly the same distance from each city, thus entailing a good two-hour drive for both parties. Jeremy agreed to depart following his final dismissal of the day, and after allocating time for a dinner stopover, they settled on seven o'clock in the hotel lobby for a precise meeting point. With neither of them thinking to offer a description of themselves, Luke closed out the conversation in the same fashion he'd wrapped up his call with Shelly: by recounting the dream from his spectacular bird's-eye view offered by the equally spectacular Martin B-26 Marauder.

The remainder of Professor Lowe's workday was lost in a collage of abstracted thought. He found himself simultaneously mapping out the route to Hartford, measuring the stranger from Beantown, and contemplating his standpoint on Shelly's involvement—whether to conform to Luke's request to keep things under wraps for the time being, or to make her aware of his impending departure.

In the end, Jeremy went with a simple text message that would suffice to satisfy both camps, stating without specifics that he'd be considerably late in his return home from the school that evening. The conscientious side of him ached to divulge the plan to vacate the city for Hartford, but for now he opted to suppress the rather speculative particulars.

Having lived in Boston his entire life, Luke Sheehan had a distinct advantage whenever manoeuvring through the city's notoriously chaotic evening rush hour. Avoiding the snail-like pace of almost every outgoing artery, he schemed his way through the backstreets until he merged with the flowing westbound interstate. Then, following an eventual southern cut onto I-84, he was just shy of an hour from the Hartford city centre.

With the hectic pace of New York City now long-dissolved in his rear-view mirror, Jeremy marginally slackened in his seat as he approached the Connecticut state line.

Now gliding through Bridgeport with the night falling fast and heavy, the waning glow generated an anamnesis of his dream from a night ago. Scattered fragments of memory were seeping back into his current conscious state. Defogged images of the refurbished warplane resurfaced from the depths, and then, like a great wave of retrospective reasoning, one of the elusive answers Jeremy had been seeking since the morning suddenly emerged: the identity of the young blonde girl.

Though the distressing account (and gut-churning visual documentation) of Isabel and Estella Fallbrook was anything but a laughing matter, Jeremy couldn't help but chuckle to himself as he recalled the story of the young twins. The sisters from Lawrence, Kansas, were the topic of a paper Jeremy had submitted some twenty years prior, while in university. He'd authored the piece for an intriguing—if not occasionally disturbing—Criminal Psychology course. Based on true events that transpired in the fall of 1980, the heinous narrative recounted the seven-year-old identical twins, and how Estella's swelling obsession to reign superior over her sister had ultimately led to Isabel's gruesome murder by means of a pickaxe. Then how shortly thereafter, Estella had become so utterly overwhelmed with remorse that she pitched herself into the accessible, murky depths of Clinton Lake—wilfully drowning her stigma in the man-made reservoir less than a quarter-mile from the Fallbrook residence.

Now approaching Meriden along I-91, Jeremy was making good time, and he'd managed to wiggle himself free of at least one set of binding chains that were prohibiting his progress. Relieved to know that the blonde-haired child sitting with him at Fenway was no more than a random wink from the past, he shifted his focus back to the mysterious warplane and its alleged passenger.

In the vague description of his dream to Shelly, Jeremy had indeed mentioned the plane and its fluent swoop over the historic ballpark, and he'd also described the vantage from which he'd viewed the maneuver. But while speaking with Luke over the phone, Luke had somehow taken the details a few steps further, pinpointing the exact location in which Jeremy was sitting, like he knew the finer intricacies of the park. "Left-field grandstand, section thirty-three, above the garage door along the wall—not thirty feet from the foul pole," Luke had stated emphatically, all but narrowing it down to an actual seat number.

Lost in disconcerting thought, Jeremy continued to put the miles behind him. The northbound traffic was light—almost eerily non-existent; this was strange, seeing as how a populous capital city was now on the horizon.

Certain that the initial moments of his meeting with Jeremy would be tense, Luke planned to break the ice with a simple introductory handshake, followed by an explanation of how he'd subliminally received Shelly's cell number in the first place. In respecting the justifiable anger that the professor would surely convey with him to Hartford, Luke was prepared to openly recount the crucial information that was generously offered to him by his tour pilot: the spectral figure flying the warplane through their interwoven visions.

During Luke's dream, when the Marauder had reclaimed the Boston sky following the Fenway sweep, the aviator affirmed that a foreign grade of radiation was seeping into the atmosphere. The imminent threat had the entire human race in peril, and to make matters worse, a growing network of evil was essentially stoking its fire. He then explained to Luke that an alliance with the man he'd just spotted sitting in the stands would be imperative to impede exposure. The name and cell phone number of said man's wife—a journalist from New York City—were then disclosed, as well as an explanation as to why going through her initially—and not the man himself—would be the best shot at the desired result in the long run. Before the sound of thunder had stirred Luke from slumber, the pilot expressed how Luke and the stranger in the stands weren't nearly the only ones being dragged into this plight. Due to recent developments in both New Mexico and Washington, there would now be a host of others caught up in the fallout.

With the charming town of Tolland now left in his florid taillight gleam, Luke Sheehan was closing in on the destined city, and he was feeling confident with what would be his approach in the Hilton lobby. Another ten miles had him veering off the interstate and into East Hartford, where he only hoped his impending meeting with Jeremy Lowe would go as smoothly as his drive in—from one New England state capital to another.

———

It was the roadside sign with its bold, white lettering indicating the short distance to the city that spooked Jeremy from his musings: Hartford 11. Unaware of his considerable progress, the signboard's retroreflective sheeting almost instantaneously aroused a focus in him that he'd need to navigate the foreign streets and ultimately locate the posh hotel.

CHAPTER 18

Janelle Revisited

A PAST LIFE AGO

Janelle Crawford had already sensed what was coming before she saw the police cruiser edging up to her curb. Her husband, Andy, always either called home or fired a quick text whenever there was even the slightest possibility of being late after a shift. It was now pushing nine o'clock in the morning: a good two hours beyond his expected return. Already anxious, the sight of the patrol car was enough to shake whatever remained of her foundation.

Assuming their master was home at last, Kody and Alias barked in deep-toned unison as a pair of officers made their way up the drive. Janelle recognized Officer Sheppard, but not his partner, who looked to be no more than twenty. Bill Sheppard and Andy had met as teenagers, furthering their friendship through the association of their respective professions. She presumed Bill had been personally assigned to deliver the bad news, seeing as it was no secret that he knew Andy on a personal level.

When it wasn't who they were expecting, the dogs altered their roar of excitement to a guttural, protective growl. Despite the horror that was brewing within, Janelle took notice of their change in temperament and ordered them back into the kitchen so she could converse with the officers out on the veranda.

The spring-loaded screen door slammed shut behind Janelle, moderately startling the officers before she met Sheppard's eyes. In that seemingly infinite moment, his woeful expression told her all she needed to know. "Janelle, there's been an accident," he said, finally severing the weighty silence in a consoling tone, all the while advancing a supportive hand to her shoulder. Just like every other officer or medic who'd ever been called upon to deliver these ugliest of all bulletins, Sheppard flat-out loathed this component of the job; it always seemed so far beyond anything he'd ever signed up for. It wasn't the inevitability of death that ripped at his heart-strings with a jagged claw; it was having to deliver the mournful news to the *living*.

Half-expecting Janelle to crumble on the spot, Sheppard pulled-up a soft-cushioned patio chair. "I'm so sorry," he continued. "Unfortunately, Andy lost his life this morning while battling a massive chemical fire just south of Hamden. I'm sure you've seen it all over the news. The blaze was unruly—far beyond what the local departments could control. Help was rushed in from every corner of the state—that's how Andy and the EHFD became involved. I don't have much more details at this time, other than that he was rushed to Yale New Haven Hospital sometime after six. I'm also hearing word on how his heroics saved the lives of—"

"Enough," Janelle suddenly interjected in no more than a murmur. She lowered into the chair like a woman twice her age. "Please . . . enough." In that moment, words were no longer required. She wondered if there would *ever* be words again, or emotions, or anything other than the suffocating undertow of despair that was already pulling her down below.

In the aftermath of the tragedy, Janelle's friends and family leaned heavily on the "time will heal" mantra. But to her, the fibres and filaments of time only took on the life of a suture—a suture repressing a lament that had no place to go but to fester deeper and deeper within.

She'd managed to find enough strength to beat the initial undertow, but waiting on the surface was a great wave of grief that seemingly washed her into her next life. Declining an overwhelming number of emotional pleas to remain in Hartford, Janelle strayed eastward, abandoning the state of Connecticut altogether. Along with Ashlyne and the two dogs, she picked up what she could of the broken pieces and took her first steps along an unlit road to recovery.

CHAPTER 19

The Rover and the Rock

PRESENT DAY

Though Mason Greene had briefly studied the Apollo program back in university, the newfound blemish on his recently acquired moon globe sparked a whole new inquisition into a *specific* space endeavour: the Apollo 15 mission. Dismissing coincidence, he knew there had to be some underlying relation between the globe's minor defacement and its precise location on the Apollo 15 landing site.

Now deep into the small hours of the night, Mason sat before his computer screen while exhausting the internet of all it had to offer on the specific moon mission. Through the lengthy search, a surplus of educative information was revealed, yet he found himself no further along than when he started when it came to pinpointing a connection.

By the time the clock struck four, Mason could feel himself caving under the pressing weight of slumber. With what seemed would be a mountainous ascent up two flights of stairs, he opted to remain down in his subterraneous sanctuary, where he'd crash in the company of orbs on his sofa. Within seconds he was drifting away from the shores of consciousness, and then remained buoyant in the vastness of a cosmic dreamworld.

Mason casually kicked stones as he sauntered along the gritty lunar surface. A pillowy wind whispered elegantly across the plain, the breeze sweeping moondust over the depressed footmarks in his wake. The ashen-grey ambience was customary—as if grass or anything else showing signs of life would be deviant in nature. Gazing out into the void as he moved, Mason observed the moon's natural satellite, known to lunar-folk as Earth-Planet. On this fine morning, the distant orb was hovering atypically large and lucid against the black backdrop of space.

Undoubtedly born of his nocturnal study, key elements of the Apollo 15 mission were percolating into Mason's subconscious and were queerly represented in the vision. First there was the lunar rover. The Lunar Roving Vehicle, or LRV, made its maiden voyage on this Apollo mission. Powered by one electric motor per wheel and a pair of silver-oxide batteries, the rover was equipped to ferry two astronauts, their equipment, life support consumables, and lunar rock samples. During the course of the Apollo 15 mission, the vehicle travelled a total distance of 17.3 miles and ran for a total time of 3 hours and 2 minutes. The rover, along with two others from following Apollo missions, remains on the moon's surface to this day.

Also making a most unusual appearance in Mason's dream was the Genesis Rock. The Genesis Rock is a renowned sample of moon rock retrieved by Apollo 15 astronauts James Irwin and David Scott. Currently stored at the Lunar Sample Laboratory Facility in Houston, Texas, the rock is believed to have been formed in the early stages of the solar system, at least four billion years ago.

While pausing to further observe the wonder that was the imposing Earth-Planet, Mason began to sense mechanical movement slowly coming on from behind. The soft, crunching sound of wheels over loose gravel emerged and grew louder until a lunar rover came to an easy halt about ten feet from where he stood. The vehicle was nearly overflowing, carting along a host of items as if it were a mobile pawnshop. Mason recognized (amongst other trinkets) what appeared to be several poster-sized prints of the controversial postage stamp covers (about 400 unauthorized postal covers that were carried into space and to the Moon's surface on the Lunar Module *Falcon*), a number of Fallen Astronaut sculptures, and resting in the rover's passenger seat was an oversized replica of the Genesis Rock.

Commanding the vehicle and overseeing the eclectic blend of space memorabilia was a forty-something gentleman, evidently out peddling his goods along the barren lunar landscape. Crammed in amongst his clutter, the operator offered Mason a simultaneous smile and cordial salute before he spoke. "*Buenos días*, moonwalker. Can I interest you in a range of curious curios?"

As Mason stood in a perplexed silence, the rover rider proceeded to reach down into a cramped compartment beneath his seat, where he casually withdrew a heavily bloodstained pickaxe. Without hesitation, he elevated the tool and then drove a sharp point directly downward upon the Genesis Rock, purposely retracting force upon contact in order to preserve what lay at the jewel's core. Archaic shards expelled through a cloud of moondust, stabbing at the shadowy void as the primitive stone shattered. The obliteration revealed a single kernel item, mercifully left resting on a bed of debris. "Looks like it's our lucky day, moonwalker," the peddler proclaimed as he seized a brass apparatus from the ruins. "Believe you me, we're in for a real treat. Once this dust settles, we'll have ourselves a stellar view of Earth-Planet." His eyes met Mason's with a cold connection. "Trust me, you haven't *seen* Earth-Planet until you've seen it through the *moonflaw* scope!"

As if a scene or two had been purged from existence, Mason suddenly found himself perched atop Mons Hadley: a colossal lunar mountain with an elevation greater than twice the height of Mount Washington. The rover was nowhere to be seen, but its operator and his extricated scope had gained the summit as well. There they sat, resting atop the towering massif like a pair of skilled mountaineers having recently conquered yet another crest.

"This peak is unquestionably my favourite of all the viewing stations," the stranger proudly stated as he aimed the spyglass out into the starry zenith. Then, after tweaking the focuser to bring Earth-Planet into sharp definition, he suddenly added with child-like enthusiasm: "Didn't I tell ya it was our lucky day? Looks like they've finally planted the seventh and final flag!" He slowly lowered the pocket telescope from his eye and offered it to Mason. "Here—it's time to peer into the magic for yourself!"

Just as Mason took hold of the mysterious instrument, he began to detect the ever-untimely claws of consciousness embedding themselves and pulling him to the surface. Clinging to the depths of slumber, he countered the unsought arousal by extracting the claws with exhausting mental exertion.

Having regained the subliminal setting, Mason and his new-found associate were still the kings of Mons Hadley. With the scope now in his possession, Mason found its brass surface extremely warm to the touch, as if it were an overheating electronic device. Disregarding the thermal impression, he trained the lens on Earth-Planet, where the resulting image only augmented an already eccentric setting.

Expecting to see a moderately enhanced perspective of the remote planet, Mason alternatively witnessed what appeared to be a floating *globe*, complete with an accompanying hardwood pedestal. "C'mon, this scope is a hoax, buddy," Mason asserted. "There's no way in hell that this—" Still focused on the baffling image, his delivery quickly fell off the shelf with what the scope now exhibited. Becoming larger and more defined with every passing second, the planet/globe now appeared to be gravitating toward the moon at an alarming rate. "Jesus Christ! It's heading straight for us!" Mason lowered the scope and turned to warn his anonymous company, but the man was nowhere in sight. It was as if he'd suddenly . . . dematerialized. All that remained in his place was residual smoke—smoke that reeked of sulphur. The disorder continued as the pocket scope suddenly reduced to a handful of dust, the powdery remains spilling through Mason's trembling fingers like sand through the neck of an hourglass.

Aghast in his sudden isolation, Mason braved an unaided skyward glance, and as he feared, the results were terrifying. Like a space shuttle jettisons its solid rocket boosters into the sea, the incoming planet/globe had whirled itself free of its supporting pedestal, thus giving it the formidable impression of an unbridled planetoid, destined to obliterate the very lunar surface on which he rested.

With the approaching orb now frenetically spinning itself into a blur, Mason had no choice but to swim for his life—swim like a madman to the fringes of the dream, hoping like hell that the icy barrier between worlds would allow him to break through and surface. Where were those ill-timed claws of consciousness when you needed them? The race was on. Approaching the periphery, yet still immersed in the dream liquid, he stole a backwards glance. Down below, distant cries of envy from the lunar-folk littered his now-semiconscious state, as though they were calling from the bed of a fathomless sea. Then, as Mason broke through the barrier and surfaced, the cries gracefully abated to silence with the dissolution of the dream.

Mason awoke groggy and coated in a clammy glaze of sweat. A vague impression of his cosmic dream still danced on its last legs somewhere in the depths of his mind. He instinctively referred to his Girard-Perregaux watch, and, after confirming the fact on his computer screen, was shocked to find that he'd not just lost a few *hours* to slumber, but that he'd somehow been rooted in the subliminal abyss for *a day and a half!*

While trying to wrap his hazy head around the fact that a full thirty-six hours had elapsed during a single sleeping session, Mason suddenly noticed a sharp, burning sensation rapidly intensifying in his upper right arm. A single glance revealed the source of the pain, as he found what appeared to be some form of medical syringe still clinging to his bruised flesh like a tenacious stinger. *What the fuck? Have I been drugged?* he speculated in a sudden whirlwind of shock and confusion before gingerly extracting the unwarranted spur.

Mason began to survey his surroundings, and something immediately caught his eye. His newly acquired moon globe had not only appeared to have been stolen, but moreover supplanted by a globe in which he'd certainly never seen the likes of before. As the effects of the anonymous anaesthetic began to wash over him like a wave, he sluggishly moved in for a closer look. What he found was not another moon globe, but rather a mystifying facsimile of Earth. The standard-sized model somehow seemed to be . . . physically exhibiting signs of life—*catastrophic* signs of life. Exasperated volcanoes were spewing red-hot lava, raging seas drove tidal waves at defenceless coastlines, forest fires raged out of control, and angry fault lines trembled and split the surface into boundless chasms.

Mason questioned his own sanity while plunging two fingers nearly knuckle-deep into a rolling Indian Ocean. A timid dab on the tongue followed, and convincingly revealed the signature taste of saltwater.

Amongst its turmoil, Mason chanced upon the only form of print that the globe openly displayed. Seemingly adrift on a turbulent Pacific Ocean, brown capitalized letters like giant wooden rafts displayed the word: Earth-Planet.

Mason began to wonder if he was still dreaming, for things were now spiralling out of control at an alarming rate. But when

he once again utilized his Electro-Optix magnifier and encountered the miniature flags, the ordeal reached a whole new stratum
of irrationality.

While surveying the Pacific Northwest through the lens, Mason
spotted a fluttering flag in the general vicinity of his hometown.
Though it was battered and torn by the wind, he still managed to
decipher its showy, calligraphic script. In glowing yellow characters
against a deep matte maroon, the flag read: RD #6. In his dream,
the stranger who'd initially arrived by means of a lunar rover had
spoken of a "seventh" and "final" flag. Now Mason began to specu-
late that if the #6 flag represented Bellevue, then there surely had
to be others—thus initiating a scrutinized study of the globe.

His subsequent find was an RD #3 flag, and it was spotted quite
easily. He swore he could actually hear the wind ruffle its fabric as
a breeze whipped along Florida's west coast. He felt confident that
the flag's precise location was St. Petersburg. Following a fruitless
search through Mexico, Mason bounced the magnifier back to the
United States, where a slow stroke over Connecticut revealed the
aforementioned RD #7 banner. *That has to be Hartford*, he thought.
The smallest flagpole imaginable was spiked into the centre of the
state as though it were a bullseye.

Still, the numbered flags failed to bring any form of geographical connection to light. That was until he spotted RD #5 just
up the way, in southwestern New Hampshire, and a glimmer of
understanding began to surface. This time Mason referred to an
atlas, and it all but confirmed his inkling. The flag was waving
directly over the city of Keene—the previous home of the now
seemingly purloined moon globe.

Though still extremely hazy in its implication, this morsel of
information was a solid lead, nevertheless. Whoever had broken
into Mason's gated estate and drugged him while he was sleeping had *purposely* left clues as to the globe's current whereabouts.
If indeed these diminutive flags tracked its course, then it had

four previous lodgings before reaching Keene. From there, Mason received his delivery in Bellevue. And now, according to numerical order, the globe had found its way back east, this time to Hartford, Connecticut.

For Mason Greene, there were still a slew of questions to be answered. Why the Connecticut capital? Who was it that had the audacity to break into his secured residence? What exactly was the drug that was decidedly still swimming in his veins? What did the RDs that graced the seven flags stand for?

Though he couldn't have dreamed it possible, the lunar globe now seemed a thousand times the mystery it had already been before he had succumbed to slumber—a day and a half earlier.

CHAPTER 20

Lobby to Bridge

As he wove his way through the unexpectedly abandoned city streets, Luke Sheehan was seeking assistance in locating the Hilton Hotel. The trouble was, it wasn't just the roadways that were entirely void of activity, but Hartford as a whole gave the impression of being a funereal ghost town. Since drifting off the interstate, he noted that the suburbs, and now the urban core, were drowned in a sort of sinister silence. The evening's light drizzle and intermittent wafts of fog only added texture to the already eerie surroundings.

Now heading deeper into the heart of the city, Luke caught a distant glimpse of the illuminated red lettering that graced the summit of his target. From his current vantage, "Hilton" was visible on both the front and side of the towering building—the pair of glowing words like beady, demonic eyes peering out through the murk. With his bearings now dialled in, Luke continued to maneuver his way forward until he stumbled upon the hotel's Trumbull Street entrance.

With his journey in from Boston having taken a little less time than anticipated, Luke was afforded an opportunity to browse the hotel in advance of the university professor's expected arrival. In stark contrast to the desolate ambience that seemingly had the city under some kind of spell, the Hilton lobby was, at least initially, what one would come to expect of a high-end hotel chain. A smattering of guests were mingling before a lengthy front desk, while members of staff were busy seeing to their needs. A majestic fireplace warmed the vast foyer that also offered a roomy resting area, a cocktail lounge, and a sports bar that was clearly biased toward New England's four major franchises.

Shortly after entering, Luke altered his plan. Rather than scope out the lobby and the deeper depths of the hotel, he chose a little liquid palliative to take the edge off before talking business.

"What can I getcha this evening, sir?" asked a dapper-looking bartender at Element 315—the Hilton's elegant cocktail lounge.

"Small glass of white, please," Luke replied as he settled onto a cushioned bar stool and fished through his wallet. With the late-night lounge having just opened within the hour, and Luke being the first to the bar, he was targeted with typical small talk.

"What brings you to Hartford?" the barkeep casually inquired while tipping a chilled Sauvignon Blanc.

Cautiously guarding his *actual* agenda, Luke responded, "Just meeting up with an old friend—should be here shortly."

With fervent, steely eyes, the bartender suddenly fashioned a leery grin and peered into the very essence of Luke's being. "An old friend, you say?" The lounge seemed to drop twenty degrees the second he spoke, like he was spitting ice. "I find that rather curious, Luke, considering you wouldn't recognize this so-called 'old friend' of yours if he parked his ass on that stool next to you and bought you a fuckin' spritzer!"

With the invaluable guidance of his Garmin GPS, Jeremy Lowe located the Hilton Hotel without any difficulty. Navigating the streets of downtown Hartford proved elementary with the device leading him through the city's unnervingly vacant course. He chose the hotel's underground parking option upon arrival, and once his vehicle was secured, he took a moment to reflect on the day's turbulent nature. He found himself marvelling at how both the storm that had conquered the morning and the ceremony at Columbia had somehow taken a back seat to this crazy out-of-state venture.

From the parking garage, a steep flight of concrete stairs led Jeremy up to a pedestrian door that opened onto the Trumbull Street walk. From there, the hotel's main entrance was no more than fifty paces up the way, and with a deep breath, he found his stride.

With the casual assistance of a doorman in a wool overcoat and velvet top hat, Jeremy crossed the threshold and found himself inside the Hilton's seductive lobby. Trying not to give himself away too easily while sizing up the room, he spotted a group of women by the front desk dressed in chic business attire, two separate elderly couples walking leisurely about the space, and a stunningly attractive woman who appeared to be a member of the Hilton staff. Though he didn't have the slightest inkling as to what the mysterious man from Boston looked like, there was no sign of anyone who even *remotely* matched the loose perception he'd drawn up in his mind.

Still scanning the surroundings, Jeremy spotted the Element 315 lounge. Coincidentally, at that very moment, a middle-aged man poured out through its grand set of glass doors like the joint was on fire. In the process he ploughed into an innocent gentleman lugging an oversized duffle bag through the lobby, leaving him stunned and leaking blood from the upper lip. As if perfectly oblivious to his destructive conduct, the loose cannon was still on the move and heading directly for Jeremy.

Though a small part of Jeremy still hoped—and assumed— this was indeed the man he'd come all the way from New

York to confront, he wasn't comfortable in the least with this riotous introduction.

"Jeremy!" Luke Sheehan barked without breaking his now rhythmic stride. "If that's you—it's *me!* We're not safe in this goddamn hotel. Follow me—we're gettin' the hell outta here!"

Jeremy, who was certainly in no mood to break into a sudden dash, reluctantly picked up Luke's pace and trailed him down the hotel's lengthy south wing. Approaching the exit, Luke slowed from a near sprint to a jog as he burst through the single door, leading Jeremy out into the ominous Connecticut night.

As if the pair of out-of-towners had summoned a cloak to conceal their whereabouts, a timely fog was now seemingly congealing into a lethargic mass. Accompanying the haze and augmenting the night's ill-boding mystique was a dose of misty, English-style rain: a far cry from the pounding winds and driving downpours the city had endured over the past few days.

Now clear of the hotel grounds, and presumably safe for the time being, Luke finally ceased his sudden burst that had commenced in the lounge and, through winded gasps, attempted a more befitting introduction. "First off, let me apologize for this rather rude initiation," he began, offering an outstretched hand to solidify their acquaintance. "Though it could've been worse, I suppose—I could've begun by sayin' 'I'm Luke, from your dreams.'"

Jeremy, equally out of breath, chose to bypass the humour and went right after some reasoning. "Jeremy Lowe," he responded sternly while accepting Luke's handshake with the little strength he had left in reserve. "Listen, why the hell did we just storm out of there like we robbed the place?"

"It was the *bartender!*" Luke emphasized, squinting back through the fleecy murk toward the hotel. "I rolled into town a little early, then sat down for a quick drink in the lounge while waiting for you. The bartender, he seemed fine at first, but then he . . . he suddenly just . . . turned."

"*Turned?*"

"I don't know how else to put it. Christ, it was blood-curdling! His eyes just seemed to turn to cold stone, like a pair of black holes—empty, yet still full of the darkest malevolence. With the transformation, his voice became gritty and metallic, as if the words were being processed through an internal speaker. He referred to me by my *name*—which I hadn't even mentioned—before saying that I wouldn't recognize *you* if you were sittin' right next to me. I knew it then and there—he was an assigned Deceiver."

"Excuse me?" Jeremy questioned with a slight shake of the head. "He was a *what?*"

On the verge of an explanation, Luke suddenly paused, deciding the exchange couldn't persist in their current surroundings. "Listen, I know this meeting of ours has already skipped off the rails, but I can't help but sense that our words are vulnerable out here in the open like this." As desperate for answers as Jeremy was, he had no choice but to listen in as Luke swiftly drew up their next move. "We need to sneak our way over to Bushnell Park. I believe it's just a few blocks away—down at the end of this street. It should offer adequate seclusion at this hour."

Anticipating a possible hitch during their confluence at the Hilton, Luke had squeezed in a quick study of Hartford's downtown layout before departing Boston. Now, seeing as how they'd already fled the hotel before a single handshake, this small bit of forethought was already paying dividends as they began to target the lush green space.

Bushnell Park, a historic oasis nestled in the heart of the city, remains the oldest publicly funded park in the country, and serves as the perfect retreat for workweek lunch breaks and festive weekend activities. It was designed in conjunction with New York City's Central Park in the mid-1850s, and though it hasn't undergone any major architectural upgrades since the early 1980s, Hartford's scaled-down equivalent has certainly seen its share of transformation in its time—most notably the rerouting of the Park River. This river once entered the park near the State Armory and then meandered along the north side beneath a seemingly endless canopy of timber and leaf. Each spring, when the Connecticut River overflowed its banks, the Park River would back up, and its journey into the Connecticut would be blocked. As a result, the waters would routinely flood low-lying areas of the park.

The great flood of 1936 not only inundated *all* of Bushnell Park, but much of Hartford as a whole was left under several feet of water. Then, in 1938, the Great New England Hurricane hit the city head-on, and it was the straw that broke the camel's back. In 1940, the Army Corps of Engineers began work on one of the largest public works projects in New England's history. Over the next seven years, they literally changed the course of the Park River, burying it underground in a huge concrete conduit, thirty feet high and forty-five feet wide. Today, the conduit runs straight as an arrow below the centre of the park before branching out into various subsidiaries beneath the city, which all connect again to drain into the Connecticut River. The system stretches for more than nine miles, and during its construction cost more than $100 million to complete.

Through means of public voting, a gorgeous pond and tributary stream were added to the park shortly after the conduit was completed. Following yet another major flood in 1955, a Cotswold-style pump house was added to Bushnell Park. To this day, a collection of massive pumps continue to do their job far below the surface by pumping the river under the park and through the concrete bowels of the city.

Romantically lit by a succession of black, cast-iron streetlamps, the park's boundary was now within sight for Jeremy and Luke. As they approached the perimeter, a clearly intoxicated beggar greeted them unexpectedly. "Shay there," the man slurred over the swooshing sound of his openly exposed gin bottle. A forty-ounce Colt

45 bottle also clung to a low pocket on his tattered and grimy overcoat. "Yous two look t'me like a coupla fine mates. Couldja spare me some change fer a waaarm cup-a-coffee?"

The foul coalescence of tobacco smoke, liquor, and neglected hygiene was enough to floor the sturdiest of men. "Beat it, buddy!" Jeremy suddenly piped up, ordering the drunkard off with an assertive fist and thumb gesture.

Then, as if a switch had been flicked from somewhere deep within his soul, the beggar suddenly shifted a stern gaze toward Luke. "Well then." His speech was now stern and coherent; his once-glazed eyes now parched like brittle slag. "Since *he's* in no mood, how about *you*, Luke? You wouldn't come all the way from Boston without a few bucks in yer pocket, wouldja?"

"Go fuck yourself!" Luke roared before squarely landing an uppercut to the Deceiver's jaw. The rigid clout sent the counterfeit vagrant tumbling backwards; he clumsily fell over a wooden bench and then collapsed into a heap, cursing the blow. During the process, the Colt 45 had slipped from its pouch and shattered into a mini lake of malt liquor. "Jesus Christ!" Luke continued emphatically, already shaking his smarting right hand. "We clearly can't trust *anybody*. This whole goddamn *city* is on to us. It's about time we start gettin' down to business." He motioned Jeremy with only his head, and the two crossed the lamplit threshold before boldly venturing into the darkening depths of Bushnell Park.

The murky glow of the perimeter seemingly lessened with every additional step into the grounds. With the mist and fog now also waning, the buildings that towered high above the green space offered a lambent service but, with a good majority of trees still lush with foliage, the light only slipped through in intermittent pockets.

Luke and Jeremy stuck to a narrow pedestrian path that initially followed the arcing trajectory of Jewell Pond before jutting out into the heart of the park. Though visibility was wanting, there were no signs whatsoever of another soul in their vicinity. Their recent run-ins were more than enough cause to keep their guards up, but the current hush gave the park the impression of an innocent forest.

"What about over there?" Jeremy suddenly proposed, pausing in his tracks to guide Luke's eye with an outstretched arm and pointed finger. "I'm not certain, but it looks like a footbridge from here, does it not? We could position ourselves atop its arch for a favourable vantage while we talk."

Quite keen on the idea of having a perched, panoramic view, Luke's vision laboured through the murk towards the presumed overpass. Without another word, they guardedly approached what was labelled Weidenmann's Bridge, where a sizeable ground plaque honouring Jacob Weidenmann—the park's chief landscape architect—was embedded in the cold concrete. A lazy stream trickled beneath the crossing, the sound a lucid melody in the stillness of the night. With their surroundings still seemingly secure, they mounted the pass and, just as Jeremy suggested, paused at the crest. Once there, they immediately caught a glimpse of the uppermost arc of a glorious crimson moon sprouting from the horizon. The men were enthralled in the moment as the prodigious satellite commenced its ascension into the night sky.

Now under the watchful eye of the emerging orb, the two began exchanging vital information about their coextensive dream.

CHAPTER 21

Gone with the Windsong

Long-faced and dejected, Ernie Cowarth moped out through The Treasure Trove's front doors and promptly cursed his luck. "All these years, dammit," the old man muttered as Linden trailed his exit. "All these goddamn wasted years, searching far and wide for a bloody scope that was right under my nose the entire time."

Not knowing exactly how to respond to Ernie's chagrin, Linden consoled him with a supportive pat on the shoulder. "Some things just aren't meant to be, my friend," he finally stated. "Come on—whaddya say we get us some breakfast? I'm buyin'!"

Deep down, Ernie knew exactly whom it was who had swooped in and snagged the pocket telescope from his near grasp—just as he'd finally gotten a sniff. Sam from the pawnshop had mentioned an "innocent little blonde-haired girl," and that was all the information he'd needed. It was Estella—the murderous twin sister of Isabel. Isabel being the child who over the course of three dreams back in 1980 had, among other things, come to warn him of the Deceivers' ways. The scope he'd possessed as a young man and had presumed lost during a grisly shipwreck had now fallen into

Deceiver hands, and it made him cringe to think of what that meant for the very near future.

Eventually, Ernie gathered himself, and he took Linden up on his offer to buy breakfast. Heading back in the direction of the university, the two agreed on the acclaimed Minnie's Pancake House: a mecca for Albuquerque residents and ravenous students for over twenty-five years.

"Say, Linden," Ernie muffled through a mouthful of blueberry flapjacks, "you have any other plans for today?"

"Well, let me see," he replied with more than a hint of sarcasm. "Since I hadn't exactly planned for *any* of this, I guess the balance of my day could be open to more random reconfiguration."

"Great!" Ernie announced with a sudden rejuvenation, clearly missing the irony in Linden's response. "I'd still like to bring you back to my place—show you the Redeemer file anyway. I figure what the hell—I ain't gettin' any younger, and now's as good a time as any to start sharing my findings."

Linden started into a second cup of coffee as he attempted to corral his unsettled thoughts, and then he carefully chose his words. "I appreciate the offer, Ernie, I really do. But from what I've gathered to this point, this situation of yours deserves more attention than someone like me has to offer."

"Exactly! You said it—someone *like* you wouldn't be able to give it the attention it *does* deserve. But *you*, my friend, *can*, and given what's recently transpired, you *must*. The simple fact that you stumbled upon that scope, then, though inadvertently, came directly to me with news of its existence and whereabouts, tells me just how *vital* you've become."

Slightly shaking his head, Linden was still trying to grasp what this all meant, and furthermore, where it was all headed. "Though I still don't have the slightest idea as to what I'm buying into, you sure know how to sell it." He downed another swig of coffee in the hopes that a quick jolt of caffeine might somehow crystallize the situation in his mind. "I'll tell you what," he continued. "I *am* interested in reading this file of yours. And since I don't *actually* have any plans for the time being, I can spare a few hours to go check it out. Shit, I've come this far—why stop now, right?"

"Excellent," Ernie replied, then pushed forward with the business. "So, what we'll do is head back to the school, and from there you can follow me up to my place in Santa Fe."

After satisfying their appetites at Minnie's, Linden, as promised, graciously footed the bill. A little more than an hour later he was trailing the old man as they angled off I-25 and into New Mexico's beautiful, Spanish-influenced capital.

Following the slow, demoralizing death of his wife, Edna, sixteen years earlier to lung disease, Ernie had downsized from a single-detached dwelling to a diminutive bungalow in the city's Pojoaque Valley. Given the unfortunate loss of his partner of over fifty years, he fought through the heartache and slowly settled into his cozy, retrenched quarters.

With Linden still in tow, Ernie approached his property on River Song Lane and immediately sensed that something was amiss. As he pulled into the driveway, he noticed that the flowers in his front garden lay trampled directly below his partially shattered bay window. With this chilling observation, it didn't need to be spelled out for him that someone had committed a break-and-enter offence—and perhaps were still in the process of it. Though the glass was fractured, it appeared to somehow be . . . controlled. Most of the sizeable windowpane remained intact, as only a meagre aperture was present.

"The file," Ernie whispered to himself as he killed his engine, knowing his chronicled research was most certainly the target of the home invasion. Meanwhile, Linden, still oblivious to the adversity at this point, pulled up to a curbside vacancy.

Rather than conducting an immediate investigation by blindly barging into his house, Ernie opted to play it safe, marching out to Linden's Cherokee and informing him of the disturbance. "More bad news, my friend," he declared in a shaky voice, as Linden began to exit the vehicle. Linden had seen the same distressed look in the old man's eyes just the night before, back at the university during the TAAS meeting when he'd first mentioned the likes of the pocket scope. "I'm almost certain my place has been broken into."

"*What?*"

"Look at my front window," Ernie said as they carefully made a move toward the house. "And the trampled garden below it. Hell, there could still be somebody in there as we speak. I got a bad feeling as to what's goin' on here, Linden, what with the timing of it all." Linden instinctively reached for his cell phone with a clear intent to notify the police. "No! Wait!" Ernie abruptly interjected, flailing his arms and nearly swatting the device from Linden's hand in the process. "Listen, I know this'll sound crazy, but I can't allow the authorities to ruffle through my belongings before I confirm the status of the file." After peering in through the bay window, Ernie mounted his front steps, paused, and then turned to Linden, who remained below. "I'm goin' in. You with me?"

Linden tarried in the moment, and found himself wondering how many more twists and turns Ernie could possibly lead him through. Making the trip up to Santa Fe was already a hasty agreement in and of itself, and now he was being asked to overstep the law by manipulating a suspected crime scene. Before committing either way, his eye was once again drawn to the busted window, where something suddenly caught his eye in the garden below. From where he was standing, it looked to be . . . duct tape, of all things. Tattered strips of the silvery-grey adhesive appeared to be affixed to the shards of glass that now littered the trodden flowerbed.

"All right, I'm with ya," he finally declared. "Not because I want to, but because I can't let ya go in alone."

Feeling uncomfortably foreign in his accustomed surroundings, Ernie guardedly led Linden on a survey of his breached bungalow. They began in the minimal living room, where fragments of window glass had settled on the hardwood surface. As they crept in for a closer look, Linden made a mental note that there was no sign of the curious duct tape on the interior. From there they moved on to the rear of the house, where Ernie gave the kitchen and his single bedroom no more than a passing glance before making a beeline for the study.

At this point he'd concluded that, save for the possibility of the study itself and peeking into closets and under beds, the house was free of the culprit. The door to the study was pulled to, but not shut completely. Without pause, Ernie swung the door fully open, and it rattled the spring doorstop upon impact. Then, within seconds of crossing the threshold, his deepest fear became a blatantly clear reality.

The room which Ernie had come to call his study was a scanty space that he filled with nothing more than a pair of vertical filing cabinets, an L-shaped desk that was large enough to make the area tricky to navigate, and an imposing, life-sized cigar store Indian that he'd received as a gift from Edna on his fiftieth birthday. And as if the room weren't bland enough, the walls were in desperate need of a fresh coat of paint, and they were void of a single picture or painting.

How could such a simple setup be ransacked into such a violent mess? Ernie initially considered, as he took in the remarkable damage on display. The paper contents of both filing cabinets were strewn about the room, as if someone had intended to cover every square inch of the floor, and the cabinets themselves were left battered and bruised, as if repeatedly clubbed with a sledgehammer. Items that had been meticulously arranged atop his desk joined the scattered wreckage on the floor, and the Indian statue was lying face down in the chaos like a fallen soldier.

Ernie knew at once that his irreplaceable Redeemer file had been lifted. As he approached the specific cabinet within which the file had been secured under lock and key, he found it knocked on its side, with each of the locking components completely obliterated. "Juusst perfect," he blurted while glancing back at Linden, who was now reluctantly edging into the room. "I'd wager everything I own that the goddamn child was *just here*. First, she beat us to the pawnshop in Albuquerque to grab the scope, and then, knowing I'd be away from home, raced up here and swiped my file. It's no big deal, though—there's only *thirty years of research* in those papers!" Ernie returned his gaze to the crippled cabinet, and then slowly shook his head as if admitting defeat.

"I guess now's not a good time to ask if you backed up this file of yours onto a memory stick or something?"

"Backed up? Christ, I'm in my eighties, boy. The only thing I have *backed up* is my goddamn colon."

Though he knew the manila folder that contained the Redeemer file would be long gone, Ernie still asked for Linden's assistance in lifting up the weighty, three-tiered steel cabinet. With the tracks and rollers warped beyond repair, the two still managed to force the bottom drawer open. Ernie surged to the pocket where his precious file would have otherwise been resting. "What the . . .?" he suddenly uttered under his breath, as he realized the folder remained in its customary slot. He delved inside, and though void of the thickset aggregate of paper that made up its contents, the works appeared to be . . . supplanted.

"What is it?" Linden asked, though he wasn't too sure he actually wanted to know the answer. "Is your file still in there?"

From the very folder that was home to years of his investigative findings, Ernie proceeded to haltingly extract an enticing, jet-black envelope, its flap sealed shut with a golden sticker the size of a quarter. The initials *RD* were fashioned into the seal in a rich calligraphic font. "RD—Redeemer Deceivers," Ernie affirmed, while pointing out the showy decal. "Fancy fuckers, aren't they?"

"Redeemer Deceivers," Linden lazily repeated the words, but found they sounded just as strange spilling from his own lips. "Sorry to disappoint you, Ernie, but that term means absolutely nothing to me. Don't let me stop you, though—go ahead and do the honours. Whatever's in that envelope certainly wasn't intended for *my* eyes."

Though the room was a sea of distraction, Ernie severed the envelope's seal with a focused demeanour. From the pocket he withdrew a single sheet of hunter green bond paper—sharply folded once along a perfect seam. In spreading the crease, he exposed the same calligraphic font that so elegantly graced the outer decal. Kneeling next to the filing cabinet, he huddled over the text, straining to study its convoluted flair.

The letter, inked in a golden pigment, read as follows:

The Great Gathering is upon us. Hark the westerly windsong.

Ride the zephyr. Your place awaits.

Still muddled? Reiterate.

The Great Gathering is upon us. Hark the westerly windsong.

Ride the zephyr. Your place awaits.

Hallowed Artefacts Reveal The Facticity Of Redeemer Deceivers.

After reading the message to himself, Ernie gained his feet and stood perplexed. "It's nothing but a load of blabbering, hocus-pocus drivel!" he then vented, his confusion giving way to outright anger.

"Mind if *I* take a peek at it?" Linden asked tentatively, scared to poke the old bear.

"Sure, what the hell." Ernie surrendered the paper without hesitation. "But I'll tell ya this—if *I* can't wrap my head around it, then you're *sure as shit* to be baffled."

Like Ernie before him, Linden struggled through its curious prose—the only difference being that he possessed the patience to endure multiple passes. Upon the conclusion of his third attempt, a conspicuous clue seemed to suddenly hurl itself off the page and become openly discernible. "Ernie, Ernie, check this out," Linden insisted with a spike of enthusiasm, all the while drawing the old man's attention to the bottom of the page by tapping the paper repeatedly. "Look at how the first letter in each word of the final sentence is capitalized."

"Yeah," Ernie grumbled. "So?"

"If you align those eight letters together, they spell out *Hartford*!"

In an instant, Ernie snatched the paper back from Linden's hold and homed in on what he'd spotted. "That's it!" He immediately confirmed the decryption as if it were his own doing. "The westerly windsong, the Great Gathering—Christ, how could I've been so blind? Linden, my friend, you need to zip back down to your place and start packin' a few things—we're headin' to Hartford!"

Linden found himself at a loss for words. He failed to decipher if crazy old Ernie was just pulling his leg, or if he were *actually* considering the cross-country venture. Finally, he broke the lull in a hardened tone that initially surprised even himself. "*Please* tell me you're not serious, Ernie, because if you are, this is where I jump off."

"Take a gander about you, son," Ernie replied in an equally earnest pitch. "Does this seem like the time or place for an irreverent remark? Of course I'm serious, and you *are* comin' with me."

With Ernie now giving orders as opposed to options, Linden naturally took offence to his manner. "Let me tell ya something, you daft son of a bitch. I shoulda just left you waitin' at the school this morning. Whatever it is you're after—whether it be here, or in *fuckin'* Hartford—you're on your own from here on out." Linden was now making his way toward the room's exit, where he couldn't help himself but to pause, turn, and then continue his rant. "And who the hell do ya think you are, exactly, dictating that I just drop everything on the spot for your extravagant quest? As far as I'm concerned, you're officially off your rocker, old man. Thanks for wasting my time!"

Having said his piece, Linden marched out through the front door, leaving behind a now-tampered-with crime scene and an unstable person he wished he'd never encountered. On his way out, he was again drawn to the garden of trampled flowers and shards of duct-taped glass. *Weird doesn't even begin to cover it*, he mused as he readily vacated the property.

———

"Didn't I tell ya it was our lucky day! Looks like they've finally planted the seventh and final flag!" Linden slowly lowered the pocket telescope from his eye and offered it to his fellow dream attendant. "Here—it's time to peer into the magic for yourself!"

Linden, now back home in Albuquerque, stirred from a late-afternoon siesta. His brief time with that eccentric old man had tested his nerves to the limit, forcing the requisite escape to unconsciousness.

With his head still cloudy, he found his thoughts wavering between Ernie's bizarre plight, and the curious dream he'd just experienced in shallow slumber. Just a few hours ago, he had been cursing Ernie for his overbearing behaviour. Now, following this most unconventional of visions, he began to feel the tug of a change of heart toward the old man and his motives. *Maybe, just maybe, he's* justified *in travelling all the way to Hartford,* Linden contemplated as he connected Ernie's travel plans to his recent dream. He recalled driving a lunar rover and sitting atop a towering moon mountain next to an unknown associate. And of course, there'd been the pocket scope, and how he'd first freed it from within the Genesis Rock by means of a pickaxe. Then how its lens seemed to naturally sharpen upon the advancing Earth-Planet, and more precisely upon a sprawling green space in downtown Hartford, Connecticut. There, a flagpole was planted firmly in the park's surface, and a red flag proudly exhibited a yellow #7 on the face of the fabric. *Ernie didn't mention anything about numbered flags, did he?* Linden wondered, though he was almost certain he hadn't. He knew at heart it was just a dream, but at the same time he could also *feel* that it was somehow something more. It all seemed to channel back to Ernie, and his seemingly perpetual quest to untangle a most intricate Gordian knot.

Linden's dreamy recollections were extinguished in an instant by a screaming ringtone. He picked up the line, and an all-too-familiar voice immediately bellowed out on the other end. "Whether you like it or not, Linden, you're already . . . *we're* already in too deep!" It was Ernie once again, and he spoke like someone who'd long ditched the word "quit" from his vocabulary. "Just hear me out a min—"

"Ernie, Ernie, hold up," Linden's words crashed into Ernie's, bringing them to a sudden halt. When Linden realized he had the floor, he drew a deep breath that emptied into a reconciliation. "Listen, I'm not quite sure what made you decide to call me back, but let's just say I'm glad you did. I want to apologize for storming out on you the way I did. I guess I just—"

"Ah, don't bother," Ernie interjected in the same fashion Linden had, hoping to skip the mushy musings in the process. "As far as I'm concerned, all is forgiven. So, I'll get right to it. In order to overthrow this enemy, I'm gonna need *you*, and likewise you're gonna need *me*. Now, there's a red-eye flight to Hartford out of Albuquerque International—leaves tonight! I already took the liberty of buying a pair of tickets. Don't worry, though, I got it covered—won't cost ya a dime. Whaddaya say?" The line went eerily quiet. To Ernie, the silence lasted an eternity as he awaited the pivotal response. To Linden, it was the time required to ponder what seemed to carry the weight of a life-altering decision.

"What do I *say*, you ask?" Linden ultimately replied. "What I *say* is that your persistence is the definition of infuriating. Your avenues of communication often come across as crass. And though I've only known you for less than twenty-four hours, you could very well be the craziest son of a bitch I've ever met. So, in light of these facts, I have but one question for *you*, Ernie."

"Well I'm glad to hear you hold me in such high regard," the old man quipped. "As for your question, I'll return but one answer."

Linden couldn't help but wonder if he'd eventually come to regret his next words: "What time is our flight?"

INTERLUDE

Excerpts from the Afterlife

So, I'm not quite ready to reveal myself, reader, but I *am* ready to open up and get personal.

In the end, it happened when I was certain that a rope leading out to the moon from my second-storey window was real. That's when I died—when I reached for something that was nothing more than my own spiralling mind spinning its final fallacy. Sadly, my last moments were spent plummeting down upon a pad of unforgiving concrete.

Though I've tarried in this netherworld for some time now, I still recall the fall like it was yesterday. Let me be the first to tell you that it's true what they say about your last living moments—how your entire life passes before you like some nostalgic slideshow. Actually, given the single second it took to complete my inadvertent plunge, it was more like a billion jesters of memory, all crammed into some cognitive jack-in-the-box that suddenly exploded—the fallout an atomic mushroom cloud of recollection.

So here I am, surely not alive, nor *entirely* dead, but rather stuck in this mid-realm where my embodiment is still required. *How* am I here? Hell, I don't have an answer for that. How is anybody anywhere? In my case, I guess I just . . . *am*. I often wonder if this is hell itself—an endless duration of infinite half-deaths, for lack of a better term, where one forever depresses into lower substrata of Hades.

Amidst the incertitude, what I *do* know is this: though not by choice, I've become what's known as a Deceiver. Technically a *Redeemer* Deceiver, but that term doesn't get tossed around lightly here in this apparitional afterlife. We primarily exist within the imperceptible crevices of the dreams of the living, obeying an Overlord's directive as to when an appropriate incursion is required.

What we are is an ever-growing army of monozygotic twins who, upon our initial death, are immediately analyzed and ultimately divided. Basically, when both members of a set of identical twins perish within a short, specified time of each other, they're simply partitioned into two groups: good and bad. There's no middle ground, as the decision is very cut and dried. One wins, one loses—and all judgements are final. Well, I lost. Shit, *obviously* I lost. Let's face it: I didn't stand a fucking chance. My twin brother was an almighty priest for fifteen years—died in his sleep the very same night I took my great plunge. Talk about having the cards stacked against you. On the surface, they see a devoted theologian. And on the other hand, yours truly: an unstable back number who eventually veered clear off the rails.

Overall, I was a good man; had my ups and downs, just like everybody else. I was a science fiction writer with three published novels, though judging strictly by the number of sales, a subpar one at best. I guess my slow derailment into the depths of madness was my ultimate shortcoming, and unfortunately that's how I'll always be remembered.

As for my brother, we'll call him Peter. I still see Peter from time to time, when we cross paths within some stranger's late-night vision by chance. But herein lies the difference between us: now that we no longer exist in what is now known to us as the "Initial

World," I have an advantage over Peter. I have the capacity—if only in brief spells—to return to the Initial World by means of what are known as Dreamducts. (A note on Dreamducts: these transcendental conduits enable Deceivers to channel from one dream to another, as well as to and from the Initial World. A Dreamduct "rider" will reattain their physical form upon entry to the Initial World, and then vanish into a return duct when an assigned task has been successfully executed.) For reasons beyond my capacity, all Deceivers deemed as "the good ones" are denied this expedient passage.

At this point, allow me, reader, to acknowledge your possible confusion. I recognize that I'm painting with cloudy, convoluted strokes; but it's an elaborate piece, and my canvas is ever unsteady.

The reason for these words, which I'm logging in the Initial World, is due to a recent strain of dream entanglements. Random people's dreams have been intertwining like ivy vines at an alarming rate. You see, the Dreamducts are weakening, like a fabric full of holes—in this case, holes induced by disseminating radiation. I have my theories on this, and they're primarily based on ionizing lunar emissions. God help the living if I'm right. I'll expand on these theories in due time, but for now, I'll just let you in on my *current* obligation.

Under the direction of our appointed mission leader, Maercus, I've been assigned as second-in-command for an operation critical to what has already been christened the "Great Gathering." As much as we'd like to, we don't ask questions. You do what you're told to do, and if you don't follow through with your assignments, you're simply deemed a traitor and subsequently pay the ultimate price: another death within death. Now, when I say "death within death," I assume that gives the impression of *less* pain. This, in fact, couldn't be further from the truth. Words fail to construe the true affliction that the Overlord will surely hand down upon a traitor. I've seen it with my own dead eyes, and the trauma nearly shocked them back to life. As for the Overlord himself—known as Zreverus to the select few permitted to use his name—I promise to get back to you soon as far as detailing who *he* is, along with sharing a few back pages from his story as well.

My current assignment is to capture a very particular, long-coveted moon globe. The authentic artefact is a moon replica with splendidly detailed volcanic maria, towering mountains, and low-lying impact craters, all sculpted into its surface with scaled precision. The globe is currently situated in the Pacific Northwest: Bellevue, Washington, to sharpen the point.

I've learned that the Deceivers have tracked the globe's whereabouts for years, always aware of its precise location, yet unable to physically seize the piece due to an unyielding barrier—a barrier only to be breached with the possession of the artefact's complementary key: a rarefied 3-draw brass pocket telescope. What I'm gathering through the latest chatter is that the scope has surfaced due to a fortuitous discovery in New Mexico. Our mission has since been deployed, and the scales begin to tip in favour of the Overlord.

As for Washington, a seasoned pilot by the name of Mason Greene is the unlucky holder of the moon globe. The plan is to await his slumber, then furtively gain his estate and inject him with a medial dose of Dream Serum V. (A note on Dream Serum V: a low-risk sedative administered by means of injection through the subcutaneous tissue of the upper arm, thus, initiating a twenty-four to thirty-six-hour somnolent period in recipients. Provisional memory loss is common during the succeeding term.) Once Mason is suitably anaesthetized, we're to not only seize the moon globe, but to also supplant it with a Vitalsphere. This fascinating Earth replica is a living organism devised to supersede the moon globe amidst Mason's elaborate orb medley. Though not nearly as significant as the moon globe itself, the Vitalsphere is indeed vital to the broad scheme. When Mason eventually awakens from his lengthy slumber, the combination of the Dream Serum and the magic of the Vitalsphere will undoubtedly entice him to follow up on his globe's whereabouts, thus leading him straight to the site of the Great Gathering.

So, allow me to try and clarify things in these final words. Since this report is entirely off the record, I'll just come right out and spill my aversion toward the Overlord, and furthermore toward his imminent, underhanded endgame. There are certainly others on board with me when I speak of his dastardly ways. He assuredly has something big in the works—some form of an apocalyptic stratagem that doesn't bode well for the Initial World. The scary thing is, he has the great majority of Deceivers brainwashed and blind, marching toward a goal they can't even remotely begin to comprehend.

All this having been said, whatever his ruthless plan may be, there's surely an underlying glitch somewhere—a weakness our band of insubordinates will soon pounce and rebel upon like mutinous wolves.

It's been a few days since we've last spoken. But just because I'm dead, it doesn't mean I can't fulfill a promise. I told you I'd delve a little deeper into what I know of the Overlord and his hierarchy over the deceased—so here it is. Having successfully completed my mission into Bellevue to seize the moon globe, I will soon be on the move once again—therefore, I must be brief with my words.

Since my inauguration into this esoteric afterlife, I, along with every other member of this corrupt cavalry, have been under the watchful eye of Zreverus, whom I named previously. A good leader is respected on one side of the coin and feared on the other, and judging by what I see from within this affiliation, that's how he's perceived for the most part. His demands are handed down and promptly seen to with no aversion.

Now, let me catch you up to speed with a short history. Once simply known as Teaghue, the leader of all Deceivers was a man of dignity and unbending principle. The bulk of his days were spent in Munster, Ireland, the country's southernmost province, where he was respected by many as a skilled seaman. Teaghue was a lighthouse keeper off the coast of Mizen Head when he suddenly passed in his sleep in the fall of 1959. The coroner determined the cause of death to be by sudden cardiac arrest. In truth, it was more a rebirth than a passing—a metamorphosis into the early stages of sovereignty.

This is a paranormal puzzle indeed, but there are hints of key information sprinkled throughout. There's a certain Apollo moon mission, radiation particles, government cover-ups, coexisting dreams, and finally, the city of Hartford. All signs seem to point to the Connecticut capital, as people are being seduced to the city through the agency of dreams—and of course by Deceiver subterfuge.

Unfortunately, for those seeking answers of greater depth, this will likely be my final written entry of the sort, so all I can do for now is to keep you apprised of my intentions. Time is dwindling toward the Great Gathering. Shortly, I'll be riding the Dreamducts into Ohio, and from there on to Hartford. Look for me in the city's nucleus—a can't-miss recreational space called Bushnell Park. From deep within the park's confines I'll be furtively aborting my next assignment of containing Mason Greene, and then relying on instincts to implement our insurgence.

PART
III

That must have been another of your dreams
A dream of mad man moon

—Tony Banks

CHAPTER 22

Seeing Red

Following his unexpectedly prolonged slumber, Mason Greene had the feeling his legs were about to buckle under him as he scaled two flights of stairs to reach the heart of his home surveillance. Undoubtedly due to his long-tenured profession, he'd dubbed this designated office space of seemingly endless wire and sophisticated gadgetry "the cockpit." Here, the eyes of his state-of-the-art home security system displayed their findings on a pair of fifty-inch Sony monitors. Each of the monitors were suspended on a wall above a grand mahogany desk, and they continuously altered between three screens apiece—each of these screens offering six individual camera views. With the thirty-six images in total that covered each and every square inch of his estate, Mason was more than confident that at least one would hold the answer as to not only who'd breached his gated barrier, but who'd also buried a syringe deep into his flesh as he slept.

"Don't you think all these cameras are a little overkill?" Mason recalled his wife's words and the mocking tone in which she'd used them as he settled into a pivoting armchair.

"Overkill, my ass," he now chuckled to himself, half-scared and half-excited by what the various playbacks would soon reveal. With his vision still hazy, and his thoughts still tangled in cobwebs, Mason launched into a rearward search for the day and a half that was underhandedly taken from him.

Going straight to the source seemed to be the logical place to begin. With a remote that switched between camera views, each of his den's "eyes in the sky" revealed their respective quadrants. From there, the plan was to simultaneously rewind the four images on high speed until the perpetrator and his immoral deeds were exposed.

With the simple push of a button, Mason observed himself from two different camera angles as he lay dormant upon his sofa, the utilized syringe dangling listlessly from his appendage. As the seconds passed, real-time minutes elapsed in reverse, yet no signs of intrusion or foul play were evident to this point.

Clearly visible during the video shakedown was the enigmatic globe that mysteriously superseded his moon globe, with its lifelike qualities that inexplicably defied all means of probability. Though the whole ordeal was drenched in uncertainty, this otherworldly sphere had generously offered a constructive clue: it had told him of Hartford. The numbered flags protruding from various cities were telling him as plain as day that his moon globe—and likely its captors—was now, or was soon to be, nearly three thousand miles away in central Connecticut. Somewhere deep down inside, Mason knew he'd ultimately venture east—first to confront his assailants, and then to reclaim what was rightfully his.

The time read-out on the surveillance video continued to tick in reverse when the four screens suddenly flickered simultaneously, then briefly dissolved to static before regaining their clear picture. Mason, spooked by the sudden glitch, frantically searched out the Play button on the remote and prepared to observe the drama in real time. But by the time his sweaty, trembling hands had found the proper key, the images had flown far beyond the slice of static, thus revealing the den as it was prior to the break-in. There he observed himself as he lay in a world of unhindered slumber—no sign of the unsolicited syringe whatsoever. Camera 3-I offered a precise view of his brand-new moon globe, which he'd placed on the coffee table to gain a better view of its peculiar scuff mark. At this moment in time, everything appeared to be in its right place.

Mason drew a deep breath and acknowledged the searing pain in his upper arm. As bad as it was, it appeared to have already peaked, and he managed to tuck the discomfort away for the time being.

Knowing the video glitch was soon approaching, Mason pressed the images into slow motion and focused in on the screen. Once again, the flicker introduced solid walls of static. The perplexed pilot's eyes never abandoned the screen as they stared deep into the snowy void for its entirety—a solid two minutes and thirteen seconds of pondering how he'd not only been both drugged and robbed, but also how the bastards had managed to cover their tracks in the process.

A part of Mason couldn't help but feel violated; yet rising above the gloom was a sense of invigoration, a blossoming energy fuelled by the prospect of adventure. No one (other than the leery voices in his own head) was around to call him crazy for such an incalculable enterprise. His wife and daughter weren't due back for another week; that was plenty of time for a round-trip to the beautiful New England region.

Sure, the option of calling the police was still there, but in the moment it just seemed like the easy way out. It would surely defuse the rush of adrenaline currently coursing freely through his spirit. He somehow needed to fly this one alone—free of burdens like high-strung passengers and cocksure co-pilots.

Following another half hour of fruitless investigation, Mason's next move was to abandon the surveillance room altogether for a physical survey of his estate. On his way out, an image on the far monitor suddenly caught his eye, stealing his attention like a thief itself. It was camera 8-E, exposing a broad perspective of the property's eastern expanse, viewed from a perched exterior lens. It wasn't the live shot of the luscious landscape that grabbed him, but rather the spine-tingling presence of the early evening moon. Insinuating an apocalyptic warning with its sinister-red glow, the circular beacon was floating modestly low behind the estate's rich foliage.

As breathtaking as the florid moon appeared on the surveillance screen, Mason knew the image portrayed through a camera would still fail to capture its true essence. He impulsively slipped a cozy Seattle Seahawks sweater over his head before venturing out into the cool autumn night for a peek, his bruised and burning arm tender as he manoeuvred the sleeves.

Outside, the air felt refreshingly clean and crisp on both his skin and in his lungs. The gloaming had a soothing stillness to it, as if time itself had booked the evening off. Highly attentive to his surroundings, Mason strolled past a fenced-in tennis court before mounting a dozen or so sandstone garden steps for an optimal view of the lunar spectacle.

There the moon hung low in the east like an accessible, bloodshot piñata. The image on the Sony monitor had been stirring indeed, yet it paled in comparison to the prodigious satellite before him now. It appeared inconceivably large, as if the bloated orb were dangerously close at hand, and the slightest pinprick might cause it to burst. It was quite unlike *any* moon Mason had ever witnessed—and he'd certainly seen his share of beauties while navigating countless night skies. "Straight out of a dream," he muttered to himself, his soft words augmented by the tranquil setting. The sight drew his most *recent* dream to mind: the one with Earth-Planet, and how it had grown continuously larger as it plummeted toward his peculiarly inhabited moon world. The moon on this evening was so surreal that he couldn't help but wonder if he were still enveloped in said slumber, or if the maleficent injection he'd received was now inducing post-dormant hallucinations. Nevertheless, Mason chose to view the carmine sphere as a divine signal—an augury image further endorsing an eastward course to Hartford.

Still arrested in the trance of the moon, Mason found himself seeking answers that wouldn't likely be arriving anytime soon. *Why the hell would somebody drug me, steal my shit, and then leave clues as to where they could be reached? And why* Hartford? *What's so damn special about—*

"The English say a red full moon is the *killing* moon." With a graceful confidence, a mischievous voice suddenly cut through the silence like a swiftly thrown dagger. Mason's thoughts were pierced. He immediately spun to discern an elderly man, likely in his early seventies, leaning comfortably against a wooden gazebo column less than fifty feet away. "Oh, pay no heed to *me*," the unknown party continued, as he casually raised an arm to aim the tip of a walking stick at the baleful moon. "I'm just taking in the wonders of the night as if it were my last."

Up yet another notch on his perplexion meter, Mason inched toward the trespasser and raised his voice vehemently. "Just who the *fuck* do ya think you are, buddy? And how'd you get through the gates?"

"Ahh, don't sweat the petty stuff, Mase," the stranger responded, holding his unruffled tone as he spoke. "Pet the sweaty stuff." He paused, as if to watch his crude words register, then continued. "Please, call me Red. Listen, here's the deal: all I ask is that you calm yourself, and that you talk civil with me here—I'm trying to fly under the radar as it is. Trust me—another outburst on your end'll be grievous to the pair of us. Now, given your current state, I understand you're looking for answers—I really do. And I *possess* those answers. But if you're gonna continue to run yer mouth at such a volume, I'll make sure to run the words right back down your throat until they spill outta yer ass in a whisper!"

Taken aback by the foul threat, Mason consciously halted beyond Red's reach as he joined him beneath the gazebo crown. From this immediate perspective, his initial deduction of the intruder's age was confirmed. Red's jowls drooped like that of an old blood-hound, and his eyes looked like they'd witnessed the horrors of multiple lifetimes. He sported a collared flannel shirt, dark brown slacks, and a grey flat cap. Then there was the cane at his side. The jet-black walking stick was overlaid with cryptic engravings, with a wolf's head for a handle and a tip resembling a silver bullet. "All right, speak to me," Mason said, resuming his interrogation, struggling mightily to keep his composure in the process. "First and foremost, I want to know why I just woke up to find a fucking *syringe* dangling from my arm like some strung-out junkie. And secondly, why was one of my globes stolen while I was under? You're the furthest thing from what I envisioned as the culprit, but you've already acknowledged your involvement."

"*Involvement?*" Red replied with a snicker. "Shit, I mainlined the serum into your bloodstream myself! Here's the thing, though. I've since jumped ship, so to speak. I was supposed to return with the others after we snatched your globe, but I've aborted the mission. Long story."

Having now heard the trespasser's cold confession, Mason was fighting the urge to pluck the walking stick from the old man's feeble grasp and bury its pronged tip four inches into his skull. But as annoyingly calm and monotone as Red spoke, he was *speaking* nonetheless. And if his cane were to soon resemble a toothpick stabbing an olive, that would surely be the abrupt end to any additional information.

For the time being, Mason thought better of his actions, and listened in as Red continued with his head still intact. "As for you, you were injected by yours truly with a non-lethal dose of what is known as Dream Serum V. Other than a tender arm that'll linger a while, the effects should have all but lifted by now. During your sedated slumber, a supplantation was executed to perfection—your moon globe swapped for the chimerical-like Vitalsphere, which I'm assuming you've already evaluated by this point."

"Yeah, I looked it over," Mason casually affirmed, as if to suggest its animate qualities were shy on piquing his interest. "And I deciphered its elementary flag sequence in about two minutes, by the way."

It was then that the stranger introduced a slow, purposeful stride toward Mason, his icy eyes like hardened rime as they beguiled the pilot. "All right, here's the deal," he began. "You were actually *meant* to crack the stupid flag sequence. For whatever reason, the higher-ups like to turn everything into a goddamn riddle. So, as you've already worked out, you basically need to get your ass to Hartford ASAP. Once you arrive, it won't take long for you to realize that things aren't exactly . . . as they should be. The city will be spiritless and cold. But don't let the desolation delude you—the enemy will indeed be lurking in the shadows and around innocent corners."

"Hold up, hold up." Mason raised his arms as if to surrender. "Either I'm still lulling in the anaesthetic void, or you, my friend, are spewing some of the most vile verbal diarrhea I've ever heard."

"Let me assure you that your slumber is through—though that freakish moon behind you belongs in *someone's* nightmare. Now, this enemy I speak of is a vast multitude, invading Hartford in support of an event dubbed the Great Gathering. And unfortunately, all signs are pointing toward a calamitous end."

Mason stood dumbfounded in the moment, and then found his voice. "You gotta be kiddin' me, buddy! Gimme one good reason why I should fly all the way across the country to a city where all that awaits me are enemies and calamity! Christ, I hope you're not lookin' for work as a travel agent."

Red chuckled before promptly closing the door on it while fine-tuning his hat. "Because you're just . . . well, you're just *supposed* to be there, okay? I know that's as vague as the day is long, but a sharp ear will notice that fate tends to whisper in the wind from time to time. Also, there will be others like yourself—strangers from distant corners flocking to Hartford. Some consciously, and others teetering along a tightrope of intuition. I can't say how, but trust me, you'll know your allies when you—"

Red's obliging words were suddenly severed mid-sentence. The residual sound (a searing hiss, like raw bacon being tossed into hot grease) and accompanying sight forced Mason to buck backwards, his spine meeting a support pillar in the process. The enigmatic stranger had abruptly vanished into thin air, like a magician's volunteer. There was no applause; just a noxious vapour that remained in his place, smouldering low over a scarred gazebo floor.

Mason couldn't help but wonder if he'd been fixed in some science fiction mise-en-scène. Any second now, Rod Serling's patented delivery would emanate from the heavens for a cryptic narration. Or perhaps the TARDIS time machine would suddenly materialize before the gazebo, and the Doctor would step forth and kindly construe the situation.

Mason was justifiably rattled by the man who'd seemingly appeared out of nowhere, then suddenly vanished while dispensing pivotal counsel. He now stood alone, feeling helplessly exposed within a current reality that had all the stability of a landslide. Exiting the gazebo, he stumbled over a slender object that nearly sent him tumbling down a pair of wooden steps. After regaining his footing, he glanced down to find a mutated shell of what could only be Red's walking stick, a black, gooey residue blotting its disfigurement like wet tar. Mason knelt next to the sad alteration, and at once considered the possibility that it had been purposely salvaged, Red having wilfully tossed the crutch to safety at the last millisecond to spare a *complete* incineration.

Mason didn't need any more convincing. It was time to head east—to Hartford! Whereabouts *within* the Connecticut capital, he didn't know in the slightest. But what he *did* know was this: he'd be leaving his home in Bellevue by sunrise at the latest, and upon landing at Bradley International, some*one* or some*thing* would stand out like the blood-red moon rising before him now and point him in the right direction. *Some consciously,* Red had said, *and others teetering along a tightrope of intuition.*

Mason doubled back across his vast property at a brisk pace. As he moved, he was inevitably drawn to the blushed orb once again and was jolted in his tracks with what it now presented. A dusky blemish seemed to scar its red face like a slanted bruise—a jarring imperfection on an otherwise flawless surface. Mason then felt his stomach priming to purge when he recognized that the deface-ment was in perfect correlation with that of the blemish on his since-seized moon globe.

Observing the moon in its current state, Mason paused to close his eyes and then rub his eyelids with some force. *Christ, am I seeing things? Am I teetering on the edge here?* In that muddled moment, he prayed to the heavens that when he reopened his eyes, a world free of the devilish magic he'd been enduring would be revealed.

His eyelids lifted, and the defect was gone, as if it had been wiped away with a damp cloth. At least for now, Mason's prayer had been heard, but all it did was open a door for more questions. *Did it just . . . disappear? Was it ever there in the first place?* Mason's mind had become a roiling ocean, stirring up muddy sediment from the deep unknown. He could feel his stability continuing to slip—a stability he'd certainly need to sustain, as the city of Hartford awaited his arrival like a snake in the grass.

———————

Mason's connections within the Delta Air Lines circle enabled a hassle-free red-eye flight booking out of Seattle–Tacoma International. After swiftly gathering enough belongings to fill a small suitcase, he'd nearly made it halfway to the airport when an impulse to return home began to weigh heavy on his mind. It wasn't a sudden reconsideration of the bold trip ahead; it was something about the seared walking stick he'd left deserted on the base of his gazebo. Less than a minute later, that notion got the best of him, and with a wheel-squealing U-turn, he surrendered to his intuition.

As the cane lay like a broken tree branch, Mason raced to a nearby shed for a pair of garden gloves before returning to gather the charred stick. He proceeded to stuff it into an oversized duffle bag that would now accompany him across the country.

Before he knew it, Mason Greene of beautiful Bellevue, Washington, was on the road once again. As he approached the point of his earlier U-turn, he felt a shiver run through his body like a kiss of déjà vu. It now felt as if he was about to pass the point of no return, with a one-way ticket to a moribund city.

Pulling up to the airport he was ever so familiar with, a fusion of excitement and anxiety ruled the night. Making his way through the Delta terminal he was met with select handshakes and hellos. Many had never witnessed the seasoned pilot donning anything other than his customary uniform. Some wondered why he was not only departing his hometown in a solitary fashion, but also with an anxious spring in his step that challenged the late hour.

The widespread city lights gently languished below as the airliner thrust upward and onward. As he climbed, Mason stole a final glance back down at the region he'd called home for over forty years. The now distant lights had melded into a solid amber glow, and in that moment, he couldn't help but liken the glow to that of a traffic signal—a signal warning that at this point it was too late to turn back.

CHAPTER 23

Dreamducts and Duct Tape

Just as he'd done every morning since The Treasure Trove first opened its doors, Sammy rolled into the pawnshop's parking lot at precisely eight thirty. With his ever-faithful extra-large black coffee secured in his left hand, he keyed the lock with his right, and then began preparations for his customary nine o'clock opening. On this day, Ernie and Linden would soon come seeking the moon-flaw scope; but as fate would have it, not soon enough.

Before he'd even gotten around to illuminating the fluorescent Open sign in the window, Sammy noticed a most unusual customer browsing along a succession of glass display cases. First off, he had neither heard nor witnessed the young girl enter the shop. And secondly, since she was the only other person in the store besides himself, he noticed that she failed to meet the requirement of an accompanying adult. "Hello there, young one," Sammy offered in a comforting tone as he slowly approached the blonde-haired child. "Might your mother or father be nearby? Next door at the bakery, perhaps?"

"There's a particular item I'm looking for, sir," the young girl replied in a sweet and innocent voice that suited her appearance.

She continued to scan the glass casings without so much as a glance in Sammy's direction. The child reminded Sammy of his youngest granddaughter, who lived over a thousand miles away in Illinois, and he regrettably saw only once or twice a year. Whatever it was she was up to in the shop, she appeared to be extremely focused on her task, like a coin collector pursuing a rare mint. "It's for my science fair project."

"Well, young lady, I'm glad to see you working hard at school," Sammy continued, holding his soft tone. "But this is a store for adults. It's what you call a pawnshop—we do grown-up business here. Now, you never answered me when I asked if you're with your parents." Sammy's eyebrows rose like a drawbridge. "Are they waiting out in the car?"

"No, sir." This time the child shifted her stance, and acknowledged Sammy through a low-spirited frown. "Mommy says we don't got enough money t'have a car—not with the rent and all."

Just then Sammy noticed a man and a woman making their way into the shop, both toting hard-shell guitar cases by their handles. "Okay, run along now," Sammy now insisted to the child, his composure slipping. "I've got business to attend to."

Foiled in her bid to attain the pocket telescope through civil means, Estella was suddenly feeling the pinch of the clock. The old man from Santa Fe wouldn't be far behind, and an encounter with him and his fresh apprentice would surely throw an untimely wrinkle into the Overlord's grand design.

Thus, she resorted to what is known to Deceivers as Hollow Hypnosis. The trance—a temporary diversion from one's own free will—was promptly cast upon Sammy and culminated with the exchange of both the coveted moonflaw scope and a roll of duct tape for a dollars' worth of rolled pennies. The beauty of the hypnosis was the perception it yielded to the victim. No memory loss ever occurred throughout the entire process, leading Sammy to believe the exchange was a conscious agreement.

As a result of this exchange, the Deceivers now possessed the imperative moonflaw scope, and once transferred to the reigning hand of Zreverus, along with the imminent moon globe seizure in Bellevue, the final chapter would ultimately commence within the fated city.

Following the sly confiscation, Estella remained a shrewd step ahead of her adversaries. It was now northeast to Santa Fe for more conniving trickery. With the precious scope in tow, she atomized into the nearest Dreamduct and, when a suitable outlet presented itself, discharged her corporeal form out into Ernie Cowarth's neighbourhood before seeking out his modest dwelling.

While Ernie and Linden were rolling into The Treasure Trove lot with the high hopes of obtaining the pocket telescope from Sammy, Estella was making preparations to inaudibly fracture Ernie's bay window. Cloaked behind a golden yellow forsythia shrub, the young Deceiver planned to not only be out of sight, but out of earshot as well. While balancing atop a wobbly garden stone, she applied numerous strips of her recently acquired duct tape to the window's sun-drenched surface. She then proceeded to pluck a softball-sized rock from the dirt, and following a cursory scan of the vicinity, struck the now-swathed window with a concise blow.

What would've otherwise been a shrill resonance of shattering glass was no more than a muffled thud. The window had indeed fractured upon impact, but it was a controlled break, as the glass remained in place under the adhesive. Again, Estella surveyed her surroundings, and then began to carefully peel back the strips of tape. The myriad shards held fast to the gummy seal as a saw-toothed aperture grew with no more than a minimal crackle. When the perforation was sufficient, she vaulted her pint-sized figure up and inside.

Estella regained her footing on the old man's wooden floor amongst fragments of glass, each sliver reflecting the sun's light in its own inimitable fashion. The Reverie Redeemer file was now practically right under her nose, and she didn't squander another second before going right after it.

For the assigned Deceiver, recklessly rummaging through bulky cabinets, private folders, and loose documents to seize the revered file was elementary in its own right; it was the cryptic riddle she was to author off-the-cuff, and then leave in its place, that drew the burden. The obligation, firmly pressed down from the hierarchy, was to entice both Ernie and his associate eastward, from the temperate comforts of New Mexico to the shadowy gloom of Central Connecticut. With the triumphant acquisition of the moonflaw scope, and now the Redeemer file, Estella knew a successfully penned inducement would all but ensure herself a choice seat at the Great Gathering.

A legion of assigned Deceivers were now ordered to take their appointed positions in Hartford. From the Dreamducts they swooped in and merged seamlessly with the Initial World. Most made inroads from the west, while others advanced from other corners. And a select assemblage was already established in the city, laying crucial groundwork for the Overlord's long-awaited final chapter.

CHAPTER 24

A Soft Voice

Given the frenzied reception that both Luke Sheehan and Jeremy Lowe were greeted with at the Hilton, the pair were content to have settled within the seemingly secure confines of Bushnell Park for the time being. "I have a bad feeling that all this is just the tip of the iceberg," Luke revealed in little more than a whisper, gazing about in surveillance while the two remained perched atop Weidenmann's Bridge. He now took his eyes off the grounds and dialled in on Jeremy. "Listen, I believe we're here in Hartford for a reason. I'm not quite sure what that reason *is* just yet, but this is definitely something more than just a pair of random strangers meeting up halfway between their respective cities."

Like an outlying overture, the rumbling of distant thunder accompanied the night's murky mystique. "What, like we've been . . . summoned, or something?" Jeremy asked as ominous moonlight washed over the park.

"Yes, but *subconsciously* summoned," Luke added, removing his Red Sox cap to feverishly scratch his temple. "Like some subliminal force had already arranged this rendezvous between us."

As he struggled to digest the ever-thickening plot, Jeremy took a moment to snip at the web of confusion that seemed to be suffocating his psyche. "Already *arranged?*" he finally said. "Arranged by whom?"

"Brace for it, my friend, keeping in mind that I'm just dealing in *theories* here—not facts. Basically, I suspect this has all been arranged by whomever—or *what*ever—has gotten inside our heads and is essentially regulating our dreams. I know, I know, it sounds freakin' absurd, but let me start from the bottom and work my way up. Through whatever means, the dreams that each of us had last night somehow became . . . entangled, for lack of a better word. We've already established that much, am I right?" With his thoughts still scrambling through a murky maze, Jeremy failed to respond. "*Am I right?*" Luke barked this time, attempting to snap the professor out of his fog, yet not so loud as to draw attention to the bridge.

"Yeah, you're right, you're right," Jeremy reluctantly agreed. "Entangled."

"All right—now stay with me. Here's what we know for sure then." Luke firmly affixed his cap upon his head as if to indicate that the *real* business was set to begin. "As surreal as all this may seem, something has definitely happened to us—and I'm almost certain that it's just the beginning of something *big*. Now, we must view our dream as a sort of . . . puzzle. There must've been integral signs, or clues, purposely offered to us. Some would've been hidden, and some should be smacking us square in the face. We just have to start diggin' a little deeper, that's all. What I need from *your* perspective is any piece of information, as miniscule and irrelevant as it may seem, that could possibly trigger a recollection in *me*."

Over the course of the next twenty minutes, both Jeremy and Luke became so engaged in their dream dissection that neither noticed the new patch of stealthy fog that had fallen over the park like a fleecy blanket. "Well isn't this just par for the course," Luke grumbled, finally conscious of the thick murk. "How the hell are we supposed to spot someone approaching if we can barely see our own goddamn feet?"

"I'd like to think that the fog is concealing *us* as well, though," Jeremy added, trying to put a positive spin on their ongoing march of adversity.

As if born of the haze, a misty rain began to kiss the grounds, permeating the creaky wooden surface of the timeworn footbridge. The visible breath of the two strangers spilled into the gloom as precarious words were spoken in muted tones. "This dream we shared," Luke continued in a measured drawl, aiming a finger at the orb of the night. "I can't help but think that the moon has some sort of influence over its . . . well . . . its existence."

Initially, all Jeremy could offer in response was a contorted expression of confusion. He then replied, "I'm not even gonna *attempt* to wrap my head around that one. But I'll give ya this: in the dream, there *was* a plump morning moon suspended over Fenway—larger than life, really. I noticed it when your plane drew my eye to the sky."

"Yeah, I saw it too," Luke acknowledged. "Larger than life indeed." The two pivoted in unison to study the *actual* moon, but it had furtively snuck behind the brume. "We're not the only ones involved in this mess," Luke continued after a moment. "There are others out there who've been experiencing similarly melded dreams."

"*Out there?* Out *where?*"

"I don't know *where*, specifically," Luke replied, "but what I'm trying to say is this: these dreams branch out from a source like tributaries—connective channels that are somehow blending dreams into extensive subliminal collages."

"Riiight." Jeremy protracted the word in a confession of ignorance. "So how do you know all this bizarre shit, anyway?"

"I can't say that I truly *know* anything. It's all mere speculation based on what I've gathered from recent dreams."

For Jeremy, the entire situation had become a stir of confusion, suspicion, and doubt. In dire need of an adjournment, he shifted his thoughts toward Shelly. *I have to give her a call, tell her where I'm at,* he said to himself as he scooped his cell phone from a pocket. *Tell her what the hell's been goin' on with this Luke fella.*

"*No!* You can't be making any calls!" Luke abruptly opposed, lunging to hinder Jeremy from his actions. "If it's your wife you're lookin' to dial, I strongly advise against it—you can't risk her coming here. Open your *eyes*, dude! This city is a spreading disease!"

"All right, you listen to *me* now!" Jeremy demanded in response, his tongue full of venom. "You may've initiated our union, but I'll be damned if you're gonna be calling *all* the shots here. Whatever *this* is, we're in it together. That being said, if I feel the need to call my own goddamn wife, I'm sure as shit gonna do it."

"Suit yourself, man," Luke replied, noticeably unfazed by the outburst. "Just don't say I didn't warn ya."

Jeremy still had every intention of calling his wife, even though Luke was dead set against the fact. But he also realized that their time cloaked in the perfect fog could be limited. He returned his phone to his pocket for the time being and continued speaking to the man from Boston. "Listen, I've got questions that need answering before we go any further. You said you've been experiencing these screwy dreams for the past little while, right? So, I want to know why *ours* was the one that ultimately prompted you to act. Why did *this one* send you off into a panic that had you desperately seeking me out?" Jeremy now cocked a pointed finger within a foot of Luke's brow. "Start giving me somethin' solid to stand on, buddy! And make it fast! Otherwise, I'm headin' back to the hotel, and then gettin' the fuck outta this creepy city."

"Listen, I feel your frustration." Luke gently placed a hand on Jeremy's shoulder as he spoke. "But right now, more than anything, I need you to calm . . . the fuck . . . down. Believe it or not, you've *also* experienced these dreams prior to last night, but unaware of their gravity, you just haven't been paying attention to them. As for *our* dream—for me, it was simply the clincher. The one that basically told me it's finally time to take action. Now or never, ya know?"

With the picture still as foggy as their current view from the bridge, and Luke's words still seemingly spinning circles in the mud, Jeremy decided he'd heard enough. The lack of concrete information was *his* clincher. He offered his hand to Luke for an honest shake. Then he'd be off, back to New York where he'd crawl home to Shelly and, following a detailed explanation of his strange stint in Hartford, would offer a grand apology for leaving her in limbo the way he had.

Before their hands even connected, a tentative, feminine voice suddenly seeped through the murk from down below. "Hello? Excuse me—you two, up on the bridge."

The soft words brushed through as if riding in on a feather, but they were unforeseen words nonetheless, and that fact rendered them electric. Following the initial wave of shock, the two men had no choice but to react to their undisclosed company. "Let me do the talking here," Luke whispered to Jeremy as he huddled close. "And get ready to run down the other side on my command."

There was a compelling quality in the woman's voice that almost instantly drew Jeremy back into the fold. As the frail innocence of her speech perforated the misty shroud, it diminished his intentions of retreat. "Maybe take it easy on this one," he muttered in return. "Don't jump to any conclusions just yet. I don't know why, but I have a strong feeling she's not here to harm us."

"Odd time to be trustful, but okay."

Before Luke could spill any words upon the woman, she beat him to the punch and spoke again. "Mind if I join yous?" Rather than wait for a reply, she found a railing and guardedly began to ascend the slope.

"Identify yourself!" Luke appealed as the approaching woman's slender frame began to clear a swath-like passage through the murk. She stood tall atop the arch with the look and physique of a runway model. When she failed to offer an immediate response, Luke pressed the issue. "I believe I asked you your name, lady. And why are you roaming the park alone like it's a Saturday afternoon?"

"*Alone?*" the woman rebutted with a fresh spirit. "Hell, I ain't been more than fifty yards behind you guys ever since you stormed out of the Hilton!"

"You're *following us?*" Jeremy probed with a sudden look of distaste. "Why?"

"Why? Because I've been in this disturbed city for a few hours now, and you two appear to be the only freakin' people I can trust!"

Luke and Jeremy glanced at each other, as if to say, "Hard to argue that."

"Okay, since you're openly admitting to following *us*, then who's to say there isn't anybody following *you?* But before you answer that, like my friend here has asked more than once now, we need a name. If you can't give us that much, then we're basically done here. This is Luke, from Boston, and I'm Jeremy, from New York."

"Janelle—Janelle Crawford, from Newport. Used to live here in Hartford in what seems like another lifetime now—place has gone to shit. As for me being followed, there's no need to worry about that. Trust me, I've been lookin' over my shoulder so much that my neck is sore."

Though Janelle's approach seemed genuine, both Luke and Jeremy continued to regard the attractive woman from Rhode Island with guarded suspicion. Given their early encounters in the city, they understood she could turn on them in an instant. "You say you used to live here in Hartford," Luke acknowledged. "So tell me, what brings you back? I mean, Christ, it seems like the Grim Reaper himself decided to settle in this hellhole."

"Well, even with the fog I'm already starting to feel like a sitting duck up here, so I'll try to make a long story short. Exactly ten years ago to this very day, my husband, Andy, was killed in a fire-fighting accident just south of the city. Plastics plant—went up like Chernobyl. Of course they tried to tell me he died a *hero*, and all that crap. Not that I don't think he had it in him, I just never received any specifics, that's all. I'm certain they just use that line—or something similar—on *every* fresh widow, to sort of soften the blow, ya know?"

"I remember that fire," Jeremy added, curious as to how this particular story would wind its way back to why she was back in town. "It was in Hamden, wasn't it?"

"Yeah, just outside of New Haven," Janelle replied. "Anyhow, where was I? Oh yeah. When I lost Andy, I basically cracked. Him being a firefighter, I always feared the worst. But you can never *truly* prepare yourself for such hardship. When it actually happened, it was like having my heart ripped outta my chest. Soon thereafter, I quit on Hartford as a whole, because I simply couldn't bear to live here anymore. Then, following failed attempts to settle in Vermont and New Hampshire, I eventually found root in Newport. Don't think I would've made it if it weren't for my daughter. She gave me the strength to push through a seemingly endless line of barriers. Oh, listen to me go—I'm giving you guys the long version after all.

"Why I came back . . . right. About six months ago, I started having these really messed-up dreams. And not your *typical* messed-up dreams—I mean dreams that have me questioning my sanity. After a while, I began to realize that as much as I loathed facing them, they simply couldn't be ignored. Each dream centres on somebody specific—somebody I've unfortunately lost touch with. People I used to know when I lived *here*, some of whom I loved and respected very much. These dreams all begin beautifully, like there was never an accident with Andy, and my life had just carried on accordingly. But in each and every instance, right before

I wake, these old friends start to cry. And by 'cry' I mean their eyes suddenly turn a sinister crimson and begin shedding tears of blood. They then wait until the blood first reaches their lips before leaving me with the exact same message—word for word." As if to add suspense, Janelle chose this moment to pause and survey her surroundings. A mischievous wind disturbed fallen leaves, while a flash of electric light permeated the city's sullen spirit. A rumble of rolling thunder followed, complementing the glow, and then tapered off into the distant reaches of the night.

"Well, *go on*," Luke urged strongly. "Don't be quittin' on us now. What do they all say? What's the message?"

"Well, I've heard it enough times to know that it's some kind of riddle," Janelle explained in a hushed manner, as if surrounding ears might pick up on her words. "What they say is, 'Ten years to the day the flame took him away, regain the land from which you strayed, seek the one from Santa Fe.'" Janelle shrugged her shoulders innocently, and then offered a simple analysis. "Call me crazy, but here I am, ten years to the day Andy passed, in Hartford, looking for someone from Santa Fe. I figured, what the hell—I'll come back here and see if these dreams carry any real weight."

"Well, considering a dream brought the two of *us* to Hartford," Luke acknowledged, pointing back and forth between Jeremy and himself, "we don't think you're crazy at all. Listen, I'm gonna throw something at you here, and see what you make of it, okay? Just hear me out, and consider what I'm saying. Now, from what I've gathered from my *own* dreams of late, I believe it's possible that at the exact time you experienced each one of your dreams in question, your coinciding friend, or loved one, was having the exact same dream as well—only viewed from their own perspective. So basically, every single one of those people has subconsciously told you to be here tonight.

"Like I just touched on, that's why Jeremy and I are here right now. Prior to about an hour and a half ago, we'd never seen each other before in our lives. Somehow our dreams last night became entangled, or fused—however you want to put it. And suddenly we're here in Hartford, sorting it out—or at least trying to. Your story, Janelle, is just proof that this whole ordeal is operating on a much larger scale than we initially anticipated."

"So let me get this straight. You're telling me that you think someone's dream can actually be in synchronization and coexist with that of another's?" Janelle queried, struggling mightily to wrap her head around the seemingly impossible explanation. "And you think this is what's happening with *my* recent run of dreams? Wow! Part of me wants to say that the two of you should return to whatever loony bin you escaped from. But then again, who am *I* to judge, when I'm here standing atop Batshit Bridge just the same?" The three chuckled in unison, and as the veil of fog sustained its hold on the city, it was quickly becoming clear to each member of the newly formed trio that they were establishing a trust in one another. Assuredly soon to be exposed in unfamiliar territory, it was agreed upon that the theory of safety in numbers was indeed a practical one.

"All right, we've determined that we're here because we acknowledged our dreams," Jeremy announced with a hint of frustration. "So now what? Where do we go from here? Christ, we're confused, the weather's shitty, and we're standing atop a goddamn park bridge in a city that none of us call home. Not to mention these *Deceivers*, as Luke here calls 'em."

Janelle was unfamiliar with the term. But having already dipped into the shell of the city she once knew, she quickly put two and two together.

"Okay, I agree we've become stagnant up here," Luke responded, while struggling through the haze to gauge the base of the bridge. "So, I think Janelle here has already answered the question as to what our next play should be."

"I *have?*" she marvelled.

"Well, in a sense," Luke replied. "It pertains to the final line in your recurring riddle—about seeking someone from Santa Fe. I'm pretty sure we don't have a clue who it is we'll be looking for—or even *why*, for that matter. But what we *do* know is this: whoever it is, they're *vital*."

When it was understood that all parties were on board, Luke led the way as the trio descended the southern half of the bridge. Not a minute later, as if they'd riled the heavens by vacating the arch, the skies suddenly unfastened and expelled a torrential downpour unlike any of them had ever experienced. The deluge, riding in on the coattails of Hurricane Allan, sent the group scurrying like mice for shelter. "Follow me!" Janelle cried out through the raging torrent. "I know this park pretty well. There should be a pavilion about a hundred yards from here. Let's go!"

In no time at all, the Bushnell Park grounds had mutated into a boggy slop. Surface drainage systems were quickly overrun as the drink spilled over onto pedestrian pathways like seawater flooding a ship deck.

Heading toward the pavilion, a fleet-footed Janelle sloshed her way through the park, as both Luke and Jeremy followed her meandering course. The three were weaving their way through what felt like a mile-long maze of timber and shrub when suddenly, about two-thirds of the way to their mark, Luke ordered a halt after envisioning a worst-case scenario ahead. "Wait! Hold up!" he shouted. "Jeremy! Janelle! Hold up!" Against their better judgement, the two paused in their soggy tracks, and then loped back to Luke. "I'm not so sure about this," he stated between laboured breaths. "I mean the pavilion—I think it's too predictable."

"Too *predictable?*" a bemused Jeremy questioned. "What the hell are you goin' on about? I don't know 'bout you, but I've had just about enough of bein' pissed on like this. I'm sure the lady agrees. C'mon, we're almost there!"

"Listen, just hear me out. All I'm sayin' is this: wouldn't you think that if there's more of these Deceivers around, they'll be a step ahead, and recognize that we'd be seeking shelter right about now? They could be lying in wait for us at this pavilion. Janelle?"

The former Hartford resident took a moment to think, as the gushing sound of the relentless rain was nearly enough to drown her reasoning. "I think you raise a valid point," she ultimately acknowledged, before catching sight of Jeremy shaking his head in dissent. "It's just not worth the risk."

"Well then," Jeremy countered, paying no heed to the cautionary advice, "while you two marinate in this misery, I'll be just over there, catchin' my breath, with a roof over my head." And with that, the professor from New York drifted out of sight, swallowed up in the night's miasmal gloom.

CHAPTER 25

Across the Night

"Good evening, passengers. This is a pre-boarding announcement for American Airlines Flight 114 to Hartford. We are now . . ."

Linden Maddox and Ernie Cowarth each felt a shiver run their spines as the verbal notice filled the terminal. "I can't believe I'm *actually* going through with this," Linden stated as the reality of departure sank inside him like a stone.

"And I thank the good Lord you chose to!" Ernie replied with a beaming grin as he clutched his carry-on bag in preparation to board. "To say a lot has happened in our short time together would be a gross understatement. The pieces of the puzzle are finally coming together, Linden. All we need now is a little bit of luck, and we'll be on our way to crackin' this thing wide open!

"I tell ya, the fact that for years the scope lay idle in a goddamn Albuquerque pawnshop—it boggles my mind. I mean, how in God's name did it ever get back here? And by 'here,' I mean America." The old man began to shake his head at the unthinkable odds. "*My* scope, Linden—that was *my* pocket telescope from way back when. It must've survived the wreck—by some stroke of luck, it must've . . . survived . . . the wreck. Come on, let's climb aboard this bird, and I'll tell ya the whole story."

As the aircraft scaled the moonlit sky like some steel-winged eagle of the night, the captain spoke in low tones over the PA system as he prepared his passengers for the possibility of some turbulent weather upon arrival.

Having settled in after the plane levelled out and seatbelts were free to unfasten, Linden figured there wouldn't be a better time than this to begin picking the old man's brain. He still needed more answers—more layers of knowledge that he wanted to peel from the wealth of Ernie's mind. "Listen, Ernie," he carefully began. "I need to ask you about a dream I had after I returned home from your place earlier in the day. First off, are you in any way familiar with the term 'they've finally planted the seventh and final flag?'"

Ernie repeated the peculiar phrase slowly, accentuating each word in the hope of shaking some distant memory from an ancient tree. "Well, the phrase, as is, fails to ring any bells. Now, that being said, I *have* heard that in certain circles, a seventh flag does indeed denote some form of an end. I also know that if it's the *moon* we're talkin' about here, and I'm willing to bet we are, an American flag was planted on the lunar surface during each of the Apollo's *six* manned moon landings."

"Okay, this is all good stuff—*great* stuff, actually," a jittery Linden said, halting Ernie from expanding on his "seventh flag" theories. Then he continued to further describe his dream in question. "This dream, it was like some . . . some ass-backwards cosmic illusion. There I was, sitting comfortably atop some prodigious moon mountain, with an unknown associate at my side. We'd arrived by means of an exploring rover, in which I'd been transporting a slew of antiquated lunar collateral."

"Must've been the pawnshop experience trickling into your subconscious."

Linden agreed with a modest nod. "This grey, desolate moon world served as our natural habitat. All the while, what was known as Earth-Planet orbited our world as its only natural satellite. In the dream I possessed the moonflaw scope, and when I instinctively trained the instrument on the distant orb, Earth-Planet, what I observed through the lens was what brought my line about the seventh flag into play. Initially there were *six* flags already planted firmly in Earth-Planet's surface—some more faded than others, as if to demonstrate a chronology. It was then that I witnessed a shadowy figure cunningly planting a stake with a seventh flag attached. The work took place in the heart of a large park that just so happened to lie in the heart of a certain Connecticut city."

An easy smile formed upon Ernie's face. "I'll take Hartford for two hundred, Alex," he said facetiously.

"But how could I have seen such precise long-range details through a *handheld scope*, Ernie?"

"Linden, it's a bloody *dream* we're talkin' about here. Logic is usually twisted six ways from Sunday. But in saying that, there's often answers in this twisted logic. If you know where to dig within the garden of the mind, the underlying truths are often the richest treasures."

Linden let Ernie's words skate around the thinning ice of his current mental state, and then he continued. "I guess the bottom line is that with everything I witnessed through that lens, it was enough to sell me on *you*."

"Well then, I guess we have our first order of business, don't we?" Ernie declared, seemingly always pushing forward. "Once we touch down, we'll find an information desk, and inquire about a large park that rests somewhere in the city centre."

"Okay, I can get behind that. Sounds like as good a place to start as any," Linden replied before gazing out into the blackness beyond the curved windowpane. "Say, whaddya think we'll find when we get there?" he then asked, his eyes still foraging deeper into the night. "To the park, I mean. Will something obvious draw our attention, or will we be scratching our heads like a couple of lost tourists?"

The old man began to scratch the side of his temple, as if acting out the aforementioned scene. "Oh, we'll find *something*, Linden— I'm certain about that. As for what that *something* will be, exactly, that's hard to say at this point."

Onward they flew, as the aircraft spilled temporary scars of exhaust across the vast canvas of night. The flight conquered skies high above a sleeping Midwest before beginning its long descent into the Northeast.

"Hey, Ernie, I almost forgot." Linden pulled the old man from his distant thoughts. "You mentioned how the telescope used to be yours—that at some point you lost it in a car wreck or something."

"No, not a *car* wreck, my friend, not a car wreck." Ernie adjusted his posture, as if to settle in for a long, detailed explanation.

"Well, I'm guessing we've still got another hour or so before we land," Linden added. "And I believe you said you'd like to share the whole story."

———————

"Ladies and gentlemen, we'll soon be descending into the New England region. As anticipated, we'll be heading into some inclement weather that's been affecting the Eastern Seaboard of late. Please secure all overhead items and . . ."

Due to Hurricane Allan's tapering yet still combative winds and rain, Mason Greene's coast-to-coast flight destined for Hartford's Bradley International Airport was rerouted to Hartford–Brainard Airport. Brainard, a Class D airspace commonly referred to as Bradley's stunted sibling, would ultimately serve Mason well with its proximity to the city's downtown core.

As the wheels lowered and met Brainard's slick runway with a collective thud and squeal, Mason considered the ghostly thief in the night that had stripped three hours from the day before it had even begun. Though you wouldn't know it by the morning's sombrous cloud cover, a quick time zone calculation told him it was already eight o'clock. Following a trip to baggage claim to retrieve his compact suitcase and Tracker duffle bag, Mason's only plan at this point was to hail a cab and head to the one hotel he was familiar with in the area.

At the Hilton Hartford, a room was both conveniently and suspiciously available upon arrival, where the view from the nineteenth floor was a far cry from what would otherwise be an optimal one; the day's sullen stance had utterly stripped the city of its colour, supplanting a cheerless masquerade of murk in its place. The peaks of surrounding buildings were lost in the gloom, and the streets below were vacant strips that seemingly dissolved out of sight in the vague distance. A vast park sat on the periphery of Mason's panorama, and with the sombre morning, lamps remained aglow around its visible fringe. Having persevered through his recent whirlwind of events, Mason settled into his new nest and spent the day lying low. When the early evening rolled around, he ordered a feast of Chinese food up to the room, and with a laptop that was a last-second addition to the trip, began to study Hartford's general layout.

The night fell surreptitiously upon the already shrouded city as a light mist kissed the hotel windows high above Trumbull Street. Mason livened the room with lamplight, and shadows awakened and stretched along walls with the warm radiance. Then suddenly, as if provoked by the light, the room's telephone began to ring. *Who the hell could that be?* a startled Mason considered in the shattered silence. After some debate, he finally chose to pick up the line when the ring failed to cease. "Room 1408," he answered in a courteous fashion, consciously revealing a false number, and disguising his voice in the process.

"*Really?*" A calm yet confident delivery spilled through the receiver in response. "Is that the best you got, Greene?"

"Who the hell is this?" Mason challenged the anonymous caller, his speech retreating to its customary accent.

"Who I am is not important at the moment," the voice retorted. "But what I *can* say is this. Despite my admittedly direct involvement in the thievery of your moon globe, I'm someone who's on your side. Now I know it sounds crazy, but I'm here to help you—so listen to me, and listen well. What I need is for you to meet me down in the lobby in *exactly* fifteen minutes. It's 6:47 right now. And I need you to bring the cane that you very wisely brought along on your journey. But whatever you do, keep it concealed in the duffle bag. Now, didja get all that?" There was no reply on Mason's end. "*Hey!* I asked you if we're clear on everything I just—"

"I got it, I got it," Mason replied, sounding like a schoolboy folding to the rules. "Seven o'clock in the lobby . . . cane in bag."

"No! For Christ's sake, 7:02! We're on a strict ticker here!"

"Okay, shit, 7:*02*. How will I know who you are?"

"Don't worry about that. Just do your part, and I'll come to *you*."

Mason held the line as he awaited further instruction, but all he heard was a click, followed by the sound of a disconnect tone. He narrowed his eyes toward to the room's digital clock, where the numbers glowed in a sinful red, and seemed to tick away like seconds—

6:49 . . . 6:50 . . . 6:51. Suddenly, the thought of confronting these cryptic strangers who'd essentially brought him here didn't evoke the same appeal it had when he'd taken flight from Bellevue. 6:54 . . . 6:55 . . . 6:56.

With the Tracker bag in tow, Mason nudged the elevator panel's prominent Lobby button, sending the lift along its smooth, downward course. A single *ding* announced his arrival, and the glossy bronze doors gracefully split from the middle like a parting sea.

An elderly couple stood patiently before the opening, clearly waiting for Mason to exit before boarding themselves. But the pilot stood paralyzed, a cold sweat chilling him to the marrow. "Everything all right, sir?" the gentleman asked. "Come on out, and we'll see to finding you some water." Mason finally pulled himself together and crossed the threshold, the elevator doors nearly clipping his heels as they closed.

Bypassing the elderly couple as if they weren't even there, Mason's initial scan of the lobby revealed no anomalous activity. A pair of clerks manned the lengthy front desk, and another member of the hotel staff—an alluring woman with a tight skirt surely cut shorter than staff regulation—caught his wandering eye as she floated through the room like a feather. Knowing now wasn't the time for carnal distraction, he continued to assess the extent of the lobby. To his left: the front desk, and a paraphernalia-stocked sports bar called Pesky's Porch. To the right: a set of doors to a conference room, a contemporary cocktail lounge called Element 315, and a grand fireplace near the entrance.

At precisely 7:01, Mason started for a leather chair near the warmth of the hearth. Then it happened. Though he didn't know what to expect in the lobby, he surely didn't expect what he received. While making his way toward the fireplace, he noticed a middle-aged man standing squarely in the middle of the foyer. The man appeared to be just as uneasy as he himself, as he was glancing about like a little boy lost in a department store.

While Mason was passing the entrance to Element 315, another man, this one presumably the same age as the other, suddenly burst out through the lounge's doors and plowed squarely into Mason like a wrecking ball. The unexpected blow jarred the duffle bag from his grasp and induced a considerable laceration just above his upper lip. To his great surprise, the man continued in his course without so much as a backward glance. Said course was a beeline toward the anxious man who had first caught Mason's attention. "We're not safe in this goddamn hotel." A slightly dazed Mason caught a chunk of his assailant's panicked report before the two men scampered off together into the depths of the hotel.

Mason slowly gained a knee and had begun seeing to his facial wound when an unruffled voice suddenly emerged from above. "Not exactly how I expected to find you, Greene. Here, put some pressure on that." A damp cloth was offered, along with a small patch of gauze.

Mason took the cloth and pressed it firmly against his wound. With his free hand he swatted away the gauze and began to accost the man who'd reached him in his room by phone. "I don't know who you think you are, buddy, or how you knew to bring these supplies, but you've got about three seconds to start explaining yourself!"

"Oh, I see, now you're puttin' *me* on the clock—well played. I promise to speak, but for right now, we gotta roll!" The stranger pointed to the bag on the ground next to Mason. "I assume the cane is in there?"

"Yeah, I told ya I'd bring the damn thing, didn't I?" Mason replied in another wave of anger, blood now seeping through the cloth and forming a cherry. "And why is it so important, anyway?"

The man offered Mason a hand and proceeded to help him to his feet. He then did a quick survey of the lobby before speaking. "It's important because what it *actually* is, is a *key*. Or more precisely, one of *seven* keys that permit access to a necromantic underworld here in Hartford."

"A necromantic underworld, you say?" Mason questioned in a mocking tone. "Sounds charming. And this carbonized excuse for a walking stick is a key to gain entry? You're completely cracked, aren't cha, buddy?"

"'Cracked' might be a little harsh, but I can't deny it all the same," the stranger countered without the slightest hesitation, as if he might even be slightly proud of the fact. "Now, like I said, we gotta roll! Grab the duffle bag and come with me—we're goin' for a little stroll in the park."

CHAPTER 26

The Gracious Host

With one book on dream interpretation published and already in stores, William Lynch's second volume of *Disentangle Your Dreams* was currently in the works and nearing completion. His talent and love for analyzing these queer concoctions of the mind had been instilled in him at an early age by his mother, Eliza, who was always sharing her insights on the subconscious.

Residing in Akron, Ohio, William had recently experienced a run of recurring dreams that were quite unlike any he'd ever endured—or even studied, for that matter. For five consecutive nights, the dreams featured the same mysterious figure who would always pause behind a floating translucent door (which was boldly marked The Host in a sharp calligraphic font) before politely asking permission to gain entrance. Though amiable and most appreciative of his "host," the figure exuded a sturdy confidence and governor-like superiority.

Over the course of the five nights, William would wake and immediately reach for the bedside lamp and then his trusty dream diary. A particular entry was hastily penned and then subsequently refined as follows:

Again, I wake in the dead of night after yet another of these most peculiar visions. In them, a cryptic visitor awaits passage into my giant conduit-like tube. The tube is hollow, and though dry, comparable to an underground waterway; dank and ominous. It's as though the proceedings can't *truly* begin until I allow him to cross the transcendental threshold—which of course I do. I'm aware that this man with whom I share the alien duct is of medium stature, yet every time I attempt to discern a face, my vision promptly blurs, and my eyes begin to flare like a flash burn. Therefore, I'm unsure as to my visitor's identity, or to what he represents. But I sense he's simply biding his time—waiting upon the arrival of another, or perhaps a delivery of some sort. With each dream, he appears to grow more and more impatient, like whatever it is he's waiting on is on the verge of being overdue.

I haven't been so intrigued by my own dreams in quite some time. These visions are indeed perplexing, but I feel there's something more, something close, but it's still just out of arm's reach. Time will hopefully tell if I'll once again regain the tube and witness whatever it is that has my recurring visitor on edge.

Days passed, and ultimately linked to form weeks. For William Lynch, the dream with the translucent door and indiscernible visitor failed to resurface. Though the broad scope of the vision remained rooted in the garden of his memory, and the finer details on the pages of his diary, he eventually gave up on the man in the strange tube, all the while returning to his common practices of writing and interpreting the dreams of others.

Then came a cool night on the tail fringes of October, when William and his girlfriend, Christine, had returned home late after attending a double feature at the drive-in: a yearly ritual for the couple to close out the season. The two were so exhausted that they were both sound asleep within fifteen minutes of trudging through the front door. During this slumber, for reasons unknown to William, the dream he'd been seeking returned at last. Once again there was the man stationed behind the crystalline portal, requiring authorization to enter. However, in this alternate version, once William had granted him access, the dream finally blossomed into the enrichment of activity he'd so patiently desired.

William Lynch, master of subliminal perception and proud author of detailed dream explication, would wake to record his most extraordinary diary entry to date:

> At last, the dream has returned from its hiatus! Just like before—with my permission, of course—this strange visitor entered the tube-like surrounding. This time around there were no burning eyes to deny me, as I was promptly granted a sharp view of the man who'd been occupying the halls of my subconscious weavings. The stranger caught my intrusive stare and somehow seemed to physically clutch it with his own eyes, seeking the source of my curiosity. I tried to look away but was powerless against his hold. His countenance was slovenly, yet dignified; his deep-set eyes were like recessed jewels, gazing back at me with enough emotion to penetrate a million calloused souls. But facial mannerisms aside, it was an old, weathered nautical cap he donned that has my curiosity buzzing.

Its brown, ragged texture spoke of lifetimes at sea. I've yet to figure out his identity, or why he's become a fixture in my visions, but I'm convinced that clues lie somewhere along a nautical trail.

The man proceeded to inform me in a thick Irish accent that since it was *my* dream, I was welcome to witness what he called "The Coalescence." He then scoured our tubular setting with those beady eyes. "Be patient, gracious host," he added in a composed, gritty voice, as if the words rolled off coarse sandpaper. "Your slumber shall soon accommodate an eternal affiliation." Then suddenly, it felt as if my body had been physically removed from the tube. My spirit remained and was authorized to observe the proceedings, but I was no longer in the game, so to speak; I was more a spectator perched up high in the rafters. It was from this lofty vantage point that I spotted a young blonde-haired girl below, standing patiently beyond the translucent door. She was accompanied by a middle-aged man, and the two were granted permission to enter the tube by the mystifying figure in the old nautical cap. From my remote viewpoint, the three bodies appeared as if hundreds of feet away, yet I could still see every detail with a sharp precision and hear every word as if transmitted through a perfectly tuned radio frequency. The young girl and the man she entered the tube with each percolated into the dream in possession of a specific artefact. The child: what appeared to be an antique brass pocket telescope. And the man: a standard-sized globe—though not your typical globe displaying seas and seven continents, but a rather intriguingly detailed *moon* globe.

Though most odd in its manner, the dream at this point felt as close to sentient life as any I can ever recall. In fact, it almost seems as though I'm recording an actual conscious experience. The man in the cap then received his company. "Thanks to your timely proficiency, the hour of the Great Gathering is nigh. For now, you shall proceed east, to the chosen city. It is there you will both be handsomely rewarded for your courage and your honour." They then presented their respective artefacts to the speaker.

"Kind sir, I also managed to secure the old man's sacred file," the young girl added in a nervous, high-pitched voice. "And I'd be most honoured to offer it to you now."

The man who'd arrived with the globe then chimed in, "Well done, young one—above and beyond the call of duty. Mind if I take a quick gander at its contents?"

"Pass it here, child!" the man in the cap suddenly demanded, his tone seemingly reaching out like a tight grip to the throat. "From here on out, the file shall be for my eyes only." The young girl obliged, and with that, as seamlessly as they'd arrived, the man and child vanished from the dream. At this point the impeccable clarity of the dream began to wane. Though once again visually indistinct, the man in the nautical cap remained.

With his pair of gifted artefacts and an old man's "sacred file" now in his possession, he barked a final message in my elevated direction. "You will be spared, gracious host, but not if you hesitate in the least." I was slipping into consciousness now, as his gravelly words began to graft with that of Christine's soothing tone. "There's still time for you to reach the Connecticut capital. Go now, gracious host. Go now!"

From day one, Christine had always supported the open-minded rationale that essentially served William's dream interpretation prose. But when he told her of this specific vision, and that he was seriously considering the nine-hour trek to Hartford, she looked at him as if he had two heads, and then spoke. "So, what you're tellin' me is that you're gonna drive that piece-a-shit clunker over five hundred miles based on the counsel of some dreamed-up sea captain? You'll truly outdo yourself on this one, skipper."

A strange medley of emotions stirred deep within William Lynch. Part of him felt confused and disoriented with his own thoughts on the bold venture. Part of him ached with the pronounced disfavour shown by Christine. And above all, a part of him felt a burning desire to just pack up and go through with it—to follow the words of the mysterious man in the mysterious dreams and immediately split for the destination he'd dubbed "the chosen city."

CHAPTER 27

Subterranean Shadows

Having deserted Luke and Janelle for the inanimate saviour that was the sheltered pavilion, Jeremy Lowe toiled through the cruel elements until the airy structure seemingly materialized into view. "Come on, you guys, it's safe!" he hollered back through the nebulous night in an attempt to reconvene as a group. He sensed his words were being smothered by the sonorous blast of rain, but he continued to challenge the conditions, nonetheless. "There's nobody here!"

Closing in on the shelter, he turned and looked back a final time. He was certain he noticed a pair of vague silhouettes shifting furtively through the murk. The figures were moving about in the general vicinity he'd just decamped, yet he wasn't so sure they matched the likes of his recent acquaintances.

Still struggling to seek out his allies, Jeremy suddenly felt an intuitive chill in the form of eyes burning holes through his back. He knew in that very instant that he should run—run straight back out in the direction he'd come. But there, in that frozen moment, he just *had* to know the source of the lurking presence behind him.

He simply couldn't fight the fact that his curiosity was outweighing what he *knew* would give him the best chance to evade this enemy.

As he turned, he guessed there'd be two Deceivers lying in wait—definitely no more than three. But what the professor came to witness through the haze was enough to make him recoil in horror. There were too many to count. Twenty? Twenty-five? It didn't matter; he was outnumbered in the worst way. They were all clad in black guise and seemed to swell into a ravenous pack as they closed in on their catch, their eyes like black marbles, glossy in the pot light glow. *Where the hell did they all come from?* Jeremy questioned his own sanity, having been certain the pavilion was vacant mere seconds earlier.

Before he could fully grasp the situation, the Deceivers were already forming a circle around him at the foot of the building.

Jeremy could feel himself being sucked even deeper into this living nightmare; it continued to wrap itself tighter around him like a psychological straitjacket. Every attempt to cry out for help was only a breathless whisper; every effort to escape by foot was a step void of motion.

"Abandoning your friends for a little shelter, Mr. Lowe? Pathetic." A voice slithered through the misty silence as a woman stepped forward from the pack to meet Jeremy's eyes. Her own eyes were like recessed tombs, buried deep within an ancient catacomb; her skin was sallow against a rich sea of black linen. "What you're going to do now is follow me as we descend into the bowels of the city."

Jeremy spun around to gauge the group of Deceivers around him, and then returned his focus to the woman who spoke for the circle. "I don't know *who*—or *what*—you people are," he said, pitching his words as sharp as knives, "but I *do* know I ain't accompanying your travelling freak show anywhere, let alone underground!" He then promptly found his step and sprang headlong for what he chanced to be the weakest link in the barrier. In his bold attempt to flee, he first absorbed a resounding blow directly to the nose. His eyes instantly welled up, and tears alloyed with the blood that followed. With his vital fluid spilling and staining the pavilion's concrete pad, a second bludgeoning clout caught him square in the midsection, stealing the wind from his lungs. Still, Jeremy persevered. But just when he thought he'd split the pseudo-human blockade, he was jolted from behind by a brilliant flash of blue electric current. From the pronged tip of a black cane that the dead-eyed woman possessed, a swift, gleaming band of electric energy pierced the gloom and mercilessly coursed through Jeremy's body, ultimately thwarting his escape.

With her cell phone clenched tightly in hand, Shelly Madison-Lowe gazed out through the fog-drenched night, barely able to make out Central Park's proximity, and pondered the whereabouts of her husband. After several failed attempts to contact Jeremy by both call and text, a sinking feeling began to weigh heavy on her spirit.

It was now nearing nine o'clock, and Shelly decided it was time to push the matter a step further. Scrolling through her list of incoming calls, she quickly found the number that belonged to the stranger from Boston. *Luke was his name,* she recalled. Coincidentally, just as she was about to make the call, she received a text notification herself. *Well it's about freakin' time,* she thought, assuming Jeremy had finally decided to let her in on his business. But to her bemusement, the message wasn't sent from her *husband's* phone; it was being forwarded from *Luke's.*

Though she knew nothing positive could possibly come of this report, Shelly steadied her hand and read the text.

Its luke sheehan we're in hrtford theres been an accident.

· Shelly froze as the words registered like individual spikes to the heart. A second notification then chimed through, surely to be the maul that drives the spikes firm. *We tried to sav him...wouldnt listen.*

The cavernous atmosphere in which Jeremy woke was quite unlike anything he'd ever seen before. Standing in a couple inches of stagnant water, he found himself groggy and shackled to something more like a natural stalagmite than a column. The spire resembled an old witch's finger as it tapered high into a vast cavity. He appeared to be in some central underground rotunda. The air in this dispiriting space was musty and hung heavy like smog. Substantial concrete conduit tunnels ran their separate courses from this epicentre of colossal pillars and giant water pumps.

He's awake!" a voice suddenly echoed from an undefined distance. Startled, Jeremy surveyed his peculiar surroundings for the source, but there wasn't a single soul in sight; in fact, he wasn't so sure that the voice he'd heard wasn't his own state of delirium screaming from within.

As his vision slowly adapted to the feeble light, he noticed that there were precisely seven of the concrete channels that either fed or fled this great open space, their births like black, eyeless sockets, all varying in size. *Where the hell am I?* he asked himself. He then wondered if he'd asked it aloud, because his inquiry was promptly acknowledged.

"Like I said before you tried to flee the pavilion, you're in the bowels of the city—or more precisely, in the hub of a great series of concrete conduits that run like arteries deep below the city's surface." It was the ghostly woman who had led the pack at the pavilion, and in these sunken quarters her sallow tinge was an even darker shade of death.

"What is it you want with me?" he asked over the rattling sound of his chains. "And could ya be so kind as to relieve me of the manacles? Christ, the iron's diggin' into my skin. Trust me, I ain't about to just pick up and scamper off into one of those giant rat holes."

Jeremy's eyes followed the pallid-skinned woman as she stalked the dingy underground, slowly circling his lofty stanchion while tapping her cane incessantly. The woman suddenly halted, and just as Jeremy noticed another sombre figure exiting one of the tunnels in the distance behind her, she spoke again. "In the underground, your trivial questions don't warrant a reply. It is us—and *only* us—who shall catechize!"

"That'll be enough, Maezra. I'll take it from here," the newly arrived figure said. An unmistakable Irish accent spilled from his tongue in a grainy fashion, filling the chamber with its resonance. As the man approached, Jeremy noticed how his eyes depressed into bony facial lineaments and were barely visible below the sagging brim of an old nautical cap. His declining skin was eerily similar in colour to that of the woman he was now addressing. "You have further business on the surface. Peak perigee shall take place shortly after midnight, and there are many yet to be detained. Secure all required underground inlets, and then seal the northern reaches of the park. Use as many as you require."

Without protest, the malevolent woman who'd mysteriously transported Jeremy underground turned and saw to her instructions. She retired out through the smallest of the seven tunnels without as much as a backward glance, her trail swallowed in a sea of darkness.

To Jeremy, it was undeniably clear that this newest subterranean shadow stood in a place of high authority. Also, he sensed that whatever it was that had drawn Luke and himself to Hartford had emanated from this man's immoral hand.

"All right, Mr. Lowe. For your own good I'll cut to the chase here," the autocratic figure announced. Aided by a black walking staff similar in design yet noticeably larger than that of the woman's—and not unlike the piece Gandalf wielded in Tolkien's Middle-earth—he leisurely circled Jeremy and the vertical skewer he remained shackled to. A ragged black overcoat sagged to his ankles, occasionally skimming the now-rising waters that were finding the hub and strengthening in force by the minute. "We're presently situated in a central underground post, directly below Bushnell Park. From here, an intricate network of concrete con-duits redirect overflow into the Connecticut River. I could give you a history lesson on when and why these tunnels were built, but quite frankly, at the rate these waters are rising, your lungs don't have that kind of time. Now, regarding you—the reason you're chained to a post like a disobedient dog is because . . . well . . . I need you. I need you to root through your memory garden and recover a few specifics from your dream last night. You can do that for me, can't cha? Soil should still be nice 'n fresh for the reaping. Let me make it simple for you. Cooperate and answer my ques-tions honestly, and I'll release you to the surface without harm. On the contrary, denying me known information will result in a most unpleasant expiration. With the unheard-of amounts of rain that the city has endured as of late, along with this most recent burst, the conduits will soon be pushed to maximum capacity. The current downpour will force water levels well above your head, and being bound in irons, you'll fail to flail free of the controlled flood. Any questions before we proceed?"

"*Questions?*" Jeremy replied with a roar, as well as a dogged attempt to bust himself free from the restricting links. "Yeah, I got fuckin' *questions*, all right! But given your ultimatum, I'd rather we get on with it so I can get the hell outta this soggy tomb."

The torrents continued to intensify and echoed sonorous *swooshes* as they surged together in the open space. Following a brief struggle to dismiss the reality in which he now found himself, Jeremy managed to rekindle the recent dreamscape as he recalled sitting in a deserted Fenway Park.

"Are you there?" the man in the nautical cap probed, his voice maintaining a sober tone yet still cutting through the sound of the water.

"Yeah, I'm there," Jeremy replied. "Now what the hell do ya wanna know about it?"

"What I *need* to know is if there was any form of communication. Did anybody reach out to you? A young child, perchance?"

As if he were right back in the exact bleacher seat on that perfect Boston morning, Jeremy was able to relive the entire dream with relative ease. Though it seemed as though a number of days had passed, it was still shy of a full twenty-four hours since the unconventional dream took flight. With vivid clarity he recalled the eerie stillness of the ballpark at dawn, the roaring resonance of the warplane fly-by, and of course, the presence of the blonde-haired child. Jeremy suspected that spilling the truth still wouldn't help him out of this most unusual bind, but considering his life was suddenly on the line, there was no other alternative. "Yes, I spoke with a young girl," he conceded. "I recall assuming I was alone in the stands. But then she . . . she kind of just . . . appeared in the row behind me."

With this piece of information, the man in the nautical cap revealed a hint of a smile and slowly began to edge toward Jeremy. "Good, good—I like where this is going," he expressed. "Now kindly tell me what the child spoke of." As he conversed, he pointed his walking stick at Jeremy's ankle restraints, and then, like some illusory magic trick, the cuffs vanished in an instant.

Though still confined to the gnarled pillar by his wrists, Jeremy now found himself able to kick about freely within the rising waters, giving him a progressive perception of freedom. "The child was both confident and wary. She steadied a fishbowl on her lap—it seemed to comfort her, like a stuffed animal might. Eventually she ran off a pair of bizarre questions: 'Have you seen my fish?' And then, 'How many people will—'"

"Did she inquire about the moonflaw?" the man interrupted, as urgent as a house fire.

Jeremy knew it right then and there. He pieced together that whatever this *moonflaw* event was, it was diabolical in nature, and was somehow tied to the city of Hartford. He knew time was of the essence, but he was also aware that his next response could very well make or break him. He wished more than anything that he knew what the moonflaw *was*, exactly. The young girl from the dream certainly did, as she openly feared its consequences. "The *moonflaw?*" he feigned puzzlement. "Can't say she mentioned *that* term at any point—not that I can recall, anyhow. Forgive me if . . . under these circumstances . . . my memory isn't exactly razor-sharp. If that's the information you're after, then I'm afraid I'll be of no help to you."

The cadaverous man was now closing in on Jeremy with leaden steps. His stature appeared to intensify with every sopping stride until the shadowy underground hub produced the illusion of a freakish giant. "I've gotta hand it to ya," he said, his sunken eyes buried deep in their caves, and his voice now a direct transmission. "A man in my position can't help but respect one's valour in the face of adversity—to stick to your guns when it's quite clear your life is on the line. But here's the thing: I believe you're lying to me. No . . . wait . . . let me rephrase that . . . I *know* you're lying to me. You see, I know things about you and your dreams that would leave you begging for the bughouse. I know the man in the warplane that you shared the dream with, and I also know that he's here in the city with us tonight. All you had to do was disclose a small piece of information that I'm having trouble with, and by now you'd be unchained and delivered. But no, you choose to hold your cards close to your chest, thinking you could deceive a Deceiver. Well, Jeremy, your weak poker face told me all I need to know—which leads me to ask: who exactly do you think you're protecting by withholding information from me? Yourself? The two you stood atop the bridge with? The *child?* What you've *actually* done is exposed everyone to a much greater risk. So, due to your disobliging actions, you've left me no choice but to act as I see fit."

The now thigh-deep waters thrashed about the concrete corpus with a relentless fury, threatening Jeremy's foothold as his arms remained fastened. Still powerless at the hands of this demoniac dignitary, he could only watch with a profound sense of dread as the man began to elevate and aim his staff in his direction.

Jeremy Lowe once again found himself in a groggy daze as he woke in unfamiliar territory. Hazy fragments of an ashen dream were floating through his mind's eye like passing clouds.

For a fleeting moment he expected to be at home in New York City, lying safely beside Shelly following a bizarre dream enacted within the envelope of a nightmare. As he began to gather his senses, he became cognizant of the fact that he was still cemented in the bowels of Hartford, and that his dash of hope couldn't have been further from the cold reality being painted before him now.

Along with Jeremy, countless souls were lined along opposing ledges in a massive tunnel, their backs seemingly fixed to graffiti-marred concrete walls. Three feet below the ledges, water merely trickled along this particular course, moving left to right from Jeremy's vantage along the minimal ridge. As he gazed in both directions through anaemic light, gradual bends, like twisting subway tunnels, wound out of sight.

He was convinced that everything that was happening was indeed real, yet still dreamlike in the way he seemed to mysteriously jump from station to station, linked only by blotted voids of memory. Lined among the stone-faced strangers, his back was also pinned to the conduit wall by an unknown force. Though he vividly recalled and was thankful to have survived the rising waters of the subterranean hub, a whole new batch of questions were begging to be answered in this latest chapter of incessant hell. "Can somebody *please* tell me what the *fuck* is goin' on down here?" he pleaded to anyone who'd listen, his voice bouncing off boundless concrete in the process.

The collective reaction to Jeremy's appeal was feeble at best. A few responded with a sluggish cock of the head and an indistinct murmur, as if heavily sedated. The rest failed to provide any response whatsoever; they just continued with their vacant stares into some deeper abyss.

Lost in his own swirling abyss of apprehension, Jeremy suddenly heard a high-pitched holler. It was a woman's voice, distant and muffled in the concrete cavity. Again, he couldn't help but consider that perhaps the voice hadn't actually emanated from beyond a bend in the tunnel, but rather from around a dark corner in his own failing mind.

CHAPTER 28

A Reflection

As the plane continued along its eastward course through the now-waning night, Linden awaited Ernie's story regarding the mysterious telescope.

"Yes, now's as good a time as any to tell you," Ernie confirmed, while readjusting in his seat and signalling to the flight attendant for a cup of water. "Once we touch down in Hartford, there won't be time for reminiscing tales of old."

Ernie's water arrived along with packets of Biscoff cookies and the airline's customary salted peanuts. The flight attendant, with a bold nametag reading Sonya, smiled and said, "Eat 'em up, fellas—snacks are a hard sell at this hour." Ernie returned her smile and added a wink for good measure.

"So, let's start at the beginning, shall we?" Ernie proposed as he tore into a package of peanuts. He figured that if Linden was going to accompany him on this venture, his fellow New Mexican needed to . . . no, *deserved* to not only know the complete story of the pocket scope and the shipwreck, but also how NASA would come to play a pivotal role in the years that followed. "I was born and raised in Camden, Maine—a small seaside town about eighty miles northeast of Portland. When I was a young lad of about ten or eleven, I had a friend named Addison Tuck. 'Addy,' I used to call him. Addy and I would frequent this old, abandoned lighthouse about a half-mile from my place. Looking back, it must've been built in the early 1800s. It was enclosed within two separate fences, each boasting their own No Trespassing and Keep Out warning signs. I mean, they were there for good reason, but you know how it is at that age—those fences just stood as a challenge waiting to be overthrown. The sense of rebellion only seemed to enhance the adventure. We'd hop the six-foot fences, enter the lighthouse through a low-lying window that Addy had broken and cleared, and then climb the seemingly endless steel spiral staircase. The salty scent of the Atlantic filled the steep rise, and the surrounding stone interior gave the impression of the depths of a great well. When we reached the wooden floor of the watch room, it creaked like old bones and threatened to cave under the slightest load. From there we'd gaze out over the ocean and pretend we were co-captains of some great vessel, stationed high above the main deck as we conquered the waters below.

"One evening, Addy and I made our way down to the lighthouse as the sun was already sinking in the west like a golden stone, and by the time we'd mounted the stairs, the day had vanished behind a furtive curtain of night. Before we knew it, a radiant moon had climbed the sky like a natural beacon, guiding our mythical ship across the sea. Then suddenly, by means of an inexplicable moonlight reflection, a pocket telescope made its presence known from its discarded place within the watch room. Addy and I both caught the shimmering glint of light off its glass eye as it winked through the hollow, stone-walled chamber. I can still recall the brief moment of stunned silence the two of us shared as we regarded the gleam, followed by Addy giving me consent to investigate the source. 'Go ahead, Captain,' he said, as his widening eyes accentuated his words. 'Your ship, your treasure.'

"I'll never forget poor Addy, and the mischief we always seemed to wiggle our way into. Regrettably, Addison died the following year when he was struck while strolling along the bloody sidewalk one night by a goddamn hit-and-run. He was only twelve. Of course, they never found the bastard who ran him down. I like to think there's a seat reserved in hell for whoever it was, if they're not already there.

"Anyhow, for whatever reason, this scope was left behind in the lighthouse when it was decommissioned and cleared of its contents. Go ahead; take yourself a wild guess as to where it was hiding."

Already immersed in the old man's tale, Linden froze in the moment, and then stumbled through a reply. "Um . . . uh . . . no idea, Ernie. Not in the slightest."

"Ah, ya wouldn't a guessed it if ya tried," Ernie quipped before throwing back a refreshing gulp of water to chase some more peanuts. "There was this eerie, gothic-style fireplace that probably weighed about two tons. It was the only thing that remained in the entire lighthouse. It was so damn heavy that whoever it belonged to probably just said, 'Fuck it, it stays.' One of its solid wrought-iron doors was left ajar by a mere two inches, and the scope's lens was scarcely peeking out through the opening, while its brass length rested in a bed of charred wood and ash."

"Why on earth would something like that be left behind in a *fireplace?*" Linden asked. "Was 'moonflaw' engraved in the surface at *that* point?"

"Whoa, whoa, slow down, my friend," Ernie replied, along with the corresponding hand gesture. "We'll get around to that. Ya know, I've never really put much thought into *why* it was left in there. There's really no way of knowing—especially now. So, I plucked the scope from the fireplace, dusted off the ash and soot, and then took a trial run at the night sky. The initial returns were unremarkable at best, but I kept the gadget regardless. I figured it carried no value, and probably paled in comparison to other models, but it was *mine*—my own mysterious find. And looking back, it undoubtedly launched my lifelong fascination with the stars.

"In the years that followed, I immersed myself in the wonders of the sea and sky. When I was in my early twenties, I was offered the opportunity of a lifetime: I was asked aboard a Scottish schooner to partake in a most prestigious seafaring expedition. *Gavinia* was her name, and she was the most magnificent ship I'd ever seen in my life—and by that point, I'd seen a few. My maritime work along the East Coast had earned me the invite, and I, alongside a dozen American seamen, flew from New York City to Renfrew, Scotland, where we amalgamated with a proficient crew of Scottish sailors.

"Long before we left America, I was advised that I'd be the youngest on the sea voyage by a good fifteen years. I understood this would render me the low-ranking gofer—or swabbie, as they used to say. And ya know what? It didn't faze me in the least. I was ready and willing to work my tail off, no matter what was asked of me. It was a dream opportunity to unite my two great passions, and if they'd've asked me to shovel shit on that boat, I'd've boarded with a spit-shined spade.

"Knowing we'd eventually be sailing out into the great open waters of the North Atlantic, I couldn't resist the urge to bring my pocket scope along to enhance what would surely be wondrous night skies. Though in hindsight, a part of me wishes I *had* defied the urge. In fact, I can't help but wonder how my life would've been different if I'd never even found that bloody thing in the first place. You may soon be using those exact same words yourself, Linden."

"Trust me, Ernie," Linden replied, "those words have been simmering in the back of my mind from the moment you chased me down in the lot."

"But we *did* find it, Linden, and both cases conquered virtually impossible odds. And now here we are, brought together by a fate that unseats even Divine Will. Anyhow, we're getting sidetracked.

Over a steady flow of some of Scotland's finest ale, we spent the better part of two days preparing for the voyage as a unified group. Before daybreak on the third day, we finally departed from Port Bannatyne, which is about forty miles west of Glasgow, if you're not up on your UK geography. We skimmed through the North Channel with grace and precision, and by eventide we were racing through the Irish Sea. That first night on the water was simply majestic. An atypically large, pinkish moon hung low and, like the moon Addy and I observed that night in the lighthouse, seemingly served as a beacon guiding us toward the birth of the North Atlantic. I tell ya, Linden, as much as I wanted to steal away and view that imposing moon through my scope, I was just too damn worried that I wasn't making a good enough impression on the crew. From the very moment we set sail, I was engrossed in my responsibilities, and surely didn't want to be caught with my head in the heavens.

"With the dawning of our second day aboard *Gavinia*, the open sea was fast approaching. I hadn't slept a wink, yet my adrenaline was still firing on all cylinders. By this point I'd already assisted in the kitchen, calibrated the crew's nautical navigation devices, learned the schooner's complex rigging system, and hoisted the mainsail."

"*What?*" a curious Linden interjected. "No offence, Ernie, but why the hell would they let the low-ranking man hoist the mainsail? I mean, I ain't no sailor, but if the ship was as grand as you say, shouldn't that be the responsibility of someone a little more . . . seasoned?"

"Well, I wasn't gonna get into that, to be honest with ya. But since you asked—you asked for it! I was quite surprised when I was pulled from the kitchen by the captain himself. Up until that point I'd received no more than an apathetic handshake from him when we were introduced back in Scotland. Little did I know that it was a tradition amongst this group to call upon the greenest member of the crew and officially welcome them aboard with the mainsail honour. How I was so blind as to not realize that some-thing sketchy was in the works, I'll never know. All but a few of the crew members abandoned their posts and gathered around myself and two others as we cranked the winch to pull the halyard. When the mainsail met the top of the mast, I cleated off the halyard to a raucous ovation. I reactively raised my arms in a feigned victory pose, and in that moment, I truly felt like I would fit in with this gang of hardened mariners.

"That was when I suddenly felt the horror of someone clutch-ing my trousers at the waist, and then yanking them, briefs and all, clean down to my ankles. There I stood before the group of mates I was to spend the next three weeks with, my arms raised high and wide, with my bratwurst suddenly the ship's new sundial. And as if *that* wasn't enough humiliation, before I could process what the hell was happening, I felt the immediate sting of a ten-pound tuna, swung like a goddamn baseball bat, as it socked me square in the keister. *Whhaaack!* Oh, how they all laughed as I struggled to hike up my drawers, all the while guarding my rump against another possible attack. Thankfully, it was a one-and-done affair.

"'You're now *officially* welcomed aboard *Gavinia!*' the captain announced above the merriment. 'Maybe one day *you'll* be the one swingin' the catch!' The laughter turned to mass applause, and the entire crew tipped their caps in my direction. Through the shock and embarrassment, I forced a smile and a bow for their antics. At that point I knew I had to at least mildly reciprocate, so I told them that since I was currently working in the kitchen, they'd all get a good taste of my rear, as that exact tuna would now be served as the main dish later that evening.

"By noon of our second day on the water, we'd reached the mighty Atlantic. It was a picturesque day, with reduced speeds and some deep-sea angling. Later that evening, I noticed the great moon once again as it lifted from the shadowy depths of the sea at a funeral pace. And I swear, though I didn't think it possible, it appeared bigger and brighter than the night before. It had lost its pink tinge, and now came dressed in an ominous crimson hue, painting the waters below with its ruddy reflection.

"Now, this is basically where the shit starts goin' down, Linden, so listen up. There was absolutely no chance I was gonna miss viewing *this* moon through my scope. I was doing no more than a little preventative maintenance work at the time, so I figured I could spare a few minutes for some well-deserved moongazing. With the moon being so bold and brilliant that night, it seemed as if the view through my scope put me within an arm's reach of it. And this is where we come to what I saw on the surface. I didn't notice it at first—maybe it hadn't even happened yet, or I hadn't quite tweaked the instrument into proper focus. Then suddenly there they were—and I swear, to this very day, I've never seen anything so . . . so bloody terrifying and bizarre!"

Reliving what he'd witnessed on the moon's surface during that fateful night, Ernie suddenly went silent, and the colour washed from his face to a waxen pale.

"Are you *kidding me?*" Linden voiced in a sudden burst, attempting to snap the old man out of his recollective hiatus. "Don't you go quittin' on me now, Ernie. What the hell didja see?"

A few more despondent seconds hung in some distant, hopeless place before Ernie suddenly recovered. "Particles," he muttered in an undertone so suppressed it was as if he feared he might hear his own voice. "I'm sorry—that don't help you out in the least. Post-impact emissions, to be more precise. And we're not just talkin' about a little atmospheric spatter here and there—we're talkin' *millions* upon *millions* of black-and-white spherule specks, spewing from a shadowy, fissure-like crevice, like some cosmic fountain.

"My first instinct was to lower the scope. I closed my eyes and took a deep breath, then glanced back at the moon to see if the phenomenon could be observed with the naked eye. The unaided view brought no abnormalities, other than the imposing size and breathtaking luminance of the orb itself. I then called upon the scope again, this time to prove that the uncanny observation had to've been conceived in my mind. And it was just then, at the exact moment I noticed the particles *weren't* just a twisted figment, that *Gavinia* absorbed a mighty surge of seawater that immediately forced all hands on deck. As if suddenly provoked, the breezeless night and temperate waters had turned without warning, catching our crew off guard and scuffling to regain control of the vessel. It was like a switch had been flicked, spurring the sea into a boiling rage as it spilled over the deck in prodigious torrents."

Coincidentally, shortly after Ernie first spoke of *Gavinia*'s peril, the first signs of air turbulence warned of unstable weather ahead in the Eastern states. The Hartford-bound plane suddenly dipped and shuddered, and several passengers were wrenched from their slumbers as the Fasten Seatbelt alerts bleeped their cautionary instruction.

CHAPTER 29

The Ring of Mortal Remains

There was no let up in the rain whatsoever as it continued to drive down upon Bushnell Park and the city of Hartford with a relentless force. From where they stood, Luke and Janelle's voices rang out into the squall in near-perfect unison, their pleas begging Jeremy to abort his mad dash to the pavilion.

"That stubborn son of a bitch!" Luke swore with a shake of his head, conceding that Jeremy's decision had been foolishly resolute.

"Luke, do you hear that?" Janelle asked haltingly, her words reeling his faraway thoughts back to the situation at hand. "I can't *see* a damn thing, but I'm pretty sure I'm hearing voices coming from over there." She pointed in the direction Jeremy had just scampered toward. "Over where the pavilion is located."

The resonant roar of the rain drowned Luke's ability to discern any voices, yet considering Janelle had managed to furtively follow the two of them all the way to Weidenmann's Bridge, he had nothing but full confidence in her sharper sense. "Okay, I know it's no picnic out here, but I think we should wait until we're sure it's safe to go in after him," he replied. "Maybe for now, just circle 'round back and see what we see."

"Sounds good," Janelle replied without hesitation. "I'd rather be on the move, anyway."

With it being just the two of them now, and both still practically perfect strangers to one another, Luke and Janelle again found themselves lacking the stability of a "safety in numbers" crutch. They were only down one, but it suddenly felt as if the wind and rain whipped a little harder, and the cool night air seemed to chill a little closer to the bone.

With the park's surface now resembling a swampy meadow, Janelle led the way once again as they trudged a wide berth around the pavilion. While slogging his way behind Janelle's moderate pace, Luke helplessly observed Janelle as she suddenly lost her footing and tumbled headlong toward the ground. Fortunately, her reflexes helped prevent a face plant, as she extended her arms just in time to break the fall. As Luke approached, he abruptly found himself stumbling blindly over the same object as Janelle had before him. He managed to gather himself mid-stagger and regained his footing before joining her in the mire.

Before examining the peculiarly placed obstacle that had tripped them up, Luke offered Janelle a hand and hauled her back to her feet. "You all right?" he asked. Then, upon her positive reply, he nudged what he expected to be no more than a solid length of fallen timber with the tip of his shoe. "What the . . ." he muttered under his breath, bewildered by the object's rather fleshy nature. A second prod proved his initial deduction. "It's a goddamn *body*, Janelle. And I . . . I think it's been here a while." As he spoke, he caught a fleeting flash of blue light coming from the general direction of the pavilion. The flare seemed to pierce through the fog with the potency of a lighthouse beacon before it dissolved in an instant. Though curious as to the source of the strange refulgence, Luke realized they were currently dealing with more important matters.

Without hesitation, Janelle dropped to her knees and, after discerning the body to be a male, sought his wrist with the faint hope of catching a pulse. The presumably deceased figure, clothed in jeans and a beat-up flannel shirt, was varnished in a thin wash of rain-diluted blood. His face appeared bloated and blotchy, with eyes wide, yet cloudy and inanimate. "You're right," Janelle agreed. "I think he's probably been dead for quite some . . ." she suddenly paused and began turning her head from side to side, as if it were on a swivel. "Jesus Christ!" Her re-evaluated words echoed out through the gloom. "Are you seein' what *I'm* seein' here?"

Luke failed to distinguish the chain of bodies at first, but as he knelt to meet Janelle's eye level, the disturbing reality began to register. The two of them shared the same first wrong impression that the bodies, for whatever reason, were purposely arranged to form a straight line—a grisly barrier of sorts; but the body they'd literally stumbled upon was actually one of many that were linked to form a giant *circle* of corpses. When tallying the dead while following the lurid trail, they soon deciphered the continuous arc. The majority of the slain appeared to be adult males, while women and even a few adolescents rounded out the ring. And as if the macabre scene wasn't enough, there were the syringes. Countless hypodermic needles were either left dangling from the cold flesh of the deceased, or they littered the route of the circuit. Exactly forty-three lifeless bodies later, the cryptic circle came to an end, so to speak, exactly where it began. "This is the guy!" Janelle announced, as if almost happy to be reacquainted. "This is the guy I tripped over!"

"Yeah, you're right," Luke confirmed. "Now let's get the hell outta here before someone tries to pin . . . *whatever* this is on *us*."

An appropriate term to define the weather on this night would be "consistently inconsistent." By the time Luke and Janelle had decamped the ring of remains and settled with a distant northwest view of the pavilion, the thick swathe of fog had all but dissipated. As for the lawless faucet of rain, it now produced no more than a scant drizzle.

For the time being, the two took refuge beneath a sweeping red oak, its colossal trunk like a barricade of ancient bark, and its leaves forming a giant, dome-shaped canopy of melded colour. A broad scan to the west revealed a secondary pavilion of sorts—a vintage 1914 Stein & Goldstein carousel. From their outlying vantage, the stationary steeds appeared villainous and sinister, like feral creatures kicking at the chains of captivity.

From the carousel they swung their glances back to the actual pavilion. With no more than an occasional waft of pillowy fog to contend with, their target was now readily distinguishable; that was the good news. The bad news was that Jeremy was still nowhere in sight. There was absolutely *no one* in sight—not a single trace of the source of the garbled voices Janelle had heard earlier. "Why do I get a sinking feeling we've seen him for the last time?" Luke asked with another adjustment to the brim of his cap, as if it were a crystal ball that required a little coaxing to induce clairvoyance.

"Because it was *your* gut feeling initially, remember? *Your* hunch that suggested the pavilion could be a trap."

"Yeah, and I still stand by that hunch, but I'm starting to think it'll weigh on me if we don't at least take a closer look while we're here. He could be just outta sight—back around the front side of the building or something. Hell, he could be standing there looking for *us*, wonderin' where *we* are. He can't be far. Come on, let's go while the coast is clear."

The pair couldn't help but feel vulnerable as they crossed the expansive, treeless plain. They cleared the soggy patch and approached the pavilion with caution. Tidy pot lights ran the building's periphery and illuminated its airy structure. Situated around wooden support pillars were a dozen or so secured picnic tables. When in operation from Memorial Day to Labour Day, the north end of the building served as home to the Capital Snack Bar, and the south end to public restrooms.

"Is that . . . blood over there?" Janelle suddenly asked in a reluctant manner, aiming her index finger down at a spattering of crimson stains on the concrete surface not twenty feet away. "Over by the base of that picnic bench."

As the two drew closer, a pot light directly above them aided their view of the scene. "Yeah, that's blood all right," Luke affirmed, now kneeling, almost certain from whom it had spilled. "Looks fresh, too. Clearly Jeremy encountered trouble exactly where we stand—but something's still amiss. It just doesn't add up, ya know? I mean, how long's it been since we saw him? Ten minutes? Fifteen at the most? I find it hard to believe that in that amount of time, he ran over here, got caught up in a scuffle, and now suddenly, *poof*—not a soul in sight. I mean, shit, you can hear a pin drop. I'm not completely doubting that what I just said *could've* happened here—I just find the timing to be rather suspicious." Luke paused in contemplation, and then continued. "You don't think it's possible he—" With his back to Janelle, he peered up over his shoulder from his knelt position, fully expecting her to be hovering over him, listening intently. But he found she'd wandered about twenty feet and was staring out into the distance. "*Janelle?*"

She held her gaze for another couple seconds, then turned and spoke in a hushed tone. "Hey, come over here and check this out. I'm pretty sure I can see a group of about three or four. They're still far away, but I think they may be heading in our direction."

CHAPTER 30

The Reminder

"We must be gettin' close now, Linden," Ernie declared beneath the rattling of overhead compartments. "Buckle up—we'll be sure to feel more turbulence as we start to descend. Now, getting back to the story . . . where was I?"

"The sea had suddenly turned violent," Linden quickly recalled, clearly eager to be distracted from the tempestuous punches they were presently experiencing at twenty thousand feet.

"Right, right. So, I see these peculiar particles spewing from what appeared to be a fresh, gaping hole in the moon's surface. Just then, the sea suddenly became enraged, and our seafaring mettle was promptly put to the test. Authoritative orders cascaded down the ranks in a flurry, and before I knew it, I found myself buried under a mountain of responsibility.

"I knew from experience that when a violent storm hits, you ain't gonna be restin' your head until well after it passes, and your ship and your mates are all in good order. In this case, I knew it would be long hours before the wind and raging waters would subside and grant me another shot at a steady view of the moon. So, call it strange—or even negligent, for that matter—but before

I saw to my duties aboard the troubled ship, I . . . well, I basically etched myself a reminder. I mean, it's not like I thought I'd ever *forget* what I'd witnessed on the moon's surface that night, but given the chaotic conditions, I couldn't exactly sit down and write a paragraph about it. So, for the time being, I simply summed it up in a single word, to be expanded upon when the opportunity arose. To this very day I have absolutely no idea how or why I came to choose the word 'moonflaw'—or if it even *is* a word, for that matter. It just sort of . . . came to me in the moment.

"Going back to my earliest days of working in various Maine harbours, I'd always carried a Wade & Butcher clasp knife. Naturally, I brought the tool aboard *Gavinia*, and that's what I used to scratch the word into the scope's brass surface. After doing so, I quickly hid the scope under a litter of other tools in a giant carpenter's chest."

Ernie Cowarth continued strong with his account of that most eventful night back in the fall of 1953. He told Linden how after he'd hidden the scope, he fought dangerously slick deck conditions as he raced off to assist with the switch to storm sails, and how he planned to simply recover the instrument from the old chest when the dust had settled. He described the sustained hours in which the sea bruised and battered the helpless schooner with a merciless fury—and then how an insidious fog had crept up on the crew like a cunning thief in the night, seemingly multiplying the crisis tenfold.

Ernie's words were abruptly suspended as the monotonous drawl of the captain announced the aircraft's forthcoming descent and estimated time of arrival. He absorbed the toneless bulletin, then glanced at his watch and proceeded, knowing that in less than half an hour they'd touch down, and the city of Hartford would inevitably greet them with all its mysterious charm.

"We knew we'd lost our course," he continued hurriedly, fearing the window to squeeze in his story was closing. "And that's about the *only* thing we were sure of. When the fog encompassed us, it was a full-on fight for survival—a struggle just to keep the incessantly pummelled schooner upright. For all we knew we were being tossed further and further out into the North Atlantic, but as we'd eventually find out in the worst way imaginable, we were conversely progressing upon Mizen Head—an extreme southern point of the Irish mainland.

"Now, forgive me, Linden, but this is where my recollection of that night becomes . . . well, let's just say understandably cloudy. Whether or not our captain was ever aware of Saferock's position— a lighthouse situated on a rocky islet seven or so miles from the coast—we'll never really know. I say 'we'll never know' because he was one of twenty-three men aboard *Gavinia* who perished when she was blindly thrust upon the sharp-toothed isle. One of the last things I recall was the great force of the initial impact—the crunch of the hull being gravely impaled by jagged rock, and then the chilling screech of steel peeling back like the lid of some oversized tin of sardines. I helplessly watched faces frozen with fear suddenly fly from the deck and plunge into the seething sea. The drink suppressed their cries in an instant as mighty surges drew them under.

"As for me, well, I'm here today tellin' ya the tale. I was one of only three who survived the wreck. How exactly I lived to tell is a miracle in its own right. Unconscious at the time, I was pulled to safety by the lighthouse keeper—so I can only go on what I eventually learned from the authorities. Apparently I was found wedged in a shallow rock crevice, a dozen feet above water level, my forehead, chest, and lower abdomen spilling blood over the cold slate. My memory completely fails me from those final moments aboard the schooner until a solid month after the incident. Yeah, you heard me correctly. You see, I spent that vacant period of recovery in an induced coma at the Bantry Bay Medical Centre in Southern Ireland. Along with severe head trauma, I'd suffered fractured ribs and a collapsed lung, a dislocated shoulder, and for good measure, an eight-inch gash just above my groin. After a total of six weeks at the Bantry Centre, I was transferred to St. Patrick's Marymount, where I spent another six weeks before returning home to America. It was there, at St. Patrick's, that the memories slowly started to trickle in. Except the memories were more like little snippets of a nightmare that I pieced together like a giant, abstract puzzle.

"Now, believe it or not, it wasn't until shortly after I'd returned home to Maine that I actually remembered the scope, and what I'd witnessed with it the night of the wreck. When the memory of the curious moon image finally found its way home, it brought about a resurgence in me, as far as probing its significance. As for the scope itself, well . . . up until you mentioned it back home at the TAAS meeting, I must say I'd long-assumed it held a permanent residence down in Davy Jones's Locker. I can't say that I've ever envisioned it to be anywhere other than resting on the bed of the Atlantic. I mean, *Gavinia* was in ruins—once we ran aground, the surging breakers chewed her up and spit her out. I presumed everything aboard met a similar fate. I guess the scope must've been flung upon the islet amidst the chaos. But think of the *odds*, Linden! Not only the odds of it surviving the wreck in the first place, but that it eventually ended up back across the ocean, and then further west, to my current home state! And then *you*, a complete stranger, come questioning your curious pawnshop discovery some sixty years later, while I just *happen* to be in your company. Astro*nomical* odds, I tell ya."

Linden contemplated the general overview of the scope's travels, and for a moment could do no more than shake his head in disbelief. "Would it be strange to compare it to a lost dog, sniffing its way back to its rightful owner?" he finally asked hesitantly.

"Maybe not as strange as you'd think."

"What does it all mean then, Ernie?" Linden felt a slight quiver with his own question, as if the answer might be more than what a simple man would be adept to handle.

"What does it all *mean*, you ask?" The weight of the question visibly pressed down on the old man like a natural force. "It *means* that the scope is not of this world, Linden. You see, something crashed into the moon that night in '53, and by some . . . preternatural design, that old instrument granted me a primary view of the consequential by-product.

"Oh, and just to clarify something—as much as there were supernatural forces at work, we're not talkin' aliens here. This ain't goddamn *Close Encounters*."

"Listen, Ernie," Linden suddenly voiced. "I must say, there's no doubt in my mind that your story here is one of the most fascinating I've ever heard—it really is. I can't even begin to imagine enduring the events on that ship. And having to spend all that time laid up in foreign hospitals must've been hell. But with all due respect, this is where you kind of begin to lose me. I mean, I do believe you saw *something* through your scope that night, I really do. But it's like you're still skirting around the meat and potatoes. I must say, I was glad to hear you abolish the alien theory, but the whole lunar impact thing still sounds a little too much like science fiction for me. I need somethin' a little more . . . tangible. Now don't get me wrong, you opened up to a complete stranger and told me some things that I'm guessing you've kept tight for quite some time, and I appreciate that very much. But what did you *really* witness out there, Ernie? Gimme the damn entrée!"

To Ernie, it was now clear as day that Linden wanted the truth—that he didn't fear the severity of the events from that distant, direful night. With the plane descending, and minimal time remaining in flight, Ernie finally conceded the grim reality to a man he'd known for less than forty-eight hours. A truth tucked away in him for years suddenly spilled out like the bursting of an ancient dam. "All these years I've been sworn to secrecy by the federal government," he began with a nervous tension. "As those first couple of years passed—the ones following the wreck—I damn well nearly drove myself nuts trying to decipher exactly what I'd seen through the scope that night. The utter bewilderment took its toll on me, as it began to eat away at everything I was. My crazed psyche held me captive within the memory of the whole experience—until, in 1956, I decided to send word of my sighting to what would later come to be NASA."

"Wait, you took your story to fuckin' *NASA*?" a shocked Linden replied, and he would have nearly hopped right out of his seat if he weren't already buckled in.

"Well, technically, no. Like I said, I took it to what would eventually *become* NASA. Ya know, most people aren't aware that NASA wasn't always NASA." Linden wrinkled his brow, openly acknowledging that he belonged in said category. "I told the people at *NACA* what I'd seen. NACA—the National Advisory Committee for Aeronautics—originated in 1915, and in '58 the agency was dissolved, its assets and personnel transferred to the newly formed National Aeronautics and Space Administration—NASA.

"I figured I'd simply mail off a letter to the NACA Headquarters in Washington, explaining in detail what I'd witnessed, and then I'd subsequently be rewarded an explanatory response. Well, let's just say that that wasn't exactly the case. I must've sent a dozen letters over the course of the next eight months, all directed at various departments within the agency, before I finally received a reply. And boy, I tell ya, when the envelope with the stamped logo arrived in the mail, the combination of excitement and anxiety nearly shook the bloody thing clean out of my hands. I took a seat, a deep breath, and then lied to myself by saying that there were more important things in life than chasing down a stupid mystery.

"An anonymous representative with the agency replied with a two-paragraph, professional acknowledgment of my account. Through the jargon, the words basically told me that what I'd *claimed* to have seen was contrary to reason, and lacked the validity required for further investigation. I was then advised not to send any additional letters to NACA regarding the incident. The response closed by stating that my letters would remain on file should an inquiry be deemed necessary at a later date.

"The rejection put me in a *baaad* state for a period, before I began to convince myself that what I'd seen was indeed contrary to reason—that my lack of sleep leading up to the event had my perception out of kilter. I went with that—I *had* to—and basically just moved on with my life. I soon left Maine altogether, and bought a little place in New Hampshire. It was there, in early 1960, when I figured the whole ordeal to be well behind me, that two members of the FBI's Critical Incident Response Group came knocking at my door. You see, as it turned out, the letters I'd sent to NACA were indeed filed, and were consequently transferred to NASA during the realignment. From there, someone at the newly formed agency had gotten their hands on them and taken it upon themselves to dig a little deeper into the case."

With the plane heading straight for the heart of the sunrise, broad strokes of dreary daylight were now painting over the black canvas of night with a slow hand. Gusty winds and early morning showers greeted the red-eye's approach, seemingly shooing the craft away as though it were an unwelcome insect.

Perhaps anticipating a bird's-eye view of the Greater Hartford area, Ernie craned his neck toward the window and struggled to penetrate the gloom. Gazing out through the triple-layered plexiglass porthole, his thoughts raced back to the moonflaw scope, and the spewing particles he'd once spotted through its mystical eye. Then, shortly thereafter, mindful of the repercussions that would inevitably now find him, he opened up to Linden and severed his long-standing oath with the Feds as if it were no more than a harmless childhood secret.

INTERLUDE

The Courtyard Garden of the Mind

So, allow me to pull back the curtain and finally reveal myself, reader—your "guiding voice." My name is Hoyt Colston, and I'd be lying if I said that all this time I haven't been communicating from within the ivy-clad courtyard walls of the Institute of Living—a distinguished psychiatric facility in Hartford, Connecticut.

Now, I'm going to leave this snippet vague, as to overly expand on my surroundings at this juncture would only be to pull the rug out from under the entire tale. But what I *will* offer is this: out in this airy setting often awash in sunlight, there's a bench that plays host to my work, an integral figure who accompanies me, and a garden—a garden that essentially nurtures my cognitive designs. The soil within is rich with nutrients and organic flavour, serving as an optimal environment to facilitate growth—the harvest then bestowed upon my courtyard companion to amend my imperfections.

I'll catch up with you soon.

PART IV

But now it's gettin' late
And the moon is climbin' high

—Neil Young

CHAPTER 31

The Covert Cruiser

A weighty combination of angst and confusion came crashing down on Shelly Madison-Lowe like an avalanche upon an unsuspecting skier. A complete stranger had just finished stating via text that her husband was in Hartford, and that there had been some kind of an accident.

Then suddenly there it was again, slicing through the silence with its chime—yet another message from Luke Sheehan, the owner of the number she now wished she'd just ignored in the first place. The text read: *Forgot to mntion . . . whatevr u do . . . stay away. Not safe here!*

As if being left in the dark regarding Jeremy's condition wasn't enough, Shelly was now being told to stay away from his current location altogether. Though even if she wanted to pick up and venture into the heart of Connecticut, she couldn't; Jeremy currently possessed their only vehicle. Left to her last resort, the only other option was to get the police involved.

All she had to offer the authorities were the bare-bones of what she actually knew: that a perfect stranger from Boston had placed a suspicious call to her cell phone, asked to get in contact with her husband, and now her husband was apparently miles away in a neighbouring state and in some form of distress. Despite the insufficient detail, the bottom line was that the Hartford Police Department (HPD) needed to be incorporated. But first she would call Luke back and demand some vital information—that is, what he meant by Jeremy being involved in an "accident," and where, exactly, they were within the city.

With the phone pressed to her ear, the ringing of Luke's cell seemed to resonate out into eternity. "Come on—answer the bloody phone, you bastard!" Shelly cursed aloud as a single tear forged a trail down her face and found her upper lip. With a trembling hand she finally tapped the End Call button. Then, following a brief interlude where the waterworks really began to flow, she tried the number again.

This time the call hadn't even rang a second time when, to Shelly's bewilderment, a *female* voice answered the line. "Who the hell is *this*?" Shelly demanded with renewed strength, wondering why it wasn't Luke, but rather a woman receiving the call.

"My name is Janelle," the woman promptly replied. "Luke figured you might call at some point and thought I might be a little . . . easier to talk to."

"Well it's just wonderful to meet you, *Janelle*," Shelly voiced sarcastically, mimicking someone in a far better mood. "Now if you don't mind, could you kindly tell me what the *fuck* is goin' on with my husband? You know anything about some kind of accident?"

"Unfortunately, I do," Janelle reluctantly affirmed. "The truth of it is, this *whole city* has gone haywire—and we believe your husband may've fallen victim to the madness."

Shelly paused amidst the confusion, her right ear still fixed to the cell. She discerned a fusion of driving wind and rain on Janelle's end. "May've fallen victim to the *madness?*" she broke the brief lull. "Stop beatin' around the bush with me, lady! Tell me what happened to Jeremy!"

"Listen, you want me to lay it out for you?" Janelle roared back while attempting to shelter Luke's phone from the unforgiving elements. "Fine—you asked for it. Something totally illogical is happening here in Hartford. And as much as I hate to be the bearer of bad news, your husband appears to be right in the thick of it. He was with Luke and myself for a small period, but heavy rains came, and he ran off on his own to seek shelter. We strongly advised against us separating, but he just wouldn't hear it. Right about now he's likely in the cold custody of a spectral-like mass who've converged upon Hartford, apparently known as Deceivers. They're overrunning the city as we speak!"

Shelly was certain she'd heard enough absurdity in this one conversation to last a lifetime. "I'm getting the cops involved," she declared vehemently, "and if you and this Luke character are right about my husband—that he's been harmed in any way—I'll personally see to it that you're both held accountable."

"I'm sorry to say, lady, but none of that matters anymore. The *law* doesn't matter anymore. I must go. Just know that we haven't given up on your husband. And please, stay clear of this infected city."

To her dismay, Shelly was disconnected before she could squeeze in another word. Shrouded in this unforeseen plight, she manoeuvred her trembling fingers back to the keypad and dialled 9-1-1.

———

Twenty-two-year NYPD Officer Danny Vicerro wasn't even half an hour into a ten-hour night shift when a more . . . unconventional call came scratching through from dispatch. The report indicated that a distraught woman in his vicinity had called 9-1-1, claiming her husband had not only been lured to, but was currently being held captive in, Hartford, Connecticut.

Vicerro was then informed that the Hartford Police Department were already on the case; therefore, his sole obligation was to transport said woman to the HPD headquarters building as quickly as possible.

After receiving the call, he headed north off West Sixty-Fifth Street along Central Park West, before settling his unmarked cruiser at the foot of the woman's swanky high-rise condo. There, a pair of colonial pillars stanchioned a sheltered entranceway with Parkview Palace lettered along the arched canopy. A sharply dressed doorman was stationed before a pair of glass-panelled doors, and a twenty-foot maroon runner boasting the condo's fancy *PP* seal rested below his shiny shoes like a washed-out red carpet.

Just as Vicerro threw the gearshift into Park, he noticed a woman burst forth through the building's front doors like the Devil himself was hot on her tail, startling the doorman in the process. Clearly distressed, the woman made an abrupt halt a few feet beyond the curb and instantly began studying the flow of traffic, as one would before attempting to flag down a cab. Only this woman wasn't exactly raising a hand to reel in any of the numerous advancing taxis. She rather appeared to be waiting on a more *specific* ride—a getaway car, perhaps, given her overly aggressive exit and beeline to the street.

"Excuse me, ma'am," Vicerro addressed the woman through a lowered driver's-side window in his Ford Crown Victoria. "Traffic's movin' by at a pretty good clip—don't wanna see ya get hurt. If you're not lookin' to hail a cab, then I'd appreciate it if you'd kindly step back up onto the sidewalk."

The woman could barely make out the officer's instructions over the steady hum of traffic, but she quickly distinguished his undercover cruiser. She marched to Vicerro's open window and spoke. "Wait a second, you're my ride to Hartford, ain'tcha?"

The seasoned cop played the situation cool, doing no more than nodding a confirmation. He was surprised that he hadn't put two and two together as soon as he noticed the woman's frantic actions.

He proceeded to step out of the car and introduce himself accordingly before opening the passenger's-side door for her.

"I'm Shelly Madison-Lowe," the woman replied. "My apologies—I just didn't expect an unmarked car. All the lady on the phone said was that an officer would be meeting me down at the entrance. I was lookin' for a standard cruiser when I was leanin' out onto the street."

A flurry of car horns amplified the busy strip as Shelly settled into the front seat. A moderate wave of comfort came over her in the moment, knowing the authorities were doing their part to help resolve this most peculiar case.

Before she knew it, they were clear of the big city, accelerating east along the interstate, touching speeds that left the legal limit to die in their wake. While en route, sporadic bouts of heavy rainfall threatened Vicerro's vision and slickened the moonlit highway—yet not once did he draw in the reins on his personally dubbed "covert cruiser." Weaving through law-abiding motorists like they were mere obstacles along a speedway, he cut through the night like a nocturnal hunter.

With the officer focused at the wheel, Shelly found herself observing the passing night through a rain-spotted reflection of her own face in the passenger window. Now north of New Haven, the only sounds were the rhythmic shrill of run-down wiper blades and an occasional blip from the cruiser's two-way radio. Despite her rampant fears, the events of the day had finally taken their toll, and the soothing patter of the rain gently lulled her into a light slumber. The transition was seamless and seemed to progress as if something large and predominantly black was slowly veering dangerously close to her passenger door. A closer look revealed a hulking Hummer H2, barrelling alongside the cruiser like a tank with highway-speed capability.

"*Christ!* This psycho's practically scraping the paint right off your car!" Shelly cried out, informing Vicerro of the immediate threat.

The officer stole a glance for himself, and then reacted by immediately easing off the gas and slightly cutting the wheel to avert the reckless road hog. To his dismay, the Hummer promptly followed suit, matching the cruiser move for move, all the while becoming even more aggressive in the process. With the beastly vehicle still riding abreast, Vicerro now noticed a set of beaming headlights closing in from behind. A tree-lined median to the left completed a trinity of probable peril, so he was left with no choice but to once again punch the gas.

Certain that the encroaching Hummer couldn't touch speeds of ninety-plus MPH, Vicerro was remarkably proven wrong when the two vehicles were still screaming down the interstate, neck and neck, like a pair of dragsters down a quarter-mile strip. A reluctant glance in the rear-view mirror told him that even at this perilous speed, the mysterious vehicle on his tail was also keeping pace. It was now quite clear that they were not only being challenged from the side by the Hummer, but they were also being *followed* by what Vicerro surmised to be a Rolls-Royce Phantom Coupé.

The cruiser's speedometer had now reached triple digits, and to both Shelly and Vicerro's absolute disbelief, the Hummer was still matching its speed. In fact, it had actually nosed ahead, and was crowding over into their lane as if to angle the cruiser straight off the highway and consequently into the bounteous wall of firs and larches.

As if being boxed in on three sides wasn't trouble enough, through the wiper-streaked windshield Vicerro suddenly noticed a glowing cluster of brake lights forming in the near distance. The radiating sea of red flooded the night as it swelled with each slowing vehicle. "Get ready to brace yourself!" he warned. "We're almost outta runway. Any second now I'm gonna jam the brakes, swerve hard to the left, and pray we don't get rear-ended or eat timber!"

Amidst the compressing chaos, Shelly strained to identify the Hummer's occupant. Her initial gaze revealed a cryptic, shadowy figure behind the wheel. The slippery survey offered something straight out of an old gothic horror tale—perhaps something Poe might have dreamed up and scribbled to life in the dark hours. The inauspicious driver donned a black sweater with a hood pulled up and over his head like an awning. Under the coal canopy, a lifelike wooden mask with an unmended slit running from top to bottom substituted for a human face. The fissure-like gash ran from the crest of its forehead, right down between a pair of cavernous eyes, then cut through the nose and mouth until it tucked under the chin. With a crippling chill, she promptly dismissed the image as erroneous due to rain-soused windows distorting a true perspective.

To Shelly's horror, a return glance toward the forbidding figure only confirmed what she'd first witnessed. Only this time, the woodface had begun to part from the furrow down the centre. The outer shell was now fanning open, as if on hinges, revealing a protruding human skull. The demon-thing's empty eye sockets were like passageways to hell itself, the dual cavities tempting Shelly's inquisitive soul to venture deeper into macabre imaginings. She resisted the luring gaze, and turned away for good, as she'd already seen enough in that blood-curdling image to haunt her until her dying day.

"Okay, showtime! Grab a hold of something," Vicerro alerted Shelly before throwing his risky plan into action. Shelly promptly took the officer's advice, employing a mighty grip around both an armrest and a grab handle overhead.

As if anticipating Vicerro's impending move, the menacing Hummer suddenly slammed into the side of the cruiser, jolting the vehicle clear off the road before the cop could implement his controlled strategy. Vicerro instinctively hammered the brakes upon impact, causing the car to flip violently, and then continue to tumble down the sloping grade and into the swampy, tree-choked valley of the interstate median.

CHAPTER 32

IFR

Closing in on the city from above, Linden and Ernie's night flight was finally nearing its conclusion. "I'd say we'll be on the ground in about five minutes," Ernie asserted as he shifted his gaze from the window overlooking a sombre West Hartford. "So, as I was sayin', back in early 1960, these two FBI agents paid me an unexpected visit. They told me that a group of NASA scientists had recently completed a thorough follow-up investigation of my case, and that based on their findings, they had a few questions to go over with me. I knew I wasn't *guilty* of anything, but boy, was I terribly scared in that moment—intimidated, ya know? Two men in sharp, black suits wielding FBI badges practically barge into your home and state that *NASA* has some questions for you—you'd be sweatin' too, Linden.

"So, these fellas state that aside from the questions, NASA would also like to start disclosing some significant information to me, essentially letting me in on what they'd discovered. But only on one crucial condition: I'd have to be sworn to secrecy from that point forward regarding the entire incident. I was definitely taken aback by the offer, but regardless, it took me all of two seconds to tell 'em I was on board—though little did I know at the time the lengths they would go to to make such a matter official. You can't just slap your hand over your heart right there on the spot and say, 'I solemnly swear . . . blah, blah, blah.' Oh no, it ain't that easy. Once I'd verbally committed to proceed and cooperate, I was promptly flown to Washington—you wanna talk about first-class travel—where I was placed before a panel of high-ranking NASA officials and government operatives. I took an oath before a judge, signed a seemingly endless line of legal documents, and then sat through a lengthy discourse that detailed the retribution I'd face should I disclose *any* of the information I was about to acquire.

"At this point we adjourned for lunch, and when we returned, the Investigative Findings Report was revealed to me in strict confidentiality, as per our agreement. NASA's administrator opened by stating—or rather *asking*—and I quote, 'What would you say, Mr. Cowarth, if I were to tell you that we've concluded that the information you've shared with us checks out? And that in due time the radioactive discharge you noticed spewing from the mysterious dark crevice on the moon is certain to jeopardize the *entire human race*?'"

"*What?*" Linden nearly choked on the word. "Talk about not pullin' any punches comin' outta the gate! What the hell did they mean by *that*?"

"Well, to be honest with ya, my initial reaction was that they were breaking the ice with a little drollery. I chuckled as I conceded that the joke was on me. 'I'm sorry,' I quipped to the panel through a sustained snicker, 'there must be a mistake. All this time I've been under the impression that I'd been summoned for a *serious* matter.' And, as you can probably guess, that was a *baaadd* idea. My digression was short-lived, as a humourless woman directly to my left rose from her seat and simultaneously slammed her clipboard down on the table. I tell ya, it cut my laughter with an ear-splitting *snap!* Through the resounding echo I glanced about the room, only to find a dozen other tension-riddled, dour faces giving me the impression that they were also gravely insulted by my total lack of etiquette. The woman now standing over me, whom I later came to know as NASA's senior space policy advisor, promptly unleashed her fury on me like I was a rebellious child. She was steadfast on abolishing every last breath of humour within the room before allowing the meeting to proceed.

"After the dust settled, the administrator basically continued where he'd left off. He asked me if I was familiar with the term 'perigee-syzygy,' which is better known as a 'supermoon' in modern terminology, as I'm sure you're aware. I told him I *was* aware of the term, and before he continued, he'd already confirmed my hunch that the moon's proximity was pivotal to what I'd witnessed through the scope that night. He went on to state that NASA had reviewed their records and concluded that, on the night of my sighting, the moon was at its closest point to the Earth in over seven hundred years! Would you believe they can calculate that shit, right down to less than a quarter mile?

"With no more than a single nod, the administrator then turned the floor over to a considerably young scientist-type. He wore nerdy glasses and a blue lab coat with NASA insignia patches on both the front and back. I never came to know this man's name or official title, as he was curiously never introduced; but it was he who was designated to disclose the critical aspects of the secret information this group had gathered. I'm gonna guess he couldn't've been older than twenty at the time, but he certainly spoke with authority and a knowledge far beyond his years. He opened by reminding me once again of our terms and conditions of confidentiality—as if I needed to hear the rundown of all *that* jargon again. Christ, I wanted to just scream out, 'Would somebody just tell me what the fuck you found already!' The young scientist then gathered a manila folder resting before him. I caught the capital letters *IFR* on the front before he fanned it open and withdrew its contents. It was the Investigative Findings Report. He skipped through a few peripheral pages, then cleared his throat and began to read, his eyes occasionally veering from the report to meet mine as he spoke. He stated that in October of the previous year—1959—NASA had secretly launched a lunar fly-by mission for the sole purpose of further investigating the curious crevice." Ernie paused for a moment, allowing his rather weighty declaration to sink in. "Thus, to this very day, Linden, other than myself, you're the first person outside of NASA and the high ranks of the United States government who knows of this covert mission that took place so many years ago now. I'd like this to stay between us, as I'm sure you understand. But don't worry, you won't be punished if it's ever revealed that I shared this information."

Linden was wide-eyed with this latest revelation. "This shit gets better and better by the minute!" he proclaimed. "So, what you're tellin' me is that based solely on the information you sent by mail—you being a complete unknown at the time—NASA actually launched one of those rickety old probes like the *Pioneer* and *Ranger* to investigate?"

Ernie took a few seconds to reflect on what he knew of those inaugural moon missions in the late '50s—how NASA had the world believe they had all failed miserably in their primary photographic assignments. "Not *solely*," the old man responded, quite relieved to finally be letting the cat out of the bag after all these years, "but I'll get to that in a minute. Those initiatory missions— they were decoys, for the most part. Their unsuccessful results were purposely exposed to the public to keep the secret launch I now speak of—and *its* results—under wraps. Believe it or not, NASA even excluded it from their *own* recorded history, but there was indeed an unmanned spacecraft launched in October of 1959 to further investigate the information I'd offered in my letters. The timing of the mission wasn't fortuitous, either, as it designedly coincided with yet another lunar perigee. And ya know what? It was successful! Successful in the fact that photographic evidence of the enormous fissure-like chasm, along with radiation and seismic tests, were transmitted back to NASA merely seconds before the craft met its end with a vaporizing crash into the moon's surface.

"The lad in the lab coat said the reason they'd gone to such great lengths with the investigation of my case was largely on account of an old scientist named Clive Snelling. Snelling worked for both NACA and NASA for many years before . . . well . . . I won't get into *that* right now. Long before my letters were even sent, Snelling claimed to not only *know* about the fissure and the radiative particles, but also that he fathomed a deeper understanding. Unfortunately for him, until my case was reconsidered by NASA, his zany theories were always slighted—pushed to the wayside, as he already owned the moniker "the deranged scientist." Turns out that sometimes the ones comin' across as crazy are the ones actually making the most sense. Snelling's story is a fascinating piece, and I'd love to share it with you, but it'll have to wait until another day. For now, I'd like to finish by letting you in on those test results, and what those photos revealed.

"So, the young NASA representative eventually returned to the IFR folder and withdrew a good-dozen black-and-white photos, fastened by a single clip. He spaced them out before me and said they were selections from over three hundred successful shots taken from the Palus Putredinis region of the moon—obviously unknown to NASA at the time to be the future landing site of Apollo 15. I'd pinpointed that specific area at the bottom of my letters, to the best of my ability, by sketching a circular moon and identifying the region where I'd seen the fissure.

"The photos clearly revealed the exact yawning crevice I'd witnessed through my scope—the same chasmal slit leading into a deep, coal-black unknown. Though not surprisingly, for six years had passed at that point in time, the spewing particles I'd seen through my scope were no longer visible. The scientist continued by saying that though they failed to capture any *photographic* evidence of the particles I'd described, their test results indicated that specific radiation levels had spiked dramatically in that particular region.

"He confirmed right then and there that there had indeed been an unforeseen impact. NASA's estimation was that no more than an hour before my sighting, an anonymous object had crashed into the moon at an inconceivable speed, embedding itself deep inside the fissure it created upon impact. And whatever it was, Linden, *it's still in there!* That's right—even to this very day, the moon continues to spill cosmic radiation that further tests show is somehow being drawn to Earth. You hear that? *Drawn* to Earth. Possibly by a supplemental force—a correlative energy that may just so happen to lie beneath the *Earth's* surface. And boy, do I have a hunch that whatever the hell it may be, it currently rests below the city of Hartford!"

The ground was coming up fast, and Ernie wanted to squeeze in as much information as Linden could possibly absorb before they disembarked the plane. "Are you *familiar* with the Apollo 15 moon mission?" Ernie asked hastily.

"To a moderate extent, I guess. No more or less than any of the others."

"Well, take everything you *do* know about it and flush it right down the crapper, because it doesn't apply. NASA has continuously kept in touch with me over the years and has always kept me in the loop whenever essential information becomes available. I learned many years ago that below the surface of the facts presented to the public, the Apollo 15 mission was primarily a manned follow-up investigation of the crevice. Space travel had come a long way since the *initial* investigation in '59, and NASA, in conjunction with the government, felt that both the timing and technology was right to go in for a closer look."

Ernie stole a final glance out the window and considered that if he didn't know they were just about to land, they could easily be flying through a cloud, given the low-lying fog. "I'll try to make this quick," he continued, "as we're finally touching down. In addition to the facts and results that the world is aware of regarding the mission, the Apollo crew was ordered to do no more than update atmospheric testing and shoot existing images of, and around, the chasm—all the while remaining a safe distance from the actual hole to avoid possible contamination. Well, as fate would have it, both David Scott and James Irwin ultimately caved to their curiosities, and came so close as to actually peer down into the sooty gorge. After taking a plethora of photos, they conducted their designated tests without a hitch. But following a scrutinized inspection upon their return to Earth, it was found that the 170 pounds of sample mass they collected for detailed analysis had been pre-exposed to various forms and levels of adverse cosmic radiation.

"So basically what I'm sayin' is that we were all destined to be exposed to the fallout at some point in time. The negligent actions of the Apollo 15 crew just sort of . . . well . . . expedited the inevitable. Also, this radiation . . . it somehow seems to lay root to a bizarre amalgamation of dreams—shared visions between complete strangers, if you will. And from your description of the dream you had yesterday—with your lunar rover and companion atop the mountain—it sounds like you, my friend, are now officially in the thick of things with the rest of us! I'd be willing to bet that the fella who shared the dream with you yesterday literally *shared the dream with you.* By that I mean that there's someone else out there—God knows who or where—who had the exact same dream at the exact same time, the only difference being that he experienced it from his own perspective. Shit, for all we know, he could *also* be aware of this whole dream enigma, and right about now he's wonderin' who the hell *you* are.

"Part of me believes that by now the government must know how all this shit ties together. They may even know what it actually *is* that buried itself deep in the moon's surface all those years ago—and how something nearly two hundred and fifty thousand miles away is managing to worm its way inside our heads."

———————————

At the airport's information desk, the middle-aged woman flung her flowing auburn hair from her eyes in preparation to greet her first clients of the young day. "Good morning, gentlemen," she offered, with the same artificial pitch and fabricated smile she'd been deploying for the last seven years on the job. "Welcome to the Bradley Information Center. How may I help you?"

"Hello there," Ernie replied. "My friend and I are on our way down into the city, and we're looking to find the largest recreational space that Hartford has to offer. If you could just give us a name, that would be great."

Just then, as if she'd been nonchalantly eavesdropping with her back turned, another woman behind the desk swung around and took Ernie's question herself. "Pardon me, Sue, I'll look after this one if you don't mind," the lady said to her associate with cold, staring eyes, the look forcing Sue to recede and then tarry in a sudden daze. Those same inanimate eyes then lazily shifted toward the old man from Santa Fe. "You'd be referring to beautiful Bushnell Park then. Now don't get me wrong—Hartford offers a handful of parks of similar size and significance, including Elizabeth Park, with its world-renowned rose garden. But it's indeed Bushnell that you're after. For your convenience, along with a flat-rate taxi service into the city, we offer discounted rates at the elegant Hilton Hotel. Shall I arrange a stay?"

To Ernie's surprise, Linden suddenly stepped forward and confronted the shifty woman behind the desk. "Why are you so keen on *this* particular park?" he barked, causing a few early morning airport strollers to turn their heads.

"Please keep your voice down, sir," the woman replied. She followed with a subtle hand gesture for Linden to come in closer, and then whispered in an eerily soft tone that only he could hear. "You wanna know why, Linden? I'll tell ya why. Simply because Bushnell Park is the answer to Ernie's question. It's no secret that it's the city's largest. Now, the two of you would be wise to take my offer and hop in a cab to the Hilton. The park is within walking distance."

A mystified Linden promptly turned to Ernie and spoke. "This crazy bitch knows our names!"

"Knows our *names?* Impossible!"

"Yeah, she just whispered both of our names to me!"

When the two men glared towards the desk in unison, they weren't utterly perplexed by what they saw, but rather by what they *failed* to see. The cryptic, dead-eyed woman who'd offered them assistance was suddenly nowhere to be found. "Excuse me! Excuse me, miss!" Linden called to Sue, the woman who'd initially greeted them. She still appeared dazed as she now sat hunched, rotating sluggishly on a black swivel stool. "Where'd your colleague go? She was just here two seconds ago."

"I'm sorry, sir," she responded in a listless drawl, as if still in the process of crawling out from under a transient spell. "Please forgive me—I must've dozed off for a minute there. I can't say that I follow you, though. My *colleague?* I've been manning the morning desk exclusively since last year's wave of cutbacks."

Ernie Cowarth was certain that at some point upon their arrival things would get thorny, but not so soon as their very first encounter. "Welcome to Hartford, my friend," the old man stated before leading Linden on their way. He continued as they moved, "What we just experienced there was something we'd better get used to. We can't trust a soul. All we can do is take heed to intuition—it'll lead us to where we need to be. For now, my gut says screw the hotel. Let's grab us a cab and head straight for this Bushnell Park!"

CHAPTER 33

Shorty

Shelly Madison-Lowe woke with a sudden jolt and an accompanying whimper. Disoriented, she quickly realized that the vehicle she was riding in had favourably come to rest right-side up. Naturally, there were other police cruisers on the scene, but the lot of them sat empty as they were all parked in tidy rows. The night around them was eerily quiet and still, save for a pattering of rain on the roof and the easy hum of Officer Vicerro's idling engine.

With her foggy head slowly beginning to clear, Shelly noticed the words Hartford Police on the side of each of the parked cruisers, and illuminated by faint overhead lighting, Hartford Police Headquarters hanging in large white letters against the brown brick wall of a two-storey building before them.

"We're here," Vicerro's voice leaked into Shelly's mental murk. "You dozed off for a little while there—just as we were comin' into the city."

"Yeah . . . sorry, I guess I did," she replied, still lagging in that voided spell of confusion following a bizarre dream. "It's certainly been a long day."

"Ready to head in?"Vicerro asked, killing the engine. "I'm sure they're waitin' on us."

Shelly hesitated a moment, slowly inhaling a deep breath before expelling it even slower. She wanted nothing more than to know the state of her husband, but on the other hand, she was fearful that the Hartford Police might just inform her of a truth she couldn't bear to face.

The two stepped out into the dreary Hartford night as strands of fractured moonlight breached the gloom. The pounding winds of Hurricane Allan had since subsided, but sporadic gusts still kept its memory alive, and currently whipped a cold rain at them on a great slant as they raced for the building's double doors.

In a gentlemanly manner, Vicerro beat Shelly to the access at the last second and reached for a handle to pull it open for her. After finding the first door locked, he tried the other—also locked. The officer found this particularly odd, for they were expected. He considered the late hour; perhaps a buzzer would allow them to signal their arrival. Again, no such luck—not a single buzzer or intercom graced any of the immediate walls. Vicerro proceeded to lead Shelly around the east side of the building in the hopes of stumbling upon an alternate entrance. Not a soul was in sight as they moved through the harsh elements, nor a single passing vehicle along the street that served the headquarters building. To their dismay, the east facade was no more than a lengthy, unsheltered stretch of brick and fastened windows. With the wind and rain now seemingly lashing them against a solid backdrop, they opted to double back for the warm shelter of the cruiser. There, Vicerro could start making inquiries as to why they'd failed to be admitted.

Not thirty feet shy of reaching the patrol car, Shelly suddenly spotted a pair of washed-out headlights peering through the murk. The dual shafts of light, like stealthy nocturnal eyes, appeared to be guiding the vehicle into the parking lot and directly toward their current position. As the prowling glow drew close enough to reveal the make and model, Shelly froze, and her blood ran cold. In an instant her face lost its colour, and her mind screamed of unspeakable horror. As if it had been plucked straight out of her recent nightmare, there before her was a black Hummer H2, the windows tinted so dark they were nearly one with the paint.

As startled as she was, Shelly found herself drawn to the inexplicable coincidence—or perhaps there was something more in play here, something along the lines of a supernatural connection. That exact notion was immediately confirmed when she stepped within a few feet of the now-halted truck and noticed the considerable damage to the driver's-side exterior. Paint had been stripped to bare steel, the metal mangled and warped as if it had recently sustained some form of impact.

"Come on, Shelly, that's no business of ours," Vicerro called over, as he now stood next to his cruiser. "I know of another station, and I'm almost certain they're open around the clock."

Just as Shelly was about to turn and acknowledge the officer, the Hummer's driver's-side window slowly began to lower. At the rate things were going, she half-expected the wood-faced-demon-skull thing from her dream to actually be sitting behind the wheel. She stood her ground, and as the window settled, she surveyed the driver. To her relief, it was not a dream-invading fiend, but rather a young man who appeared to be in his mid-thirties. Promptly introducing himself simply as Shorty, the Hummer's sole occupant had a terribly faded Hartford Whalers mesh-back cap pulled down snugly over bushy red hair that threatened to burst the hat at the seams. A thick red beard concealed most of his face, and he spoke through the thatch with a sense of urgency, claiming he'd not only been sent to help *her*, but the New York City cop as well.

"Miss Shelly, Officer Danny, may God help you if you don't come with me right now!" Shorty warned emphatically. "And I mean *right now!* In less than a minute, you'll be swarmed by Deceivers, and it'll be too late. Get in! I'll explain while we're rollin'.""

"It's nice to know the nut jobs aren't *all* in New York," Vicerro mumbled to himself, and then spoke to Shelly. "Let's go—we don't have time for this nonsense."

Shorty quickly replied as if it were he who had been addressed. "You're right, you *don't* have time. Last call to save your lives!"

It was evident Vicerro wanted nothing to do with this distraction. He had a task at hand, and their time in Hartford had already gotten off on the wrong foot. The last thing he needed was some unhinged stranger telling them their lives were in danger. Until he personally handed Shelly over to the Hartford authorities, she was *his* responsibility—and by no means were they about to hitch a ride in this unannounced and defaced Hummer.

Vicerro opened the cruiser's passenger door and gestured for Shelly to get in. As for her, she couldn't help but find herself at a crossroads. She saw Vicerro's point of view, and respected it, as he was just doing his job. But he hadn't yet learned of the city's malignant state, and he certainly hadn't experienced the sudden rash of premonitory dreams. Dreams like the one Shelly endured when she'd drifted off in the cruiser, ultimately foretelling the Hummer's arrival.

"I think . . . maybe we should go with this guy," Shelly said to the cop sheepishly, knowing very well her words would do little to convince Vicerro to agree.

Shorty revved the Hummer's throaty engine and offered a final cast of deliverance. "There's no time for debate. It's now or never, and in this case, never means forever—as in death! Shelly, don't waste your one and only chance just because he ain't buyin' it. Save yourself! Live to see your husband again!"

Now resolved to the last resort of taking Shelly by the wrist, Vicerro began a slow tread toward her. "Get in the car, Miss!"

he dictated as he moved. "I don't wanna get physical, but you're leaving me no choice."

"He knew our names, Officer!" Shelly retorted, her tone now unwavering. "He addressed us by our *first names!* Didn't you catch that? He knows about Jeremy, too. How can all of this be of no relevance to you?"

As the two sparred, Shorty began to set the Hummer in motion, as his patience had clearly expired. With Vicerro closing in, Shelly instinctively made a dash for the rolling truck, waving her arms frantically for Shorty's attention before he left the lot.

Some thirty yards from where he'd first brought the truck to a halt, it wasn't Shelly's flailing arms but rather her high-pitched cry of desperation that stalled Shorty's exit. "That's cuttin' it close, lady," he affirmed while marginally poking his head out the window. "Hurry up, hop in—we gotta bounce!"

Shelly narrowly made it into the front seat before a multitude of Deceivers, now swarming the vehicle like a pack of ravenous zombies, could deny her attempt to flee. The second her door was secured, Shorty punched the gas and ploughed through the few that had gathered before the grille.

As he began to forge his bulky ride forward, the two were suddenly taken aback by the sound of erratic gunfire. "*Christ!* Is he shootin' at our tires?" a tense Shelly questioned, eyeballing the side mirror for a glimpse of Vicerro. Committed to be completely in the clear before engaging in any form of conversation, Shorty barrelled on without a reply.

Now free of the shitstorm blowing through the police headquarters facility, and cruising up an eerily desolate Jennings Road, he finally asked casually, "Did you know the cop?"

Shelly hesitated before responding, "Whaddya mean, *did* I know 'im?"

"What I meant was, were you *close* to him? You know, a friend? A family member, perhaps?"

"Well, no, then—I just met him a couple hours ago. He drove me here from New York. By *here*, I mean the police station we just fled. I was supposed to be received there, but for some reason the doors were—"

"Yeah, yeah, I know," Shorty's words barged in. "I'm well aware of it all. Listen, I'm gonna be blunt here. I asked you if you knew him because . . . regrettably . . . he's sure to be dead by now. In fact, I'm *also* dead—but I'll get to that in a minute. Those gunshots we heard back there definitely weren't shots aimed at our tires; they were the officer's desperate attempts to stave off the mob of Deceivers we left behind. Unfortunately, he'd've needed an automatic rifle to even begin to stymie their ruthless raid."

From the cold precincts of Jennings Road, Shorty swung the Hummer south onto I-91 for the quickest route into the city's core. For Shelly, it was the second time in as many hours that she'd been whisked away by an unfamiliar face to an unfamiliar place. "Wouldja mind tellin' me where we're headed, exactly?" she asked in earnest. "Because you certainly appear to have a strict agenda. And why do you keep sayin' 'Deceivers' like I should know what the hell ya mean by that? Are they a gang, or some kind of army?"

"In a transcendent way, yes, they *are* like an army," Shorty replied. "Technically speaking, I'm a Deceiver myself, but not in the same vein as the immoral masses that have recently converged upon this very city. That's what I meant when I said I'm *also* dead. Deceivers are the reanimated by-product of an incomprehensible lunar event that originally took place way back in the '50s. Yeah, you heard me right—the '50s. Then, some years later, the government only made matters worse when their investigative measures went inadvertently awry.

"Anyhow, we've no time for the whole story, as things are about to get hairier than this face before you. For now, here's what you need to know. We're headed downtown to a large recreational space called Bushnell Park. It's not far. Barring any setbacks, we should be there in no more than ten minutes. Up until about an hour or two ago, before he went out on his own and found trouble, your husband shared the allied company of two others within said park. From the point of their split, I'm sure of only one thing: when he was alone and vulnerable, he was seized and taken underground by Deceivers into a labyrinth of concrete conduits that run beneath the city."

With a myriad of questions swimming to the surface, a distressed Shelly wanted to ask them all at once. She was mentally wrung, and could feel herself coming unglued. "None of this is making and goddamn *sense* to me!" she suddenly screamed at the top of her lungs. A tear held fast along her lower eyelid, unmoored in the limpid gloss, and then slowly slipped down the course of her cheek as she continued to vent. "If you say there's shit goin' down in this park with these *Deceivers,* as you call 'em, then why the hell are ya takin' *me* there? Don't get me wrong, I wanna know where my husband is, but I'm not so sure I'm comfortable headin' straight into the den at this point."

"We're goin' in for two reasons," Shorty replied, as cool and calm as ever, quite unfazed by Shelly's sudden outburst. "Me, I intend to rally with a select few who, along with myself, have been secretly devising an insurgence for some time now. As for you, well, through no fault of your own, you're consequently in deeper than you'd probably care to know. What I'm basically sayin' is, because of your connection to Jeremy, you've suddenly become vital to our revolt."

Shelly threw her arms up and could only smile wryly, as if to say, "Of course I have!"

Though he'd called Hartford his home all his life, the Trumbull Street exit snuck up on Shorty faster than he'd expected. Following a bold lane change to gain the outlet, he wove through an S-bend that eventually drew south, past the Hilton, and directly toward Bushnell Park's northeast entrance.

CHAPTER 34

The Story of Clive Snelling

Though he maintained his official title of aerospace engineer following his transfer from NASA headquarters in the early spring of 1959, Clive Snelling's moniker of "the deranged scientist" also followed him across the country to NASA's Ames Research Center in the southern San Francisco Bay Area. For Snelling, the relocation west was a homecoming of sorts, as he'd spent the first seven years of his life in six different dwellings within the Silicon Valley region.

As the '50s rolled along, Snelling's reputation as a top-tier engineer diminished with his persistent claims of some inevitable lunar threat. From executives, all the way down to the night shift caretaker, Clive would spew his off-kilter theories to anybody who'd feign even the slightest interest. He'd catch employees off guard in the hallways, suddenly throwing himself at potential followers with the emotional fervour of "Doc" Brown from the *Back to the Future* trilogy. Though the films premiered after his time, Snelling could have easily stepped in as Doc's double, with his bulging eyes

249

and unkempt white hair that did nothing to temper his growing reputation as a delirious individual. "After four-and-a-half *billion* years, our satellite has finally spoken!" he'd proclaim in a boisterous tone, assuming his space jargon made perfect sense to his fellow cosmologists. As though he were quoting aloud from a bizarre newspaper headline, he'd offer outlandish phrases such as, "The sick lunar lungs have finally coughed up the ghost cancer," or, "Guard your dreams against the spilling orbital venom."

As if his pretentious words of wisdom weren't enough, there was the eventual existence of, and rather curious connection to, his moon globe. For most, the globe was the clincher—the *physical* proof that sealed the certifiable deal. For a six-month period leading up to his transfer west, and then during his time at Ames, Clive Snelling was seldom seen in the absence of his self-made lunar model that he'd boastfully dubbed "My Lunacy."

On a brisk morning in October of 1958, Clive Snelling had woken considerably earlier than his conventional hour. A dream was still very much alive in his mind, and like a strong undertow, it strove to pull him back under for a re-examination of sorts. Succumbing to the drag, it was as if he were suddenly observing the proceedings from a precariously high perch in a cold, alternate reality. It was from this roost that he watched his previous dream play out before him, as though he were watching the familiar scenes of an old rerun. He observed himself sitting on a rustic wooden stool before a sizeable carpenter's table. A crackling fire threw dancing shadow figures on surrounding cabin walls, and a wood-framed window permitted a choice view of the luminous moon he was set to replicate. All the necessary tools and supplies were neatly laid out atop the table for the creation of the lunar model that would require the precise definition and detail that only a dream could so graciously afford.

From on high, Snelling watched himself meticulously shape the wooden globe using a lathe and a segmented winding technique. A thorough sanding session followed, and then he went to the window to study the archetype with the aid of a brass pocket telescope. Then, with the steady hand of a marksman, he carved and shaped the great intricacies of the lunar surface into the face of the wooden sphere. A world of ashen hues and a glossy varnish were applied, and then the finished product was gently placed upon a wooden pedestal, awaiting its prize in the corner of the cabin.

A hard rain began to rap against the cabin/bedroom window, stealing Snelling from his slumber. He was certain he'd been dreaming once again, but this time around the memory was muddy and fleeting, then lost to that gossamer void where dreams go to die. He woke to find the house quite cold, and considered the possibility that his furnace had failed overnight. The morning weather was sour, as leaden skies depressed and ruthlessly blanketed the sunrise. A whistling wind stirred the gloom, rattling gutters that conveyed fresh rainwater.

Though disinclined to do so, the engineer threw back the covers and rolled out into the chill that became even more evident now that he was mobile. He was shocked to see his own breath, and guessed the temperature had somehow dipped as low as fifty degrees. Charged with a weighty headache, Clive not only sought the source of the icy bite, but some medicinal relief as well.

While en route to the bathroom along a narrow hallway, he ambled past the open frame of a spare room that curiously produced a stiff blast of cold air. He halted in his tracks, then turned and faced the draft head-on, and thereupon reckoned that whatever was morphing his house into a meat locker must be situated within this particular space.

Still too groggy to fear whatever foul revelation the vacant room might divulge, Snelling flicked the light switch. Once his eyes adjusted, he found the source of the mysterious chill to be alarming in its illogical nature. He surely didn't know what he expected to find behind the darkness, but what he saw was certainly lost on a list of possibilities. There, resting innocently on a French Empire pedestal in the room's far corner, was what appeared to be the exact moon globe he suddenly recalled crafting in the depths of slumber.

Initially, he couldn't help but wonder if he was wrapped in yet another dream layer, the globe serving as some talisman-like entity at the core of the subliminal tiers. That thought was promptly expelled when he approached the curious orb and felt the glacial sting with his palm—an icy bite that certainly would have shattered even the strongest of dream enclosures.

Snelling leaned in and examined the cold beauty of the piece. It was entrancing in its precision—the masterwork of an artist whose skill defined the trade. *Could I have actually created this in my sleep?* The preposterous thought suddenly seeped in through the pores of the moment, evoking an invigorating sense of wonder as he regarded the possibility.

Lost in that distant headspace for an unknown time, he eventually returned to find that the chill had thawed considerably, and was even bordering on a comforting warmth. Everything was suddenly different now—there were no more questions to be asked. To Clive Snelling, the reality of any situation was always how *he* chose to perceive it. And in this case, the reality was that the moon globe was indeed resting before him. Though the details regarding its existence were sketchy at best, the bottom line was that it *did* exist, and that it *had* to have been *he* who'd created it. To think any differently would be to think along the jagged lines of a crazy man.

"Not only do we *create*, but we proceed to schlep our own insanity like a stone," Snelling would reply assuredly when someone bold enough at NASA would inquire about the globe's significance. "We inadvertently weave and then tighten the threads of madness until we eventually choke on our own design. The globe just . . . let's say . . . grants me a little wiggle room within the noose."

Most of the time, perplexed employees would just walk away without a verbal response. Eyes would roll and heads would shake, as they would all wonder how the once-revered engineer still held his position—or any position at all—with the esteemed agency.

Upon his transfer to the Ames Research Center, Snelling was appointed a position in the Unitary Plan Wind Tunnel: an extensive research facility used to design and test new generations of aircraft. There, he and his moon globe remained inseparable, even during laborious working hours.

Fanatically wrapped up in the globe's aura, Clive was inattentive to the new batch of cages he was rattling with his zany ways. An electrician of nineteen years named Franklin Smart was the first person—and, as the damning hand of fate would have it, the *only* person—to take action against Snelling's unprofessionalism. To Smart, the newcomer's incoherent ramblings and peculiar rituals had quickly grown old.

Franklin Smart stood at five foot nothing and weighed in at a hundred and jack, but his strength was in his crafty actions, and the pleasure he took in messing with a fragile mind was indeed a force to be reckoned with. In this case, knowing how Snelling would go to pieces if his globe happened to "go missing," the electrician went straight for the jugular. His tactic was to dedicate two days in which he'd closely monitor the engineer's tendencies and patterns. If the white-haired wacko so much as took a leak with his back to the globe, Smart would make note of it.

Careful not to give himself away, he sauntered about the facility with his electrical tools in tow, occasionally fidgeting with things in Snelling's vicinity that weren't exactly broken. Though periodically close at hand, he made sure to avoid any eye contact with Snelling whatsoever; any form of association would just risk making him a suspect when the shit eventually hit the fan.

When he was confident that the time was ripe, Franklin Smart made his move. He didn't go as far as to actually follow his target into the john, but what he did do was distinguish a seemingly reliable early morning window where Snelling would part with the globe while he'd stroll down to the cafeteria for a coffee.

Like clockwork, Snelling would roll into his office at six-thirty in the morning, eyes bloodshot from a lack of sleep, globe tucked under his arm like a beach ball, and whistling some simple ditty in the highest of annoying pitches. He'd go directly to a cupped support stand situated next to his desk, where he'd rest the globe on the stand like a trophy on display before heading out for his caffeinated shot in the arm. After returning to his office to tackle the morning's paperwork, he'd carry the globe out onto the floor, as it would accompany him for the balance of his shift.

Smart clocked in at work an hour before Snelling on the morning of the big heist. He staked out the engineer's office from a safe distance as he watched and waited from a nearby maintenance lockup. Then there he was, not a single minute early or late, casually drifting down the narrow hallway before disappearing into his private office. Smart heard him coming before he saw him, that grating whistle announcing his presence as it bounced off the corridor walls like a poorly tuned instrument. After completing his globe placement routine, Snelling whistled his way back down the same hallway toward the cafeteria.

Eventually, the shrill note faded out of earshot. A single bead of sweat suddenly tickled Franklin's temple and triggered him into action. In one fell swoop he found himself through the office door and face to face with Snelling's replicated moon. A pair of oddities immediately jumped out at him. The first was the globe's size. It seemed deceptively smaller than what he'd been accustomed to seeing the loon tote around the grounds, as though its form had contracted from the size of a basketball to that of a soccer ball. The other oddity was the biting temperature emanating from the orb. When he cupped it into his hands, he nearly dropped it right back onto the stand, as it felt as if he were lifting a spherical block of ice.

Quickly dismissing the curiosities, Franklin Smart was in and out of Snelling's office in no time at all, the globe swallowed in a large leather sack used primarily to handle electrical supplies. He scurried back to the maintenance lockup, where he promptly stashed the lunar model in a deep nook within the storage space.

And that was that. Two days of preparation had boiled down to a mere ninety seconds of adrenaline-fuelled action. Smart had pulled off the petty theft without a hitch, and now all that was left to do was to sit back and enjoy the exhibition that would be Snelling's reaction. Unfortunately for Smart, the show would have to wait a few hours though. He would have paid good money to catch that initial look on Snelling's face when he returned to his globeless office, but his presence in that place and time would be a dead giveaway. His plan was to be openly spotted by fellow employees doing electrical work in another building altogether, and when he felt the time was right, he'd mosey back over and check in on the festivities.

Contrary to the design, word got back to Smart before he had the chance to "happen upon" things for himself. He was in the process of dealing with a tangled mess of wire in a nearby facility when he first caught wind of some news that hit him like a high-voltage shock. He pivoted from his cobweb of cable and noticed a handful of people in his vicinity who seemed to be talking in hushed circles, each of their faces swimming in a sea of confusion and disbelief. "Yeah, apparently over in the Pre-treatment Plant,"

Franklin overheard a woman mutter, her voice trailing off as if she wanted the disturbing rumour to die along with her words.

"Word has it that it was that strange fella who's always walkin' 'round with that globe," a young man added, his expression an open display of distress.

Another man appeared to be a little more in the know. "Some people are sayin' before he hung himself, he kept repeating the same phrase over and over like his goddamn needle was stuck."

With a warm rush of self-condemnation suddenly flooding the halls of his mind, Smart found his way into the conversation. "Sorry to interrupt," he said informally, "but did I catch one of yous sayin' that somebody *hung* themselves? *On-site?*"

"It's all still hearsay at this point," a curvy woman acknowledged the electrician. "But the rumours appear to be carrying some weight."

And with that, Franklin Smart had heard more than he could stomach. He immediately found himself in prayer as he departed, holding out hope that this was all just someone else's idea of a sick joke.

The trek to the scene felt like a personal death march. Sweat leaked from his brow, and he found himself gasping for air that only seemed to elude him. No matter how he sliced it, something had gone horribly wrong. He'd inadvertently laid the blueprints for this living nightmare, and he was about to descend into the depths of its grim reality.

Smart arrived at the Pre-treatment Plant to find a throng of curious bystanders dispersed within a maze of emergency response vehicles and personnel. With the building's entire perimeter secured by the authorities for investigative purposes, the winds of the rumour mill were now whirling at full force, as everybody seemed to have their own embellished take on what had actually happened to Clive Snelling.

Again, Franklin found his way into a group discussion. This time it was a familiar clique of electricians and other maintenance staff. Just like everyone else, they all seemed to be tossing their speculative theories into the breeze. He sharpened his ear in on what Winston Lowell—a fellow electrician who'd worked alongside Franklin on occasion—was offering. Lowell appeared to have witnessed some of the fallout first-hand, and Smart knew him to be a reliable source on most accounts. "I'm tellin' yuz, crazy son-bitch was runnin' round like 'e had a firecracker up 'is wazoo," he recounted in his lazy Texan drawl, his eyes bulging, impersonating Snelling's frenzied state. "Kept sayin' over and over, 'May the one who lifted My Lunacy be forever burdened by its weight.' Musta heard 'im say it twenty times. People tried to restrain 'im, but 'e slipped through 'em like jelly. Rumour has it someone snatched 'is precious globe, and when 'e couldn't find it 'e went right off the deep end—finally hung 'imself out in the open for all ta see."

"*Hung himself? Really?*" Smart questioned in horror, as if it were the first time he'd heard the news. "Has any of this been confirmed by the authorities? Does anybody know who might've instigated this?" He suddenly caught himself in the act of firing off too many questions at once: an act that even he, pinned under his fresh canopy of fear, realized would only come across as suspicious. Sensing a fainting spell slowly coming over him, he slipped away from the masses and then vacated the scene altogether.

Franklin found some shade beneath a Monterey pine that was a ten-minute walk from the chaos. There, he dropped to his knees, and promptly varnished the base of the generous tree with his vomit. The disgorge helped momentarily, but a fresh wave of repentance was already rolling in, and it seemed to bear Clive Snelling's final words on its back—the words he'd allegedly repeated over and over again before tying the hangman's knot: *May the one who lifted My Lunacy be forever burdened by its weight.*

Before he knew it, Smart was back down in a crouch, spewing another round of regret at the foot of the pine. Hunkered in this hopeless state, he was suddenly struck with an impulse to sneak back into the maintenance lockup, where he'd pluck the evidential globe from the secluded nook and abolish its very existence before the investigation broadened. The thought brought some much-needed relief, but like a cool breeze cutting a sweltering heat, it vanished just as fast as it arrived. As if the truth of the situation were carved into the sticky bark before him, Franklin could see the writing on the wall. He no longer required validation that Clive Snelling had indeed taken his own life. What was done was done—a little mild japery had come back on him and exploded in his face. He had meddled with a brilliant, yet acutely fragile mind, overstepping a line that had been scratched in the sand by the hand of madness.

Franklin Smart left work early that day and headed home, knowing he'd be forever burdened by the weight of his actions, for he'd been the one who'd lifted My Lunacy.

It didn't take a forensics expert to draw a relation between the suicides of both Clive Snelling and Franklin Smart. Less than twelve hours after Snelling was pronounced dead at the Ames Research Center, the burdening weight of Smart's culpability was lifted in an instant with a self-inflicted gunshot blast to the temple. The combination of Smart's subsequent absence, and the eventual discovery of Snelling's beloved globe in the maintenance lockup, drew investigators to the electrician's nearby residence, and to the cold conclusion of the case.

Following a short stay in a police storage facility, the confiscated globe wasn't destroyed, as Smart had fleetingly envisioned, but rather donated to a Salvation Army Thrift Store. Thus, the devious object continued its tour of misfortune, zigzagging between a number of stops along its cursed course—a course that began on a tempestuous morning in October of 1958, when Clive "the deranged scientist" Snelling woke to a supernatural chill and the unearthly artefact it emanated from.

CHAPTER 35

Two and Hugh's Army

"Bushnell Park, please," Ernie Cowarth politely directed the cab driver toward the sprawling green space. As they set in motion, the dispiriting morning weather continued to cast its gloomy mood over the day. The sky moved sideways as the low ceiling floated along like a lofty funeral procession. Intermittent wafts of fog seemingly swam below, and the rains, which had drenched the city of late, were currently no more than an ethereal mist that could coat one's clothing without ever threatening a full saturation.

"Bushnell Park, huh?" The cabbie suddenly sprang to life a quarter-mile into the fare, snapping Linden out of a justifiable lull that already had him on the edge of sleep. The unmistakable tongue of Italian descent rang true as he spoke. "Hope yer not plannin' a picnic. They say we're not outta the woods just yet, as far as the heavy rains go."

From the back seat, Ernie began to study the driver through the rear-view mirror. A cigarette dangled from his lips, and a long

261

appendage of ash hung in the balance. Smoke billowed in the reflection like inescapable smog. He appeared to be just shy of Ernie's age, and was therefore working well into his retirement years.

Ernie found the cabbie's eyes to be curious, but not cold. They were safe *human* eyes—eyes that lacked the cadaverous chill that defined the decayed lenses of a Deceiver. Both Linden and Ernie had experienced that empty gaze back at the airport with the woman at the information desk, her barren eyes like windows to a black soul.

It was as if the deeper they advanced into the city, the greater the fog thickened around them. The shroud continuously tightened as it lowered over the jagged array of stately high-rise buildings, seemingly banishing them from existence.

Eventually, the cab approached the park's northeastern lip as it drew up to an entrance along Jewell Street. The driver collected the fare—which voluntarily came out of Linden's pocket—and then offered up some free advice before going on his way. "Listen up," he said intently, twisting his body within the smoky soup towards the back seat to make respectable eye contact. "I'm gonna tell you fellas the same thing I told my first few fares this morning, and yous can take it as you may. Basically, alls I'm sayin' is just to keep a keen eye about you today. I been spinnin' my wheels through these streets for more years than I know, and though I can't quite put a finger on it, somethin' just ain't right with the vibe right now. City seems . . . infected. People are actin' real strange, and this godforsaken weather just keeps feedin' into the plague. Wish I could be more specific, but I feel obligated to at least forewarn my fares, ya know? Like I said, take it as you may."

With that, Ernie's thoughts ran a quick lap around a track of sarcasm. *Yeah, yeah, we're way ahead of ya on this one, Pasquale. You think me and my friend here just came to this dirge of a city for a scenic getaway?* "Well, thanks for the heads-up, sir," were the words that came after crossing the finish line, delivered in an appreciative tone towards the driver as he began to exit the cab. "We'll be sure to keep an eye out for anything that might look a little suspicious."

As both rear doors closed with a simultaneous *thud*, the cab pulled away and was almost instantaneously consumed in the mouth of the mist like a tiny yellow pill. The two found themselves standing alone on the threshold of the park, the deafening silence and flat-out eerie atmosphere confirming the cabbie's ominous impression of the day. "Well, here we are," Linden finally announced in a voice that seemed destined to carry all the way to Providence, his arms extended outward at his sides to embrace the expanse of the grounds. "Now what?"

Ernie drew a deep breath, his vision labouring through the murk. "Well, we're not exactly following any plans here, but that's part of the rush, ain't it? We just have to keep following the signs— should we be lucky enough to spot 'em. And more importantly, we gotta continue to trust our gut."

"I don't know about you," Linden promptly reacted, "but right about now, my *gut* is grumbling somethin' severe!" He spun toward what he guessed was a bagel shop opposite the park. "I think we owe it to ourselves to hit the pause button for twenty, grab us some chow, and then our *guts* can be trusted on a full stomach."

Ernie chuckled, and then took a moment to weigh the idea. He had no argument against a hot cup of coffee and a quick bite to eat—but at what risk? A casual appearance in some shop could precipitate endless possibilities of ruinous fate.

Still chewing over their next move, their bubbles of indecisive thought were suddenly pierced by a sharp whistle. The shrill blast had clearly come from within the park's boundary, and was followed shortly thereafter by a direct, loud whisper. "*Hey!* You idiots got a death wish or somethin', millin' around out in the open like that?" The voice was close, but its source remained out of sight. "For Christ's sake, get yer asses under cover before ya draw the Double-Dealers!"

From their current post along the perimeter, both Linden and Ernie gazed into the park and surmised that they detected a slew of shadowy figures behind the foliage and the milky curtain of fog. Linden then looked to Ernie to confirm the whisperer's intriguing choice of words. "Did he say 'Double-Dealers?'"

"Certainly did," the old man replied in a whisper of his own. "Makes sense, too. Sounds like another way of saying Deceivers."

The two stood perplexed. They were still finding their feet in the foreign capital and were suddenly entertaining the pivotal counsel of an obscured unknown. "Ya know," Ernie continued, all the while easing into a cautious stride toward the voice from within the park, "whoever the hell he is, the man's right—we need to start keeping a low profile. As for now, we have to trust that if somebody's willing to warn us of potential danger, they must at least be somebody we can talk to, don't ya think? Besides, aren't we due a little inside information? Come on, follow me."

Though skeptical of the move, Linden had no choice but to tread on Ernie's heels. His stomach coincidentally announced a disapproving grumble, as if to proclaim that there'd certainly be no rejuvenating morning meal in *this* direction. The pair crossed the park's threshold in close tandem and were promptly met by a group much larger than they'd anticipated. Ernie estimated the rugged assemblage at forty to fifty strong; the lot of them huddled close together in the mist. A sharper scan revealed the majority to be grown men, with women and adolescents mixed in the cluster.

Without delay, a burly man stepped to the forefront as Ernie and Linden approached. Evidently the leader of this tight-knit group, he gave the impression of an overworked ironworker. The straps of his grimy brown overalls wrapped up and over massive shoulders, and time had blanched his once-orange construction T-shirt to a near coral pink. "Name's Delabar," he stated in a gruff voice that suited his towering frame to a tee. His prodigious stature and thick black beard reminded Linden of Bluto from the live-action film

adaptation of *Popeye*. "*Hugh* Delabar, and this gang behind me is
the final thread of sanity remaining in this unravelling city."

Ernie and Hugh connected on a firm handshake. "Ernie
Cowarth, and this here's Linden Maddox. Pleased to meet you and
your . . . people."

Though he was oblivious to his own strength during the
process, Delabar finally relinquished his grip that had Ernie's
arthritic hand begging for deliverance. "You see, none of us are
from around here. We're a buncha unassociated guests who
are . . . who *were* . . . staying at the Hilton." He motioned toward
the lofty hotel as if it could actually be spotted through the murk.
"Over the course of the last twenty-four hours we've basically had
to join forces against—for lack of a better term—the giant stroke
that this city seems to have suddenly suffered. People at the hotel
started acting really strange, to put it mildly. It was as if they were
becoming more and more—"

"Deceitful?" Linden interrupted with a sudden start, his eyes
wide and confident. "We know all about it, Hugh. I mean, not so
much about the people at the Hilton, per se, but these Double-
Dealers, as you call 'em. We've been in the city less than an hour,
and we've already had the pleasure of dealing with one first-hand.
The two of us are fresh off a red-eye from Albuquerque."

"How'd you know we were safe?" Ernie suddenly asked, glancing beyond Delabar's boxcar frame to examine the gathering
behind him. "And by 'safe' I mean, to borrow your expression, not
a pair of stroke victims? And is there any reason you and your
people are hiding out in *this* particular park?"

Just then, another man stepped forward and stood alongside
Hugh. Dwarfed by the group's leader, this probable second-in-
command appeared as though he'd been dragged through the mud
by a pickup truck. He met Ernie's eyes, his own eyes steely in the
dismal dawn, and proceeded to answer the old man's questions as
if he were among the conversation from the get-go. "These people

we've come to call 'Double-Dealers' certainly wouldn't travel by means of a bloody cab," he stated firmly. "*That's* how we knew. A few of us noticed the taxi pull up, and Hugh here read the situation perfectly—told yous to get the fuck off the street. As for the park, well . . . I guess we're back here because the grass is greener than the alternative.

"You see, we've already attempted to flee the city, but all that did was cost us lives. Once you get out there, man, the streets appear to be deserted, but deep in the shadows the city is crawling with these tricky fuckers. They're not there, and then they just . . . *are*, like they materialize out of the fog the second you turn your back. They basically railroaded us back into the centre of the city by exceedingly violent measures—been stirring here within this park's boundary since just before daybreak. For whatever reason it seems to be the safest place. We've only had a few minor run-ins."

"They're called Deceivers," Ernie abruptly announced, catching Hugh and Mud Man off guard in the process. He disagreed that Deceivers wouldn't travel by taxi, and considered starting with this, but instead chose to brush it off as irrelevant. "I don't mean to dismiss your judgement by any means, because you're on the right track, but these people you're calling Double-Dealers, they're actually called Deceivers. And if you're willing to hear us out, we'll tell you everything we know about their fraudulent ways."

Hugh and his subordinate exchanged muddled glances before Hugh said, "All right, enlighten us, Albuquerque."

Ernie nodded his gratitude, then began what he thought would be an extensive analysis of the enemy. "Okay, first off, you and your group here will continue to fight a futile battle unless you begin to follow *our* lead. You see, my friend and I have—"

"Whoa, whoa, whoa, Grandpa," Hugh said, slaying Ernie's words with a sudden change of tone and demeanour. His chest seemed to inflate like a pufferfish. "Your friend here just finished sayin' that you guys are from New Mexico—did he not? We're not all from Hartford per se, but most of us are at least from this state. So, tell me, how exactly is it that you're gonna tell *us* what we should or shouldn't do? Or where we should or shouldn't go? Shit, your senile ass doesn't even know enough to stay off the bloody streets!"

"Okay, okay, let's all just take a step back here," Linden intervened. "All he's trying to say is that we've gathered a little background information on these people, and we think we may know what it is that makes 'em tick. We respect your suspicions, but you have to trust that we wouldn't purposely lead you and your group into any danger. Come on, if we're not one of *them*, we're one of *yous*."

A handful of Delabar's men began to creep forward from the pack. One of them was resting a hefty crowbar over his shoulder, while another wielded a lengthy fire iron with a six-inch protruding hook. It seemed as if all Hugh had to do was give them the word. And if it came to such an extreme, it would be an even twelve hours since Hugh and his army were first forced into violent action.

There would be no bloodshed here, as Delabar only began to recount the harrowing events of the previous evening.

When Hugh and his troops attempted their getaway, they were met in the south end of the city by a militant band of Deceivers as they approached Cedar Hill Cemetery. "End of the line, folks!" they were coldly informed by one of the dozen or so demonic dream infesters. "The time of the Great Gathering is nigh, and the chosen domain shall remain secured!"

This particular clot of Deceivers posed as gravediggers, brandishing their shovels, mattocks, and even scythes strictly as weapons to defend the city limit. Hugh's army had the Deceivers outnumbered at better than five to one, but their reluctance toward the imminent conflict diminished their advantage considerably.

"We don't want any trouble here," Hugh declared, speaking on behalf of the apprehensive throng now huddled twenty feet to his rear. "We just want to continue on with our course, and quietly close the door behind us."

As expected, the gang of gravedigging Deceivers took exception to the flight. With a sudden start, they were seemingly unleashed like a pack of predatory wolves, driving at Hugh's party in the name of a dark, divine spirit. Delabar, still spearheading his crew, stood his ground as he wielded a bat autographed by Wade Boggs that he'd ripped from the wall of the Hilton sports bar.

The gruesome events that transpired at the cemetery entrance left Delabar and his allegiant followers scrambling for their lives. The two factions charged at each other, but the Deceivers were masters of their handheld armaments, slicing at vulnerable human flesh with inspired speed and precision, cutting down anyone who dared challenge their barricade. Delabar and his crew were quickly overwhelmed; the impenetrable Deceiver juggernaut swiftly and lethally defended their sacred fringe, while what was left of the feeble human regiment retreated in the direction of the city's moribund core.

Those who lagged in the chase were the unfortunate ones. Three not so fleet of foot were run down and gravely maimed. Another five were designedly captured. As the other forty-plus scampered north, knowingly abandoning their peers in the process, the five captives were gathered by the unscathed group of Deceivers and ushered eastward like slaves to the nearby Metzner Recreation Center—an early childhood learning facility. There, they were led to a secluded, green janitorial door located along the back exterior of the building. Below a spiritless light, the door was veiled behind thick, unkempt brush, giving it the impression that it hadn't been accessed in ages. A Deceiver promptly stepped forward and cleared the undergrowth with a few radical swipes of a bloodstained sickle.

Once the thicket was passable, another Deceiver stepped to the neglected portal. In his left hand he carried a black mattock that suddenly morphed into a cane. He placed his right hand over a padlock so rusty and corroded that it appeared to be oozing some vile contagion. He then touched the tip of the cane to the back of his hand. A white glow began to shimmer from within the Deceiver's palm, and then spilled out from between his loosening fingers like translucent rays. When the radiance expired shortly thereafter, he removed his hand entirely, and all evidence of the lock's existence had vanished. Without pause, he was already opening the door.

After the Deceivers and their five detainees had entered, the door slammed shut behind them with a heavy *thud*. Along with the sound came a sweeping loss of light, leaving nothing but the low resonance to permeate the dark unknown.

As if they were blindfolded, the captives were marched down an immediate flight of stairs. There were no railings to conduct them along the cavernous decline—just the helping hands of those who had, only twenty minutes prior, slaughtered three members of their company. The stairs led to a small platform that enabled another flight to fall in the opposite direction. This pattern repeated until they finally settled nearly a hundred feet below the south side of Hartford.

There was a sliver of light spilling out from beneath yet another door—this version rustic and arched—revealing a feeble glimpse of the dusty gravel that appeared to be the bottom of the pit the captives had just involuntarily been led to.

Unlike the latent access they'd entered from above, this door wasn't fastened in any way to prevent entry. In fact, when the final Deceiver joined everyone on the coarse landing, the door slowly yawned open, the motion producing a prolonged creaking of hinges.

The light that consequently flooded the foot of the stairwell was blinding, initially, and as five pairs of human eyes slowly adjusted, it disclosed the cramped pit for what it dreadfully appeared to be: some foul underground injection site.

Resting on a small, rectangular stone slab table, seemingly awaiting their arrival, were five perfectly arranged medical syringes, each containing a russet-tinged fluid. One by one the captives were ruthlessly jabbed in the arm, plunged full of the mysterious rusty liquid, and then tossed like expired meat through the close rustic door and into an appointed division of the city's underground network.

High above and north of the city's sunken bowels where five of their own were now subjugated, the remaining members of Hugh's group spent the inclement autumn night winding their way back into the heart of the city. Not long before the day began to dawn its first shade of grey, they stumbled across the Bushnell Park boundary, and until Hugh eventually spotted two noticeably unsure individuals exiting a cab, he swore he'd never trust another stranger in the city again.

———

Oddly enough, it was a *lack* of trust that ultimately prompted Hugh to direct both Ernie and Linden on their way, and to never affiliate with his group again. "The last thing we need is to be taking orders from a coupla tenderfoots like yourselves," he stated sharply. "So beat it! And do yourselves a favour—keep yer asses under cover!"

To that, Ernie and Linden didn't protest. They each gave Hugh and his withered army a subtle nod, then were on their way. Rather than risk the scanty cover beyond the park, they agreed to venture deeper into Bushnell's secluded depths. Hugh's right-hand man had mentioned that compared to the city streets, the park offered minimal incidents as far as Deceivers go—and though they had just been dismissed to their own battles, this bit of information only seemed practical.

CHAPTER 36

The Lamplit Intersection

By the time William Lynch's beat-up, old Jimmy squeaked and sputtered into West Hartford, it was quite evident that, like his scrap heap on wheels, the city was in a grave state. It had only been twenty-four hours since the published dream interpreter from Ohio, and his girlfriend, Christine, had tested the same vehicle's stability in a rather different fashion, waiving the majority of a second drive-in showing for a steamy, impromptu back-seat showing of their own. And now here he was (consciously against Christine's wishes), over five hundred miles from home, chugging eastward along Farmington Avenue like the dying breath of a black lung.

———

To his dismay, the young man who'd introduced himself simply as Shorty quickly realized that his plan to enter the Bushnell Park grounds by way of the Trumbull Street access would have to be . . . revised.

As his beastly Hummer roared south along the desolate lane through stagnant pools of rainwater, he noticed that the approaching T-intersection before the park inlet was currently flooded. Not flooded as in an inundation of rising waters, but rather an over-whelming flood of *Deceivers*. Hundreds—perhaps even as many as a thousand—had gathered in and around the Trumbull and Jewell Street junction, seemingly guarding the park entrance by means of sheer volume. "*Sshhiiiitt!*" Shorty cursed, his voice heavy with disbelief. Now less than a quarter-mile from the end of the line, he eased his foot off the gas, but didn't brake. "Gird up, girl," he alerted Shelly. "I'm gonna go straight at 'em, then attempt a hard right onto Jewell. Once we're in the clear we'll—"

"Fuck it! *Ram 'em!*" Shelly suddenly screamed with the hard authority of a battle cry. "No more dickin' around. My husband is somewhere in that park straight ahead, and this thing is like a goddamn tank on wheels—let's use it as such!"

Still trying to wrap his head around Shelly's dauntless proposi-tion, Shorty charged the brakes and brought the Hummer to a crawl. "Okay, lemme get this straight," he said, his expression as serious as a heart attack. "You actually want me to try and hammer this thing right through that giant clot of Deceivers up ahead, and then keep rollin' straight on into the park like they were no more than a few bugs against the windshield?" As he spoke, Shorty had abstractedly brought them to a standstill, and then furthermore had the "tank on wheels" creeping in reverse in order to afford the necessary runway for such a bold attempt.

"Precisely!" Shelly replied without hesitation. "Seems like you're already preppin' for the run. When you think we've got enough road, you're gonna bury that pedal so hard it'll pin our backs to our seats! And don't be easin' off until well after we've punched through the pack!"

"You're crazy, lady!" Shorty stated, shaking his head at the realization that he was actually about to take a run at this. "But I gotta say, I like your style." He once again brought the truck to a temporary halt, this time coming to rest before the towering City Place building at the corner of Trumbull and Asylum: a sufficient distance from where the Deceivers choked the T-intersection to capacity. From this outlying vantage, the multitude appeared through a frothy fog like a thick coagulation, lingering in the glow of the park's peripheral lamplight.

With the brake still depressed, Shorty shifted into Drive with his right hand, and rotated the beak of his Whalers cap from front to back with his left. He indulged in a deep breath, and then followed it with words. "Okay, Shelly, you've basically dictated our next move—and I'm about to make it happen. But I need to get one last thing in order before we roll." He reached for the truck's radio tuner and began to scan through the stations. "Ain't no way this is goin' down without somethin' *heaavvy!*"

Classic 99.3 offered Aerosmith's "Sweet Emotion." *Helluva tune,* he thought with an approving grin, *but lacking the required* punch *to lead such a headlong surge.* The River 105.1 was all aboard Ozzy's "Crazy Train." One could argue that a more appropriate song to usher the forthcoming events had yet to be written. At this point, the chugging opening riff was just heating up. *This'll definitely do if Old Faithful doesn't have anything to say about it.* "Old Faithful" was The Axe 106.9—a balls-out, kick-'em-in-the-teeth rock station that had been serving the Greater Hartford area for over twenty-five years. When Shorty summoned The Axe, the song filling the slot was already a good four minutes deep. But the timing didn't trouble him in the least; in fact, it actually couldn't have been planned any better if he'd tried. "Attention, passengers," he suddenly said, keeping the mood light in the weight of the moment. "Please fasten your seatbelts, as we're about to *ram* these fuckers!"

Shelly drew a deep breath of her own, exhaled slowly, and then offered Shorty a delicate smile. "Thanks for all your help," she simply stated, and then threw her game face on before bracing for yet another chapter in a seemingly endless nightmare.

Shorty was through with words. With a final act he jerked the stereo's volume knob to its absolute limit, filling the Hummer with the window-rattling aggression of Metallica's "One."

———————

It was long before William Lynch was arcing onto Jewell Street that he'd realized his spontaneous venture into Hartford was an epic misstep; he'd known it from the moment a ghostly chill found his spine as he'd seeped into the dark, seedy slums of the city's western sector. Every brain cell that had a say in decision-making had wanted to turn around right then and there, abandoning the odyssey entirely while leaving the memory of this wretched place to choke on his homeward dust.

Yet here he was, still pushing eastward against the current of his will, skirting along the northern rim of a massive park that seemed to rest like a polychrome carpet at the foot of a dozen high-rises. This was where William first noticed the soupy lamplight that kindled the northeastern curl of the park's perimeter. Though the misty fog smothered the glow, it was still welcoming in the sense that until this point, every mile seemed to swallow him deeper into the night's darkening cavity.

The same subliminal calling that had drawn him this far now whispered: *Where else to go but to the light?* And so it was toward the light he proceeded until he was forced to a sudden standstill. He hadn't noticed the mass convergence of people in and around a lamplit intersection until he nearly took the legs out from under a few strays. It was as if the fog had suddenly lifted like a curtain, revealing some staged, nighttime production with a mega-cast of damn near a thousand.

William Lynch found this sudden accumulation all too peculiar. Leading up to this point, the streets of Hartford had appeared desolate and forbidding—a capital city turned inside-out like a dirty brown bag, exposing its infectious inner disease. Granted, the hour *was* late, and the recent weather was some of the worst the state had seen in years, but he hadn't witnessed more than a dozen moving cars since he'd arrived, and even fewer the number of people on foot. And now *this*—a throng of night owls cramming a specific intersection like an outdoor concert was in store.

Baffled, William eased off the brake and slowly wove his Jimmy through a handful of other seemingly directionless souls. He approached a point where the streets met at a *T*, and he drew up across from the 55 on the Park apartment building. It was here that the crowd really clumped together, as they gathered in front of what appeared to be one of the park's main entrances. Drenched in vaporous light, hundreds of ill-defined silhouettes filled the intersection, while others had frayed from the pack and found the park's immediate patch of sodden grass.

Lynch doused his headlights, and then silenced his wonky engine, fearing it may never turn over again. With stiff legs and an aching back, he laboured out of the vehicle and shuffled toward the crowd in search of some answers—answers to why he'd not only been drawn to this derelict excuse of a city by means of the almighty dream, but to this centralized horde of night-folk, as well.

What he found when he advanced upon the group was a wave of cold, waxen faces that were collectively swinging northward, directly away from the park. Their dead eyes certainly weren't inquiring *his* encroachment, but rather that of a bigger, bolder threat that led with a pair of bright eyes and filled a lengthy stretch of road with the guttural growl of an angry engine.

With the backing union of Kirk Hammett's galvanic guitar riffs and Lars Ulrich's machine-gun double bass drumming, Shorty turned a desolate Trumbull Street into a thundering personalized drag strip. By the time he'd reached Pearl Street, he was already pushing what would soon be a seven-thousand-pound battering ram close to its limit, ripping south toward a tightly packed target at speeds unheard-of this deep in the belly of the city.

Just like she'd braced for impact in her dream when she'd dozed in Vicerro's cruiser, Shelly clenched her armrests, and with stiffened legs, fortified her position in the leather bucket seat. At this whirlwind speed, the passing buildings to her right had merged into a sustained blur, and her stomach seemed to be climbing up into her throat as if she were hurtling down the steel track of a roller coaster.

Now approaching impact, it was as if the militant tongue of Metallica's James Hetfield cleared the dormant fog and shocked the mob of Deceivers into a frozen fit of fear. For a fleeting moment, those strewn along the . . .

(*Darkness imprisoning me* . . .)

front line and those directly in the line of fire . . .

(*All that I see* . . .)

stiffened, as they considered the source of the rolling thunder.

For Shelly, when the sea of faces . . .

(*Absolute horror* . . .)

surfaced into perfect focus, she closed her eyes and clenched her jaw so tightly she feared she might grate her teeth to dust.

Unlike his passenger, Shorty went in with gaping, *crazed* eyes. He saw the sea of faces as a sea he was about to part with a ninety-mile-an-hour head of steam.

William Lynch had already accepted the cold fact that his days were numbered. A roaring machine was careening his way like a wartime blitzkrieg, and his ill-starred steps had positioned him front and centre among this group like the headpin on a bowling alley. Despite his inevitable demise, Lynch stood by his decision to undergo this venture. Interpreting the subliminal mind was his life's work, and it was from deep within his subliminal *self* that this city had come calling.

His final moments were spent in a prayer that never stood a chance. *Lord*, he began his holy petition, all the while catching a cursory eye-to-eye connection with a woman riding shotgun aboard the oncoming truck. *Shit, she looks to be more terrified than I—*

When the Hummer's polished grille first connected with the cluster of Deceivers, it pulverized through with the brute force of a locomotive. With an inflexible . . .

(*I cannot live . . .*)

stab, the truck cut a swath-like passage of ruin. The perpetual impacts thrust both Shorty and Shelly forward, their seatbelts holding fast, securing them in place. Countless bodies flew . . .

(*I cannot die . . .*)

up and over the vehicle like rag dolls, their blood varnishing the failing windshield like some ghoulish artistic splatter.

Though the propelling music continued to blare, the underlying noxious crunch of snapping bones could not only be . . .

(*Trapped in myself . . .*)

heard, but felt as well, as if driving over a craggy, drawn-out rumble strip of masticated flesh and skeletal remains.

Nearly through, Shorty continued to hammer the throttle, but he was slowing considerably due to the thickset unity of the Deceiver outfit. As broken bodies thumped onto and over the hood ad nauseam, the battered and blood-imbued windshield finally began to cave. Fearing that the glass would submit under the pressure and spill knife-like shards onto her lap, Shelly challenged the . . .

(*Body my holding cell . . .*)

unfazed Metallica frontman with a piercing cry.

Directly obstructing Shorty's line of vision, the windshield was now shattered into a mass mural of spider web patterns, and as Shelly suspected, was on the brink of imploding. *How many of these fuckers are—* Shorty began to ask himself, when the condensed mob suddenly diluted significantly, and he could sense slick grass under his wheels.

The mutinous Deceiver and his rider from New York City had pushed through the pack indeed, and save for the Hummer sustaining its share of scrapes and bruises along the way, they'd reached the park's interior in one piece. But just when they thought they might be out of the woods, a stubborn obstacle had other ideas.

While attempting to gain a true perspective beyond the mangled windshield, Shorty clipped a red oak, and the jarring impact sent them careening blindly down a bank of coliseum-style concrete steps. Luckily, the grade was gradual, but awaiting their involuntary descent was a scanty strip of walkway, and then the chilly depths of Jewell Pond. All Shorty could do amidst the chaos was pump the brakes and steady the wheel, but the truck's momentum carried them crashing through a rather deficient chain barrier (which was surely never intended to prohibit local traffic) before they plunged headlong into the drink.

For Shelly, the idea that they'd suddenly stalled and were now slowly sinking in a body of water was one that simply didn't register. At least not until Shorty's frantic pleas hauled her back into the moment, where she found him maneuvering at her hip to free her from both the restriction of her seatbelt, as well as the sudden state of shock that had seemingly clamped down like a vice.

Though the stupor was short-lived, during those precious few seconds Shelly's mind's eye had flashed back to the initial moment of impact. *There was a face,* she recalled. *For a split-second, right before I closed my eyes and we began ploughing through the pack, I made direct eye contact with an innocent man who stood squarely in our path.*

He'd sensed that death had already called his number, yet he was still somehow . . . content. Who the hell was he? And how did our troubled paths come to—

"*Shelly!* For Christ's sake, snap out of it! We're *sinking!*"

They were sinking indeed, and a great number of Deceivers who weren't obliterated upon the truck's approach were now rushing to the lip of the expansive pond; from there, they just had to watch and wait, ready to pounce if the pair somehow managed to cheat their demise. And if the hand of death were firm enough to hold them under, they'd just stand by and cheer the hometown traitor and his out-of-state associate to their watery graves.

CHAPTER 37

Bandshell Blues

By the time noon rolled around, the day was already taking on a shadowy, gloaming tinge. The sky to the east was darkening like an apocalyptic omen, and the winds conveying the gloom west brought with it the salty flavour of the sea. There was an undeniable sense in the air that Hurricane Allan was priming to unleash her last hurrah, and the Greater Hartford Area was in line to absorb the onslaught.

It was shortly after one o'clock when the pressure finally gave, and the rains once again thrashed down on the city. More mindful than ever of Deceivers and their shifty ways, Ernie and Linden warily sought shelter in a location where they could rule out a blindside attack. Having already scoped out the potential refuge when the skies were beginning to swell, they holed up under the half-dome cover of the park bandshell, where they watched the conditions worsen from deep within the harbour.

"Are you hearing that, Ernie?" Linden suddenly asked, shifting his regard from the sight of the watery spectacle.

"I think a *deaf* man would hear it, Linden—sounds like bloody Niagara Falls!" the old man replied with his typical biting sarcasm, totally oblivious of the fact that Linden could actually be referring to something of consequence. "And not only does it *sound* like the Falls, but it feels like we're in one of those tunnels behind the Horseshoe Falls—you know, where you watch the surging water through the portals."

"Thanks, I'll keep that in mind for my next honeymoon. But I don't mean the rain, smart-ass. I'm talkin' 'bout people screaming! *Lots* of people screaming."

Linden left Ernie to the bandshell depths and ventured forth to the unsheltered fringe of the stage. From his new post, he could not only *hear* the desperate cries of horror through the raging downpour, but he could also *see* the source of the commotion. To divert the rain from his face, he held a flat horizontal hand to his brow, like he was shading his eyes from a glaring sun. A great mass had assembled a good thousand feet from their current position, and from what Linden could discern through the harsh elements, there appeared to be an all-out battle taking place. "Ernie!" his voice echoed back into the shelter as he hollered. "Get yer ass up here and check this shit out!"

The prospect of forsaking the dry haven to stand out in a drencher for the ages was one that didn't appeal to the old man in the least. But he'd heard the vigour in Linden's tone, and he went over in his mind how much he owed it to this gritty companion from his home state. For Ernie, this venture had certainly been a long time coming, and this stranger had seemingly surfaced out of the blue and ignited its fire—a fire they'd need to keep burning strong as they tramped through the bleak nature of this foreign land.

When Ernie reluctantly crossed the threshold where the bandshell stage was no longer under cover, the rush of rain that engulfed him was every bit the drink he'd expected. "This better be good, friend!" he asserted above the hissing torrent.

Linden wrapped an arm around Ernie's shoulder, pulling him in close, and then steered his eyes out toward the struggle with a pointed finger.

To Ernie, the study was dank and inconclusive, but he now heard the shrill cries as they pierced the fabric of the fog. "Sounds like hell's rising over there, but Christ, I can't make damn near heads or tails of what we're lookin' at," he declared, shaking his head, and then promptly retreated to his place beneath the concrete canopy.

Linden had also seen and heard enough for now, and he followed Ernie's lead. The two spent the next five minutes or so wringing out their outer layers of clothing, all the while assessing the formidable violence still proceeding in the distance; then, as if they'd wrung out the clouds in the process, the rain subsided to little more than a drizzle, and they once again found themselves at the edge of the stage, gazing out over the open lawn through the day's signature murk.

With the memories of the previous night still like fresh wounds, Hugh Delabar and his hybrid band roamed the Bushnell Park grounds during an obscure noon hour. Tired and understandably wary, the group loafed along aimlessly like a herd of lifeless zombies. Hugh still uttered periodic rallying calls, but the amount of time between each was growing, and at this point the words just seemed to drown in the undertow of their plight.

Just after one o'clock, a jolting thunderclap seemingly split the bloated sky wide open, dumping its stock over the city. When the cloudburst hit, they were caught in the middle of a vast, unsheltered region of the park. "Well ain't this just *perfect!*" Hugh said to the heavens, his arms raised to his Maker as if to add, "*Enough already!*" When he turned to look out over his group, he expected to see destitute souls getting drenched to the bone, anxiously awaiting direction. But what *actually* filled his eyes was something that simply didn't sink in until after the first few acts of savagery had sparked the mayhem.

Seemingly out of nowhere, as if born of the torrent, a massive circuit of Deceivers had materialized, and now had Hugh and his undermanned pack fully encircled. Ruthless in their approach, they stormed forth for the collective kill, directing not guns or other assorted weaponry, but rather charged syringes, at all forms of exposed flesh. Desperate appeals were lost in the resonant roar of the rain as the scene rapidly came to resemble the fields of past wars. Some attempted to flee the tightening Deceiver barrier, while others tried to defend from within it. But in the end, all cases drew to the same cold conclusion: once the needle's toxic drip was driven home, it was essentially lights-out within a matter of seconds.

Hugh Delabar—the man who'd rallied these tyro-troops back at the Hilton, and in a short time had come to speak on their behalf—was one of the first to fall. His blindsided injection straight to the jugular was surely enough to topple him, but he sustained an additional needle jab in the crook of the elbow for good measure.

As if following his lead right until the very end, when the big man went down, the others soon fell victim as well. A mere six minutes had elapsed from the moment the Deceivers first pounced to the moment the last of the forty-three heartbeats stopped pumping life. When it was all said and done, the grisly remains sprawled out over the muddy lay of the land like a pile of lifeless earthworms.

For the Deceivers, there was imperative work yet to be done. The next order of business was to marshal the deceased into the first of two arrangements called Perigee Paradigms: ring-like formations that embody the almighty orb of the night. The "surface" arrangement—consisting of the fresh corpses—would be the preliminary operation. Its correlative design, the "*sub*surface" arrangement—a comprehensive, subterranean collection of animate captives—was well underway by this point, but it was still roughly twelve hours from its true realization.

With more than two Deceivers per body, each lifting and dragging their share of dead weight along the spongy surface, the first Paradigm quickly began to take shape. There, one by one, in the centre of the great open space, the Deceivers laid the bodies in place, constructing a continuous arc until the final corpse conjoined with the first, fusing the ring of mortal remains.

The Deceivers then scattered like mice to tend to further duties—all but one, that is. A single, beguiling figure endured, standing at the centre of the silent circle like a gothic sundial. It was a woman draped in a long black robe that dusted the earth with the breeze. Her jet-black hair fell long and straight and became lost in the shade of the gown.

The woman's soulless, sunken eyes spared short time to scan the lifeless revolution around her before she drew a red article from the depths of an interior pocket. The item, clenched within her skeletal claw, was a bound flag secured by a single strand of golden string. Far from a quintessential banner one would hoist high atop an aluminum pole or fly from the mast of a great ship, this flag was invisible to the human eye. Known to Deceivers as Illusory Flags, these unique markers exist in two distinctly dissimilar forms. To the living, they dwell deep in the gardens of the mind, as they are only perceivable through the subliminal windows of dreams. They also inhabit the physical world, but can only be discerned through the eyes of the Deceivers.

With the single pluck of a raw-boned finger, the woman untethered the string. From a slightly protruding golden steel rod wrapped within the velvety material, she then unfurled the flag. She raised the rod upright and high, and then released a catch at the base. A resoundingly sharp mechanical *snap* nearly woke Hugh and his army from the dead as the rod extended earthward in a lightning-quick telescoping fashion, piercing the soggy ground like a necromantic dagger. Below wafts of rising smoke that augmented the flag's mystique, the singed ground crackled and hissed like a dying fire.

The woman in black stepped back to take in a broader scope of her work. And then, as if on cue, a stiff breeze ran the open field and exposed the flag's seductive charm like some monumental unveiling. Not even the weighty gloom of the day could subdue its vigorous appeal—its *life*. Dancing in the wind and rain on its plush vertical stage were four majestic characters of a golden calligraphic font:

RD #7

The witchy Deceiver could feel the pulse of the flag's cryptic energy as it radiated from the core of the chosen city. With the first Perigee Paradigm now complete, and the seventh and final Illusory Flag in place, it was time for the occult woman in black to move on to the next phase of the grand scheme. With one hand now clasping the handle of a black cane previously cloaked beneath her villainous vestment, she turned her back to the banner. Behind her the flag continued to stir, whispering a malevolent fortune into the crisp breeze.

"You seein' what I'm seein'?" Linden asked softly as he gazed out into the misty silence from the fringe of the bandshell stage.

"Oh, sweet Jesus, are we goin' down *this* road again? You're aware of the fact that I'm older than dirt, right? Shit, some days I struggle to get a good read on my own bloody watch! Why don't you spare me the trouble and just *tell* me what you see out there."

Linden wasn't hearing a single word the old man was blathering on about. His focus was fixed on what appeared to be the peculiar aftermath of the distant assault. "I could be wrong," he began hesitantly, as if his words were mere shadows of themselves, "but it looks as though a *lot* of people have been seriously injured over there. I'm not seein' any movement. They're all just . . . lyin' on the ground in a giant circle, as if they've been designedly arranged as such."

"Is it possible that they could be . . ." Ernie paused, and then gazed to the muddy skyline, where giant freestanding structures huddled in the mist. The thought of Linden's "arrangement" theory danced in his ballroom with an ever-growing troupe of his own theories. ". . . our pal Hugh and his tragic company?"

Rather than chance a closer look at the carnage by day, they agreed to avoid the scene until the cover of night could mask their actions. As they hunkered down within the sanctuary of the bandshell, the remaining hours of daylight seemed to drag out into an eternity. Their empty stomachs rumbled like rolling thunder, and Linden joked that the resonant echo would ultimately be their undoing. Apart from a few pocket-friendly packages of airline snacks, neither of the two could say they'd had an ounce of sustenance since New Mexico.

Finally, the darkness swallowed the last breath of daylight, and with it they vacated the shelter that had served them rather adequately. Like nestlings finally set free yet tentative to fly, they inched down a set of stairs that flanked the stage. As their feet met the squelchy lawn, the night around them seemed to take on an ethereal quality, somehow both eerie and divine. The stillness afforded a prime window of opportunity to gain their target—to get to the inexplicable circle while the getting was still good.

Over the moistened grass and patches of slimy leaves they marched. Linden led the way with his senses trained on the shadowy circle site, while Ernie kept pace and—to the best of his abilities—gauged their surroundings. As they approached the scene, they braced for what was sure to be a graphic lesson in Deceiver savagery. Linden found himself thinking, *All I wanted was to join a laid-back astronomy group, yet I've somehow become an impromptu sleuth, working the wrong side of the country with a geriatric sidekick. What in Christ's name have I gotten myself—*

"Linden! Look!" Ernie had suddenly stopped in his tracks to fire the order. "Look over there!" He pointed a finger at a pair of ambiguous figures progressing in the distance.

"Yeah, okay, I see 'em," Linden replied after a quick study. "And it's a miracle that *you* can see 'em, given your spiel about how your vision is sketchy on a good day."

"Just be thankful I *did* spot 'em, kiddo, 'cause they're comin' this way!"

In this case Linden hoped that the old man's perception *was* erroneous, but he quickly found that the pair of silhouettes were indeed advancing in their immediate direction. "Ahh, shit. You got some more gallop in ya?"

Ernie remained in his place, squinting out into the obscurity. "That would be the plan if I didn't already have one foot in the grave," he then replied, "and we actually had someplace to run *to*. Besides, I'd rather take my chances with these two than spend another bloody minute cooped up in that bandshell!"

The shapes continued to close in without hesitation. Now a mere ten yards away, they finally appeared as they were: two men, presumably in their early 50s, both of medium height and build, with one of them toting a duffel bag low to the ground. The other man paused, and then spoke with an unwavering confidence. "Trust me, yous don't want any part of that infernal circle." He glanced toward the deceased, and then swung his eyes back to Linden and Ernie. "Now listen up, unless you wanna become supplementary links in that chain, I'd strongly suggest you abandon whatever it is you're planning to do over there and accompany my friend Mason and me over to that pavilion." The stranger directed their focus toward an outlying shelter, vaguely visible through the wispy veil.

Again, the two from New Mexico found themselves at a crossroads. They weighed the possible ramifications of their next move like the city of Hartford had become an impossibly large chessboard. Had they fortuitously stumbled upon some essential reinforcements? Or were they being underhandedly ushered into an inescapable corner?

"What's at the pavilion?" Ernie inquired with cold, suspecting eyes.

"The question isn't 'what's *at* the pavilion,'" the stranger replied, and then paused a moment to let the suspense hover. "But rather what's *beneath* it."

As Linden and Ernie considered the comparatively bleak Hobson's choice, Mason Greene stood equally apprehensive. The nameless associate who'd curiously escorted him from the Hilton lobby was standing at his side, warning a pair of strangers to avoid the hazards of a nearby incident, and then advising them to follow their lead, presumably underground.

Still carting the duffel bag that evidently contained an imperative article—a cane that was mysteriously left to him back in Bellevue, and was supposedly a key to unlock God only knew what—Mason suddenly felt an inexplicable connection to the younger of the two men before him.

Linden was experiencing a similar enigmatic pulse, himself—a hazy sensation of familiarity as he studied the man with the duffel bag. *I've seen this guy before . . . and just recently. But where? Wait! Is it possible he's—*

"All right, let's go with 'em!" The sharp tone of Ernie's voice was enough to yank both Linden and Mason from their respective moments of ruminative uncertainty. The old man then further addressed his travelling companion. "Like the man said, we'd do well to avoid the scene over there. Cripes, we've become so caught up in this venture that we've heedlessly let our guards down—forest for the trees, ya know? But, I think we were still somehow meant to've nosed our way out into this field—meant to've met these two so they could basically give our heads a shake. I can't see why we shouldn't at least follow 'em over to the pavilion, and then just play our next hand accordingly."

Though justly hesitant, Linden was ultimately sold on Ernie's angle. The concept of proceeding as a foursome held a reassuring appeal, and an extended opportunity to place the man with the duffel bag was a welcome one.

INTERLUDE

Cool in the Loam

Hoyt again.

We're getting there, aren't we, reader? Or what I should say is, *you're* getting *here*—to the Institute of Living. Hopefully when you arrive, the calendar will have had time to flip to autumn though; it's currently summer here in the Connecticut capital, and the days are bathed and blistered in unsparing heat. For the other patients and orderlies, the courtyard, with its high surrounding walls, must feel like an open casket that lowers into hell as the sun rises. But not for me and my companion—whom will be properly introduced in due time. The two of us are rather comfortable as we rest on our bench in the shade, next to the garden of cool loam, where we continue to reap from the sand, silt, and clay.

Quick question before I go, reader: Are you ready for some magic? Please step through the door and proceed.

PART
V

And if your head explodes with dark forebodings too
I'll see you on the dark side of the moon

— Roger Waters

CHAPTER 38

Floating Font and the Synchronistic Door

Of the four men who'd been drawn together in the park by a mysterious hand, only one of them could discern the fluttering flag in the shadowy distance. Not only could he *see* the velvety banner waving within the ring of cold corpses, but he could also *hear* the song it was dispensing into the breeze. Knowing that time was now certainly of the essence, he chose this moment to share some key pieces of information with the three out-of-towners.

"I'm gonna make this quick," he began. "Before we break for the pavilion, you'll all have a better understanding of things if I come clean to you about who—and *what*—I actually am. So, to put it quite bluntly, my name's Hoyt Colston, and I'm the head mutineer against the Devil incarnate. Right now, he's a lot closer than you'd probably like to know, as he's currently lining this city up for an epic undoing."

"The *head* mutineer?" Ernie suddenly questioned with a puzzled stare. "How many of yous are we talkin' about here, exactly? Because if that circle of death over there was part of your rebellion, then we're *all* up shit creek!"

Colston appeared to sniff the wind like a wolf before he replied, "They weren't part of our rebellion, specifically, but I guess in the grand scheme of things, we're all up against the same adversary. You see, we're what you call Deceivers. But like I said, we're—"

"Whoa, hold up, buddy! You're a goddamn *Deceiver*?" Linden violently broke in on Hoyt's words. All the while, Mason Greene suddenly began to feel as if he was more than a little out of the loop. These people were starting the toss the word "Deceiver" around like a traditional title.

Hoyt Colston planned to have already been on the move again by now, but he understood the circumstances. He spent the next few minutes explaining that, though he was indeed a Deceiver, his agenda was defined, and his actions were dead set against what the Deceiver Overlord—his supposed leader—had in store. It was here that he offered up a simple ultimatum: "Come with me right now and give yourself a fighting chance against this evil, or end up dead and bloated like that unlucky group over there."

Whatever the man who'd led him from the Hilton had claimed to be, Mason wasn't about to relinquish his assistance at this point. And Linden and Ernie had already agreed to continue rolling the dice in their growing game of intuition.

The pair from New Mexico and the solo act from Washington followed Hoyt Colston's lead as they gained the targeted pavilion. The hike was a relatively short stretch of open space over a slight incline. As they approached, Hoyt called upon Mason to kindly remove the cane from his duffel bag, as its alchemic spark would soon be required.

When the group attained the airy structure, they found it cold and deserted. Apart from the listless candles that were the pavilion's banked pot lights, the shelter possessed all the warmth of a case of frostbite.

Hoyt promptly guided the three men around the side of the building, where he paused before a pair of forest-green public restroom doors that stood about fifteen feet apart. A single pot light hung directly above each door, the weak glow revealing the bold Men and Women placards. A weather-beaten notice clung to the surface of the women's door, rustling in the chilly autumn breeze. It read as follows:

attention:

to Further serve the busHnell pArk commUnitY, oUr rEstroom FaciLities are curreNtly undergoing a renOvaTion process, With a targeteD completion date set For earlY apRil. In the mEantime, wE apoLOgize foR any inconvEnience.

—hartford parks and Recreation Division

"Now listen up!" Colston announced as he tore the bulletin from the door with a sweeping stroke. "I reckon this next bit'll come across as quite absurd, but I suggest you look at it as more an introduction to what certainly lies ahead." He held the paper up like an unfurled scroll for the others to study, then continued. "To your eyes, this piece would pass as no more than a common announcement with a peculiar arrangement of block capitals. Correct? Where in *my* reality, I recognize it as an invite into the subsurface of the city, left by those who have already breached this particular ingress."

It was at this point that Mason was asked to hand over the cane. Following a brief hesitation and a quick glance toward Ernie, as if the elder statesman should authorize the deed, the pilot obliged. The trio then watched in wide-eyed wonder as Colston, now handling the bulletin in a flat, horizontal position, held the charred cane to the text like a pointing stick, prompting the initial stage of the script's cryptic conversion. The cane's tip was seemingly mimicking a magnet, as it peeled every one of the twenty-six block capitals clean off the page with a distinct, Velcro-like ripping sound.

Before three mouths agape, the letters hovered six inches above the paper, floating fast like hummingbirds. Then suddenly, the lowercase letters remaining on the page vanished in tiny plumes of smoke, as if they couldn't go on living in the absence of their capitalized companions. The floating font then plunged back down upon the page without the cane's assistance, and Hoyt lifted the notice vertical to reveal the capitals as they now rested:

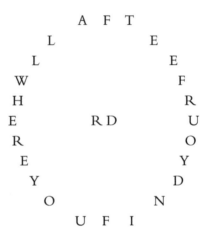

The trio huddled in close to Hoyt and his mysteriously modified bulletin. After a good ten seconds of studying the wizardly word circle—one that eerily resembled the contour of the corpses resting in the distance—Mason was the first to decipher its counterclockwise arrangement. He went over the curious phrase three times in his head, and just as he declared himself ready to speak it aloud, two unfamiliar figures cautiously crept out of the shadows and announced themselves.

A middle-aged man drenched to the bone and donning a sopped Red Sox cap led the approach. An attractive woman about ten years his junior followed on his heels, equally soaked, her long hair falling straight and heavy, and still dripping from the tips. "Please excuse our shifty approach," the woman began. Her tone was delicate, though her demeanour exuded confidence. "The last thing we need is for yous to mistake us for the evil that surrounds us. I'm Janelle—Janelle Crawford. And this here's Luke Sheehan. We're lookin' for our friend who—"

Mason then caught everybody off guard when he suddenly lashed out in a verbal attack—not toward the woman who currently held the floor, but toward the man she'd just introduced as Luke. "*Hey!* You're the *fucker* who ran me down in the lobby!" Mason snarled as he aimed a pointed finger to his facial wound before edging in Luke's direction. "Gave me a nice little gash, then scampered off with some other gutless wonder!"

It was plain to Hoyt that things were on the verge of spiralling out of control, and seeing as each passing minute felt like a lifetime of missed opportunity, the timing of such a delay would almost certainly prove costly in the end. He sensed these two men might even come to blows if he didn't intervene and explain that they were in fact on the same side, and fighting the same formidable enemy. "Eeeasy now," he stated in a calm yet assertive voice, his arms outstretched between Mason and Luke, keeping them out of striking distance of each other.

Since the moment he and Janelle had respectfully advanced upon the group of four, Luke had yet to utter a single word. He had absolutely no intentions of partaking in any form of a fight, but he also couldn't deny that he wasn't without fault in the matter. When he'd fled the Element 315 lounge in the Hilton lobby, he'd done so in such a flurry that his hard contact with Mason had practically gone without notice. Now standing within five feet of the man he'd inadvertently struck, Luke could see the damage he'd inflicted upon his face, and a pang of guilt washed over him.

"Let's let bygones be bygones," Hoyt declared firmly, and then gave each of the two men a scathing glare and held it strong until he felt it fit to lower his arms. "We need to simmer down and understand that there are bigger matters on the table here." When tensions abated, Hoyt looked to Luke and Janelle and spoke with a composed air. "Listen, I'm gonna assume the two of yous aren't out here at this pavilion because you're scouting a future cookout site."

"We're here because we've lost someone who should still be somewhere in this vicinity," Luke finally broke his silence while removing his cap to wipe his brow with the back of his hand. "And we couldn't help but wonder if you guys might know somethin' about that."

Hoyt Colston didn't know the specific person these two were after. However, he *did* know that whoever it was, they'd presumably been taken through what was known to Deceivers as the Synchronistic Door, and then from there, ushered down into a concrete rotunda that rested below the park's surface like a prodigious underground bunker. Rather than share that grim reality in such terms, Hoyt proposed that they simply tag along with him and the others, as they were on the verge of making their move into the underground themselves. For the benefit of the two newcomers, Hoyt rehashed how he was leading a mutiny against the malevolent force now eating away at the city from the inside out, and that the pair of them would surely stand a better chance of survival if they joined their imminent descent.

Luke and Janelle furtively conversed, and concluded that if they'd had any *other* plan, this one would be too risky. The surface of the city had wasted into a widespread epidemic, and they could only imagine what kind of damnable world awaited below it. But they were fresh out of options, and though the offer presented to them was anything but inviting, it at least tripled their head count, and could possibly offer insight as to Jeremy's whereabouts.

Luke wagered a step toward Mason and offered a reconciling hand. He admitted fault in his aggression and sympathized with Mason's wound, but asked for understanding given the state of the Deceiver-infested hotel.

Mason took a step forward of his own and met Luke's offering with a firm grip. "Must say, you pack a pretty good wallop . . . for a Red Sox fan," he joked, and with that, the tension around their engagement seemed to lift and float away on the cool, whispering breeze.

Hoyt Colston offered a single nod to the resolve, and then quickly brought things back around to the business end. He brought Luke and Janelle up to speed as far as the cryptic bulletin he'd swiped from the restroom door, and then Mason took this opportunity to pick up where he'd left off before he was suddenly interrupted. "Fall where you find your feet!" he stated with a proud sentiment. "The circle on the sheet—read it counterclockwise from the top! Fall . . . where . . . you . . . find . . . your . . . feet."

"Nice work!" Hoyt confirmed the relatively simple decryption, and then regarded the five uniquely inquisitive expressions that sought an explanation. "But unfortunately, that was the easy part. As for what the hell it actually *means*—your guesses are as good as mine. Right now, I can only assume that when we get on the other side of that door, the message will somehow come into play at some point." While the others ran the ambiguous instruction over in their heads, Hoyt went on to explain how the *RD* at the centre of the word circle was a prime example of how Redeemer Deceivers love to flaunt their identity. He glanced to the fresh flag in the distance that only his eyes could perceive, boasting its *RD* seal in a sharp calligraphic flair.

With everybody now on board, Hoyt announced it was time to move forward—then he corrected himself by stating that *downward* would be the more accurate bearing. He promptly marched over to the women's restroom door and touched the cane's tip to its surface. The others formed a semicircle before the entrance in anticipation of the next act of inconceivable sorcery.

Hoyt began to trace an outline of an arched door within the rectangular frame. Then, down from the peak, where the arch met in the middle at a single point, he drew a straight line all the way to the ground. Following his seemingly invisible sketch, he took a dozen backward steps, and strongly advised the others to do the same. He still had possession of the cane, but when it suddenly began to glow to a vermilion hue and burn like hot coals, he cast it to the ground. Awestruck, the group observed the spoiled walking stick as it hissed in the grass, and then lost its flare as quickly as it had materialized. "The *door!*" Hoyt cried out. "Forget the bloody cane! Keep your eyes on the *door!*"

When Hoyt had traced the Gothic-style outline, nothing seemed to come of it—not a charred streak of ash, or even the faintest of scratches left in the surface of the restroom door. Then, about twenty seconds after the outline was complete, with the cane now established on the lawn like a fallen branch, the *new* door began exhibiting the first signs of its inception. As if on a time delay, a small, blazing glow suddenly appeared where Hoyt had first touched the tip of the cane to the surface. The refulgence then slowly scorched its way along the exact course the cane had taken, bringing life to the Gothic design. The trouble was, as much as the initial sketch was an imperceptible blueprint, this delineation quickly became enough to burn their retinas blind. Instinctively the group turned away at once, shielding their eyes from the dazzling glare in the process. They all held the pose for the duration of the framework, where the light then dissolved as if it were on a dimmer switch.

A momentary hush gave way to a swelling resonance like snapping wood that incised the foggy autumn night with the chorus of a million strident splinters. At a collective loss for words, the group rallied toward the source. What they found and observed in a stunned state was the remainder of the Gothic door's fabrication process. Rustic planks of wood were seemingly forging into existence through the cold steel of the restroom door, their vertical forms slowly filling the arched outline one by one. Once the final plank had settled into place, an ornamental array of steel fretwork bled out from within the wood, complementing the new surface with its elegance.

The group was so entranced by the spectacle unfolding before them that no one noticed Hoyt as he strolled back to retrieve the depleted cane from the ground. "Behold! The Synchronistic Door!" he proudly announced with sudden excitement, as if he were a stage magician whose grand illusion had just gone off without a hitch. "Shall we see what lies behind?"

CHAPTER 39

A Doctrine of Demons

As he travelled the unconquerable road that was the passage of time, he went by many names, and an even greater number of faces: Satan, Beelzebub, and Lucifer—to name a few. But in this idiosyncratic incarnation, the Devil reigned as the Deceiver Overlord.

Though he failed to recognize what the equally evil entity was that had embedded itself into the lunar surface when the event occurred, the demon spirit still praised its design and fed off the fallout as any devil would.

The passing years had whispered the finer details of the radiative emissions to the demon: how the human mind was the prime target, and how *multiple* minds were consequently connected through an intricate network of dreams; as well as how a deeper realm of wisdom concerning the lunar event could only be attained through the utility of two material artefacts: an enduring, hand-etched brass pocket telescope and an intricately designed, ill-starred moon globe.

The demon had embarked on a quest to find the two artefacts that were unquestionably linked to whatever was spilling the cosmic poison, but the hunt proved futile. Foiled, he reasoned that the search must persist, but reinforcements would need to be conceived and then promptly called upon to expand the scope.

And so in death, the Redeemer Deceivers were born, and the Deceiver Overlord was born as the Devil incarnate. As the demon had done upon the death of the Saferock keeper, spectral embodiments of a lesser standing began to flood the Initial World and, through the weakening fabric of the Dreamducts, also sifted their way into the dreams of the living.

The often miraculous and always predominating hand of fate would eventually unearth the pocket scope in New Mexico, where a sly Deceiver would practically steal the piece from the near-clutches of a previous owner. Then, after years of cutting a jagged trail of misfortune across America, the moon globe was seized in the state of Washington, where a team of Deceivers managed to secure the orb.

Slowly, the Overlord's followers amassed in the Connecticut capital. Though the two Reverie Redeemers were now situated in the depths of the city, the Overlord had them perched up high on pedestals like sanctified entities. The moon globe rested atop a skeletal, five-foot plinth like a giant golf ball upon a tee. Roughly thirty feet away, the pocket scope was positioned upon a similar stand, its lens angled slightly upward to accommodate the tunnel's gradual grade, where it was trained on the globe's minuscule black scar.

These placements within the underground waterway were anything but random; they were precisely stationed to receive, of all things, the moon. And not just *any* moon, for the glow that would irradiate this specific night would emanate from that of a perigee-syzygy moon.

Directly above the globe was a tight, vertical passage that ran some ninety feet to the surface of Bushnell Park. Having served the Army Corps of Engineers in the 1940s as a direct route to both lower and raise working supplies, the cylindrical cavity has long been capped by a manhole cover nestled in the lawn.

On this night, the plumb passage was set to serve an imperative role within the Overlord's scheme, soon to commence as follows: during the approaching midnight hour, as the moon's glow penetrates the gloom, an assigned Deceiver will remove the steel cover and enable the toxic rays to spill down into the channel. In a short time, the occulted globe will draw in and absorb enough sour emissions for the entirety of the proceedings. When the globe is charged, the next phase will not only employ the pocket telescope, but also a multitude of subjugates, whose sentience has been stripped by means of a tranquilizing injection for the sake of the most heinous of scientific enterprises.

CHAPTER 40

Aquarium Decor

Though loose ends were still being tied up on the surface, the pieces had fallen into place quite nicely down below. For the Deceiver Overlord, the long-awaited hour was finally nigh, and a simple test run was all that stood between the groundwork and the real McCoy.

Like the adrenalized energy coursing through the Overlord's spirit, the rushing water that, in an earlier era would have wreaked havoc on the city's lowlands, surged through the conduits with a turbulent force. Blasts of resonating sound filled the channel as the cold concrete sustained the flowing fury. The pedestals that supported the precious artefacts remained poised in the current like stable tree trunks absorbed in floodwater. The pocket telescope and moon globe were in proper alignment, and it was high time for the preliminary run-through to iron out any wrinkles in a plan that could ill afford any untimely setbacks.

"I'll take two of your finest," the Overlord said, casually requesting the assistance of his inferior Deceivers as if simply asking a butcher for a pair of premium sirloin cuts. The compliant subordinates wasted no time as they mounted the channel's narrow ledges and retrieved a detainee from each of the two sidewalls. As the captives were peeled from their positions, they left smouldering black patches on the concrete behind them. They were docile in their restraint, lost in a sort of fugue state as they were assisted down the mirrored, three-foot ledges and then ushered through the drink toward the mounted telescope.

The Overlord had sloshed his way to the pedestal before his subjects arrived and placed an eye to the ocular lens. With a subtle twist of the wrist he tweaked the moon globe into sharp focus, dialling in on its single black blemish situated precisely at the Apollo 15 landing site.

When he concluded that everything was perfectly in line, he stepped aside to allow his subservient followers to place the first captive before the scope. From there, the Overlord opposed the current and the slight gradient as he made his way toward the globe that rested directly below the lengthy vertical chute. He then promptly aimed his cane up into the circular hollow, where its tip took on a phosphorescent glow in a matter of seconds before an auroral surge pierced the cavity with an alluring blue brilliance. Despite its splendour, it was nothing more than a deliberate signal—a cue for an entrusted member of the Deceiver corps stationed on the surface to indicate that the pieces were in place for the dry run.

As the full moon continued to scale the night, the steel-plated cover capping the vertical channel suddenly took on a bluish glow of its own. A half-dozen individual rays stabbed skyward through quarter-sized drainage holes, while the cover itself throbbed rhythmically with its newfound energy.

The assigned surface Deceiver would know very well what this specific glow represented, for it was the one and only task attached to his name: it was the Overlord's indicator to marginally—and for no longer than ten seconds—slide the cover from its resting position for the test run. If all were to go according to plan, there would be a second signal just after midnight, this of the glowing *red* variety, which would declare the onset of the genuine article.

The only problem was, for the entire duration of the test signal, the surface Deceiver's attention had been pried away from the prompt. A sudden commotion had erupted to the north of his post, as a rumbling hellfire shattered the silence with a profusion of grisly, crunching impacts, culminating with a resounding splash in a nearby body of water.

"*Shelly*! For Christ's sake, snap out of it! We're *sinking*!"

With Shorty's strident words, Shelly finally snapped out of her muddled state, only to realize she'd slipped into a waking nightmare. If they failed to take immediate action, the nightmare would soon dissolve into an eternal blackout.

After slowly submerging on a relatively level plane, Shelly sensed that the nose of the vehicle was now slightly starting to tip upward, and the rear was leading them under. The surface of the murky water was now meeting the top of the Hummer's windows, and with that, Shelly broke into a panic. She went for the handle, and when the door wouldn't budge, she used her shoulder to assist in the task. Shorty was immersed in his own critical endeavour, but when he realized that Shelly was unwittingly creating a worst-case scenario, he sprang over the centre console to prevent even the slightest aperture.

Too late.

In her frantic state, she'd already managed to force the door open enough to seal their fate. Pond water instantly began to pour in and was now filling the cabin with an irrepressible surge. Shorty, now sprawled out over Shelly's lap, managed to clutch the handle amidst the chaos, but with everything working against him, he could neither pull nor push the door in either direction.

Even though they only had an extremely short time before the Hummer would become fully submersed, Shorty still had the presence of mind to fire off the crucial information Shelly would need to survive. "Listen to me!" he hollered in an urgent, yet somehow still composed tone over the rush of incoming water. "This pond can't be much deeper than ten feet. At the last possible second, I need you to take a giant breath—and you're gonna have to hold it! We'll quickly sink to the bottom, and at that point the pressure will equalize. That's when we're both gonna push open your door and then swim up to the surface!"

On some distant level Shelly was receiving the message, but she could do no more than nod and whimper in response. She was freezing cold and experiencing a degree of terror that she'd never imagined possible. Still positioned in her seat, the chill of the water tickled her neck as she prepared to inhale the biggest, most vital breath of her life. Shorty offered a final word of encouragement before words would no longer be feasible: "We got this, Shelly! Piece-a-cake!"

The Hummer's rear wheels were introduced to the bottom of Jewell Pond with a soft thud, and then the front end touched down right after. Now resting like a piece of aquarium decor, the truck sat stationary and silent below the surface. For the two trapped on the inside it was time to act—and it was time to act fast. Dealing with minimal light, Shorty and Shelly worked in tandem to produce a big enough opening through which they could escape one at a time.

Shorty frantically waved Shelly on through as she squeezed her slender frame free of the vehicle. He then followed with a headlong plunge through the narrow opening.

For Shelly, the underwater crawl felt like swimming through the cloudy fabric of a dream, yet along her breathless ascent she realized her deliverance was imminent. Finally, after what felt like an eternity of stifling suppression, she surfaced with a series of desperate, convulsing gasps. Shorty emerged from the depths some five seconds later and ten feet away. With the aid of the lamplight that lined nearby Jewell Street, he promptly sought her out and swam to her side. "Breathe, Shelly, breathe," he coached as they began to tread water with some ease. "Nice 'n easy now."

While Shelly was in the process of gaining her composure, a scan of the pond's periphery told Shorty that they were far from being out of the woods. A wall of onlooking Deceivers had formed along the edge of the water: a wall that looked to have no less than the entire northern lip of the pond's perimeter covered. He was already being forced to work out yet another escape. "Don't look now, but we seem to've drawn ourselves quite the audience."

Naturally, Shelly glanced along the fringe, and what won her attention wasn't the unfavourable mass along the northern rim of the pond, but rather an attainable open space that graced the south. To Shorty's astonishment (given their current trauma), Shelly then swiftly proposed a workable strategy. "We need to swim for that gap directly behind us," she began with a sudden gleam of confidence in her eyes. "But if we just openly break for it, they'll practically be waiting for us when we get there. We need to continue to face them, make a convincing move in their direction, and then casually dip *completely* below the surface. From there we pull an underwater U-turn and go as far in the opposite direction as our lungs'll let us. Wherever we resurface, we just go like hell for that opening and hope our legs aren't like rubber sticks when it's time to run!"

Shorty was impressed to say the least. Shelly had drawn up a long shot; but in their short time together, they were seemingly in the *business* of running long shots. "Okay, helluva plan," he stated with an assuring nod as the two continued to tread the numbing pond water. "But that open space will clog up on us if we don't do this like *right now!* You ready?"

The terror that Shelly had tasted when they'd first plunged into the pond had dissolved, and in its place was that dogged tenacity she'd shown when insisting that they ram their way straight on into the park. She nodded herself, and then uttered familiar words: "We got this! Piece-a-cake!"

As planned, the two faced the multitude of Deceivers, which they swore had nearly doubled since their last survey. "Deep breath, Shelly," Shorty counselled, and then made the initial break in the direction that they'd promptly counter once they'd dipped below the murky surface. Shelly followed, and then with a single pull of precious oxygen, became fully submerged before twisting back toward their target.

As she challenged the seemingly endless underwater course, Shelly, not daring to open her eyes en route, prayed her subaqueous stroke was enough to both get her at least *close* to the edge, and to keep a relatively close pace with Shorty. After a gruelling sixty seconds (the final ten of which she truly thought her marbles were being scrambled in a submersible microwave), she had no choice but to pop up for air. Her perception of her surroundings was unreservedly shot; the world a shadowy blur, and her body felt like a depleted mass of jelly.

Suddenly, a garbled voice not far from her could be heard pleading. As her vision slowly sharpened, a dubious figure stood alone about thirty feet away, on the edge of the concrete walk that skirted the entire pond. *Shorty?* she dazedly considered.

She was reeled back into the moment when Shorty emerged from the water only a few feet behind her with the stealth of an alligator surfacing for a kill. With the pair now conscious of each other's position, Shelly promptly made Shorty aware of the unidentified third party.

The voice from the edge was now directing its urgent yet deliberately muted tones to both parties. "Let's go, you two! You've come too far to stop now! They're gonna swarm us like flies on shit! Keep swimmin' toward me, and we'll lose 'em in the park!"

The Deceiver Overlord's obscenities rang out over the liquid surge that roared at his feet. When he'd gathered himself, he fired another wave of the blue brilliance up through the vertical chute from the tip of his cane. The steel plate that capped the drop was once again aglow with the voltaic light, but with no indication whatsoever that his appointed Deceiver was receiving the cue, empty seconds ticked away until they filled yet another costly minute. The Overlord's obscenities recommenced, as this piece of ill-timed negligence had already thrown sand in the gears of the grand scheme.

CHAPTER 41

Logic?

Right on cue, as if the archaic door could perceive the spirited tones of its creator, the two halves swung open laboriously from the centre, both sets of hinges creaking and groaning like relics being wrestled from a century-long slumber. Ernie, eager like a child to proceed, stepped to the cryptic threshold and thought, *Cripes, it's a good thing* both *halves opened up, otherwise we'd all have to shuffle in sideways.*

The old man's next observation was enough to promptly quell the fire of anticipation that had drawn him to the opening. From deep within the darkness a diminutive flame appeared to flicker to life, as if it were situated along a wall well over a hundred feet into the access; then, as if on some form of sequential timer, another fiery glow, deeper still, was born a few seconds after. Not liking the illusory representation of the restroom interior in the least, Ernie retracted his steps and joined the others once again.

"What is it?" Linden asked, reading the sudden apprehension in the old man's eyes. "Whadja see in there?"

As if Linden's inquiring words were never spoken, Ernie looked to the man who'd seemingly created some form of alternate dimension inside the restroom. "All I have to say is this: I've come too damn far to *not* drag my ass through that door, but there's no chance in this hell they call Hartford that I'll be the one leading the way!"

"Fair enough," Hoyt calmly replied, then promptly started for the portal. "My door, my lead."

Though Ernie had made it quite clear that he wanted no part in being the first one through, he still found himself tight on Hoyt's heels as they penetrated the shadowy space. Linden followed, while Mason paused to cross himself before slipping through. Luke and Janelle then stepped to the opening in unison. Both sensibly hesitant, Luke gestured with an outstretched arm as if to say, "After you," and Janelle accepted with a head full of doubt.

On the inside there were no signs of toilet partitions, sinks, or any wall-mounted fixtures that were standard in a typical ladies' room. What they'd accessed was a disagreeably dank, slightly downsloping passageway lined with sconce-supported torches that hung from mossy cobblestone walls. The space appeared to stretch on for a great distance, as the glints of flame reduced in size and strength within the deeper depths of the tunnel. The group found themselves inadvertently kicking up dust, as the ground was a mix of sand and fine gravel. Thick, musty air hung heavily, and Janelle had the neck of her sodden shirt up over her nose within seconds of entering.

Trying to keep the gang moving, Hoyt took the first few steps along the descending grade. The group followed, and when they had covered about thirty feet, the restroom/Gothic door suddenly slammed shut behind them with a resounding crash, the echo spilling through the narrow passage like a ripple of sound, shooting chills through its wary occupants. The report drew a shriek from Janelle before she whirled around to face the entrance. Expecting to not only see the backside of the cryptic door, she presumed she'd find Luke standing directly behind her, also analyzing their unforeseen confinement.

Janelle had known Luke Sheehan for less than an hour, but when she'd spun and found nothing but the cold, cavernous shell of the tunnel, she suddenly longed for his presence like she'd lost a lifelong friend. "Luke?" she questioned the void, and then spun back around to find only four souls receiving her troubled gaze. "Uh, where the hell is Luke?"

Standing frozen at a collective loss, the group could do no more than exchange muddled glances. With the echo of the slamming door now only lingering in the halls of their minds, the silence was as dense as the tunnel's stagnant air. Then Mason reluctantly spoke on their behalf. "I think we all assumed he entered with *you*. Did he not?"

Janelle's head was now a swirling squall of uncertainty; trying to comprehend the last few minutes of her life felt like trying to crack an ancient Egyptian hieroglyph. "I don't know. I mean . . . I guess I never actually *saw* him come through behind me, but I'm almost positive he did. He kind of just . . . motioned for me to go in ahead of him and . . . and I don't know . . . Christ! Can't we just go back through that creepy-ass door and see if he's out there?"

Adding to the perplexity of Luke's sudden absence was the current state of the door itself. It no longer held the cane-induced Gothic guise; instead, it had reverted to the solid green form that was the restroom entrance.

"Ya know, maybe he actually *did* enter along with us," Linden suggested. "Took one look at this . . . this catacomb, and then scampered right back the way he came. Hell, it was probably him who slammed the door on his way out! Can't say I blame 'im if he did."

Hoyt abruptly stepped forward and called attention to himself. "Listen up, folks. I'm afraid I've got some bad news." Though he spoke for all to hear, his eyes were pinned on Janelle. "Regardless of whether or not Luke was ever in here, we need to move on from this predicament. And by 'move on,' I mean onward through this passage, and not back the way we came." He once again raised the cane like a pointer stick, aiming it sharply at the transposable gateway. "You see, that door's a one-way ticket. Once it's closed, it immediately takes on its original form, and will only open from the *outside* into a women's restroom. The only thing that can change that would be if someone were to come along on the other side with one of these." Still flourishing the transcendental cane, Hoyt now stabilized it level to his eye with both hands, as if to mimic taking aim with an assault rifle. He spun and pointed the tip into the shadowy, far-reaching unknown. "Now let's roll."

Against her better judgement, Janelle followed Hoyt and the others as they recommenced their venture into the torchlit passage. But she didn't set in motion without a final glance to the door, and a hope that she hadn't seen the last of her newfound ally from Boston.

For the better part of the next fifteen minutes, the gradual downslope kinked and snaked like the Amazon River. Now deep in the hold of the dismal tunnel, the wall-mounted torches were still present, but they were infrequent and barely clinging to life, as if oxygen were waning.

With the funereal spirit of the winding course sinking into the group's collective consciousness, Mason suddenly shattered a run of silence. "I'll tell you all one thing," he began as they continued to shuffle onward, their steps still stirring dust in the process. "If I'da known that that goddamn door back there was the last toll before the express route to Hell, I woulda bailed along with Luke, back while I still ha—"

"*Stop!*" Hoyt suddenly bellowed, the echo bouncing off the walls like a pinball. Everyone came to a halt as Mason's gripe was severed clean like the work of a guillotine. With the versatile cane, Hoyt indicated a slew of footprints that all led deeper into the passage. Upon a close inspection, the group concluded that there were five sets of tracks, each mysteriously matching the size and tread of their own shoes. "I certainly don't know how, but apparently we've already been here." Hoyt declared, fully aware that the observation defied every form of rationale. "This illusory maze has got us chasin' our tails!"

"Impossible!" Ernie countered without missing a beat. "From the moment we entered we've been maneuvering this cave on a continuous downslope. The concept of us coming full circle defies all logic."

"*Logic?*" Hoyt scoffed at the word. "You mean to tell me you just watched me burn an accessible door into existence, and you're still stuck on *logic*? Welcome to the champion of all funhouses, folks, where logic—pardon the pun—gets left at the door. All you see, or *think* you see, is part of a grand design to distort perception. So, on that note, here's where the fun *really* begins."

Hoyt withdrew the now-folded bulletin from his back pocket and reminded everyone of its decoded message: *Fall where you find your feet*. In a rather disorienting sense, they had indeed *found their feet*, and now Hoyt assumed that somewhere in the near vicinity there'd be a place to *fall*—or, more agreeably, safely descend.

He proceeded to drop down on all fours and immediately began sweeping away layers of the fine gravel. When the others failed to assist, Hoyt promptly gave them an earful. "If you're all just gonna stand there like a buncha city workers, then at least *kick* some dirt around. I mean *Christ*! Do I have to spell it out for yous? Somewhere under this grimy coating there has to be some kind of capped vertical access—like a hatchway!"

Linden considered joining Hoyt on his hands and knees, but he opted to query the man instead. "Say, Mister Colston, no disrespect here, but can'tcha just use your little wand there again and, you know, sketch one in the dirt like you did the door?" As Linden alluded to what Hoyt had dubbed the Synchronistic Door, he turned and, seeing as they were supposedly retracing their own steps, considered the possibility of distinguishing the backside of the portal in the distance.

The torches around them had surreptitiously found life, as the passage once again gleamed with dancing fire. And to Linden's astonishment, the light revealed the entrance resting almost mockingly in its place, a mere fifty feet away. Staring at the access, his eyes were suddenly pierced with a dagger of brilliant light. A searing heat accompanied the glow and filled the tunnel in a wave. The others squinted and cowered at the blinding flash, and it was Hoyt, still working through the dirt, who made the disconcerting connection.

"We got company!" he announced with urgency in his tone. "That little twinkle is the work of another cane burning through from the outside!" The heat continued to pour in as the Gothic shape began to take form. Now up on his knees, Hoyt shielded his eyes from the glare and continued to speak in a pressing tongue. "Now I know this ain't an optimal time to bring this up, but yous need to listen, and ya need to listen well. This wounded staff I possess is one of *seven* similar canes—and unfortunately, it's the second weakest of the bunch. There's only one that ranks inferior to mine, and though it can still burn an *impression* of the Synchronistic Door, it lacks the juice to unfasten it. So basically what I'm sayin' is this: if our uninvited guests here are using any of the five canes that trump mine, and we don't manage to find a downward passage within the next minute or so, let's just say that shit creek'll seem like a lazy river compared to this."

The fear of facing whatever was attempting to breach the door was enough to put a charge into the group. Within seconds, they were all scouring through the silty surface like crazed archaeologists. Even Ernie, at his tired age, wasn't about to face the consequences because he couldn't get his ass down to the ground to help with the search. And it was a good thing he did, too, because shortly into his dusty forage he uncovered a rusty pull handle. The grip ran flush with the ground, bridging a minimal dirt-filled cavity. Just as Ernie ecstatically announced his find, the effulgence emanating from the door seemed to peak, as it drenched the tunnel with dazzling white light.

With their backs to the glow, the group swarmed to where the old man was now sweeping dirt from what appeared to be a circular manhole cover. An embossed strip of letters ran through the centre of a checkered pattern that made up its surface, revealing two words in a rather baleful scrawl:

THE RECESSES

In the short distance from where the group huddled over the steel cover, the glaring light suddenly diminished, and the door's wooden panels slowly began to swing open with a familiar creak. Hoyt knew their time was running dangerously thin, as a ruthless band of Deceivers would be bearing down on them at any moment. From a kneeling position, he went straight for the rusty handle. "I think it's safe to say their cane isn't the one I'd hoped for," he regrettably conceded before rising to his feet and exerting every ounce of strength into a pull. The cover budged, but only in the slightest. It was immediately evident that this would have to be a two- or even three-person haul. Hoyt pointed to Linden. "You! Help me with the handle!" Then to Mason. "You! When we lift the plate, I need you to get your fingers underneath and help us heave this sucker up!"

Now that she was no longer blinded by the fierce light, Janelle could make out several shadowy figures filing in through the entrance. "Better hurry, boys!" she warned, but they could only move as fast as the cover's weight would allow.

Despite the load, and a pair of corroding hinges caked with grit, the trio managed to raise the cap to where it held in an upright position. The hole that now awaited at their feet offered no more than a fixed ladder and a cold darkness that, by comparison, made their cavernous tunnel seem warm and cozy.

There was no time to stand around and ponder the unnerving depths of the shaft. Ernie was the first to act, and he did so by freeing a fiery torch from its mounted sconce. He promptly passed the flame to Linden and then hit the ladder like a man half his age. When his head was all that remained above the dusty surface, he paused and had Linden hand the torch back, and then advised the others to shake a leg.

Linden followed Ernie and his high-octane candle down into the hollow depression. Eager to flee, Janelle didn't dare risk another glance at the advancing riot; she attacked the cold steel of the rungs like a gymnast, dipping into the void in the blink of an eye.

With the horde now pressing in like a stampede, it was undeniably clear to both Mason and Hoyt that only one of them would have time to slip away through the hatchway. They exchanged despairing glances, and then Hoyt took the decision upon himself. "Take the cane down with you!" he insisted. "It still wields a trick or two. I'll try to buy yous as much time as I can. Now *go!*"

And so down the vertical chute Mason fled, reunited with the cane that, having witnessed its black art efficacy, he now felt unworthy of possessing.

The second Mason's head was clear, Hoyt gave the steel cover a mighty shove, its sheer weight bringing it slamming down in a deafening cloud of dust. After kicking a few strokes of dirt over the plate, he turned and found himself face to face with a barrage of traitor-spurning Deceivers.

CHAPTER 42

Engines

When the cold, clammy flesh of a cupped palm began smothering his face from behind, Luke Sheehan could feel his own suppressed roar resonating from deep within his chest. Having just allowed Janelle Crawford to pass before him through the cryptic ingress dubbed the Synchronistic Door, he was ruthlessly pulled away from the access and into the restraining clutches of an inconspicuous figure. Then, like hunters converging upon a catch, three others swarmed in and assisted the initial attacker, collectively wrestling Luke to the soppy ground. From this inferior angle, he caught sight of yet another trio of what were certainly Deceivers as they hurriedly approached from around the corner of the pavilion.

With his back now pinned to the earth, Luke continued his fight to free himself. Beyond the cold reality of his losing battle, he recognized that the two halves of the arched door were right at his feet, as they had swung outward to permit entry. To serve the progress and safety of his allies, he was able to extend his legs just enough to simultaneously kick each half of the door shut.

With the clunk of the impact, the group of Deceivers who'd pounced on Luke all shifted their focus to the now-sealed access.

What had been a portal of wooden planks and fancy fretwork was now in the process of re-establishing itself into the colour and shape of the women's restroom door. If only for a second or two, each of the four Deceivers securing Luke in his place loosened their clenches to behold the transformation.

Seizing his captors' transient moment of vulnerability, Luke wriggled his left arm free with a sudden start and swiftly wrapped it around the ankles of the single Deceiver fixed on his left side. Then, with a mighty tug and a hard roll into his legs, he forced the Deceiver to crash down over the pack, disrupting their collective arrest. From his roll, Luke bounced to his feet and sprang free of the octopus of arms that had confined him mere seconds earlier.

To his pleasant surprise, as he broke into a mad dash for destinations unknown, Luke failed to hear the squelch of footfalls in pursuit. With the silent symphony of the night fanning out before him, all he could heed in his wake was a single pronouncement: "Let the pissant go! It's that traitor Colston we're after!"

It was indeed Hoyt Colston, who was still technically one of their own, that this band of Deceivers were after. But having watched the defector cross the cryptic threshold with cane in hand, leading a pack of mortals into the depths of the city, they were now forced to obtain a cane of their own—one of the five canes not only capable of burning the required Gothic frame into the otherwise drab restroom entrance, but *breaching* the said barrier, as well.

In the short time it took this particular mini-cluster of Deceivers to locate a key/cane and begin the esoteric entry procedure that once again lit up the surrounding area with brilliant white light, Luke had managed to wind his way through subsidiary pockets of Deceivers and eventually make it to a seemingly secluded nook along the northwest edge of the spacious grounds. From there, the opportunity to flee into the streets was there like an open door, but his thoughts ran back to the small group of strangers he'd come to trust since gaining the city, and the idea of abandoning their plight was simply not an option.

Relishing the idle wink, Luke propped his weight against a bronze-cast sculpture of a common man kneeling to pet his dog. The statue gleamed in a wash of light from a ground fixture. A plaque at the man's feet simply read: Where There Is Love There Is Life. Luke pondered the renowned Gandhi quote and sharply concluded that such optimistic words currently held no place in Hartford.

Clearly the park—and presumably the entire city—was crawling with malevolent souls, and a rash decision could have him right back in their grasp. So, feeling like a timid child, Luke remained in his little division of the park that seemed to hide him from the vast open space. Adding to the appeal of the refuge was the thick course of shrubbery and trees around him, and the lamps that lined the park's northeastern rim were too distant to throw their ghostly glow on this remote sector.

After a little less than an hour of biding his time behind the veil of scrappy hedges and brush, Luke was spooked out of his quiescence when the ailing racket of an approaching vehicle began ripping through the velvety night. Without thought, he skipped over to an evergreen hedge that lined the park boundary along Asylum Street. In this moment, he realized that before now he hadn't seen but a single vehicle since he'd left his own set of wheels back at the Hilton.

The sound of choking emissions and an engine in disrepair now peaked as an old GMC Jimmy laboured past him and continued to sputter along its eastward course. The truck was moving at little more than a crawl, and Luke was certain that if this shitbox were to ever attempt highway speeds, it would simply implode on itself and go up in a violent blaze of neglect.

Whatever this diversion represented, it was enough to tow Luke's curiosity along with it amidst its foul discharge. With the pace of an easy jog, he was able to keep the Jimmy in sight as it followed the southeast bend where Asylum Street became Jewell Street. Still jogging within the park perimeter, Luke began to ease up when the glow of brake lights suddenly inflamed the soupy fog. He came to a full stop when he spotted a sizeable body of water resting some fifty feet ahead that was set to impede his course at any rate. As he further approached what was either a giant pond or a small lake, he ducked behind a wooden bench flanked with steel armrests. From his current vantage point, the stretch of water appeared to be a good two hundred feet in width, and the length seemed to be at least twice that distance.

Thanks to the engine's orchestra of guttural groans, Luke once again picked up the Jimmy's position. It now appeared to be settling at the side of the road, below a tidy progression of lamps that lined the outer perimeter of this division of the park.

As he remained crouched behind the backrest of the park bench, something else suddenly caught his eye that demanded more attention than the intentions of the terminal clunker. In the distant mist, a little further on up from where the Jimmy had parked, there appeared to be a great abundance of shadowy silhouettes clogging the road—hundreds of them, he conceded, as his vision strove to penetrate the brume. *No wonder he pulled over.* There were also several figures straying from the pack, like workers out foraging away from the nest. "What the hell is *this* all about?" Luke's inquisitive thoughts had formed into whispered words, and with the Jimmy's engine now silenced, he heard them as if they'd have the strength to carry clear across the water.

After further assessing the scene, Luke considered moving in for a closer gauge of the crowd. That was precisely when he first heard a deep resonance growing somewhere in the distance. He closed his eyes and concentrated on distinguishing the source, and found it seemed to be in the proximity of the tight gathering up the way. It was louder now, and quickly louder still. It was another *engine*—an engine clearly running on all cylinders and seemingly hell-bent on blowing a gasket before ever abating.

Luke disregarded the possibility of being spotted when he not only rose to his feet, but also climbed atop the seat of the bench to give himself an extra foot-and-a-half of vantage. What he initially discerned from his new altitude was the same foggy wash of tenebrous forms beyond tree trunks and foliage; then, suddenly, he heard an indescribable bone-crunching racket that lasted about ten seconds and would forever echo in his memory. "*Jesus!*" he spouted after the raw carnage had ended, practically puking the word from his mouth.

The thundering conveyance had charged through the sea of bodies like a diesel-fuelled locomotive, and then, as if remorseful of the deed, promptly plunged headlong into the drink below to wash away the sin. Luke bounced off the bench like a cat with the sound of the splash. Though the calamity had occurred at the opposing end of the body of water, he'd caught sight of a dark truck careening down a slight bank before hitting the water in a whirlwind.

Instinct was now leading Luke to believe that the cluster that had gathered in the street were indeed Deceivers. It then suggested that if whoever was piloting that truck had purposely struck a good chunk of them down, they were on *his* side.

Planning to keep the water between himself and the dispersing Deceivers—who were now leaking down upon the pond's northern rim—Luke broke into a scuttle for the south side. The stretch was peppered with champion trees, and they served as station-to-station posts until he'd covertly put himself in a position to better appraise the predicament. Peering out from behind the mammoth trunk of a turkey oak situated fifty feet from the water, Luke quickly distinguished the grave state of the truck, as it had already been lost below the surface. All that was left to observe was the tightening wall of Deceivers as they continued to stack on the north side.

Torn between remaining in his place and attempting some form of hazardous rescue, Luke suddenly spotted not one, but rather a pair of heads near each other out in the middle of the water. Commending their resilience, his first impulse was to holler, but he refrained when he realized he'd only draw the enemy around the fringes to his still-deserted segment of the pool.

Luke ducked behind the oak and quickly tried to conjure up a plan. Then, after taking his eyes off the two who had escaped the sunken vehicle for less than ten seconds, he was baffled when his return gaze offered only the flat surface of the water. He figured they'd almost certainly dipped below by design, and he guessed they were likely making their way in his general direction.

Playing on his hunch, Luke raced down to the concrete path and anxiously began to scan for their emergence. Both the timing and positioning were impeccable, as one of the two surfaced before him, just short of the mark and in a fit of exhaustion. It was a woman. "Come on, lady! Keep swimmin'!" He repeated until a man emerged directly behind her with some stealth. Luke now directed his urgent words toward both parties, as a quick glance across the water revealed the Deceivers scattering like mice to make their way around to the very spot he now stood. "Let's go, you two! You've come too far to stop now! They're gonna swarm us like flies on shit! Keep swimmin' toward me, and we'll lose 'em in the park!"

As the seconds passed, Luke began to lose faith that there would even be an *opportunity* to lose them in the park. The Deceivers were closing in fast, and the pair in the water were seemingly mulling over their next move as if time was on their side. Finally, they came to their senses and freestyle-stroked the minimal gap between themselves and where Luke was now down on a single knee with arms extended outward.

With the joint effort of Luke pulling the woman's arms, and the man pushing her up by the rump from within the shallow water, she found her unsteady legs on the concrete walk in no time. The man then followed by hopping up and out without any assistance whatsoever. "That was straight outta Hollywood!" Luke stated to the winded pair. "Now, I know you're spent, but we gotta keep rollin'!"

Still swimming out of a fog of trauma, the woman thought she caught a ring of familiarity in this latest stranger's voice. Was it possible this was the bastard who'd instigated this whole mess by first calling her at work, and then later luring her husband to this wasted city? Their entire bizarre phone conversation then seemed to flash through her memory in an instant. She desperately needed to confirm her suspicion, but she was also well aware that this wasn't the time for a cross-examination. It was time to tighten her wobbly legs and *run*! And run they certainly did—like the hounds of hell were nipping at their heels.

CHAPTER 43

The Mad Descent

As the freshly acquainted foursome of Mason, Janelle, Linden, and Ernie lowered themselves into the cold depths of the mysterious hatchway, the sudden report of its steel-plated cover being slammed shut overhead sent an echo that washed over them like a waterfall of sound. From within the tight confines, they all gripped their respective rungs a little tighter, as if the reverberation could physically dislodge their clasp on the ladder. The air in the vertical channel was disagreeably dank, and the encircling walls were matted with moss.

With nowhere to go but down, Ernie continued to lead the way with his flickering torch in hand. To say the glow was essential to their descent would be an understatement, but with the old man basically having no choice but to forgo an extremity in the process, the others were at the mercy of his protracted pace.

With time to study his own steps, Linden was slowly becoming certain that their already-tight quarters were furtively closing in on them. Like the delusory bends and slopes of the tunnel above, the hatchway was seemingly distorting their perception. He was finding the drop to be progressively constricting, like a cone shape that would eventually choke their progress if they continued to tackle the depths. To supplement the design, the ladder was ever-so-slightly narrowing in proportion with the contracting walls, maintaining the illusion of a perfect cylinder.

Seeing as the steel cover—now a good fifty feet above Mason's position on the ladder—remained secured in place, the group unanimously agreed to take a breather and discuss their most unusual plight. It was here that Linden chose to make the others aware of his rather deflating observation. Following a few seconds of silence where the three pondered his theory, Janelle was the first to reply. "I guess when you consider our course to this point, nothing can be completely ruled out. But on the other hand, I really don't believe this ladder will just taper down to a dead end. It's here for a reason—there's a lot that goes on below this city."

"The lady's right," Mason piped up while adjusting his hold, allowing him to gaze down at the trio below and the unexplored emptiness beyond. The cryptic cane that had permitted them passage (and technically gotten them into this mess) remained clutched in his right hand. *It still wields a trick or two*, the equally cryptic Hoyt Colston had stated before sending Mason down into what the circular cover had labelled The Recesses. "Logic suggests—I know, there's that word again—logic suggests that there eventually has to be a connection to the city's underground maze of sewer channels. I briefly read about them in my hotel room— quite the complex network."

Having lived in Hartford for the better part of her life, Janelle added to Mason's summary of the concrete conduits as she clung to the cold rungs. "The story of the Park River runs rich in the veins of long-standing Hartford residents. At the time, the rerouting process was a marvel of modern engineering. But from what I gathered in my time here, the sunken channels have also spawned their share of urban myths."

"*Urban myths?*" Linden questioned from his position below Janelle. He began to feel the cursed timing of a calf cramp biting into muscle, and he adjusted his footing to shake the stitch as he spoke. "What kinda myths are we talkin' about, exactly?"

"Oh, Christ, I've heard everything from haunted auxiliary tunnels to sewer gators. I remember this story of some nut-job who supposedly purchased thirteen baby alligators in Orlando, and then drove them all the w—" Janelle's tale was rudely interrupted by a sudden grating sound from up above. The ladder seemingly served as a conductor of fear, as a chill found the foursome at once. As the steel cover lifted like a lid being peeled from a tin can, it sent the group scurrying deeper into the dark unknown like startled rats.

After whisking the others down into an ulterior hatchway, Hoyt Colston now stood alone and defenseless before a mini-cluster of his own kind.

A total of seven Deceivers had eventually flooded through the Synchronistic Door after losing their hold on Luke Sheehan, and then charged at the five infiltrators like a stampede. As they bore down, they witnessed four figures escape a Deceiver-designed circuit known as a Treachery Tunnel—a perpetual course of knavery and illusion. Only one remained on the surface, and sure enough, it was one of the known renegades conspiring against the Overlord.

"Where's the cane, Colston?" one of the Deceivers questioned in an easy tone, while the others cunningly began to form a band around Hoyt. "Tell me you didn't send it down with those worthless maggots you're protecting."

Hoyt knew the speaker as Maercus, the two having just completed their assignment of capturing the moon globe in Bellevue, Washington. He also knew that Maercus would surely see through any lie that he could devise like it were a spotless pane of glass. His only option was to speak the truth, yet somehow stonewall the process for as long as he possibly could. Every second he kept the Deceivers standing in the tunnel meant the others would be further challenging the depths of the hatchway and beyond. "Well, considering you don't see it on me now, Maercus, then I guess I did," he openly admitted in a taunting fashion. "But it's a dead issue—at this point, it ain't worth its weight in firewood. It was already debilitated when it reached Hartford. And now, after burning through the door back there, its charge has been sucked drier than Death Valley's ass."

"Just like the movies," Maercus promptly countered in his sly, raspy voice, "there's always the goddamn traitor who thinks he's above it all. Well, the truth of it is, you and all the other turncoats who think you're rainin' on this parade are in fact just playin' with fire. Your desertions are well documented, and aside from the grand scheme at hand, we're working to banish you all from the equation. As for now, we're gonna pay the big man a little visit down below and watch him make an example of you. And hey, maybe if we're lucky, we'll meet up with your maggot friends somewhere along the line!"

All it took was a subtle nod from their superior and the other Deceivers moved in from their tight circle to secure Hoyt. The defector put up a struggle, but right now it wasn't about escaping Maercus and his six-pack of thugs; it was solely about *time*—the amount of *additional* time he could manage to keep the steel-plated cover firmly in place.

When it was all said and done, Hoyt was able to buy the others an extra thirty seconds of drop time. Sure, thirty seconds wasn't much, but in a case where every second was vital, thirty of them could add up to be the difference. With Hoyt now collared, Maercus aimed his cane down at the circular cover. Then, with the slightest flick of the wrist, he let the magic do the rest. In a flash of white light, the cumbersome steel peeled back as if it were a piece of cloth, kicking up the dirt and grit on its surface that then gently fell into the vertical passage like dusty rain.

———————————

Little did the foursome know that when they had paused along the decline to ponder their next move, Ernie, the first to penetrate the hatchway, was only twenty rungs from yet another perplexing portal: their third such ingress since gaining the park's pavilion.

With danger looming at the height of the musty chute, Ernie and his now-waning flame once again led the downward charge. Mere moments later, when the old man first touched down on an unforeseen, peculiar landing, he thought that either his eyes—or his mind—were surely failing him. He was quickly reassured that he hadn't left his sanity at the top of the ladder when Linden met him face to face as they stood on what could only be some kind of floating floor. Before they knew it, all four were huddled close together in the cramped space on what appeared to be a transparent landing. Looking to their feet, they surmised that both the hatchway and the ladder within continuously depressed beyond their current stop, into a cold, immeasurable abyss.

Now seemingly no more than rats trapped at the bottom of a rat hole, they gazed upward in horror as the Deceivers were now clanking their way down the ladder with authority. In that powerless moment, it suddenly dawned on Mason that if the cane did indeed still hold a trick somewhere within its charred shell, there'd be no better time than now to utilize it. He recalled how Hoyt had not only called it a *cane*, but also a *key*. A key to its user's imagination, perhaps? With no other choice but to run with this credence, he promptly conceived an image in his mind.

Now whether it was actually born of this cognitive design he would never know, but the mere thought of another escape portal suddenly brought about a brief but potent convulsion within the hatchway.

When Hoyt Colston found himself surrounded by the double-crossed Deceivers, he knew the odds of his deliverance were stacked against him. His only hope was the cane; but he'd passed it over to Mason, who'd immediately slipped underground like a retreating mole.

With the steel-plated cover now once again propped up in the open position, Hoyt was forced to descend the hatchway ladder. Five Deceivers hit the rungs before him, and Maercus followed him down, and then one more brought up the rear.

After about a dozen downward steps, Maercus let his guard down, and Hoyt capitalized on his lapse. With the top of his head no more than a single rung from Maercus's dusty soles, Hoyt abruptly paused, then reached up and snatched Maercus's cane with an animal-like reflex. Then, right at that exact moment, like his actions had somehow provoked a disruptive tremor, the surrounding wall began to tremble violently. The ladder shook along with it, threatening to dislodge its load like leaves from a tree. The sudden shudder quickly receded, as the corroding stone wall began to spill dust and fine gravel in its wake.

The curious seismic jolt had left Maercus wavering and vulnerable. With the Deceiver's cane now in his possession, Hoyt corralled Maercus's ankles with his free hand and wrenched him free of his hold on the ladder with a mighty haul. Maercus tumbled awkwardly behind Hoyt, his hands flailing desperately for any form of purchase as he fell.

Miraculously, the Deceiver managed to prevent a full-on free fall by grasping Hoyt by the waist. As he held on, he violently tried to shake Hoyt off the rungs and down into the depths with him. With

Hoyt struggling to merely maintain his position on the ladder, the mix of Maercus's riotous exertion and sheer weight began to raise doubts about a possible flight back to the surface.

When Hoyt had seized Maercus's cane from below him, he'd noticed its tip was quite sharp—almost spear-like. With one hand still clinging to the ladder, he suddenly used the other to drive the cane downward, embedding the spike six inches into the Deceiver's skull. An ear-splitting shriek followed the soft crunching sound of the gruesome puncture, and the arms that were clutching Hoyt's waist fell limp in an instant. Maercus's dead weight promptly dislodged from the cranial implant as he plunged into a deeper hell, taking out a fellow Deceiver along the way.

Rational thinking told Hoyt that the only way out of this jam would be to challenge the single Deceiver above him. Scampering up the rungs, he once again went for the ankles. The Deceiver kicked at Hoyt's approach, but they were feeble attempts, as it quickly became evident that he was unsteady along the drop. Hoyt went for the plant foot, and unlike Maercus before him, this Deceiver fell without so much as a grasping attempt to recover.

With the now gore-tipped cane in hand, Hoyt frantically cleared the circular opening above, and then fled for the Synchronistic Door that providentially remained ajar.

———————————

From the very top of the vertical passage to where the group of four now stood on the transparent landing, the walls shuddered and shook about rock fragments and detritus matter. With no place to hide, they shielded their heads and faces from the falling threat.

The hatchway's peculiar landing quickly became coated with a crunchy overlay of fine rubble. Within a milky swirl of dust, Mason was the first to perceive the semi-protruding form within the wall that markedly resembled the size and shape of a submarine door.

The design was rectangular with rounded corners, and also like a submarine door, was resting about eight inches off the ground. "Will wonders never cease?" the pilot muttered to himself in amazement, and then shared his discovery.

The others marvelled at Mason's find, but a collective curiosity hung over their heads like a dark cloud. The timing was perfect; just when they were starved for a way out, a sudden tremor shook a layer of grimy crust from the walls, revealing a bypass. The timing was perfect indeed—*too* perfect.

Like a pickaxe to stone, Ernie cracked into the silence. "Twisted logic strikes again!" And though the words didn't explain a damn thing, they were somehow enough to push the foursome to proceed.

Before heading down into the hatchway, Ernie's quick-action thinking had afforded them a fiery beacon to light the way. But now the flame was little more than the glow of a Zippo lighter, and it was waning still. In the hopes that the light could still penetrate the dusty rise and disclose the position of their trackers, the old man gazed upward and held what was left of the flare high.

Meanwhile, both Janelle and Linden made a move for the suddenly exposed portal. "Let's see what lies behind door number three, shall we?" Linden quipped. Only half-expecting the door to budge, he tentatively nudged the handleless, solid steel surface. He was then shocked when it not only began to move, but it swung open as if it hung on freshly greased hinges. Without the slightest clue as to what might await them on the other side, the foursome shuffled through the debris and crossed the threshold in a matter of seconds. Just as he was the last to enter the vertical hatchway, Mason was the last to pass through the opening at its base.

Before he'd even had the opportunity to slam the submarine-style door shut behind him, the small landing at the foot of the hatchway was suddenly met with a pair of sickening *thuds*, followed by a third shortly thereafter. An eruption of dust choked the cramped space once again, with some carrying through the door and into their new surroundings. The other three had failed to hear the revolting clumps of the impacts behind them, as the resonating roar of flowing water had now taken their attention.

As much as Mason wanted to secure the door and put a wrap on the hatchway chapter, he couldn't help but verify who it was that had come within mere seconds of crashing down upon him from an unknown height. The dissipating dust ultimately revealed the trio of bodies lying in a heap, broken beyond repair. Their torsos had ruptured on impact, and limbs were snapped and splayed like those of mangled puppets. Whoever they were that had come to such an end, Mason was certain that Hoyt wasn't one of them, and that was enough to proceed.

Hoping to suppress their pursuers for good, Mason closed the submarine-style door behind him, before wedging a thin piece of slag into the jamb.

The group now found themselves tucked into a graffiti-laced concrete alcove that recessed from a voluminous underground river. A dozen short steps brought them out to the lip, where they overlooked a stream of surging water.

"The Park River!" Janelle asserted above the aqueous clamour, though the others had already made the connection. Below the alcove, a three-foot drop fell to a one-and-a-half-foot ledge. The ledge, and another on the opposite side of the channel, gradually arced out of sight in both directions along with the course.

Careful not to overshoot the mark and meet the fury of the river's force, the four hopped down onto the narrow projection. When they were all secure in their footing, Linden asked, "Which way should we go?"

Again, in a voice opposing the sonorous torrent, Janelle replied, "I'm pretty sure the direction of the flow leads to where the water eventually empties into the Connecticut River. That being said, given what we've gone through to get *this* far, why would we be looking for a way *out?* Though I still don't have the slightest idea as to what it may be—we're all down here for a reason." She then pointed along the ledge in the direction that would lead them against the underground current. "And my gut tells me that that reason lies thataway!"

Ernie and Linden pulled their eyes from the entrancing flow and briefly stared at each other. No words were needed here; they'd been consciously following their gut every step of the way, and there was no reason to start questioning what the woman was proposing at such a critical juncture. "No objections here." Linden spoke for both himself and the old man.

Mason had flown across the country in search of both his moon globe and adventure; taking the easy way out at this point would be like quitting a marathon with the finish line just around the corner. "Against the flow it is!" he boldly pronounced, putting any indecision about direction to rest.

In the hopes that their pursuers weren't challenging the door behind them from the foot of the hatchway, Janelle reluctantly peeked back into the alcove. What she both saw—and *didn't* see— filled her veins with ice and left her cold. The submarine-style door had seemingly vanished from its place along the back wall. After the initial shock, she notified the others in the form of a simple question: "Uhh . . . fellas, where the hell did the *door* go?"

Remaining balanced along the ledge, the others turned their backs to the angry underground river and joined Janelle in a state of bewilderment. Cryptic swirls of graffiti stained the nook from top to bottom, and in the exact place of the door that had permitted their passage mere moments earlier, a legible, aerosol-fashioned memo read like an opening line fit to the sombre works of Lovecraft:

FROM WITHIN THE
BOWELS OF DARKNESS
WE WATCH THE MOON RISE

CHAPTER 44

Monstrous Impact

Jeremy Lowe knew he was dreaming.

He knew he was dreaming because he'd been here before: *It was a beautiful autumn morning, and I was seated high up along the left-field line in Fenway Park, at the foot of a column supporting the upper deck.* This time around, though, he felt more in control, as if he'd been lowered into a familiar movie, the script resting on his lap to be revised at his leisure.

As he sat in the bleachers, Jeremy was cognizant of the fact that his *actual* physical form was roughly a hundred miles away, pinned to a wall of cold concrete somewhere below the sickness that had become Hartford, Connecticut. He was also aware that he'd been anaesthetized, and that this dream was the undercurrent of its influence. All he could do for now was delve deeper into the vision and hope that some subliminal answers would take root along the way, and then ultimately germinate in the soils of consciousness.

Jeremy was back in the left-field grandstand: section thirty-three. As in the initial dream, the setting was simply breathtaking, as golden sunlight drenched the jewel at the heart of Boston. The faint, distant drone of an approaching aircraft leaked into the serenity of the morning, informing of Luke Sheehan's imminent swoop aboard what would surely be a majestic Martin B-26 Marauder warplane.

Soon a young child named Isabel Fallbrook would rest her hand on his left shoulder from the row behind. During the initial dream, it was Isabel asking the questions, but this time around Jeremy had some questions lined up of his own.

The buzz of the approaching warplane grew louder, as it was about to swoop down between a pair of light stanchions. But something was suddenly . . . amiss. As his eyes struggled to pick the plane out of the bright sky, Jeremy felt a soft hand over his *right* shoulder. He turned, and as expected, it was young Isabel, but he then noticed a few *more* alterations. Her once-pink Red Sox cap was now blood red, and the familiar blue circle of the NASA logo no longer graced the front of her T-shirt, but had rather dulled to a detailed image of the moon. She once again had an arm wrapped around a fishbowl of muddy water, and with her free hand she followed the trajectory of the approaching plane with a pointed finger.

Finally, Jeremy caught sight of the warplane in all its historical glory, as it was now flying dangerously low. "Isabel," he said, beginning his bold cut to the chase, all the while realizing his following words would need to be spoken louder. "I need to know what a moonflaw is. This would all make so much more sense to me if you could just elaborate on it a little."

Careful not to spill a drop, Isabel rose to her feet and then bent to place her fishbowl on the ground. After straightening, she then lowered her head and touched the tip of her finger to what appeared to be a specific region of the moon on her T-shirt. "Now this'll sound absurd," she replied while pointing out to deep left field with her other hand, "but picture that big green wall over there as the surface of the moon—particularly, the Apollo 15 landing site." The droning hum of the plane was doing its best to drown out the child's words in a sea of twin-engined propulsion.

Perplexed on a whole new level, Jeremy did as Isabel requested. He bounced out of his seat as if he were a Sox fan following a deep drive off the bat of Big Papi and imagined the Green Monster as the desolate grey of the lunar surface. "Now picture the warplane as an undetected asteroid travelling at more than 75,000 miles an hour," Isabel continued. "An asteroid boiling with internal radioactivity that, to this very day, laughs in the face of modern science."

Jeremy didn't like where this was going. The dream had clearly veered off the rails of familiarity and seemed to be spiralling toward some calamitous end. The steel-winged bird had dipped within ten feet of the dirt infield before finally levelling out, and it was now heading straight for the Green Monster like the prodigious wall was the target of a kamikaze attack.

As much as he wanted to, Jeremy couldn't peel his eyes away from the imminent disaster. "Pull up, pull *up*!" he heard himself holler, as if his plea might actually reach the cockpit. The Marauder remained parallel to the ground for a short stretch and then, with minimal room left to maneuver, finally began to climb. From where he stood in the bleachers, Jeremy could read the plane's now-fatal trajectory. It was too late; the pilot had waited too long to pull out of the swoop and clear the towering wall.

In a sort of decelerated clarity, everything suddenly slowed and turned hauntingly silent. As though time itself were dragging a weighty ball and chain, Jeremy discerned the exact moment in which the silver nose of the rising Marauder kissed the hard plastic of the Green Monster. The proceeding impact then continued to play out before him in slow motion and, as if the calamity required commentary, came dressed in the muted undertones of the young girl. "'Moonflaw' is basically a code word used by both NASA and the United States government for an astronomical event that occurred way back in the 1950s."

Where there should have been a blinding ball of fire where the impact occurred, there was instead a colossal cloud of billowing grey dust. The entire grandstand trembled, as if a quake were rocking the Boston area, and within seconds the entire ballpark was choked in the leaden haze.

Isabel casually continued to speak as if the ashen fallout was to be expected. "The event and its mysterious details were withheld from the public due to general uncertainty and, perhaps more importantly, NASA's negligence in the wake of the incident. Surprisingly, 'moonflaw' was coined by neither a NASA employee, nor a member of the government. The honour belongs to a long-standing astronomy ambassador named Ernest Cowarth, who, believe it or not, is currently meandering the same underground tunnels in which you're currently being held captive. He's seeking a long-lost artefact that's pivotal to this entire ordeal: a preternatural pocket telescope through which he'd actually witnessed the emissive by-product of the lunar event all those years ago."

With what resembled a fine layer of volcanic ash, the familiar greens and reds of the historic ballpark were now dulled with a coat of colourless desolation. Brushing the dust from his clothing and skin, Jeremy struggled to comprehend the nightmarish scene all around him. "Oh, that won't hurt ya," Isabel announced with certitude. "It's only moondust." With the cloudy haze having nearly settled, she then aimed her tiny index finger at the now-visible impact site. "Look at what the old plane did to the giant wall!"

Jeremy wasn't sure he even *wanted* to see, as he knew nothing good could come of this. But just as humans are seemingly programmed to gawk at a car accident, he couldn't resist the urge to rubberneck the result.

The wall remained upright and firm, but what used to be the Green Monster was now suddenly the *Grey* Monster. The entire vertical surface had morphed into a precise replication of the moon's, with everything from hardened lava patches to impact craters gracing the new face. There wasn't a single piece of evidence lying at the foot of the wall that would indicate an aircraft had just flown directly into it. It was as if the Marauder had completely disintegrated upon impact, the ashes then instantly scattered over Fenway like a cremation gone awry.

And then he noticed it.

Precisely where the nose of the plane had met the wall, a fissure-like black slit remained, scarring the barren surface. Once his eyes found the mark, it seemed to hold his gaze in place, hostage to its mystery. "What's *that?*" he asked while pointing, his curiosity heightened.

"*That* is an exact reproduction of what the toxic asteroid did to the moon's surface," Isabel replied. To Jeremy's surprise, her once-murky fishbowl was now polished and full of crystal-clear water. A brilliant-orange goldfish swam in circles within, as though it had just found the open sea. Given recent events, the fish was by far the most vibrant object in the entire ballpark. "Over the course of time, when asteroids have crashed into the moon, they've almost always left your typical round, bowl-like craters. This particular asteroid in the '50s, however, left a most unusual crevice—both by way of its cleaved configuration, and its untold depth."

Considering the madness that had become Fenway Park, Jeremy never lost sight of the fact that he was in the depths of a drug-induced dream—a dream that wouldn't go for naught. Though they came wrapped in the queer fabric of subliminal weavings, he was getting answers—answers he'd need to retain when the drug faded, and the dream slipped away into a foggy memory.

Still submerged in the depths of slumber, Jeremy was still focused on the impact site, where he began to witness some strange emission spewing from the dark aperture. Countless black-and-white particulates were jetting from the hole before slowing to languidly rain over Fenway like cosmic mist. "Dream Particles," Isabel stated as softly as the mist itself, doing absolutely nothing to ease the weight of confusion from Jeremy's mind. "Technically, radioactive excretion from the buried asteroid."

"*Dream particles?*" Jeremy was still stuck on the initial designation.

"Picture them as more like atmospheric seeds, if you will—seeds that, over time, found Earth and germinated in the minds of its human occupants. These *seeds* then flourish into what are known as Dreamducts—a complex network of subliminal passages through which dreams can become interconnected."

As bizarre as the information was that Jeremy was receiving from Isabel, it wrenched his thoughts to Luke, and the initial dream they'd shared—the one that resembled this one before it drifted off course and became absorbed under a blanket of ash.

The charged asteroid, the lunar impact, the deep crevice, the radioactive emissions, and the interwoven dreams: the answers were starting to tie together like knots along a dangling rope. A rope he'd soon need to climb, and then quickly pull up behind him into consciousness.

CHAPTER 45

The Luckiest Man Alive

Emerging from the depths of Jewell Pond, Shelly—whose life had descended into non-stop horror—now found herself in a mad dash along a sloshy carpet of grass that led deeper into the unknown. Shorty and the stranger who'd mysteriously met them at the lip of the pond flanked her stride as the sound of their footfalls squelched like echoes in a diluted dream. She didn't have the slightest idea where they were running to, but given that the only other option was to stop and challenge the hard-charging throng of Deceivers behind them, continuing deeper into the depths of the park seemed as viable a plan as any.

About two hundred feet from the pond, as if the tracks in his train of thought had come to a divergence, Shorty suddenly began to veer to the right. "The Memorial Arch!" he shouted while making his move. "There's passage to the underground through the east tower. Follow me—we're not far!"

Both Luke and Shelly had absolutely no idea what the Memorial Arch was, or why they'd need to seek underground passage—but a plan was a plan, and it was surely better than running blind.

With the multitude of Deceivers still in pursuit, Shorty led Luke and Shelly to the foot of the imposing structure that was the Soldiers and Sailors Memorial Arch. Built from city treasury funds in 1885, the 116-foot Gothic Revival monument consisted of two conical-roofed medieval towers joined by a lofty walkway inside crenellated parapets fronted by a classical frieze. The brownstone and terra-cotta memorial was dedicated to all the men who had served in the American Civil War. A one-way street ran through the arch, theoretically splitting the park into two halves.

Feeble floodlight washed over the monument from a short distance, giving the impression of some mystical English castle lost in an ominous fog. Wasting no time, Shorty went directly for the east tower, and the other two followed. He led them to a camouflaged door around the north side that blended seamlessly with the tower's exterior.

Luke suddenly found himself in a familiar situation and couldn't help but to wonder if some form of cryptic magic would be required to breach this portal as well. To his surprise, the door was latched at both the top and bottom but didn't appear to be locked. Both he and Shelly gazed up at the towering memorial and wondered how exactly this doorway would lead them *below* ground.

Shorty manoeuvred through both latches in a matter of seconds and was now pulling from a recessed handle. Initially the door wouldn't budge, but when Luke moved in to assist, they were able to open it just enough for them to squeeze through. Now inside, warm light filled the steep, rounded space, the glow revealing a rustic wooden floor, walls decorated with commemorative plaques, and an ascending spiral staircase of cold stone. An interior handle enabled Luke and Shorty to collectively pull the weighty door closed behind them. When it lodged into place, Shorty could only hope its cloaked exterior would buy them enough time to escape.

"Didn't you say somethin' about heading *under*ground?" Shelly questioned Shorty through a shortness of breath, her eyes following the staircase that twisted to dizzy heights.

"Yeah," Luke added. "Looks to me like this elevator has nowhere to go but up."

"In case you haven't noticed during your pleasant stay in the city," Shorty replied after a friendly smirk that stirred his bushy beard, "*looks* can be deceiving."

Shorty told the two to take a step back, then went down on one knee just in front of the staircase's first step. Similar in a sense to the door that allowed passage into the monument's east tower, he suddenly pried open an access hatch that was camouflaged within the wooden floor. He proceeded to chaff Luke's elevator remark by reaching up to push an imaginary button. "Going down?"

Below the hatch was what could only be described as an underground continuation of the spiral staircase. With the tower's pale light spilling through the square hole, the stairs could be seen winding downward to an unperceived depth, the walls enclosing the drop now void of commemorative decor.

Peering down into the dispiriting access, the trio suddenly began to hear muffled voices behind them. The mob of angry Deceivers had reached the monument and were probing the base of the east tower in search of entry.

"We need to move!" Shorty asserted before offering Shelly the first descending step. She quickly complied. He then motioned for Luke to follow, but the Fenway groundskeeper appeared to be lost in thought, as he was once again gauging the elevation of the tower.

"Where do these stairs lead?" Luke finally questioned, his neck craned upward at the spiral.

"*What?*" a perplexed Shelly replied, with only her head and shoulders remaining above the surface of the wooden floor. "Why the hell would you—"

"You guys head underground!" Luke continued, brushing Shelly's words away like loose paper. "I'm gonna climb to the top of this thing and then make these fuckers think we're *all* up there. I'll be okay, just *go*! Go and find your husband!"

Shelly took a second to absorb what she'd just heard. This stranger had just confirmed her suspicion. "It was you on the phone, wasn't it?" she called to Luke, who was already a half-dozen steps into the rising spiral. "Hell-bent on reaching Jeremy!"

As Luke paused in his ascent, the Deceivers were discovering the camouflaged ingress below. The door began to inch open and, knowing their time had dwindled to an expiration, Luke left Shelly with an unreserved reply: "It was solely about contacting your husband. I had no intentions of ever dragging *you* into this mess. Hence my current plan to bail you out of it. Now both of yous— slip under and be gone! Close the lid behind ya!"

Though reluctant to leave a man behind, Shorty saluted Luke for his bravery and then threw himself down the hole before gingerly pulling the hatch down over Shelly and himself. With the cover now secure, he recalled how Luke had asked where the set of stairs would lead. Given the angry horde now certainly pressing in from the outside, the lamentable answer that suddenly weighed heavy on his mind was that the ascending staircase could only lead to certain death.

———

As he shuffled close behind Linden along the narrow ledge of the concrete conduit, Ernie Cowarth kept muttering the cryptic phrase they'd found spray-painted in the place of the submarine-style door: *From within the bowels of darkness we watch the moon rise.* The words were lost on him, but he couldn't help but figure that the reiteration might at least eventually help him punch through to some underlying clue. *From within the—*

"Hey! Check out *that* creepy tunnel!" Leading the foursome along the minimal projection, Mason Greene stole the group's focus as they approached a considerable opening on the opposing side of the channel. Three stately pillars seemingly guarded the mouth like inanimate sentries, and as they drew closer, they spotted a corroded ladder climbing a sidewall that fed up through a small aperture.

"This place is like a maze through the gutters of madness!" Janelle noted as the group continued past the unsettling artery.

"Yeah, and we're down here winding our way home to the nuthouse!" Linden replied swiftly, and then embellished the statement with maniacal laughter.

As the Park River flowed toward them down to their right, it occasionally carried random objects that one certainly wouldn't expect to see this far below the surface: a car bumper rode the flood like a surfboard, a shopping cart floated through the course faster than through any grocery aisle, and a lawn chair that remarkably remained upright looked ready to take a daring passenger for a thrilling ride along the rapids.

Having snaked their way along the ledge for a good quartermile, Mason suddenly stopped in his tracks and hastily shushed the others behind him. The tunnel ahead took a sweeping curve to the left, and though he couldn't be certain, he sensed they were about to encounter company just beyond their current sightline.

———————————

Having conquered the spiral steps of the Memorial Arch's east tower in short time, Luke Sheehan reached a primarily enclosed landing. Now peering through a narrow, doorless outlet, he noticed it led to a fog-drenched stone walkway that spanned both towers, while raised parapets guarded against a fatal fall.

Luke knew that by now the tower and its twisting flight would certainly be crawling with Deceivers, and he intended to keep it that way; if they were chasing him to such heights, then Shelly and her companion could continue to forge their way underground without pursuit. "Hurry up, you two!" he cunningly hollered down from the top of the climb. "You're almost at the top!" He then proceeded through the slender opening and out into the noticeably cool air, the fog brooding in the moonlight.

Luke snuck to a south embrasure for a bird's-eye view of the park and beyond. Down through the haze, the anaemic light revealed what he guessed to be over a hundred Deceivers, savage in their approach as they jostled in through the base of the east tower like wolves after raw meat. Any second now the multitude would begin to reach the high landing, then spill out onto the bridge.

Luke glanced to the west tower where, unlike the east, an actual door led to and from the elevated walkway. He envisioned a timely retreat down the west spiral, followed by a swift, undetected escape into the nebulous night. With an exit strategy in play, a quick thought ran through his mind and left a vapour trail of apprehension in its wake: if the door were fastened, or if it were just a dummy, he'd suddenly find himself cornered in the worst possible way.

———————

While Luke was tensely mulling his limited options some ninety feet above the ground, Shorty and Shelly had reached a landing about the same distance below it. With a series of motion sensors lighting the way, the spiral steps led them along an uncontested descent that concluded with a pitted patch of concrete. A doorsized gap in the wall was all that remained, and a distant yet resonant *chug-swoooosh, chug-swoooosh* sound could be heard as it leaked through a tight passageway beyond the opening. "The pumps are runnin' at full tilt," Shorty asserted, referring to the massive underground pumps that maintain proper flow of the river. "That means the water'll be movin' at a good clip once we get out there."

"Once we get out *where*?" Shelly promptly demanded.

Shorty considered offering an abridged explanation of the waterways that ruled the depths of the city, but in the end, he went with a more efficient approach. "We're pretty close—I think I'll just let you see for yourself. Take my hand and follow me. I doubt we'll continue to be so lucky when it comes to lighting." Shelly wilfully complied, as the thought of being left behind in the dark, musty underground made her skin crawl.

Moments after the two passed through the space in the wall, the last motion sensor that threw light upon the spiral staircase clicked off behind them—and with the sound came a drowning wave of darkness. Shelly caught herself mid-scream, and simultaneously squeezed Shorty's hand a little tighter. Shorty instinctively raised his free hand out in front of him and slowed his pace considerably.

After about forty feet, the pitch-black course gradually began to snake to the right. With senses heightened, high-pitched squeaking sounds could now faintly be heard up ahead, freezing Shelly in her place. "*Jesus Christ!*" she cried out in horror. "Tell me that isn't what I think it is!"

Shorty snickered at Shelly's reaction, and then replied, "You didn't expect kittens and puppies down here, didja? Don't worry about 'em, they're harmless. Besides, we're almost outta here."

Another bend took them back to the left, and shortly thereafter they were startled by the click of another motion sensor. The device was directly over their heads, and it filled the passageway with a soft glow that was initially blinding.

When their eyes adjusted, their reactions to what they first noticed couldn't have been more dissimilar to each other. For Shorty, it was a feeling of relief, as the winding passageway had ended abruptly with a concrete wall and a small, square hole in the ground about twenty feet ahead. A rusty ladder fastened to the back wall poked up through the vertical passage, inviting underground adventurers down into yet another stratum.

All Shelly felt was absolute dread, as a swarm of swollen rats were seemingly guarding the hole, squeaking and hissing as if the final leg of the passageway was theirs to defend. "There is *nooo* way I'm—" she began to express her thoughts on the situation, but Shorty took her by the wrist and stole her words with his actions.

Shorty promptly alleviated his grip, but he still led her straight into the clot of perturbed rodents. The motion sensor switched off behind them, leaving only a faint shaft of light peeking up through the rat-guarded hole.

Still progressing toward the ladder, Shelly was thrown off-balance as her step came down heavy upon a cushiony lump. She closed her eyes and cringed as a shrill squeal pierced the space. Shorty did his best to clear the way by booting the hissing rats like mini soccer balls against the walls, or down into the very hole they were approaching.

With the square hole now at their feet, the distinct sound of rushing water could be heard below. A single plump rat paced back and forth along the ladder's top rung like an overweight gymnast on a balance beam, the sound of its nails making a light clicking rhythm against the cold steel. To Shorty's disbelief, Shelly suddenly skipped in front of him and hopped over the hole and onto the rusty iron. She then began descending without so much as a single glance at the top-rung rat. The moment he knew he wouldn't be stepping on her fingers, Shorty was on the ladder and following her down into the Park River tunnels.

After a good twenty-foot drop, the rails of the ladder expired a foot shy of an elevated concrete landing. A few feet below the landing, angry water flowed before them through a massive channel from right to left. A shopping cart seemingly greeted their arrival as it swiftly bobbed on past.

Directly behind them appeared to be the mouth of another tunnel. A trio of massive, graffiti-stained concrete pillars stood like giants before the opening, and an unspeakable darkness was the only sight beyond. Though wounded, a good number of their furry friends had survived the boot and the fall, as they hobbled like a defeated army for the caliginous void. "Well, I know which way I'm *not* going!" Shelly declared before turning her attention to a pair of small ledges that ran along the sides of the waterway.

Again taking the initiative, Shelly cautiously hopped down onto the ledge and, immediately pondering direction, looked both ways as if she were about to cross a flooded street. She then turned and looked up to Shorty, who was now standing at the lip. She locked in on his eyes and spoke in a jittery tone that nearly got whisked away in the current: "Tell me the truth. Is my husband really down here somewhere?"

"Do ya think I would've brought ya this far if he weren't?" Shorty replied over the sonorous surge. He then bounced down onto the ledge beside her, and promptly began moving against the flow of the underground river as if it were the only direction afforded.

———

Like a plump piñata hanging from an invisible celestial cord, the mad moon ruled the night, its roseate glow washing over Bushnell Park like a baleful omen. By the lunar light, Luke Sheehan crossed the elevated walkway to the Memorial Arch's west tower, only to find that his biggest fear had become a stark reality: the door that would be his only way out was indeed a fake. The detail in the paint job was unquestionable, as even a handle was shaded to suggest three-dimensional depth. There, in what would now surely be his final moments, he still found time to appreciate the artful depiction.

Coinciding with Luke's cold realization of the counterfeit exit, the first wave of Deceivers stormed through the opening atop the east tower and onto the stone walkway. A lazy waft of fog crossed their path before they emerged in abundance in the flush moonlight. Now face to face with his lamentable fate, Luke found himself incidentally slipping into a memory of better days: *It was just shy of an hour before the first pitch was set to fly, and the Sox were taking their pre-game hacks down on the field. The Royals were in town, and it was shaping up to be a picture-perfect night for baseball. That mystical twilight glow was slowly creeping in over the city, and the smell of the fresh-cut outfield grass came with the soft breeze. John Fogerty's "Centerfield" played over the park's PA, and the majestic sound of the crack of a bat echoed only until it was drowned out by another. Autograph-seeking fans frantically lined the front rows in search of their heroes' attention, as desperate calls of "Papi! Papi!" rang out from the mouths and hearts of Red Sox Nation. Leaning against the batting cage as Dustin Pedroia peppered the Green Monster, Luke had been here countless times before—but until this day, it had always been a* job. *He was the head groundskeeper for one of the few remaining shrines in baseball, and keeping the playing surface in pristine condition was no easy task. But for reasons unknown, this was the day he realized he was the luckiest man alive—the day he acknowledged that this wasn't a* job *anymore, but more an absolute* honour *bestowed upon him.*

As swiftly as Luke had found himself immersed in the golden memory, he'd lost it just the same, the sound of a throaty voice tugging him back into the grim reality at hand. "Where are the other two?" a slender man cut straight to the point, for it was they—Shelly and Shorty—who had unmercifully ploughed through his people in the intersection. He wore baggy jeans and swam in a brown sweater with rolled-up sleeves. The other Deceivers were still piling onto the bridge, but failed to overstep the speaker.

"They never even entered the tower, you blind bastards!" Luke retorted, offering them a taste of their own deceit. "Just kept on runnin' through the arch—probably clear of the park altogether by now."

"Lyin' son of a bitch!" a voice wailed from deep within the pack. "Toss 'im over the edge!" cried another.

The Deceiver in the brown sweater calmly raised a hand and the bellowing promptly ceased. He then stepped toward Luke, confronting him head on. The man's face was pitted with pockmarks, and his eyes were lifeless cataracts. "Let me lay it out for you as simply as I can," he began, his breath like a punch to the face. "We're gonna play a little game called Fast or Slow. Do ya like games, Luke?" When Luke only stood and stared, the Deceiver continued. "I'll take that as a *shit yeah*! I *love* games! Now, both you and I know that the three of yous entered the tower together. So here's the rules. They're quite simple, really. Tell me where they're hiding, and we'll do you the favour of killing you quickly. On the other hand, lie to me one more time, and you'll be digging your own grave with a teaspoon."

Luke shook his head with revulsion. "Fuck your game!" he then bellowed into the night. "Whether you believe me or not, like I said, they're long gone. And while you walking corpses continue to waste time up here, they're busy making things happen— busy seeking others who've gathered here in the city to thwart your scheme."

Unperturbed, the speaking Deceiver abruptly gazed up to the peak of the west tower. When he appeared to find what he was looking for in only a matter of seconds, he then swung his eyes to the peak of the east's. "Pick an angel," he casually demanded, as if it were a conventional request.

"*Excuse me?*" a confused Luke asked.

The Deceiver's dead eyes remained fixed upon the east tower's conical roof. "Over here we have Gabriel, and over on the opposite tower we have Raphael. Now *fucking pick one already!*"

Luke stood there, utterly perplexed. He noticed there were indeed bronze finial angels resting atop the towers like finishing ornaments. One was clenching a pair of lengthy trumpets, and the other appeared set to clash cymbals.

Though he had absolutely no idea as to where things were heading, he chose to play along with *this* game. "That one," he said, pointing toward the sculpted angel atop the east tower. Luke's selection was met with a spattering of both boos and applauded praise. He then watched in disbelief as a Deceiver promptly bounced up atop the parapet, and from there onto a minimal ledge that circled the tower's cone-shaped crown. Now leaning forward and resting against the slope, the Deceiver seized and then snapped the angel from its mount like a twig. Struggling with the sculpture's weight, he lowered it down into the waiting arms of two other Deceivers. Together, they schlepped the four-foot figure through the restless crowd and then balanced it upright before Luke.

"The Angel of Revelation," the pockmarked Deceiver began. "Wise choice. You see, Gabriel here was once a messenger of God, but luckily for me, he now serves a darker spirit." He then hunched over and placed a cupped ear within an inch of the angel's mouth. After finally straightening, he continued. "The message Gabriel has been kind enough to share tonight is that he's always aware when people enter his *fucking tower!* He tells me you're still lyin' about the other two, and therefore loves the idea of your demise being a long and painful one."

While Luke was busy trying to wrap his head around the increasingly bizarre situation, the Deceivers had formed a band around him and the desecrated angel. He glanced to the sculpture, which had tumbled over and come to rest on its back, and was certain that his fate wouldn't have differed in the least had he chosen the other. He'd mounted the Memorial Arch for one purpose—to buy time for the other two to escape below the surface—and now he could only hope his efforts had bought them enough.

By this point he'd accepted death, but in order for it to be a quick and painless one, he'd evidently have to find a way to depart this life on his own terms. Without a list of options, he decided a lengthy nosedive onto the paved road below would have to suffice. With a sudden start, he charged through the chain of Deceivers like a bull and made for a gap in the north parapet near the west tower. Like hitting a springboard, he bounded through the opening. He felt a gust of wind whip through the path of his jump and prayed that the inevitable impact that awaited below would offer an immediate departure.

With his eyes closed, he was surely shocked when, not twenty feet into the fall, his left foot came crashing down upon an unforgiving, horizontal metal pole. Before he knew it, he found himself face down with a *thud* on a wooden platform. The structure wobbled slightly as searing pain instantly shot through his left ankle, knee, and right wrist with the abrupt landing. Through the affliction, Luke began to comprehend the stroke of luck that had seemingly swooped in from the high heavens and found him amid his final act. Clearly unaware of any obstructions that might impede his fall, he'd miraculously found the top plank of a substantial scaffolding structure that hugged the northern curl of the west tower.

Still an easy seventy feet above street level, Luke did his best to swallow the pain and gather himself. A tentative glance to the ground revealed a sector presently void of Deceivers. *Is it possible that every single one of these bastards is either still in the tower or above me on the bridge?*

The generous moonlight revealed horizontal bars on the opposite side of the scaffolding that acted as ladder rungs. Moving through a litter of masonry tools, Luke promptly crossed the high plank, every step worse than the one before as the pain in his knee barked a feral bay. He tackled the side of the scaffolding as fast as his throbbing joint would allow, passing five other wooden platforms along the descent.

The Deceivers up on the bridge had pieced together that their target had caught a fortuitous break, as they promptly withdrew from the high perch in a frenzied state.

As Luke touched down on a walkway that wound around the base of the west tower, he gazed to the street that ran through the archway like a linear river and imagined the gory landing that could have been. A chill brought him back to his blessed reality and sent him hobbling into the darkness before a single Deceiver could catch sight of his direction.

After sending Mason Greene and the others underground and then evading a band of Deceivers in the hatchway, Hoyt Colston cleared the Synchronistic Door and promptly headed south, leaving Bushnell Park and all its malevolence behind him. By the time he'd travelled nearly two miles on foot and reached the Institute of Living, the midnight hour hung high like the ominous moon above.

The building's exterior was quite fitting for what one would expect of an aging psychiatric facility. The century-old hospital stood five storeys high, the bottom three of which were blanketed in thick ivy. Cloudy windows were choked within the growth and peered out into the night like the eyes of the lost souls they contained. A dozen stairs within a Gothic-style alcove led to the front entrance, where the sturdiest of wooden doors welcomed the unhinged.

On some level, Hoyt knew that this was where he belonged, yet at the same time he wondered how long he'd been away. He closed his eyes and drew up a familiar tightrope in his mind, and then cautiously began to tread across. When he bestirred from the reverie, he was no longer out on the street before the exterior of a mental hospital; he was on the *inside*, and the recognizable ivy walls that enclosed the courtyard were now drenched in an apocalyptic crimson glow.

CHAPTER 46

Apogee

With the other three halted behind him and conversing in tight whispers, Mason Greene chanced another dozen steps along the stingy ledge. As the tunnel gradually curved away into the distance, there now appeared to be a great number of people lining the opposing ledge with their backs to the wall in an orderly fashion. Since the tunnel hooked to the left, it was yet to be determined if the same peculiar configuration awaited them up ahead on their own side.

The water still flushed toward them, but it seemed to have suddenly lost most of its vigour, as if the underground pumps had been dialled back considerably. A misstep into the drink at this point would do no more than submerge the ankles.

"They're all just lined up against the wall like a buncha mannequins," Mason began after shuffling back to the others, his words wrapped in trepidation. "A whole slew of 'em, from what I could see—none of 'em moving at all!"

"Which side of the tunnel are we talkin' here?" Ernie inquired.

"I only got as far as to see 'em on the opposite side, but I wouldn't be surprised if they're eventually on ours as well."

Linden absorbed Mason's report and then gauged the river below. While the others pondered the presence of their company, he broke the silence with a bold strategy. "Ya know, considering the water has slowed to the pace of a backyard creek, we could hop down and go right up the middle."

Ernie chuckled, and then dropped some humour on their rather eerie plight. "Yeah, and maybe if we're lucky, these cellar-dwellers will greet us by handing out rubber boots!"

Janelle was in no mood for laughs, as she promptly edged her slender frame past Mason along the narrow ledge. She continued beyond the point where he'd first ventured before turning back herself. The others had hesitantly crept in her wake, hoping that an actual plan was what suddenly set her in motion. "If we have to hop down into the water, then so be it," she stated authoritatively, while the others were collectively drawn to a rather disturbing, unclothed doll drifting languidly past their current mark. "But until we're forced to, I say we keep movin' along on our own side of the tracks."

———————————

As Shorty ushered Shelly along the limited projection, Shelly struggled to shake the rats from her psyche. She could still hear the furry critters spinning their squeaky wheels through the halls of her mind, like they'd taken up residence in her attic and would forever gnaw at her sanity.

The ledge above the seemingly abating flow was a good foot-and-a-half in width and hugged a stable concrete wall, but she felt as though she were traversing a tightrope high above a canyon and raging river. As her equilibrium wavered, she thought of Jeremy. *Where the hell could he possibly be down here? Is he even alive? Will I be alive when this nightmare finally ends?*

They'd been creeping along at a snail's pace for some time now, and Shelly began to wonder if the winding underpass would go on forever. She envisioned an eventual straining process somewhere down the line that permitted only water to pass, collecting goodies like the disturbing naked doll that she wished hadn't just caught her eye as it floated on by like a bloated corpse.

――――――――

The same moonlight that guided Luke Sheehan and his throbbing knee down the side of the scaffolding now spilled through a vast canopy of foliage in tiny pockets. Having miraculously escaped the lofty heights of the Memorial Arch, the Fenway groundskeeper now aimlessly limped his way through a timbered concealment.

Needing more than anything to relieve his knee of some weight, he plopped himself down with a grimace and settled with his back to a sizeable tree trunk. The unexpected landing upon the scaffolding structure was truly a blessing, but it came stamped with an excruciating price. He knew at the very least that he'd severely sprained both his wrist and ankle, but considering the pain shooting through his knee, both cases were currently triaged to a lesser degree of urgency.

Luke pictured himself as a member of his beloved Red Sox, writhing in agony out on the outfield grass, soon to be carted off the field in one of those dreaded rides that usually represents a season-ending injury.

A swirling dizzy spell suddenly forced him to close his eyes. When he opened them again, he noticed through blurred vision that the glow of the moon was passing through a significant gap in the trees, finding him like a spotlight. For a moment he thought— or perhaps *wished*—that it was *the* light, here to free him from the unspeakable pain and the ongoing nightmare that just wouldn't let him wake.

As the familiar, ancient walls of the courtyard were doused in sanguineous moonlight, an encompassed Hoyt Colston had gone from wondering how long he'd been away, to had he ever even left in the first place? One thing he *was* sure of was that in all his time at the Institute, he'd never been permitted to visit the courtyard during the witching hour.

Surrounded by the night, he looked to the sky and saw the moon like he'd never quite seen it before. It was as if it were . . . *alive.* The colossal orb pulsed in perfect harmony with his own beating heart, pumping lifeblood through his veins like rainwater through thirsty subterranean channels.

When Linden suggested dipping into the river to avoid the wall people, he was speaking from a worst-case scenario point of view. Yet here the group of four now found themselves, up to their shins in flowing water that was every bit the frigid bite they'd expected. To their dismay, roughly fifty feet ahead, the ledges on *each* side of the waterway were lined with the strange configuration of seemingly sedated souls, their eyes closed, arms limp at their sides, and backs pressed firm to the wall as if magnetized.

Unlike their single-file route along the ledge, the group now trudged against the flow side by side. From their current vantage, the people along the walls formed solid lines until the tunnel curled around the corner and out of sight.

Walking with high steps to counter the current, they began to split through their comatose company, incessantly gauging their eyes as they passed. They looked and dressed like common folk, everyday people drawn into the depths for some undisclosed—yet sure to be unsettling—objective.

Mason suddenly stopped cold. "The peddler in the rover!" he then voiced assertively before the others even noticed he'd paused. The echo pulsed through the conduit, sounding like *over, over, over* . . . Two of the three others turned on the spot and threw puzzled expressions back at Mason.

"*What?*" Janelle asked. "Say that ag—"

"He said, 'the peddler in the rover,'" Linden arrested Janelle's words with an assured tone. "He was referring to me. Don't even try to make sense of it, though—all I'll say is that I think the two of our paths may've crossed in one of these intertwined dreams that seem to be such a hot topic." He turned to Mason. "The pocket scope, the moon mountain—it was *you* up there with me! And now here we stand together in the depths. This is some kind of bizarre. I don't know how I never put two and two together."

"It just suddenly came to me," Mason replied. "In our defence, we've been a little preoccupied."

"Ah shit," Janelle abruptly uttered while shifting her stance within the flowing water. "Turn around, Mason, I think I'm seeing shadows inching toward us along the wall."

Mason spun with a small splash to face the direction they'd already conquered. From his vantage, he not only saw the augmented shadows, but he discerned the two figures who were casting them.

———

Focusing on their footing more than anything, Shorty and Shelly continued to slowly press forward along the ledge, their shadows slinking across the wall like floating ghosts as they progressed. Surveying the long, sweeping arc ahead, something down in the water in the distance suddenly caught Shorty's eye. He came to a halt, and had Shelly do the same. Four figures stood shin-deep in the fluent river and appeared to be assessing *them* in the same fashion. The ledges up ahead were lined with a great number of people until the tunnel curled out of sight. "One of 'em in the water has a cane!" Shorty emphatically stated, his echo contesting the current.

"Uhh . . . should I know what that means?" Shelly acknowledged, the point clearly lost on her.

Shorty failed to reply, as he further gauged their company, leaving Shelly to only sink deeper into the sands of uncertainty. "They're safe," he finally indicated in a low yet confident tone.

The four strangers in the distance remained in their place as the water sluiced around eight ankles and a single cane. Confused, Shelly demanded further assurance before taking another step along the stingy ledge. Shorty appeared to have an explanation ready to spill, when a deep-rooted rumbling sound suddenly stole his full attention; Shelly was certain that the entire tunnel had begun to shake with the resonance. It came on like rolling thunder, and in a matter of seconds sounded like a dozen 747s were simultaneously using the Bushnell Park grounds above as a drag strip.

With a subordinate Deceiver having already failed miserably with the one-shot trial operation, the incensed Overlord had regained the park's soggy surface, taking it upon himself to make sure the simple yet essential chore was executed properly.

Basking in its ruddy glow, the Deceiver Overlord lifted his head from his knelt position over the steel-plated cover and acknowledged the moon gracing the night sky. A curt, sinister grin received the baleful orb before he reverted to the task at hand.

With the touch of his cane's blue tip, the cover was scorched into non-existence. A sulphuric-smelling smoke was born of the alchemic process before wafting away in the breeze.

Resting patiently on its pedestal directly below the vertical chute, primed for its consummate kiss of misfortune, the lunar globe awaited the moon's emissive surge.

The Overlord scurried back down into the depths of the city, found his place within the maze of conduits, and then promptly positioned his eye to the pocket telescope like a keen astronomer. He spared a brief moment for Clive Snelling, knowing how proud the deranged NASA employee would've been when the globe he'd crafted finally absorbed the initial wash of lunar radiation.

The Overlord tweaked the scope's focus in on the now-fissure-like blemish that graced the Apollo 15 landing site. He then watched in wonder as countless black-and-white particles infused the vertical chute from above and then were essentially sucked into the globe's gash like inhaled smoke. A high-pitched whistle accompanied the prodigious vision, growing louder as the globe continued to draw the toxic plume at an accelerating speed. After a minute's worth of the radioactive ingestion, the globe's larger mountainous projections began to not only redden, but throb like a frog's pulsating throat, their peaks like active volcanoes yearning to spew lava and rain ash.

Still focused on the enthralling actions of the moon globe, the Overlord began to sense a steady rumbling all around him. Knowing that the source of the tremor was the very spectacle occurring before him, he merely secured his footing and kept his eye on the prize. The convulsion continued to grow in magnitude, as the globe further swallowed the lunar particles.

Resolute in its rage, the seismic shudder ultimately threw the Overlord from the foot of the pedestal and spun him down to his hands and knees in the water. When he lifted his head, he spotted six figures standing abreast in the tottery distance, observing his actions while fighting their own battle against the steady spasm.

Initially, Luke Sheehan thought that the pain shooting through his knee was what was causing his vision to flush to a bloodshot hue. But when he felt the ground start to convulse like the onset of an earthquake, he knew something unspeakable was suddenly taking place. A warm wind had cut through adjacent trees, and it bore a noxious odour, like ozone. Surrounding lights on high-rises flickered through the turmoil, the sporadic flashes like desperate distress signals thrown out into the night.

Luke fought the torment of what now resembled a gunshot to the knee and, with the assistance of the steady tree trunk he'd been resting against, forced himself back to his feet. The plan was to venture beyond the trees to catch a better sense of the danger, but the pain was now calling the shots, and it rudely told him he wasn't going anywhere.

He hoped a deep breath might begin to fill in some of the blanks, but all it did was stab both his throat and lungs with the now-toxic atmosphere. His eyes then began to burn as if hot sand had been rubbed into his corneas. Suddenly the pain in his knee was a secondary issue, as it felt like invisible hands were choking the life from his windpipe. His legs then buckled beneath him, and he fell unconscious before his body settled in a queer contortion.

Though the tunnel continued to endure the intense vibration, Shorty insisted that he and Shelly advance upon the four strangers up ahead. Seeing as the figures standing down in the water were unfamiliar to him, Shorty was playing on his hunch that the cane in their possession had been somehow forwarded to them at some point by his fellow defector, Hoyt Colston.

From the ledge, Shorty and Shelly touched down into the chilly flowing water, and then, like a pair of fly-fishers strolling against the current, they cautiously pressed forward.

As they approached, Shelly studied the rows of seemingly comatose souls that lined the ledges now slightly above them, hunting in vain with her eyes for her missing husband. The bodies appeared to be somehow fixed into place along the walls by their backs, their countless number now permeating the channel beyond a distant reach.

Shorty went directly for Mason, pausing in his watery tracks before the cane holder. "Despite all I'm sure that your group has been through to this point," he began, "you must trust that the two of us aren't here to cause you any harm. I just need to confirm my hunch that that cane came from a man named Hoyt Colston."

"*Trust?*" Mason promptly replied with a raised brow and wrinkled nose. "I wouldn't trust a *nun* in this city. And this cane is none of your god—"

"Where the *fuck* is my husband?" Shelly suddenly shrieked, her words grabbing everyone's attention like an invisible lasso, the echo pulling the noose tighter and tighter until she owned the floor. "We're not the bloody enemy here, okay? My husband is being held captive somewhere in this . . . this dungeon!"

Janelle could hear the desperation in this woman's voice and see it in her eyes—her *living* eyes. If she was a Deceiver, then an Academy Award should be presented on the spot for Best Actress. "Is your husband's name Jeremy, by any chance?"

As if Janelle's inquiry enhanced the intensity of the subterranean tremor, the channel suddenly began to shake with yet another elevated degree of anger. Mason had the luxury of the cane to help steady himself, while the others struggled like first-time surfers bound for an ugly dismount.

Shelly shuffled her way over to Janelle, and the two found some stability in each other's hold. "Yes! Yes, it is!" Shelly ultimately replied hysterically. "What do you *know*?"

"I know you didn't take our advice when we advised against coming to Hartford," Janelle countered forthright. "But I get it. If it were my husband, I would've done the same."

"Oh my god!" Shelly was quick to make the connection. "So, when did you and Luke get separated? I just met up with him in the park prior to coming down here. He basically sacrificed himself at this war monument to save me and my friend here."

While the ladies were busy piecing together their indirect relation, Mason had lowered his guard and was conversing with Shorty about Hoyt, and about how the cane had essentially fallen into his possession not once, but twice. Meanwhile, words didn't seem to concern Linden in this moment, as he was busy not only dealing with his own footing, but also with keeping Ernie upright.

Shortly after they became six, Shelly was the first to continue against the flow. She called out for her husband as she advanced, but the rumble seemed to shake the vigour from her voice. The others followed, standing shoulder to shoulder and close in her wake.

After not even fifty feet of plodding through the trembling waterway, Janelle and her keen eye spotted a figure literally down in the water in the distance. She was certain it was a man on his hands and knees.

The group halted.

Just behind the fallen man, a slim, pedestal-like piece jutted from the surface like a stunted spire, and a throbbing ruddy glow from an unknown source pervaded the tunnel beyond.

The Overlord was certain that the six people standing ankle-deep in the water weren't just another band of his subservient Deceivers.

It was too close to the moment of truth to assume otherwise—that they wouldn't attempt to halt his actions at any cost.

He regained his stance amidst the ongoing convulsion by propping himself up with the support of his cane and the sturdy pedestal. The view through the enigmatic pocket scope was all that mattered now.

What the Overlord initially witnessed when he steadied himself and pressed his eye to the magnifier once again was a refined exhibition of a globe being pushed to the brink. The lunar model was remarkably still consuming the moon's toxic emissions at an accelerating rate, now slowly mutating to a high-coloured red in the process, as if it were being boiled from within.

But suddenly the view began to . . . change. The now cherry-red moon was front and centre before a pitch-black, starry backdrop that had somehow replaced that of the tunnel's dank interior. It was as if he wasn't looking at a *globe* anymore, but rather had a more telescopic view of the *actual* moon. Only adding to the phenomenon was the fact that the perspective wasn't offering that of the *present-day* moon; this was somehow a glimpse into the *past*—a private screening of the lunar event in 1953 that produced the great crevice, and consequently sent federal agencies on a futile search for answers.

———

With the group having progressed another fifty feet along the channel bed, Mason and Ernie spotted their respective artefacts in a synchronous flash of discovery. "That's my freakin' globe up ahead! I *know* it!" Mason announced to the others with utmost confidence, a strange coalescence of joy and anger making up his tone. "What the hell's goin' on down here, anyway?"

It had been well over a half-century since Ernie had last seen his treasured pocket telescope—the night *Gavinia* ran aground off the coast of Ireland—and now here it was by some miracle, resting atop an exotic pedestal as if it were on display at some strange subterranean museum of reclaimed relics.

For Mason, the absence from his moon globe had been much shorter—less than seventy-two hours—but the search had been nothing short of a fascinating journey that led him all the way across the country, and ultimately down into the bowels of the anomalously flag-marked city.

"And that's my scope if I've *ever* seen it!" Ernie added, studying the familiar brass casing from a safe stretch—the one he'd once scratched the word "moonflaw" into with a trembling hand.

A man was now standing before the pedestal on unsure legs, gazing intently into the pocket telescope that was aimed directly at the inflamed globe in the short distance. He appeared to be utterly transfixed by the resulting image, just as Ernie had been that fateful night out on the Atlantic, when he witnessed strange particulates spewing from a gash in the low-lying moon.

Knowing there was absolutely no time for any dissension on the matter, Shorty cordially asked Mason to hand over the cane. "His back is to us," he continued, "and he's currently engrossed in the magic of the scope. This could be our only opportunity!"

Mason glanced down to the walking staff held tightly in his hand and once again heard the voice of Hoyt Colston ringing in his head like staticky audio feedback. *Take the cane down with you! It still wields a trick or two!* And then, as if Hoyt's words sanctioned his actions, Mason obliged Shorty's request.

There, deep in the underground, the Overlord was lost in the heavens. Wholly invested in an open sky of anticipation, he began to perceive a faint light forming in the starry reach, growing in vitality and size, and seemingly pushing through the vast ebony of space like a plant pushing up through soil.

Drawn further still to the blossoming manifestation, the Overlord was suddenly yanked back into the present and again down into the flowing rainwater.

———————

Shorty went for the waist, violently wrenching the entranced Overlord away from the scope and pedestal with ease. Though the water had only been up to his ankles, the Overlord tumbled down into the drink with a mighty splash. The cane never left Shorty's hand during the manoeuvre, and he now had it cocked and ready to strike as he stood over the sodden Devil incarnate.

The Overlord rested face down and motionless in the water, his own cane dislodged from his grip and now floating toward the others with the light current. Then suddenly, as if jerking awake from a nightmare, he spun violently and began to rise from the river like the pre-eminent adversary he was.

———————

The moment Shorty pulled the Overlord down into the river, Ernie pounced toward the pedestal and reunited himself with the brass artefact that had been at the root of his life's work. *The . . . fucking . . . odds,* he reminded himself once again, more astonished than ever, before putting a hand to the scope's curiously warm shell. He ran a finger along his own seemingly immortal engraving. *Moonflaw*: a word that had come to him on a whim in the heat of a direful moment; a word that literally sent NASA to the moon in search of a deeper understanding; and now, a word that was on the verge of shedding its skin and finally baring its soul.

Like he'd done countless times in his youth, Ernest Cowarth pressed his eye to the eyepiece and adjusted the focus. He'd certainly seen a lot of things through this specific lens, but nothing quite like the vision it offered now. Both time and space had seemingly sucked his headspace clean out of the tunnel and out of the present-day like a unified vacuum. Ernie knew exactly when and where he now was. As illogical as it all seemed, there was no fear whatsoever—just a warm blanket of infinite space that assured him he was meant to observe whatever was surely imminent.

He stood aboard *Gavinia*, the sea a turbulent swell, spilling onto the deck and meeting his ankles like swashes upon a shore. But there was a calm in his heart that permitted a steady hand as he gazed skyward. He was quick to spot a dazzling white light on a direct course for the moon, scratching its way across the black backcloth of night at a celestial speed. As the luminous streak progressed, a *second* glow suddenly emerged high above it, initially a mild jade, and then a toxic green within seconds, angling its way downward on a forty-five-degree slant and seemingly destined to meet the moon as well. With simply inconceivable odds, a pair of meteoroids were not only bound for a collision with the lunar surface, but they were to do so while synchronously striking each other.

With the stunning realization, Ernie struggled to wrap his head around the true nature of the event before it had even occurred in the preternatural viewing. Foreign radioactive elements from distant stretches of the galaxy had been forced to knit together in the fresh crevice—just like entangled dreams within the minds of perfect strangers. The discharge that followed the brief confinement was what he'd actually witnessed back in '53 through the scope, and what members of the Apollo 15 crew inadvertently conveyed back to Earth in '71.

The view began to soften, as if the lens was receiving a fine dust. Ernie could sense the image slipping away, and his present-day place down in the tunnel leaking back into existence. He tried to remain rooted in the past for as long as he possibly could—to witness the actual impact that defied even twisted logic.

The view of the night sky suddenly began to shudder violently as he struggled to steady the scope against the trembling tunnel. Though indeed unwavering along their respective paths, the two flares of light rapidly skipped up and down through the lens like they were tracing the serrated teeth of a blade—a blade on the verge of carving a fathomless gash into the moon's Palus Putredinis region.

As the converging meteoroids slammed into the moon as one, the tunnel's lengthy convulsion suddenly ceased, and Ernie was afforded a steady view of the immediate fallout. The simultaneous impact generated a splash of luminance so bright that, if only for a few seconds, it washed the ruddy glow from the entirety of the moon's visible surface.

With Shorty having already secured his stance firmly within the flow, he used the purchase to meet the Overlord's advance with a resounding drive directly to the left eye.

The staff depressed through the socket like butter, and then further still, as Shorty angled the cane up into the cranium with continued force. A wail of agony filled the spillway and was met with a surge of dazzling white light that began to flow down along the stick. The tawny skin-tone of the Overlord's skeletal face began to illuminate with the electric current, and his emphatic wail sharpened into a shriek so loud and piercing that everyone but Shorty covered their ears and formed painful expressions.

Shorty was too focused on the task at hand to be distracted; all he heard was the staticky white noise in his head that accompanies all-out exertion. As he continued to fry the Overlord's brain from the inside out, Shorty quickly glanced over his shoulder to assess the state of the moon globe. What he saw was enough to bulge his eyes and make him shudder with dread. The globe's shell was beginning to fracture under the strain of the intense radioactive ingestion within. With a chilling sound resembling cracking ice, the orb was shedding its vermilion crust in fitful patches. Shorty then pried his eyes back down to the still-shrieking Overlord, only to discover that the demon's head was now sloughing layers in a similar fashion. Brief images of his former incarnations appeared in flashes, as if illuminated by strobe light. Dozens of facial embodiments terrorized the tunnel in a matter of seconds, each representation its own unique contortion of horror.

Shelly, observing the cranium cookout, swore she saw a familiar image flicker in the face during the voltage. It was the wood-faced-demon-skull thing from her dream in Vicerro's cruiser. Rather than ponder the portentous connection, she could only wince and turn away.

Given the acute state of the globe, Shorty knew it was far too late, yet he still turned to the others and hollered with every ounce of energy he had left in him. *"Ruuunnnn!"*

Collectively frozen with the otherworldly spectacle playing out before them, nobody took as much as a single step in any direction. They all just stood and watched in childlike wonder as the demon's head and the moon globe simultaneously exploded in a fusillade of radioactive release.

———————————

With the discharge, an unfathomable, seething wave of heat immediately surged through the tunnel. The group, ultimately unified at the eleventh hour, whose timing was both impeccable and cursed, received the blast at once. Collectively—there was the incinerating burn in the lungs. And then the irrefutable disequilibrium. And then the bleakest shade of black. And then the soft, gauzy fabric of a dream. And then . . .

. . . the twilight sky was an ethereal marriage of pinks and purples, like a visual announcement of the passing of a powerful storm. The softest of cool breezes rustled dry leaves in the ambient half-light, but the psychiatric facility's courtyard walls kept the litter imprisoned.

Roaming the open space in a drug-induced haze, Shelly Madison-Lowe tried to clear her intellectual windshield and quest for Jeremy Lowe, knowing on some level that she'd been yearning to find him.

And somewhere deep down below the waves of his own shattered intellect, like an undisclosed shipwreck, Jeremy was yearning to be found. But in the moment, the high walls around him engrossed his spirit. A particular wall, solid green with Boston ivy, like a spiny-leafed monster, pricked holes in his perceptions and teased at a familiar flood.

Linden Maddox's headspace couldn't be contained within four walls. He'd spotted the moon creeping over the crest of the enclosure, the orb like a crimson hot air balloon primed to lift his spirit high into the night. From his lofty perch, he'd soon be gazing into the past, as the ghosts of long-dead stars would host a haunting over Hartford.

Just like every other day since his admittance, Ernest Cowarth was desperately seeking some unknown entity—something long-lost, something deeply cherished. The clues were few, as the lens in his mind's eye had grown foggy with age, and with it the search had grown bleary and disoriented.

Though she couldn't for the life of herself comprehend why, on this evening Janelle Crawford found herself drawn to the garden that ran at the foot of the courtyard's north wall. She knelt to one knee before the lengthy patch and scooped up a handful of loose soil. It was rich, evocative soil—cool and comforting to the touch, stirring the soul. She brought it to her nose to catch the essence of the earth. Still no closer to understanding the allurement, she lowered the loam and slowly let it trickle through her fingers like the sands of time.

Like Ernie, Mason Greene was looking to recover something lost, or perhaps something *stolen*. He didn't trust his own shadow in this joint, and now that the all-encompassing shadow of night was rolling in, every soul, living or dead, was a suspect. Lost in his own head, he nearly tripped over Janelle as he wandered along the courtyard garden. She was down on a knee, scooping dirt like a child lost in the wonders of a sandbox, when Mason considered that perhaps he wasn't the only one digging for answers.

Feeling as if he'd already consumed his nightly meds, Luke Sheehan felt utterly revived—weightless, in fact, as though a great burden had been lifted off his shoulders. Merely meandering about the enclosure, he spotted Jeremy across the open space and made a line for him with a limber stride.

After weaving his way through spiritless obstacles, all donning matching garments quite like his own, Luke found Jeremy standing squarely on a manhole cover that was nestled in a patch of grass. A look of sudden enlightenment was all over Jeremy's face, like a revelation had slipped up from the sewers below. "Somethin' on yer mind, friend?" Luke queried Jeremy's palpable expression.

Without a reply, Jeremy crouched down and softly ran his fingers over the steel-plated cover. He then mumbled a few words under his breath before returning to his feet. He was standing there, swathed in the last pale light of the day, a great proclamation seemingly loaded and ready to fire, when a pair of husky orderlies suddenly appeared. One promptly clutched Jeremy by the forearm, and the other took a firm hold of Luke's wrist. "That'll be all for tonight, fellas," Jeremy's orderly asserted, his head swaying back and forth between the two patients like an oscillating fan in high speed.

The orderlies were quick to loosen their grip on their respective patient, but weren't about to release them until they'd cleared the courtyard and were administered their medicinal nightcaps.

———————————————

Hoyt Colston sat with one leg crossed over the other on a white bench that blended seamlessly into the colour of his garments. A violet aura of dusk had infused the courtyard, and an early moon had already taken to the lavender sky. An orderly was sitting next to Hoyt on the bench, hanging on every word that Hoyt had to offer, occasionally jotting down notes into a small, leather-bound notebook.

The orderly shifted his focus to acknowledge a pair of fellow orderlies passing directly in front of their bench along a paved walkway. They were escorting a pair of patients back into the building.

"Hey!" Hoyt suddenly shouted out at the men rather ungraciously after they had passed. The orderlies paused and then glanced back toward the bench before Hoyt continued. "Maybe trim Frick and Frack's dosage some tonight, huh? We got ourselves a beauty-of-a-moon on the rise! Wouldn't want 'em to sleep through the show!"

EPILOGUE

A Fine Line to the Moon and Back

So here it is, folks. It's time to lay the cards on the table.

My name is Evan Caldwell, and I've been employed as an orderly at the Institute of Living in Hartford, Connecticut, for seventeen years. I met Hoyt Colston about three weeks after he joined us here at the psychiatric facility, and I began jotting down notes within days of that first encounter, when he sat down next to me out in the ivy-clad courtyard. That was some time ago now—close to eight years if I had to spin a guess. And now here we are, resting on the same bench, both a little older and wiser, deliberating whether we've reached the end, or if we've just come full circle.

Mister Colston approached me one sunny afternoon while I was pencilling through a crossword puzzle on my coffee break. I'd seen Hoyt around the facility here and there, but he wasn't assigned to my wing, and we had therefore yet to formally meet. I was sitting alone when he just plopped down next to me out of the blue. He didn't introduce himself initially; he just simply dove into the fact that he needed a medium to the outside world. *Oh, is that so?* I thought to myself, before peeling my eyes from my puzzle to see who was stealing a bite out of my daily slice of sanity. *And I need a four-letter word for a Sicilian volcano.*

"Rumour has it you used to write," Hoyt continued brusquely as I now faced him. "Before your river of ingenuity ran dry, of course."

I was indeed a failed writer who'd succumbed to the "block" some years prior, essentially relinquishing the craft in the process; but how was this new patient of ours mindful of my desiccated pastime?

I didn't care for his ill-mannered approach, so right then and there I stated that if we were to proceed in any capacity whatsoever, then the next step would be a respectable introduction on his end. "Hoyt Colston," he promptly complied with an accompanying firm handshake, before basically starting over from the top. "Forgive my demeanour, sir—I tend to get ahead of myself when I'm anxious. What I mean to say is that, as far as your writing goes, I want to get you back in the saddle. I have what I believe to be a compelling story to tell, and I want *you* to author it. And when it's complete, you can stamp your name on it and call it your own— only if you deem it worthy, of course. Let's be honest, ain't no one gonna line up in the *nuthouse* lookin' for an autograph."

I was admittedly intrigued, but at the same time cautious of the greasy games our patients tend to play from time to time. I was due back inside from my break, but first I told Mister Colston that I'd meet him on the same bench at the exact same time two days from then. I said that if he could commit to that much, then I'd at least consider the proposition, and maybe even start taking a few preliminary notes.

With my empty coffee cup and crossword in hand, I'd made it about a dozen steps before Hoyt called to me from the bench. "Etna!"

"Huh?" was all I could muster after I paused and turned. The word was lost on me.

"You were looking for a Sicilian volcano—Etna!"

I stood perplexed, certain I hadn't spoken those words aloud, and my next meeting with this curious new patient suddenly couldn't come soon enough.

———————

With his right leg crossed over the left and gently bobbing up and down, Hoyt Colston was patiently waiting on the bench when I arrived. Punctuality carries a lot of weight with me; I was already impressed. I was happy he showed up because I'd grown eager to start stringing some sentences together on paper for the first time in what felt like an eternity. God only knew what kind of tale Hoyt had ready to flood from the dam of his surely troubled mind, but I was ready to catch it with buckets—buckets I'd stowed away in the fathoms of my mind and certainly thought I'd never use again.

We started by establishing the particulars of the project; though it was technically *his* story, I was the medium, and therefore could shape, shake, or shave it any way I pleased. The flexibility was liberating, and we hadn't even begun.

"I can only work out here in the courtyard," he proclaimed at this point, his expression very matter-of-fact. The remark had me figuratively scratching my head. "I require both the moon above and the garden below. You see, the moon is my beacon of inspiration, and the story it produces is nurtured by the rich soils of the garden. But once I head back inside, my creative spirit disappears. *Poof!* Dust in the cold stone hallways of confined madness."

Hey, at least he knows his company, I thought.

"All I have to look forward to are my daily pair of forty-minute adjournments out in this open-aired sanctuary, where I shake off the dust from the inside and then lose myself in the tilling of the fertile loam."

This was good stuff he was introducing—*certifiably* good—and I was set to reap the rewards. But was I truly willing to step inside this man's psyche, and then refine the works into a polished entity?

"Where do we begin, Mister Colston?"

Our first official session was shortened by rain. The sky had grown angry on the sly, and with it the air became cool and earthy. Winds began to swirl within the courtyard, stirring fallen leaves and rousing trees from their fixed stances.

"Feels like a hurricane's rollin' in," was the last thing Hoyt said before his personal orderly, Allan, ushered him inside and out of the threatening elements.

And with that, Hurricane Allan was born. We sailed in its slipstream, so to speak, for what had to have been a solid month, before I decided it was time to pump the brakes and take some inventory. We'd flown out of the gate like gangbusters, and I feared we might be getting ahead of ourselves. I already had over fifty full pages of notes, so I told Hoyt we'd reconvene after a few days.

Like scattered puzzle pieces dumped fresh from the box upon a dining room table, I took this time to structure my jottings.

Almost as if the hiatus had spawned a vast change of scenery and location, Hoyt had shifted the narrative across the pond when we recommenced. We dropped anchor at Saferock—the lighthouse-employed islet some seven miles off the coast of Ireland. He then had me captivated with the introduction of *Gavinia*. My grandfather was a seaman, and when I was young, he used to hoist me up on his thigh and mimic the swaying motion of the sea while recounting tales of nautical adventure.

Hoyt and I fell into a systematic routine where we'd work together for two months and then recess for two weeks. He told me once that those intervals were extremely hard on him, but on the other hand he understood the necessity. There would never be a story if all I ever had was a growing mountain of notes.

In addition to using Allan as the name of a hurricane, Hoyt was weaving actual patients here at the Institute into the fabric of his tale. The reason being that he required corporeal faces to evoke his characters. *No offence, John Doe, but your face is truly an inspiration for the Devil in this macabre tale I'm currently working on.* For obvious reasons, other than Hoyt, who simply couldn't resist inserting himself into his own adventure, the names in the story have all been fabricated.

Whoever happened to be present out in the courtyard on any given day would almost always be the subject of that day's writing. It didn't matter where we were within the story—Hoyt could always switch gears on a dime and pick up exactly where we'd last left off with a particular character. I see it as that he was always looking down over his story from a lofty, big-picture perspective, where a sudden skip of the chronological needle wasn't nearly enough to derail the process.

To say his storytelling style was unique would be an understatement; the entire journey his mind traversed along that fine line between genius and insanity. Perhaps the early tightrope reference *is* said line, and I've been just lucky enough to follow his lead without slipping into the abyss below.

———

Seeing as that we would only ever work outside in the courtyard, writing slowed significantly during the frigid winter months, but never came to what I'd consider a standstill. We knew we had to keep that stone rolling—even if it became a frozen clump of ice and snow on its travels. We'd brave the elements in short stints, as I'd jot down my notes with numb hands onto paper that simulated a cold slab of granite.

I was pleased to see the story wind its way home to Hartford, and then down into the storied tunnels that further meander below the city like flooded catacombs. Hoyt may be marooned here on the inside, so to speak, be he certainly knows the ins and outs of the Connecticut capital enough to lead a guided tour.

Looking back, Hoyt Colston led us *all* on a guided tour, didn't he? A grand expedition culminating with the Great Gathering, hosted in the ballroom of his dotty attic—where dusty relics rest on brittle wooden planks below low-lying rafters that creak and groan with the slightest of breezes. I guess we were always headed there, right from the onset, when Hoyt rose in the night to a wash of brilliant autumn moonlight; we just didn't know we'd been formally invited. For a time, our backs were *all* pinned to the wall down in the cold recesses below Hartford, captive as we pondered the twisted logic of our dreams.

Thanks for having us, Hoyt. You took us on a trip to the moon and back—the entire journey along the finest of fine lines.

ABOUT THE AUTHOR

Following in the same vein as his first book, *The Turnstile*, Steve Godsoe writes tales of adventure that leak into realms of the supernatural. The author lives with his wife, Lindsay, in Stoney Creek, Ontario. Visit Steve online at www.stevegodsoe.com.

Lightning Source UK Ltd.
Milton Keynes UK
UKHW010705240520
363742UK00004B/154/J